POTENTIAL

For Katt

POTENTIAL

x

KEITH BRADBROOK

Matador
9 Priory Business Park,
Wistow Road, Kibworth Beauchamp,
Leicestershire, LE8 0RX
Tel: 0116 279 2299
Email: books@troubador.co.uk
Web: www.troubador.co.uk/matador
Twitter: @matadorbooks

ISBN 978 1838591 847

British Library Cataloguing in Publication Data.
A catalogue record for this book is available from the British Library.

Printed and bound in Great Britain by 4edge Limited
Typeset in 11pt Minion Pro by Troubador Publishing Ltd, Leicester, UK

Matador is an imprint of Troubador Publishing Ltd

For my beloved family

Daryle – Elliot, Sarah and Reiss – Tom, Beth, Tommy and Betsy.

And in memory of Uncle Bert – for the chess and the stories.

'Every child is an artist.'
Pablo Picasso

'Man needs colour to live; it's just as
necessary an element as fire and water.'
Fernand Léger

Part One

November 2006

West, north, east, south, then west again.

On and on into the night.

Driving, the driving rain. The car, foot down, fantastic shapes in the headlight beams. Tears blinding his eyes. The drive to get away, get anywhere, get away from the red.

Out of the old harbour town, the glare from its multicoloured night lights distorting in the late autumn storm, B swings right at each junction, no knowing why. Speeding away, spray jetting out behind along the roads hugging the coast. A dark Atlantic pounding away somewhere out there. Waves smashing the shores. Turmoil crashing inside him.

Get away from the red.

The red of the little boy's blood, trickling and oozing out of his limp body. A red shadow of a long-ago day on a Belfast street, re-enacted with equally grim results on a Parisian boulevard. The past blasting into the present. A dark memory exploding into the now. A memory as black as the ocean battering the beaches and rocks beyond the rain-washed car windscreen.

More turns, more blind choices on the road and B stays right. Iron-hard rain pounding down. His field of vision cut to a few phantom metres but not enough to stop such reckless speed.

Get away. Get away from the red.

Blood running through his fingers, dripping silently onto the ground. Blood, the colour of a lady's lipstick, another echo in time. The little boy and his mother lying on the pavement, his head twisted at a sickening angle, her arm and half a leg hanging over the curb, a handbag's contents scattered across the road. Victims of clashing worlds, politics and religions. Ancient rivalries played out in the everyday life of the French capital. That city of romance, degenerating into a metropolis of death in a few seconds of thunderous gunfire.

Town and village signs rushing towards him, gripping the wheel even harder. Words flying past unnoticed in his extremis. Flashing place names momentarily lit up on a Normandy road to nowhere.

Pennedepie, Villerville, Hennequeville…

B had reached his bolthole, a little apartment in Honfleur, thinking he could take time out and try to come to terms with the terrible events in Paris. A friend's keys to the one-bedroom sanctuary in *Rue Haute,* just a stone's throw from the peaceful cafes and quaint restaurants overlooking the boats at rest in *Le Vieux Bassin*, he hoped for some peace, some calm, to gather his savaged nerves and put things into a kind of perspective.

Perhaps there was a chance of plotting a way ahead, a forward course. Perhaps it was just possible to salvage something from his life, his job. For, as he knew all too well, they had always been the same thing. Guardian and protector, the job he had lived in various guises since joining the army at sixteen. That day he left his mother, the market town on the two rivers, the mystical colours of his beloved lakes and hills and his terrible anger to serve Queen and country. The red, white and blue of the flag.

And for a while the charm of the little French port two hundred kilometres north-west from Paris had worked its quiet magic. Sipping an espresso, a beer or two, another cognac while the peaceful life of Honfleur passed him by, B was indeed comforted. There were shades of sympathy in the fresh sea colours and bustle of the hardy post-season tourists strolling in and out of shops, patisseries and bars. Boats bobbed, the sky-blue sky was unseasonably cloudless and a cold, yet benign, sun shone down on the little harbour, each day giving way to evocative moonlight glistening off the historic *quais*.

Six days of ease had lulled him and B's world began to wear a softer face. A man of reserve, preferring solitude to crowds, a seeker of detachment not engagement, he even surprised himself on this unsought sojourn. On two occasions, once at a bar in the early afternoon, and later at dinner, without any invitation B had struck up conversations with total strangers. First a German with a military background, no doubt detecting a kindred spirit.

Then a recently widowed Englishwoman delicately putting her toe back into the outside world. From the outset, B realised a more physical engagement with the widow was eminently possible and, who knows, this may have been welcome therapy for them both. But at the pivotal moment after coffee he shut the idea off. It had been a long time and mourning was not yet done.

But suddenly, following a light lunch on the *Quai Sainte Catherine*, this fleeting, fragile, picture-postcard seaside cameo dissolved in an instant and sad, bruising reality crash-landed. Wednesday afternoon, the sun gleaming, a slight breeze, B saw red. Strolling along, hands in pockets, thinking about nothing in particular, a little girl no more than six or seven passed him by.

Wearing a red sweatshirt and white shorts with little red dots on them, the blonde-haired youngster was pulling on her father's hand. Perhaps she had been denied a present or an ice cream, it wasn't even a serious show of petulance, more a momentary moan, but the father's response was so savage, so out of proportion and brazen, B was hand-to-his-mouth shocked. Yes, B, who had seen plenty of violence in the army and then more plying a highly successful career in the international world of personal security. A career, his life, culminating in crushing, guilt-ridden death in Paris.

B watched almost in slow motion as the father, his face remaining perfectly impassive, brought his hand up high and smashed it down on the little girl's temple. In a moment the strike was repeated, then repeated again, the force of the last blow driving the girl's little frame five feet away into a shop doorway – stunned, bleeding and silent.

Completely emotionally separated, the father stood perfectly still telling the girl to rise and come to him. Yet even as these words left his mouth, the full force of a fist drove into his face, jaw cracking and teeth popping. B acting in disgust and an instinctive need to protect. The slender little girl in red. The powerful, callous man.

Punches continued to rain down as wild, pent-up frustration and pulsating grief exploded. B saw and felt enraged by red, his favourite colour, the colour of action and at that moment the red of intense and uncontrollable retribution. Punch after punch, the man's nose pumping blood, the dull thud of his head striking a shop wall, his groans as he reeled at the mercy of a strong, highly-trained professional.

In real time the attack lasted only about fifteen seconds but the man's life would surely have been in danger had a shrieking voice not pierced B's red bubble. Glimpsing a woman in the doorway with her arms around the little girl, the madness in his mind flew back to his Principal's wife lying in the street – victims, violence, mothers.

The punching stopped, the screaming halted, the man slumped deadweight to the ground and cuddling each other tightly the woman and the girl cried in mutual distress. B looked down at his bloodied hands, saw the red, and after a few seconds held his face in them as he too began to cry. Heaving sobs of deep, inner fatigue.

A long time passed before B felt a hand on his arm, a tender touch, a soft, female act of concern. The woman, still with her other arm around the wounded girl, stroked B's bare skin with her thumb and reaching upwards gently kissed him on the cheek.

'*Merci...*' she whispered. '*Merci*. It is OK. *Partez, maintenant*... leave. I can deal with him... *mon mari.*'

B looked into the woman's brown eyes and through his own tears and hers saw understanding shine back. He nodded, tapped his hand on hers, and feeling every one of his fifty-one years, slouched off to his apartment a hundred yards away. Amazingly, there were no onlookers, no outraged witnesses in the street. Except for him, it had been an exclusively family affair.

A key in the door, a painful shower, slugs of red wine and a warm duvet but B found little peace inside his bolthole. More tears, more anger at the father of today's family, more guilt about the poor boy and his mother lying dead in Paris. They had been his own adopted family, his responsibility, a decade dedicated to their safety, yet their silent bodies were a testament to his failure. B's Principal, the world-renowned diplomat, husband and father, who over the years had become a close friend, speeding across town after the shooting with the rest of the security team. Alive? Possibly. Hurt? No way of knowing.

Inevitably, the questions came too. The same sort of questions that dogged every single day of B's life, today their unsheathed claws sharpened by new pain and violence.

Why? How did this happen? What should he do? What could he have done?

Never-ending questions and never any answers.

Sleep did come off and on but when B awoke for the

third time the apartment was dark, a strong wind blew at the windows and heavy rain hammered the glass. Rising and padding to the bathroom, the hallway clock revealed it was 11.45 pm. Hours gone but his climax still lay ahead.

With a hand on each silver washbowl tap, the bathroom mirror stared back and B looked himself in the eyes. How sad and obviously vulnerable he was, how alone and cast adrift. Yet even now, colours would not let him be. Cream soap, white flannel, blue towel, he saw the red toothbrush tube. Red, blood, the girl's cute clothes. Helpless tears began to fall once more and B knew, like he was drowning, he had to get out, get anywhere, get away from the red.

Rain continued to slam down as B drove on. The ocean still to his right, the windscreen wipers slapping full speed. Kilometre after kilometre, working down the coast.

Deauville, Benerville-sur-Mer, Villers-sur-Mer…

Out of the wild night, suddenly a huge flash of lightning flared up the road and B realised with his first conscious thought since leaving the apartment he was driving alongside a vast beach. Huge areas of sands stretching beyond houses on his passenger side were momentarily illuminated like a sinister blue-black lunar expanse then just as quickly cloaked again.

Jolted out of his tunnel vision, B reacted instantly by ramming his foot down on the brake causing the car to skid for a considerable distance on the rain-soaked tarmac. Juddering to a stop, the engine still racing, frantically he fumbled for the door handle, leapt from the car and began gulping in air as huge winds battered him. Groping against their massive force, he stumbled a little way forward eventually grabbing the top of a waist-high wall to steady himself. Drenched, rocking and weeping, B threw his head back, screamed in lost, wild abandon and remained there, venting his soul, until at long, long last the storm gradually lost its force, his panic and rage finally began to ease and his terrifying red images slowly faded.

The next thing B knew was waking up in his car with a hand positioned as a pillow against the side window. Painfully opening his eyes, he couldn't place where he was at first. Then leaning forward as he looked through the misty car window out across a sandy beach in the dawn light, he remembered.

The car door opened again, this time to a sunny, peaceful morning so changed from the savage stormy night, and B got out, stretched stiffly, his clothes still wet, and looked about him. A quiet seaside town yet to come to terms with the new day that was obvious, but where was it? How far had he driven? He felt very hungry. So breakfast quick and he could work things out over eggs, toast and coffee.

Walking forward a few paces, B was intrigued by a curved white wall in front of him and dimly he remembered it from last night's storm. It ran in an arc for a few metres and at its middle a tourist's pay-per-view telescope pointed out to sea. Another two steps and he focussed on a blue vertical line running from its top to the ground and some blue words laid out on its rendered surface.

Incredulously, he spoke the words out aloud.

'Méridien de Greenwich'.

B crept up to the wall and bending down ran his hand

over the lettering, stopping on the vertical line running through the *de*. Then kneeling, as if by some primal instinct, his fingers felt for the rumble of drumbeats, of rushing rivers and galloping herds of animals.

It was the Greenwich Meridian, the line that ran around the globe from pole to pole, top to bottom, bottom to top. The Prime Meridian, circling the world, denoting the world's meeting of east and west.

B sat down on the floor with his back to the Meridian marker, the line's first strike on another country after leaving England's shores, and closed his eyes, his brain bombarded by a host of mental connections. Words, names, people, memories.

Greenwich, observatory, Wolfe, telescope...

The park, the swings, the bandstand, the river, the brown Thames...

The flood continued... Nelson, Trafalgar, Barbra Streisand...

The invisible Meridian Line ran out between B's outstretched legs just as it had done on a chilly autumn London day in 1965, the same 'muddy line' running down to all those penguins who lived at the bottom of the world. He pictured it all. Memories which in the sunny French seaside morning seemed clear and cleansing.

B marvelled at the serendipity propelling him to this spot. The chance of Honfleur, the little girl, the mother and her tender touch. It even sprang to mind if the killing of the little boy and his mother had been part of the journey too, but he felt a flicker of shame to think it. Now was not the time to debate that one with himself.

Instead, he stood up and quietly turned to look out to sea. *Villers-sur-Mer*, although he didn't know that yet, and a vast array of colours were displayed before him. Blue-green water, yellow-gold sand, wispy-white waves, the myriad tones of the sky and, yes, a red marker out to sea.

Red.

B saw red.

October 1965

East meets west.

Across a thin brass strip inlaid into cobblestones and running the entire width of the courtyard, thirty pairs of young legs straddle both sides of the Earth.

Laughter, shouts and squeals fill the air and Miss Andrews smiles. Despite the din, the teacher is having a good time too, lapping up all the fun with her young and very eager charges.

For most of the children in her class it's enough to be simply huddled up playing this exciting game of crossing the worlds. Yet not for B. For him, what's happening is far deeper than a mere game. Like all the others, he's standing with his feet on both sides of the muddy line (well, that's what the old man calls it) but there's more, so much more. Here in this special place something very significant is unfolding – even at ten years of age he can sense that. Something he knows he will remember and lock away right down inside for the rest of his life.

What a magic feeling to be perched so high up overlooking the huge expanse of London. A powerful magic churning so many things together. Brand new things revealed only in the last half hour... Observatory, muddy line, hemisphere, Wolfe, stars and time. All of them mixing with the stream of normal things constantly flowing around inside his head every second of his life... colours, lines, shapes and patterns.

With voluminous grey clouds looming over the city, a cool autumn wind on B's cheeks, the chaos of giggles continues to jump from one side of the world to the other. Such delight in the power to skip between hemispheres (although the children have no idea what hemispheres are, despite the old man's explanation).

The Royal Observatory high up in London's Greenwich Park is a very familiar sight for the youngsters. Being so near their school, all of them have visited it before – family fun, family outings. All except B. A new boy, he's only lived in the area for a month, but he knows he could have been born here and his parents would still never have brought him. They just didn't do things like that and certainly never to magical places like this with its muddy line.

According to the old man, the line cuts the world in two and stretches right out across the park and as far away as the eye can see, never stopping, running right down to the end of the world where it's so cold only penguins can live. And B knows what penguins are because he's seen them in a magazine. Penguins, with lovely contrasting colours. Black and white with touches of yellow and red.

Red.

His favourite colour.

Red. Always standing out, like a lady's lipstick, like buses and cars, like flowers in gardens and a shirt he has. There's even a big red ball on the tall pole above the old building across the cobbled courtyard and B starts to daydream. A fiery fireball dangling in the sky...

Arriving earlier at the observatory, Miss Andrews stood all the children in the middle of the courtyard and introduced an ancient-looking man who proceeded to lecture them for a quarter of an hour while all the time flailing his arms around his head like a mad magician.

The observatory, he declared, was a very important place and kings and queens had built it especially so that famous and very intelligent people could look at the stars in the sky to see what they did. Stars, it was firmly believed, held secrets about time and if the famous people could only uncover them then the world would be a better place for everyone. The famous people had been in charge of the observatory for centuries and were under strict orders to find out about stars by using all the telescopes and other old equipment kept in the various buildings.

The old man carried a slim black telescope in his hands and paraded in front of the boys and girls showing it off. But B already knew what it was because he had seen one on the telly only a few weeks ago, something about pirates and a flag. He remembered a pattern on the screen. A pure white skull and some bones crossed against a black background.

Flapping his arms even faster, the old man told the children to stand alongside a muddy line as it crossed the courtyard and then explained how people at the observatory had put it there to ensure everyone in the world knew where the two halves of the world met – how east and west were divided up. B couldn't understand much but caught something about how people found out where they were at sea. He pictured wild waves and huge monsters rising from the deep, attacking ships because their captains had steered the wrong course.

Like so many before him at the observatory, B imagined this line as a physical thing running out around the world. Right now, were people in other countries stepping over it in the street, crossing it in fields or rivers or somewhere up mountains?

But the big question was, why was it muddy?

When the old man finished, Miss Andrews stepped forward asking the children to respond in the usual way. Thirty pairs of lips rang out 'Thank you!' then, at her clap, the class was set off hemisphere dancing and the teacher soaked up their young delirium – her vocational reward. Eventually, reluctantly, Miss Andrews clapped once more for the children to stop. It was now nearly noon and school dinners awaited them but they could spend just a few minutes exploring the courtyard before they had to go.

Time at the home of time had passed quickly. The class left the school gates at ten o'clock sharp in a nice, neat hand-in-hand double queue, a multicoloured snake slipping through the breezy Greenwich morning. And just as the snake was forming in the playground, B felt his hand being grabbed, squeezed and held up into the air all in one motion.

'Hello!' a girl announced, 'I'm Molly. I'm funny!'

and just as suddenly she drove their arms back down to their sides. Taken off guard, B could only stare in silence. Evidently, she was his partner. He didn't seem to have much choice.

B knew of this girl but hadn't spoken to her yet. She had come to his notice through a curious incident a week ago when Miss Andrews went out of the classroom for something. Humming loudly while standing perfectly still on one leg, without warning she sprinted to the front of the class, jumped up on the teacher's desk and shouted, *'Emergency Ward 10!'*. B was deeply impressed by the girl accomplishing her recklessness and arriving back at her desk a second before Miss Andrews's return. What timing! But he couldn't make sense of it. *Emergency Ward 10*? He had seen the hospital drama on the telly, his mum never missed it. What had it got to do with anything?

From leaving school up to the Greenwich Park gates, their conversation had been only by hand, every now and again Molly squeezing B's as if in reaction to something she had just thought of or seen. But he couldn't wait any longer.

'What d'ya mean?' he blurted. 'You said you're funny.'

'F-u-n-n-e-e...' Molly mouthed back elaborately. 'It's what my dad says. I do mad things.'

'You did a mad thing last week. You jumped on Miss's desk.'

'That *was* funny. Everybody laughed.'

'Why'd'ya shout *Emergency Ward 10*?'

'Well, what else?'

B hadn't a clue.

At the top of the park, with the observatory directly ahead, Miss Andrews clapped her hands for the class to stop and form a huddle around her. High above them on a pockmarked pillar of white stone stood a dark, caped man looking out across the vastness of London.

'Children!' she said, pointing a hand upwards. 'Anyone know who this is a statue of?'

A pause, then a squeeze on B's hand.

'It's General Wolfe, Miss! My dad brought me here. He told me his name and I started howling like a real wolf.'

B visualised his partner leaping around holding her head back and letting go.

Miss Andrews slanted her head in surprise. 'Well, that's a very good way to remember things. But did your dad tell you what General Wolfe is famous for? Anyone?'

Silence, except for the breeze in the trees. Molly's unexpected knowledge obviously didn't stretch further.

'Well. General Wolfe won the country of Canada for Great Britain. Making us more powerful. Wolfe was a hero.'

Then, adding with a self-conscious smile, 'Canada is a very long way away. But I shall be going there soon on my holidays and I will bring some photographs back to show you.'

Another clap started the snake moving towards the observatory but as it slithered away B lagged behind continuing to stare up at General Wolfe. Black figure, three-cornered shaped hat, shock white stone – colours, patterns – here was a hero fixing his glare across the capital and his own gaze was only averted at some length by the firm tug of Molly's impatient hand.

Now having spent some time learning about time

and the jumping game over, B turned away from the other children and retreated to some metal railings at the edge of the courtyard. The broad expanse of the park stretched out far below him. A huge area of green grass, criss-crossed with paths laid out before the elegant white buildings and columns of the landmark National Maritime Museum.

A little way behind the museum B saw the river – the brown, slow Thames he had quickly come to know in his short Greenwich stay. No school or other mates yet, no brothers or sisters (he doubted very much whether his mum and dad wanted another one like him), he had already come to look upon the river as his friend – something to walk alongside, imagine things with and talk to. Waves constantly rolling across the brown, murky water, birds bouncing off its surface, forbidding, gloomy barges, there were always so many shapes and colours. The river felt like a non-stop living thing which somehow was always listening to him.

'What's caught your eye then?'

Gazing out over the railings, B heard a voice from behind and a light touch on his shoulder.

How he liked her. Nervous on his first day a month ago, how softly she had spoken to him after his mum simply handed him over like a dog on a leash, span on her heels and left without a word. Kind Miss Andrews, holding his hand, smiling and listening to what he had to say. He never got that at home.

B whispered. 'There's so much to see, Miss. Always. It's bonkers.'

Bending down to hear him, his teacher looked into the boy's face and saw what she saw every time – a great sense of concentration, of fighting to keep things in, of a little boy fit to burst with whatever was inside him. It wasn't merely a child's natural enthusiasm, as a teacher for eight years now she saw that all the time. No, high spirits were one thing, what was going on underneath B's outer shell was something entirely different, altogether mysterious. He was a child apart, that was clear enough and she wished she could pinpoint why. So far, she had drawn a blank.

B took the lack of response as a cue.

'Miss, why do they call it the Muddy Line?'

Miss Andrews looked puzzled.

'Muddy Line, Miss. That's what the old man said. Goes right around the world because of time and ships and telescopes and things. But it's not muddy here. Why?'

Miss laughed.

'You are funny. He didn't say "muddy". He called it the "Meridian" line. Can you say that? Meridian?'

B stuttered. 'M-e-r-i-d-i-a-n.'

The teacher ruffled B's hair. 'It tells us what's east and west.'

'But it does go right around the world, Miss, doesn't it? Even if it isn't muddy?'

'Yes it does, right around.' She paused. 'Does that interest you? Do you like the idea of that?' for one glorious moment thinking this was a breakthrough. B looked away quickly and shuffled around again to face the sweep of the park below.

'Lines are all over the place. They're in the shapes of

everything and join up with other lines to make things. Lines and colours. Do you like colours, Miss?'

'Um, yes I do.' But he kept going.

'I like red best but I'm not sure what one. There's lots. Red cars and flowers. My mum's lips are red when she goes out. My blood's red. All different. You got bits of dark red in your dress, Miss.'

Miss Andrews smiled, indeed she did, but realising in that instant she had temporarily forgotten the rest of the class, she darted away clapping and calling for the snake to form again. As the children started to assemble, B twisted away from the railings and his red images faded. Scanning the courtyard, he searched for Molly spotting her in a few seconds in a far corner. Standing bolt upright, she held her head high, flapping her hands about.

'Join the queue!' Miss Andrews shouted at her as she passed. A madam in the making that one, despite knowing General Wolfe.

Eventually, Molly came up to B and without a word scooped his hand up, squeezed and started to swing it back and forth.

'What's all that flapping about?'

Molly stopped their hands at the forward apex, holding them both high.

'Playing kings and queens. Waving to the crowds.'

'Why?'

'Was fun. Kings and queens came here, didn't they? The old man told us, didn't he?'

Suddenly, Molly swung their clasped hands back down to their sides so violently the two burst out laughing. They were still in hysterics when the snake slithered out of the observatory gates and stopped once again in front of General Wolfe.

'We shan't be going back the same way as we came,' Miss Andrews declared. 'We'll walk straight down this big hill here on the grass. It'll be quicker and more fun. But be careful. It's very steep and I want absolutely no running, do you all understand? Take your time and keep behind me.'

Two by two the snake started off downwards and Molly and B duly followed at the back still giggling. But after a few steps, B felt a sudden pull of his hand and a loud shout.

'Come on, let's go!'

No time to think. Molly yanked him to one side and they started running full pelt down the grassy hill. Wind ringing in their ears, in seconds they shot past their teacher, and by the time they heard her high-pitched wailing from behind they had covered another twenty-five yards going even faster. Inevitably, their flight couldn't last and, crossing a footpath, their speed refused to take the ground's sudden change of angle and they careered to the grass, rolling and tumbling further down the hill. Amazingly, when they finally came to a stop both lying on their backs, the two were still holding hands.

Within moments Miss Andrews was upon them shrieking at the top of her voice, crashing to the ground, checking for injuries. In time, satisfied there was none, she hoisted the runaways to their feet with an arm around each waist. But she was shaking very badly and despite the madness of the moment the children were both shocked at her obvious distress. Never had they seen her so upset, so frightened before.

Molly took a gulp of air as if to speak, to make amends. Immediately, B realised she was going to own up to starting the run, to say it was her fault, to take the blame. Somehow he felt he had to protect her, to save her, and before he could stop himself he was shouting.

'I just saw red, Miss!'

December 2006

Running.

Up from the steep rocky path from Newlands Hause. Running towards the green horizon, the green grass-line above the lush green Buttermere valley. The Lake District, the hills, valleys and rivers. Old friends.

Running.

That torment yet again. Guns firing, running hard down the corridor, through the hotel lobby and out into the glaring Parisian sunshine, just in time to see his Principal's limousine speeding away, tyres screeching, rubber burning. His eyes off the ball in a back room dealing with some government official. A routine exit, no apparent danger, no recent threats, nothing suspected. B not essential. Go back in the support car.

Now on the pavement and in the road lay the consequences. Boy and woman, son and mother, stretched out in a grotesque pairing. The body of one of his team face-down several feet away. Fumbling a hand to his radio earpiece and shouting but just hiss and static. No knowing if his Principal is alive. Yes or no, his family lay in ruins.

Breaking the horizon, B arrives at the top of High Snockrigg, his precious, hilltop sanctuary in those boyhood days of ferocious, pent-up anger with everything and everybody. B is remarkably fit, his job, his way of life, demanding (demanded?) it, but the years between his last visit here and today are unalterable facts. Hands to knees recovering his breath, B hawks in air and slumps to the cropped green grass, a few mounds of rock showing through, some ubiquitous Herdwick sheep nosing around in the distance.

When he starts breathing normally again, B pulls himself up and takes in the cinematic Lakeland panorama before him. A vista so familiar all those years ago which in today's cold December sunshine is remarkably snow-free. Mountains he has climbed, paths he has trod, sunny days and black nights, shouting anger into the winds and frustration to the rains.

Mighty Grasmere away to his right and sweeping west, the tops of Rannerdale Knotts, Melbreak, Red Pike, High Stile, High Crag, before lowering to Haystacks. Next in the circle, Fleetwith Pike, Dale Head, Hindscarth and right behind him the sheer bulk of Robinson. Then the lakes, the dancing water patchwork running through connecting valleys. Far away in the afternoon light, silver sparkling Loweswater, a little nearer the grey-blue of Crummock Water and down below him, deep, green, smooth and forever magical, Buttermere.

The loving comfort of High Snockrigg, a few miles down the Lorton Road from his old home in Cockermouth. A walk up from Buttermere village and, the reward on achieving its moderate height, a vast vantage point across Lakeland. So many hills as they meet the heavens, low level but remote, more sheep than people, so many days and nights, his wide-open, secret place. His living kaleidoscope of red sunsets, orange sunrises and skies of blue, grey, black or whatever colour the temperamental Lakeland weather might throw at him.

B had driven straight from Paris in the early hours. Motorway to Calais, the Shuttle, driving from Folkestone, orbiting London, the A1 north, the A66 across high, bleak moors and he was in Cumbria. Out of the bustling market town of Keswick, along the twisting Newlands Valley road passing little farms and errant sheep the wrong side of fences, rising hills on all sides, at length he reached the hause. Parking in the wide lay-by, he donned a warm red jacket, strode up the side of High Snockrigg over the dashing, waterfall sound of nearby Moss Force before reaching grassland and starting to sprint.

For so many reasons, there had been no return to the Lakes since that day he left for the army so long ago. But with the shrill chords of the Meridian Line at Villers-sur-Mer still striking inside him, the inquiry into the shootings still fruitless and getting colder by the day, politicians and factions in various countries still saying nothing and his resignation confirmed on his return to Paris from Honfleur, B had been drawn back by sirens of his past. Sirens from which he had no power or wish to ignore.

Naturally, he had thought about the Lake District many times over the years. On each mountain topped all over the world, he had surveyed the view and felt distant stings of memory. But as always, he told himself it was a place with its place only in his past. Leaving for the army had meant leaving everything, all that he had hated as a teenager – his mum, his anger and, sadly, the Lakes and hills, his friends. Going back would only open up old wounds.

Yet Villers-sur-Mer's clanging bell, its raw, insistent toll, had utterly consumed him, its ceaseless reverberation drowning out the day to day. His first thoughts of return had come right there standing on the Meridian Line, that morning after the storm, but the final decision had emerged only out of dark days and even darker nights back in Paris. Eventually, B had concluded, if he was to dampen the incessant bell and find any answers to the questions that plagued him then he must return to the Lakes and let the chips of his future fall where they may. There was no other place. And like an arrow, straight and true, he had flown to his target.

Nothing had changed, except the arrival of wispy white wind turbines away towards the coast. High Snockrigg looked just the same, the hills were all in the correct order, as were the three lakes, and the little outpost of Buttermere was as it had always been, beautiful and serene. B sat for a very long time taking it all in, letting his mind go completely blank. No sounds except for the gentle breeze and some dreamy birdsong. The same peace that used to calm his old anger. Then, when he had emptied himself as much as he possibly could, he allowed the ferocious, competing chaos of the world to rush back in.

Life in France was over now, there was no going back. His Paris flat let, farewells bade to a few acquaintances in and outside his tight professional world, a midnight call to a woman he had been seeing of late but bereft of any emotional or physical ties, B had kept his *au revoirs* short with no hint of his destination.

His Principal, the man he had steered beyond harm's way for a decade, his friend the diplomat, the political fixer, the international negotiator respected in the east and west and almost everywhere else, had told him face to face and in the presence of others he did not blame him for the death of his wife and son. The murderers were the sworn enemies of his world stature and influence, his family and his country, his religion and his god.

Publicly exonerated perhaps, but B blamed himself completely. Poor decisions, a false sense of security (Security? Ha, that was rich!), perhaps finally getting old, he may have been pardoned with grim generosity but B knew the truth. A golden, basic rule had been broken. He had got too close to the family. He had become too emotionally involved. He had loved too much. And in the end he knew this had been the key weakness, the deadly flaw, the soft spot which had spawned complacency.

Born only weeks before he was hired – highly recommended, hand-picked, all the experience plus the essential personal chemistry, perfect – B watched the boy grow up. First steps, learning to swim, birthday parties, family visits, holidays, hundreds of car journeys, happy talk, even on occasion some words of wisdom, the son lived with his protector as a central part of the family – a rock, a fixture. B realised the boy felt more for him than just another of his father's employees – there was respect, a little hero-worship. And for his part too, despite his training and years of detached professionalism, there was something about the boy that drew B in, submitting him to the quiet and sensitive charm of the man-child relationship. He could never forget what the boy had said to him once when he was no more than six or seven – bright, intelligent, eager.

'What makes colours? *Savez-vous? Rouge mon préféré!*' And a car journey home from somewhere was spent exploring their views on the subject.

Later that day, B slipped a red-coloured stone into the boy's hand, a piece of red amber, something he'd had for years. The lad laughed adoringly, turned it over in his fingers, put it to his lips then from that day onwards kept it in his pocket whatever he was wearing. Sitting on the lush Lakeland grass, B twiddled that same stone in his own fingers now. Eventually, on that terrible day when he had lain the boy down softly on the ground outside the hotel having taken him in his arms for the last time as a protector but the first time in the admission of love, B slid his hand into the boy's pocket and took his gift back. A gift as red as the boy's blood pooling on the pavement.

France, tragedy, his life as it had been, questions about his past, more questions about his future, these were what B had returned to the Lakes to try and put into some semblance of order and resolve. The killings, his flight to Honfleur and his uncanny stumble upon *Méridien de Greenwich*, were life-changing events which had driven him back.

Back on High Snockrigg, once more B felt the weight of being cast adrift, cut off from all he had come to know. All his adult years had been spent protecting people, looking after others, making sure they survived, that they lived and were safe. Now everything and everyone had gone and he had only himself to focus on. Looking out over Buttermere and back over his life, B considered the conclusion he had reached walking the lonely streets of Paris. All those famous people – all the actors and the pop stars, the politicians and business chiefs, the religious leaders and even the odd royal – his every thought for however long he was hired had been for them. What did they need? What would make them secure? Death threats, blackmail, the fear of a sad, lonely, fame-obsessed fan, a religious zealot or faction, no matter what the job, B's feelings, his own personal needs and wants never entered into it. B had existed to serve others. He had lived his life for others. He had forgone himself.

Then, working for his Principal and his family over the last ten years. Yes, B had loved the job, had loved the people, and yes, he could even admit now, had loved the boy, but it was still a decade of living his life through others. Wherever the non-stop, international schedule demanded – the UN, Moscow, Washington, Tel Aviv, Beirut, Beijing – B went too. His Principal and his family were the principal lives.

The army didn't start out that way but it ended up the same.

B joined the services to escape his anger, an inexhaustible fury making his life a misery in Cockermouth. Such destructive anger, only finding solace and abatement by roaming the colours and shapes of his familiar fells. His Lakeland mentor and only human friend, Miss Hattiemore, had put forward the idea. It was she who saw the army as an answer, a positive channel for B's bottomless negative feelings. Signing up would give him an outdoor life (B's love of the hills proved this was essential) and the opportunity at sixteen for a clean break from everything he loathed – his mum, school and his utter frustration at always feeling this way. More practically, it was also the chance for him to steer clear of the petty crime and associated mischief B had no doubt already dabbled with.

Green eyes, greying hair, his saviour all through his Cockermouth years, Miss Hattiemore had opened him up to all the majesty and magic of the fells. His friend in angry times and whose home was his haven, she was the mum he never had and the one he loved as if she was. Miss Hattiemore had told him to go into the army and leave everything behind – everything, including herself – and that's precisely what B had done, never looking back. Never, until Villers-sur-Mer, until the line around the world hooked him again. Until today when returning to High Snockrigg.

Joining up didn't prove an immediate panacea. B's anger persisted and he rejected his initial training with its noisy, brutish, in-your-face discipline. The army offered no change, no escape and there were fights, charges for drunkenness and insubordination. Not the ideal soldier then when his first posting to Northern Ireland came through in the early 1970s.

Drab, drab Belfast. Subdued colours, gritty browns and blacks alleviated only by sudden outbreaks of red-hot violence and the white, icy antipathy of almost everyone, Catholics and Protestants alike. Patrols, roadblocks, day-to-day fear on the streets, occasionally a mate blown apart by a bomb or picked off by a sniper's shot. Yet gradually, through the relentless grind, B's anger began to temper. There was more caution, fewer outbursts and red mists. Then one day it all died, killed on a street corner leaving behind the severed hand of a little boy in a black jacket and the rest of him covered in red blood in the middle of a road.

Red. Colour even at the moment of horror.

The close comparison of two needless deaths of children in Belfast and Paris, separated by many years but unified now in his mind, had filled the dark hours between Villers-sur-Mer and B's flight to the Lakes. Young boys, lives to lead, victims of misplaced passions, he had cradled them both so early in death and both marked a major turning point in his life.

In Belfast the change was dramatic. Suddenly, he became disciplined, dedicated, professional, cool, on the button. All at once negative, internal anger was replaced by a positive, outward concern for others, a need to protect. Driving from Honfleur to Paris, crossing bridges over the Seine in the early hours, packing his bags for England and even mounting the track to High Snockrigg once more, B kept thinking how much his life had been shaped by that little Belfast boy lying in a pool of red in the street.

Then living for others becoming a way of life – a doctrine, a mantra – and ultimately, a distinguished army career was realised on its iron theme. The squaddie who looked after his pals and covered their backs, the corporal watching out for everyone on patrol in Belfast or Derry or Omagh, the beloved young sergeant yomping across the Falkland Islands during the Argentine war and, finally, the captain who always put his men first and foremost. Years of service to selflessness.

So, when over dinner one evening at a gentleman's club, a former colleague proffered a friendly invitation to join a new, high-class private security company based in Paris, B acknowledged the timely need for a fresh professional challenge and accepted with gusto in complete comfort it was an entirely natural move. Protection for Queen and country merely exchanged for the more commercial kind.

A change of country perhaps but the business was just the same, the bottom line no different. Others before himself, other people's lives before his own. And that same doctrine remained his personal watchword until another little boy's death, a boy with red in his pocket, forced this latest step-change in his life.

And here B sat, recalled by a timeline calling time on him, facing the daunting prospect of having no one but himself to look after. Certainly, there were disturbing unknowns to confront, with the most fundamental being, who exactly was he? What did he want and what the hell was he going to do now?

Cast adrift indeed and B shrugged at the irony of

coming full circle. In Paris he had been able to say his goodbyes, there was time for parting drinks at his usual bar and farewell walks along the Left Bank bookseller stalls. Back in 1966, however, there had been no such luxuries. Then he never got the chance to say goodbye to anything, not even his friend the brown Thames. One morning B got up, was told to get dressed, pack a bag and ordered into a car. Hours and hours, miles and miles later, he arrived at his mum's sister's house in a place called the Lake District and all B had known and loved – the park, the observatory, the Meridian Line, the alley and the river – was gone.

Full circle. He had lost Paris, his way of life, and sitting on High Snockrigg he recalled losing everything dear to him as a deeply unhappy eleven-year-old. Clipping a few blades of grass with his fingers, he let out his breath at the memory of the dearest of all. B held the name on his lips for a few seconds as another pulse of wind stroked his face making his already glassy eyes even more watery.

Putting his hand into his red walking-jacket pocket, he pulled out a slip of paper, a computer printout, an easy task of research when in addition to the Internet you knew all the tricks and methods of the trade. He read the lines again.

Molly Larnder. Stage name Venus. Actress. Now appearing at the New Theatre, Hull...

B studied the facts – the address, the history as far as it went – and the voice of Barbra Streisand came into his head.

October 1965

Running.

Out of the red-brick school, all the way home. Running hard, beating heart, pounding pavement.

Usually B walks, very slowly, taking his time, savouring every single moment before going indoors. Since moving to his new house, he often delays that inevitability by detouring off to the river to see what's happening. Always something going on, especially at high tide when the brown water lies just below his feet. Chunks of driftwood sloshing up against the bank walls, strange contours of mud and oil floating at the top. Shapes like the outlines of unknown coastlines.

There's no fear of going home, no threats of violence or other physical horrors, simply an understanding his parents couldn't care less about him. Mostly ignored, generally told off when he isn't, blamed for anything going wrong, shoved out of the way, always talked over, never to,

B feels maybe he's living with the wrong family. His mum often calls him a "spare part". He doesn't know what that means but it sounds right. Molly holds his hand and his teacher talks to him in that nice, kind way. No one ever does those things at home. No one touches him, not even to smack. Perhaps he doesn't matter enough even to be hit.

But it's different today.

Must get home, fast. Must. Despite everything, despite the daily dismissals and rejections, surely they will want to hear about the observatory, the muddy line and Molly.

School bell, school gates, Molly's mum there on time to take her daughter home, and although B now lives only a few hundred yards away he has a twinge of envy. Nobody ever picks him up, no one's at the gates for him. Protection from a grown-up doesn't matter, he can look after himself, but mattering enough to come for him does. But no big deal now. A quick wave as Molly turns her head to smile and B tears off home at top speed, the sheet of paper in his hand flapping noisily in his sprint-wind, his fingers gripping tightly to stop it blowing away.

Miss Andrews had been adamant. *'Make sure you show it to your parents'.*

Zigzagging a couple of backstreets, B speeds into the narrow alley where he now lives. A row of small cottages sits across a pavement only a few feet wide just down from a pub and the side wall of a part hotel-part restaurant he knows is very old indeed. Both buildings look out on their other sides directly onto the brown Thames. How good to have his friend the river, now one of two new friends, flowing so near.

Breaking fast to his cottage in the middle of the row,

B jerks up the mat on the step, grabs a key and rushes into the house slamming the door. Despite the running he's hardly out of breath, sheer excitement and expectation fully compensating, but his heart is pounding in his ears.

'Mum!' still gripping the paper hard, running into the living room, 'Mum, you there?'

Silently she appears behind him, exiting the kitchen. Dark green dressing gown, white towel wrapped around her just washed hair, a cigarette held softly between her lips, B's mother doesn't look at her son but instead focusses her gaze above him into an indistinct middle distance. It's her way.

B goes to speak but for some reason he hesitates for a tiny instant. A wafer-thin shadow of a doubt races across his mind as his mother breezes past.

'That father of yours... late again. Work and pub, work and pub. Makes me sick! Do you have to slam the door?' Her first recognition B is there and he seizes the opportunity.

'Mum! Look, Mum! It's a picture. The observatory in the park. I drew it today...'

The precious drawing offered upwards as if in tribute to his mother is simply ignored like it is meant for someone else. Turning away, she takes her cigarette from her lips, jabs it angrily into an ashtray on the mantelpiece hardly missing a beat.

'I don't understand. He knows I want to go out. I don't know how many times I told him. Nothing gets through, does it? Does no one listen to me?'

The palpable irony is lost on her and B is not old enough to understand the nuance. He tries again.

'Mum, it was great today. The observatory's a great place. I saw lots of things and a line right around the world, although I thought it was muddy. Then Molly and me ran down this big hill and fell over and Miss was very angry but she let us off and I drew this in the afternoon. Miss said it was very good and told me to show it to you.'

For the second half of this speech B watches his mother slowly depart the living room returning to the kitchen. By the time he ends it she has gone completely, water running from the sink, a few bangs and crashes, her bad mood being taken out on the cupboards. Surrounded by the living room's faded colours, he carefully places his picture on the table, pulls out a chair and sits down.

Staring down at his work – black lines and shapes, one spot of vibrant colour, a deep and violent red – B feels a tear trail down his nose and drop silently onto the paper. Blobbing exactly where the Meridian Line crosses the black and white hashed courtyard, the water smudges and the line does indeed look muddy. B is taken aback. He never cries and certainly never over the insensitivity of either of his parents. Why now?

Suddenly, he wants the river.

Jumping up, he grabs his drawing and tears out of the house as fast and noisily as he entered it. Into the alleyway, leaping left, sprinting the eighty yards or so to the end, he breaks right past the entrance to the old restaurant and out onto the cobbled river walkway.

Breathing hard, B stands at the sturdy black fencing fronting the Thames. The tide full, the brown flow swelling just below his feet and he begins to rip the drawing up, first into halves, then into quarters, then into as many pieces as his young strength allows. When he can't tear any more, he throws the pile of paper into the river and watches as bits shrivel in the water, disappear or float away. A flash comes to him and he holds his head right back and howls like a wolf.

Howling...

The day coming back as an entirety, all of it at once. Thoughts merging and dovetailing. Colours gelling together.

Molly's smile, their raised hands locked, the old man's flailing arms, the fiery red ball, the grey threatening city, the huge, dark warrior above the white plinth, the speed of the flight down the green hill, Miss Andrews's kind hand on his shoulder.

Howling...

The snake arrived back at school tired but glowing from the walk and the children moved through to the hall to start their school dinners. Giggling the whole time, B ate with Molly, every now and then jabbing their arms out in different directions. This represented a new, shared secret code between them. It stood for adventure, for Molly being funny and for getting away with it.

Back on the grassy hill, Miss Andrews had wrapped her arms tightly around herself trying to stop shaking. In all her time teaching she had never lost it before. She had experienced many scrapes and accidents with her children so what was more shocking about this one?

It was the boy. Despite her professionalism, on which

she prided herself above all things, he had got firmly under her skin. She cared more than she wanted to admit. A sign of weakness? B said he had seen red. Where had that come from? Did he even know what that meant? Was he trying to play games with her after their talk up at the observatory?

No, it was Molly leading him astray. B was the innocent party. Molly, a developing force of nature, who no doubt would end up either a film star or a burnt-out neurotic, or both, was the culprit. Reluctantly, the teacher decided to let the whole thing pass and unwrapping her arms in confirmation, she clapped her hands to reform the snake which, subdued and silent, slithered back to school.

After dinner the new friends spent a few silent minutes apart in the playground as if the intensity of their togetherness was temporarily too much and they needed a little time on their own to reflect. But by the time the afternoon bell went they were back holding hands again, both bubbly, laughing around Miss Andrews, ready to return to their classroom.

Inside, all the children were sat down and told to draw a picture to capture what they had seen and learnt at the observatory. Large sheets of white paper and pieces of charcoal were handed out to the usual flurry of excitement.

'Remember,' urged Miss Andrews, 'all the things we saw today. The observatory, the Meridian Line, General Wolfe, jumping between east and west...'

But B was already at work, drawing, creating lines and forming shapes, the whole of his picture already there in his head. Certainty. Charcoal passed over his paper like wind, strokes streamed from his hand like blood from a cut. Head down, eyes focussed, from deep within came an unconscious, intensive release.

His scene was of the observatory as seen from the courtyard gates, slightly elevated in outlook with the line around the world spanning the paper. At odds with the events of the day, when everything teemed with shouts and laughter by so many, B fashioned only one figure. Standing with her feet on each side of the world, she looked outwards as if greeting the viewer, waving to imaginary kings and queens. And for a boy so enmeshed in the world of colours, so conscious of their constant impact on him and his struggle for their meaning, some unexplained instinct told him his drawing should have only one explosive splash, one piece, one element. Red. The observatory's fireball dangling in the sky.

No thoughts except for his picture, looking up only when at last he needed it, with blackish, charcoaled hands, B looked around scanning for a source. The classroom was quiet except for scratching on paper and Molly yawning, absentmindedly twirling her hair. His chair scraped slightly as he rose and walked forwards.

Miss Andrews looked up from her seat at the front of the class. She hadn't seen B arrive and was surprised as usually if a child wanted anything they put their hand up and called from their desk. Twisting her head, she acknowledged him.

'Please, Miss. I need some red.'

Initially, she thought the boy was referring to the events back on the hill but looking at his eyes she realised what he was after. Prodding about in her pen pot, she picked one out and offered it to him.

'Will this do?'

B nodded, smiled, turned and walked back to his seat.

Sitting down, he resumed as if he had never stopped. Engrossed in an instant, he began to colour in the fireball with the red biro in a hashed, criss-cross style. Lines meeting lines, forming the shapes and patterns he wanted. Finishing quickly, B pulled himself up in his chair and grasped the paper in both hands to view it. Slowly, a tiny smile bent his mouth and deep inside he felt the flicker of a new and very satisfying sensation. Placing the drawing down softly on his desk, he put his hands under his knees and closed his eyes wallowing in the euphoria.

After what seemed an age, a loud clap brought B back to the present. Miss Andrews was calling for all the drawings to be handed in telling everyone not to forget to put their names at the top of the paper. School was nearly over and while the children were washing their hands at the basin by the store cupboard at the back of the room the teacher flicked through the work announcing that tomorrow they would write stories about their visit, putting their pictures into words. As the bell sounded, Miss Andrews dismissed the class but with a finger stopped B for him to stay behind. No time had been lost in teaming up with Molly again but with a shrug she agreed to wait for him outside school.

Alone together, the teacher leant back on her desk and met B's anxious gaze. The boy had affected her so much throughout the day it was as if she needed some kind of closure with him before she could go home. Reaching behind, she turned to hold out his picture in front of her then reversed it so he could see it himself. She watched him run his eyes over the paper.

'Do you know what this is?' she asked in her soft tone.

Fearful of being in trouble again, B shook his head so the teacher answered for him.

'This is the best drawing I have ever seen by one of my class. It's wonderful. Do you know that? Wonderful.' B remained silent.

The teacher leaned forward to be closer, remembering the mother who had deposited her son on her like he was some kind of infestation.

'I want you to take this home now and make sure you show it to your parents. Tell them I said you could, the only one in class allowed to do that. Do you understand? They should see how marvellous it is and feel proud. Then bring it back tomorrow for your story.'

With a touch to his arm Miss Andrews sent B on his way and as he disappeared out of the door she pushed up from her desk to walk to the chalkboard. What a full day, she sighed, one fixed with thoughts and wonderings mostly about this little boy. It could have been a fluke but somehow she didn't think so. The drawing had been more than good, more than a ten-year-old's good. There was real quality here, a keen vision, a sharp eye, a deeper eye perhaps than she had seen in any pupil before. The beginning of understanding? But was it for him or for her?

She picked up a piece of white chalk and with care wrote one word in the top corner of the board.

Red.

Molly at the centre
of B's world

Molly.

Standing in the centre of the bandstand situated between Greenwich Park's flower gardens and the observatory.

Head to one side, one arm held straight out from her chin, the other curling upwards to the other arm, pumping away at an imaginary violin.

Spinning on her heels, B jogs in a circle around her making her movements seem twice as fast. The round shape of the bandstand, its red metal pillars and iron railings, the haze of the surrounding green grass spilling into view, visualising the light brown wood of the fantasy instrument in her hands.

'Ladies and gentlemen!' she announces. 'The best violin player in the whole wide world. Molly, here for one day. Off to Paris tomorrow… beautiful music!'

B keeps circling. 'You're mad. Mad as a fruitcake. Can you play anything else?'

Without a break, Molly stops twisting, starts to jig from one foot to the other and bringing her hands to the side of her mouth starts playing the flute.

'Like this?'

'That all?'

In a second she transforms from a flute to a trombone, one hand clenched tightly to her mouth, the other rapidly punching out to tap the beat. After a few seconds making a gurgling noise she thinks must be like a trombone sound, she starts laughing and, as if spent from all the action, collapses onto the bandstand floor with her arms and legs splayed like a snow-angel.

'Thank you, thank you, everyone! I love you all. You're the best audience I have ever had. Thank you!'

'You're mad!'

'I know... and as my dad says...'

'F-u-n-n-e-e-e!'

'Yesireee!'

* * *

Molly.

Sitting on the playground step holding B's hand. Not in her usual, playful way but tenderly, with care, with concern. Her eyes fixed on B's face as he looks down at his black plimsoll shoes between his legs. The words ringing in his ears – lost, picture, hard to believe, where, how...

Angry Miss Andrews.

Miss, in her sand-coloured dress, with her black shoes and blue jumper, holding the white chalk. That B should have been so careless, so wilful. She had allowed him to take his picture home especially and now he was the only one in the class not to have a drawing to write their story. Well, he would jolly well have to do another one instead – some paper, a piece of charcoal and, as an afterthought, a red pen. Her anger is really frustration. She so wanted B to repeat the triumph of yesterday. She had discovered something here.

But B's desire, the need, the inner feelings are gone, floating away on the dirty brown Thames. Howling at the water, howling at the sky. B will not recreate his vision of Molly with one foot in each side of the world below the fiery red ball. No shapes, no lines or colours today. Just a vague gesture.

For Miss Andrews there's no eye, no subtlety, no explanation. A picture like every other ten-year-old's picture. Acceptance passes with a resigned sigh. No doubt it had been a fluke. The possibility a tantalising play on her mind at the end of a long day.

* * *

Molly.

Standing centre stage, bathed in the golden glow. Angel Gabriel shining his beneficence down on an incredulous Mary.

No lights in the school hall except for a single spotlight with its coloured filter flowing onto Molly's cardboard wings making her shape stand out like the bright star in the night sky. A star the famous people at the observatory would have wanted to see from their telescopes.

Silence though the hall is packed. Boys and girls awed by the sheer wonder of it all. Parents (all except B's who are absent doing something else) with overcoats and handbags on clenched-up knees sitting in the dark, aching with pride at their sons and daughters no matter how insignificant their parts. Teachers glowing from within because the show, despite all the calamities of rehearsals, is actually going to work. Every single eye on Molly as she glides before them like the angel she is. Molly, the godly presence, the bright star in the firmament, the bringer of glad tidings, the golden girl of the Christmas moment.

Although his job as a shepherd is to watch his flock by night, slightly discomforted by the itchy false beard hooked over his ears, B is watching his friend instead. Lying down behind one of the stage-set screens, he can see her through a gap. She is clear, she shines, she radiates and like everyone else he is captivated.

Molly holding court in her element, as always the centre of attraction. Not through arrogance or conceit but by her sheer character, presence and confidence. An ordinary school hall showing the same nativity play being played out in thousands of other schools, and here is a precocious talent plain as day, plain as the starry, starry night on the road to Bethlehem.

B sees all this and knows it. Molly's colour, the same gold as the jar of marmalade at home, liquid and rich, outlined against the blackened cloth at the back of the stage. Angel wings splaying out from her back forming an appropriate "M" shape above her head and shoulders.

Applause for Gabriel exiting stage left having carried out his heavenly duty of informing Mary she will have a Son of God. But just as Molly reaches the edge of the stage, suddenly she spins around and parades back into the centre glare. She stops, carefully lifts both arms, and with a flick of her hands goes down into a low and slow curtsy. As the clapping continues, Molly repeats her encore three times before blowing a very un-archangelic-like kiss to the audience and exiting finally to the searching grimaces of her teachers.

B closes his eyes and in his darkness all he can see is gold.

* * *

Molly.

Standing at B's door in the alley as a waft of cooking steams and streams from the restaurant. Pop music twanging from inside the pub. B stares at her like she's a phantom. She is here, at his house, Sunday morning, out of the blue, somewhere out of the deepest blue B can imagine. A shaft of light into the dark, lonely home he shares with two adult strangers.

B can only smile, shock taking his voice away. Only days from the day at the observatory and his new friend has come to see him. To play? What, here, where he has never played with anyone?

'Surprise!'

Molly makes to jump into the house but a figure appears behind B and she stops with a start.

'Hello!' she laughs backing down.

B's dad brushes his son aside and stands before her. Black suit jacket flowing out undone, red tie hanging forward like a long, bloody gash, black Beatles-type hair, a sticking plaster on one hand and pointy shoes, he hovers above the little girl like a dark menace. B can see Molly isn't scared, she isn't frightened of anything, yet he knows she will not be stepping one foot inside his home.

'Can B play, please?' Molly asks politely. 'Can I come in?'

'No! Who is this?'

'She's my friend. We're in the same class.'

'Well, not inside. I'm off out and your mum is upstairs asleep. Don't care who she is. Hear me?'

B hears. He hears and they never listen.

'We'll play out then.'

'Do what you like…' pushing past Molly into the alley already thinking of something else.

B moves to the middle of the doorway and the two friends gaze at each other understanding everything. Molly isn't to come knocking any more, the house is not a place to play, not a house to be friends in, not a place she can be spontaneous in.

'Come on, let's go down to the river. I'll show you my shore and we can throw stones.'

B runs inside, gets his blue jacket and slamming the front door behind him winces for fear of waking his mum, then laughs because at that very moment he doesn't care.

Molly is here, she has knocked for him in her green coat, yellow and pink striped skirt, white socks and black shoes and she means the world to him. Jumping down, he puts his hands on her shoulders and keeps them there. They stand, locked like this for a long, soul-to-soul minute until Molly shouts.

'*Emergency Ward 10!*'

And pushing B away hard she turns and sprints off down the alley laughing like a banshee. He tears after her, so happy there will be three friends together now. B, Molly and the river.

* * *

Molly.

Standing in the east, B in the west. No class, no teacher and no old man today. Just the two friends at the place of time, with more time to learn about each other. The observatory still standing proud overlooking London like an ornate watchtower. One eye on the city, the other on the sky.

Molly and B starting to criss-cross hop from one hemisphere to the other, landing apart in tandem like mating water birds. Lost in the world of their own where the world splits in two.

When they reach the end of the metal Meridian strip, Molly veers off and begins to dance in a circle across the courtyard, arms above her head, twisting and gyrating in wide sweeps. Stopping back in front of B, she places her head forward on his chest and he rests his chin on her blonde hair.

B turns his head up. 'I started to look at the stars after we came here with school. At night I go outside into our garden, sometimes even down to the river because you can see more of the sky from there. When it's not cloudy you can see millions of them, silver and shining. I looked at a book in school and you can join the stars up with lines and make pictures of lions and giants and bears. That's where people ages ago thought they lived, in the sky. People stand on the line all over the world and see the same things I see. They might be doing it right now.'

Molly pulls away, walks a few paces towards the railings where B and Miss Andrews talked about reds and starts to balance on one leg. After a little while, B bends down and puts his fingers on the brass of the Meridian Line as if trying to feel for the rumble of drumbeats, rushing rivers, or galloping herds of animals across the world.

16 July 1966

Waiting for the 2.20 to arrive.

B feels very strange standing at Maze Hill Station having never been on a train before in his life. In fact, apart from extremely rare local outings with his parents, he doesn't travel at all. Well, where can he go? To see family? An only, rejected child, with no relatives, maternal or paternal, that he knows of, who could he visit or wonder of wonders take him somewhere?

Consequently, returning with Molly to her blue house after playing in the park, B was completely dumbstruck when her mum and dad came to their black door and invited him on Molly's special trip to London that Saturday. Tongue-tied and shuffling his feet for a while, somehow he managed to accept.

Although he and Molly were now inseparable friends, B never felt comfortable with Mr and Mrs Larnder. Whenever he called they made him feel as if he was stealing their daughter away or had interrupted something important. They looked at him strangely too. Curious, critical eyes. Yet this was nothing much out of the ordinary – he was used to it at home. There he was accepted only because he happened to be his parents' son, apparently. At Molly's, no doubt he was tolerated just because he was her friend. So, being offered to go to London and have an expensive theatre ticket too, had quite stunned him.

Of course, when B got home there was scant delight in his good fortune. His mum smartly retreated to the kitchen to bang pots and cupboards and his dad was too interested in the World Cup. England was playing Uruguay in the opening game at Wembley that evening with the Queen there and everything. Actually, in all the excitement, B had temporarily forgotten England's big kick-off himself, quite a feat since all the talk at school, at the swings, in the street, indeed in the whole country had been of nothing else for weeks. With the start on telly only an hour away, B tried to focus on the game. England must win, they had to, but even his growing nerves couldn't dampen his anticipation for the weekend.

B's mum was jealous – deep, grass-green, cupboard-banging jealous. '*Funny Girl!*' she shouted from the kitchen. 'They're taking you to see Streisand? You? I don't believe it. What a waste!'

Her being amazed over anyone taking him anywhere was no surprise, but to see Barbra Streisand, in her hit London musical, in person, was beyond her understanding. She came out of the kitchen once with '*Funny Girl*? Funny family more like!' and B wondered if she meant Molly's or theirs.

The atmosphere in the house didn't improve either as England fought out a boring 0-0 draw with the South Americans. His dad swore and shouted at the telly a lot and at the final whistle found solace in the pub across the alley. Maintaining her frustration all night, his mum crashed around until she went to bed in an even angrier mood over her missing husband.

Now, finally, Saturday had arrived and here B was standing at Maze Hill ready for the off.

'Come on!' said Molly, taking up his hand and pulling him along. 'Let's run to the end of the platform.'

'Be careful!' Molly's dad warned. 'You know now, don't you?'

He knew his funny daughter sure enough but they hardly heard him as the children trotted down the platform westwards. Stopping when they had gone as far as they could, B looked down at the track and was struck by how much the metal strips reminded him of the Meridian Line up at the observatory. Lines – one going up to London, another to cities and towns across all those countries.

'It's great you're coming!' Molly beamed while starting to walk in a circle, placing each foot immediately in front of the other and holding her hands out as if balancing on a high wire. 'Dad's been calling me his Funny Girl all week.'

'I can't believe it,' watching her. 'Dunno what London's like. Never been to a theatre.'

Molly was on her second lap. 'I've not been to one as big and posh as this either. Mum and Dad have, they're always going, but tonight's a really big thing.'

B turned away and peered up the track towards a black void looming under a road-bridge. He began to imagine a magic tunnel running all the way up to town, only coming out into the glare of sunlight at Buckingham Palace where the Queen lived. London! He had been dreaming of it all week. So massive from the view up at the observatory. Millions of people, cars and lorries, lights and noise. New sights, new sounds, new colours.

And the line that would connect him to it all now seemed to crackle and rattle into life. B spun around to see a green train approaching from the bend in the far distance and Molly's mum and dad waving for them to come back. Sure enough, he felt his friend's hand scoop his up and start to pull him towards them.

A loud screech of brakes, a dusty, heavy door opening, the children leapt in and sat down opposite each other by the far window. In seconds the train was moving off and entering the magic tunnel. A plunge into darkness from July summer sunshine.

'Only a few stops. Won't be long!' smiled Mr Larnder, tapping his jacket inner pocket and beaming. 'Got the tickets! Safe and sound.'

'You're more excited than Molly!' chided his wife.

'Well, I still can't quite believe Harry came up trumps.'

This was a reference to Mr Larnder's close friend who had, finally, come through. Harry had been hinting at success for weeks but nothing was happening. *Funny Girl* at the Prince of Wales Theatre just off Piccadilly was the show everyone wanted to see and as Molly was their own Funny Girl they just had to take her. Ever since the musical started in London in April they had been making promises but for a string of reasons – bad timings and a total lack of ticket availability (seats were like gold dust) – they feared they would miss out.

So when Harry, Molly's godfather, the one with the special theatrical contacts (some said he even knew Noel Coward), strode up to her dad's desk at work flashing four prime circle tickets for the final performance no less – Barbra Streisand's last appearance as the celebrated New York entertainer Fanny Brice – the relief was as great as the consequent anticipation. The only question was who was getting the fourth ticket.

Molly's near neighbour and school-friend Sharon was the immediate choice. Such a nice, well-behaved girl (a calming influence?) and their parents were lovely people. Certainly, by mutual, unspoken consent, it was accepted the boy down by the river shouldn't be invited. There was definitely something about him. Not the thing and despite Molly and his ever growing closeness over many months, they maintained the fervent hope their bond would soon begin to break. Molly needed other friendships which were, well, less intense. But, alas, their relationship had failed to wane and when Molly heard the great news she was vocal and adamant. Funny Girl wasn't going to budge. B was coming with them and that was that. No games, no arguing. So here they all were, on the train, on the way and waiting with bated breath for Barbra.

Past Greenwich Station and out into sunlight again, B looked up at Molly peering out of the window. He was always fascinated to catch her unawares – her so identifiable shape, her familiar lines and how she frowned in concentration at a sudden sound or movement, tightening her forehead and screwing up her eyes. Always too, her delight in the way she would realise, as if by some sixth sense, that B was looking at her and she'd swivel around with a big grin to meet his eyes, like she was playing a game. But then he knew very well that Molly was almost always playing a game, playing a part.

For once, however, there was no extra sense. Molly, in her blue jacket and blue and pink striped dress, white socks and brown shoes, didn't turn around. No big grin, she kept on staring out of the train. No wrinkling up her eyes, just her normal, pretty face at the window.

At the window...

It was the picture of Molly he always conjured now when he thought of her. Molly sitting on the front windowsill of her lovely blue house just down from Greenwich Park. Legs dangling back inside her front room, all aglow in her snow-white party dress, sparkling and shining, looking out of the fully raised sash window to greet the world as if challenging all it could throw at her.

Leaving his lonely home without a word of goodbye, B had walked up to Molly's for her birthday party a little anxiously. He knew there would be lots of other children and family there so he understood he would have to share her with others. But then B turned the corner of her street, caught her shape and colours at the window, and realising she had been waiting just for him, he didn't care any more. The more the merrier.

Birthday card in hand, B stopped in front of the window and the two friends looked at each other in silence for a very long time. Molly, eleven years old today, her face angled towards him. B, blue jacket and brown jeans with a buckled orange and black striped elastic belt, wanting to stand there forever and simply absorb her.

Before they met he had questioned everything. What was this for, why did that look the way it did, why was this green, why was that blue, or yellow, or red? And with this questioning came unending worry and frustration. Why didn't he know these things and where could he find the answers? Meanings were always disappearing around the corner, out of reach. Always chasing, never catching, he lived in a maze of colours, shapes, patterns and lines, never finding the centre.

But with Molly his questions disappeared. There was no confusion. Colours and the shapes of things made sense. She made his life simple to understand. Funny, brave, caring and carefree, Molly gave him comprehension and huge happiness.

'Hello!' said Molly, eventually. 'Is that card for me?'

'Er, yes… yes, it is,' B stammered offering it up to her. 'Happy Birthday!'

She turned her eyes back to the street corner and nodded.

'I was waiting for you. I knew you were coming.'

'Yes, I'm here, Molly at the window.'

At the window…

And she invited him in and everyone played games and ate cake and jelly and ice cream and listened to Molly sing and the adults drank tea and the children drank lemonade and everything was perfect.

Then B felt his hand being scooped up, Molly's familiar soft touch with its firm, determined drag, the force of his insistent friend as they ran through the house packed with people, bumping off furniture and elbows, until they reached the open front window where Molly jumped up onto the sill as B dropped to the floor before her.

'Here!' Molly laughed, breathing hard, handing B down a long, log-shaped object. 'It's one of my presents but I reckon you will like it more than me. Know what it is?'

B looked vacantly as he took the thing and rolled it around in his hands.

'But this is yours. It's your birthday. I can't...'

Molly's face became serious and she lowered, cupped B's hands in hers putting her face close to his.

'This is for you,' she whispered. 'Special. Lots and lots of colours.'

And gently, slowly, Molly showed B how the kaleidoscope worked. How, at a twist, an eternal world of shapes and patterns and colours was his. Ever-changing visions of colours he could play with at will. The gift of colours from his friend at the window.

All that night and so many times since, B entered the sumptuous and multicoloured world of the kaleidoscope. At every turn he saw new and undiscovered landscapes, at each further twist another chaos of colours merged into complex, beautiful new orders and his fascination never ended nor his pleasure dimmed.

Molly at the window…

'Here comes London Bridge. Not far now. Couple of stops!' announced Mr Larnder breaking the trance.

Molly turned from the window and leaned against her father who, smiling, put his arm around her.

'Are we going to walk around London when we get there? The show doesn't start for hours.'

Her mother leaned over, smiled too and tapped Molly on her knee.

'Well, we thought we would pop into the National Gallery first before having a quick bite and going on. The theatre's only round the corner.'

'Didn't we go there once before?'

'Yes, a couple of years ago. When Aunt Meg came to stay.'

'I remember!' said Molly grabbing B's hand. 'You'll like this. Lots and lots of paintings. Famous ones. Won't be boring!'

Thus her parents were forced to split their attention.

'Yes,' Mr Larnder sighed at the boy, 'you're in for a treat.'

B looked nervous. 'No. Yes. No, I don't mind. If Molly wants to go…'

The arrangements settled, Molly's parents started to talk between themselves and in a short while the train duly began its approach into London's Charing Cross Station, launching across the bridge over the Thames leading into the terminus.

B looked out of the window and gazed down on his other friend, the river. It was completely new territory.

He had never seen the Thames this far upstream or from such an elevated view before. The full tide and the sheer expanse of the water emanated a sense of huge power, an all-pervading dominating force with waves and eddies glinting gold and silver in the summer afternoon sunshine. B watched the water in awe all the way over the bridge until he disappeared into the vast and dark expanse of the station's depths.

Down from the carriage, Mr Larnder checked his watch.

'Three o'clock. Bags of time.'

Three o'clock? A snap went off inside B's head. Unbelievable. Not a moment's thought to it all day. The excitement of London and *Funny Girl* had swept it from his mind.

Saturday! England v Mexico at Wembley! World Cup, three o'clock, kick off.

They had to play better than the other night against Uruguay, had to. But no sooner had butterflies begun to flap in his stomach, than B emerged from the station out into the bright London bustle, remembered the game was an evening start, and forgot all about England again.

He could hardly take it all in. Red double-decker buses floating by, black taxis lining up on the ranks, brown cobblestones criss-crossing the Charing Cross forecourt, multicoloured shop signs, huge and dirty white and grey buildings. People were going here and there, hundreds of them – blue jackets, red skirts, brown trousers, white hats, noise, shouts, laughter, a baby's cry mixing with the distant echo of a station announcer. All the colours of the capital, so bright and electric, lay all about him and in his open-mouthed wonder, B could never have imagined how much the next few hours would affect the rest of his life.

'Off we go, Funny Girl!' signalled Mr Larnder and Molly's parents took their daughter's hands in theirs, turned left and marched off.

B smiled. Without question Molly was the centre of her mum and dad's world. Without a whisker of doubt, he knew she was the centre of his.

Molly at the centre
of B's world

Molly.

Standing before three men sitting on a wooden bench just outside the gates of the Alamo – a small, white, foreign-looking building with a bell in its tower a hundred yards or so from B's alley house.

Its white glistening frontage facing the river at the beginning of the long eastward bend towards the industrial horizon of Blackwall, a skyline outlining gigantic gas tanks. The Alamo, a little hospital dwarfed beside the massive menace of Greenwich Power Station. Huge metal leg-struts supporting the building's extension out into the Thames disappearing into brown water. Their feet only to be revealed by the mud and slime of low tide.

Molly singing to the men. Her clear voice ringing out

to her trio audience as they smile and nod to her time and their pleasure.

Under the looming shadow of the power station, a little girl in her white frock and orange top entertaining the men arrayed in their blue dressing gowns. B leans on the river wall, his eyes flowing from Molly, her voice as liquid as the water below him, up to the Alamo's beautiful, dazzling gold clock as it catches the afternoon sun's rays. Time lending a few minutes for him to gain another memory and for the men to recall happy memories of their own.

B listens and in his mind sees marching armies of moustachioed soldiers blasting the brave little Alamo to bits – flags, cannon-fire, gunshots, screams, galloping horses and long knives on the end of rifles. The film with John Wayne he saw once. Wave after wave of men, bearing down on a fort he likens to this old white place looking so incongruous in its urban river setting.

John Wayne – tall, deep American voice, cowboy, hero. The man at the end of the film said the Alamo and all its heroes fighting on the battlements were dying "buying" the time he needed to defeat the armies led by the fat Mexican man on the white horse who let the pretty lady and her little girl go free when everyone else was dead. Such a sad ending with the lovely music. So many heroes.

Molly's beautiful voice ends her song and B wonders if the time the heroes were buying was the same sort of time the famous people had tried to find out about at the observatory.

* * *

Molly.

With B, swinging on the swings a stone's throw over the park wall from her blue home. Lots of other children there, some schoolmates, playing all around them and the chants of '*England, England!*' ringing out. Tonight's the night, England v Uruguay. Wembley, the World Cup, England's heroes. Bobby Charlton, Roger Hunt, Gordon Banks...

Swinging past each other on alternating arcs and only for the tiniest instant when they are level do they say something, more a whisper against the wind the swingers are generating between them. And every time they make a pass, they whisper, laugh, swing up to their highest, hum with back-of-the-throat guttural voices until they pass and whisper and laugh once again.

Then the whole game starts once more and repeats and repeats and repeats...

* * *

Molly.

Whistling a tune as she stands on the twilight river shoreline holding a long, wet piece of wood thrown up by the sinister water. B, ten yards away, trying to see what she's found and taking in her silhouette against the gloomy background of the Thames as it bends upstream towards the city. Deptford on the left bank, the Isle of Dogs on the right.

Molly and B scavenging the stone and mud-encrusted shore below the steps leading up to the gold-studded black iron gates of the Royal Naval College. Beyond its tall colonnades a mighty vista flowing onwards towards Inigo Jones's white Queen's House of the Maritime Museum. Then up, up, and up through Greenwich Park to the high, lone General Wolfe warrior statue and the observatory.

Two children mudlarking at the spot where in 1806, after his death at the Battle of Trafalgar, the body of Lord Nelson was carried down to a funeral barge for the national hero's last voyage upstream to London – fleets of ships and little boats deployed along the Thames attending in strict and reverent respect. But all the history lost on Molly and B as they hear gently rippling waves and the bells and clinks of river life colliding around them.

Molly lifts the piece of wood high into the air and B sees her shape resemble the outline of a statue in America he saw on the telly only a few nights ago. A giant figure on an island in the middle of a big bay, with a huge upright arm raised skywards holding a sword-shaped lamp.

'What would you do with this piece of wood, Mr Wood?' Molly asks in an affected high-pitched voice. 'You wouldn't throw it back into the river, would you?'

'No I wouldn't,' B replies, 'I'd take it back to the woods where it came from … it would be safe there, wouldn't it?'

'Would it?'

But the words barely leave her mouth before she drops the piece of sodden timber in a fit of giggles, runs up the shore to the steps, vaults the first few before turning on her heels to face B now standing just below her.

'I am the River Queen!' she announces. 'Come here, my prince, and bring me my crown.'

Holding out a silver and gold crown with red sparkling diamonds straight out in front of him, B begins to mount the steps slowly, each footstep rasping out the sound of his black plimsolls on the green, river-soiled wet stone. Finally, he reaches her and raising his arms aloft brings the crown gently down on her head.

'Your Majesty!'

'Ta very much, mate!' quips the Queen. 'Got to go now! Bye!' and sprinting up the rest of the steps, she bolts left down the river walkway towards the warmth of her happy home.

B lets his will-o'-the-wisp friend go and completing the steps himself, he stands before the college gates just as she disappears around the bend near his alley. The spot where he once ripped up his picture of her.

Looking out across the water over to the murky Isle of Dogs, B thinks he can actually hear hounds barking.

Howling.

He remembers his rage that day he met Molly and first saw the muddy line. He lifts his head back but this time his howl is one of homage to the girl who has brought so much colour to his bleak, young life.

* * *

Molly.

Standing at the black railings of the concrete dry-dock enclosing one of the famous maritime landmarks in Greenwich – *Cutty Sark*. In the bowels of the dock, long, sturdy prop arms help hold the old ship in place. Set in a wide piazza, it's only fifty or so yards to the river, a short distance between the concrete chains that bind and the freedom of open water the celebrated three-rigger, the fastest tea clipper the world has ever known, must yearn for.

B, beside her, looking up from beneath *Nannie Dee*, the ship's figurehead, named from Robert Burns' poem *"Tam o' Shanter"*. Looking like porcelain, the white, bare-breasted witch faces forward at the prow, pointing the way just as she did between those exotic climes and Great Britain in the ship's heyday. Distances once at the mercy of this icon of old Empire now idling her days as a river-front tourist attraction.

Ignorant of such poetic references and its illustrious past, despite their many visits to play around the ship, B peers down to the bottom of the dock. Once again he remembers the famous men at the observatory. They must have found out about the stars and time to save this big, old boat.

* * *

Molly.

Stick-still and grinning in the playground. Ten minutes before the bell goes for the end of playtime, B receives the ball out wide near the fence and darts towards goal. Two men rounded, a skip past a third and the goal is at his mercy. But an unseen, filthy leg splays him to the ground and he skids a couple of feet scrubbing his knees along the gravelly ground.

No linesmen, no goal lines, no referee but the boys all know a penalty when they see one. Nobody disputes a thing as B gets up, stares out every player set against him and places the ball down on the imaginary penalty spot measured at the imaginary but totally correct distance to take the kick.

B backs away from the ball and looks up. Breathing hard, a red-blood graze on his knee and his cheeks burning with the heat of the game, he takes in his challenge.

She stands there, hands by her side, holding her tummy in, a spontaneous goalpost. When the game started, Molly ran to one end of the pitch and stood there ramrod straight. The players just accepted it. This was Molly after all.

The goal is assured. B is a very good player and knows it's already scored – the confidence of a boy at home with a ball. His only question to himself is how close can he shoot and give his friend the goalpost the fright of her life.

His mind made up, B starts his run-in. Five paces, a shot high to his right, the orange ball spinning with curve starting straight at Molly's face and he has a tiny moment of regret. But mid-flight, the ball moves slightly, curves inwards and with a rush of wind like a strafe from a fighter plane, it whizzes past her nose and into the goal.

A roar goes up. His teammates all jump on him and the last person hanging from B's neck in congratulations is Molly.

16 July 1966

'Come down! You're going to fall and hurt yourself.'

Mrs Larnder's shouts lost on the steaming air. A merciless orange sun pounding down on wide-open African plains and her daughter's feet tapping to far-away distant drums. Head up, ears pricked, eyes bulging like a fragile antelope scanning the horizon for a predator's threat, Molly's in a different land, a different time, a different world.

Born Free.

She is Joy Adamson – blonde, determined, a wild, animal majesty pulsating from deep within – standing proud with Elsa, her queen of the jungle (although to most people in the real world it is most definitely a king – he has a full mane and everything).

Molly might be together with her big cat on another continent, but to her parents and the rest of the crowd in London's Trafalgar Square she is sitting rather dangerously on the head of one of the huge lion statues surrounding Nelson's famous column.

Born Free.

Molly had seen the film with her mum only months ago and the sheer romance of life in Africa was at times too much. How easily she slid into the make-believe world of Joy and the lioness. The blood-pumping music, its searing crescendo. How she felt like crying when Elsa departed the human world with her little cubs at the finale. The sound of her mate's roar calling her back to their natural domain.

As soon as they crossed the road towards Trafalgar Square a few hundred yards down from Charing Cross, Molly had caught sight of the lions. *Funny Girl* was instantly forgotten and Mr and Mrs Larnder's own Funny Girl swept into character and sprinted off towards them already sensing the baking African heat, the roar of the pride and the clap of the clapperboard.

In a world of his own at that moment, vivid London colours all around him, B snapped awake and tried vainly to run after his friend but she soon disappeared into the middle of some tourists and was lost.

At first, Molly's parents didn't worry too much. Used to their unpredictable daughter running off whenever a whim took her, the easy sunshine of the day gave them no cause for alarm. Strolling arm in arm, they headed off to one of the square's famous fountains while trying to escape the hordes of pigeons hovering just above their heads.

A few minutes later, however, their tranquillity ended abruptly. Suddenly, they saw Molly way up high balancing precariously on top of a lion's head and darted off frantically pushing through sightseers, shouting for their daughter to get down. Now Mrs Larnder was wailing from the pavement for Molly to be careful as her huffing and puffing husband was climbing gingerly onto the body of the lion ready to save his flesh and blood from a fatal fall.

'Don't be silly now! Hold on! Come here to me!'

Instead, the plea broke Molly from her dream. The heat, Elsa, Virginia and the lingering strings of the soundtrack all dissolved in a flash and she peered quizzically at her father's nervy outstretched hand.

'Blimey! How did I get up here?'

In one agile movement, she skipped nimbly off the lion's head, slipped effortlessly down the cat's flank and jumped the few feet back to ground level in front of her mother. Mrs Larnder went to speak but Molly got there first.

'Have you seen B? I'd better go after him. See you in a minute!' before she sped off leaving her mum open-mouthed and her dad clambering down to earth with extreme caution.

Molly ran for a few seconds before stopping to spin around on her heels to get her bearings. Scanning the crowds, a hand masking the sun from her eyes, she quickly caught sight of her target standing at the foot of Nelson's column itself and trotted over to stand behind him.

B had his neck thrust all the way back looking straight up to the very top of the mighty column where Nelson stood proudly, sword drawn, tipped to the ground. Molly laughed to herself. Time for a game they loved to play.

'Look! If you keep looking up like that you'll end up looking like nothing to look at!'

B snapped his head down twisting to face her. Molly wore a haughty face and with an accusatory finger pointed at him, he stabbed a finger back.

'Look! Don't look at me like that. I'll look at what I want to look at.'

'Look out!' Molly cried, and the two interlocked fingers in a mini sword fight which quickly merged into a ring-a-ring o' roses dance for a few seconds before they sprang apart laughing.

'Where did you go? All I saw was you running off. What was so good?'

'I saw the lion and, dunno, felt like climbing it. Keep thinking about *Born Free* and feel I'm in Africa. Blimey, lions on every corner!'

Nelson was indeed guarded by four kings.

'You're mad, Molly!'

'F-u-n-n-e-e-e!'

'Yesireee!'

B turned and looked up to the top of the column once more. Molly put her hands on B shoulders and moved her head forward close to his.

'What are you thinking?' she whispered. 'What do you see?'

'Reminds me of General Wolfe in the park... a dark man on top of a big block of stone looking out across London, towering over everything just like at the observatory. A tall tube pointing at the sky with a man at the top blown out of the hole at the end.'

'A tall tube?'

'Yeah! Or a big telescope looking for stars.'

'No stars now though. It's daytime.'

'But they are still up there, hiding.'

She started to sing. *'Twinkle, twinkle little star...'*

B's eyes traced the column down and stopping at the base he fixed on a large metal picture panel facing him. He studied it for a while trying to make out the scene. Men were pulling a rope and one man was falling over and being caught by other men. More men were standing around staring at the man falling over who B thought must have been shot by an arrow or something. Looking deeper into the picture, he saw how each figure depicted was raised out from the surface and he imagined his hand running over them, feeling the different shapes of their bodies, their faces looking so sad.

'Here you are!'

Mr and Mrs Larnder came up behind the two children shaking B from his reverie. Clearly her dad was still agitated over his rocky rescue attempt.

'You could have really hurt yourself...'

'Sorry!' purred Molly taking her father's hand in hers and swinging it back and forth playfully. As usual, forgiveness smiled.

'What are you looking at?' asked Mrs Larnder.

'B thinks it looks like a tall tube with the man on top being blown out of the other end.'

Even for an eleven-year-old this was rather fanciful. Once again, Mrs Larnder wondered why this little boy irritated her so.

'Is the man in that picture going to die?' B asked pointing at the scene before him.

Mr Larnder moved forward to get a closer look. He hummed an understanding hum and took a deep breath before explaining. He never felt at ease with B either.

'That man, as you call him, is Lord Nelson and yes he is going to die. He's just been shot on his ship *Victory* at the Battle of Trafalgar against France. It's why this place is called Trafalgar Square. Nelson was a great sailor and is one of the country's greatest heroes.'

Mr Larnder peered a little closer to read some words under the picture plate.

'Ah yes! See! It says '*England expects every man will do his duty*'. Nelson's famous message at Trafalgar.'

Then surprising himself at offering B anything extra, he turned and added, 'In fact, you might be interested to know Nelson's funeral started right down on the river where you live. His body was carried out of the Royal Naval College, put on a barge and sailed up the Thames to London.'

But his bonus only lasted so long. 'Now, can we get moving, please?'

The group starting to walk away from the column towards the fountains but B's head was teeming... Nelson, shot, Trafalgar, war, France, hero, gunfire, a ship glowing in orange flames, people rushing and decks stained in red blood.

Nelson.

A hero who had died in a place called Trafalgar. *Trafalgar*? That was what the building at the corner of his alley next to the river was called, wasn't it? B had read the word written high on its river wall a hundred times never knowing what it meant. Nelson, the hero who was carried down to B's own part of the river where he often played with Molly and where he once thought she looked like a statue in America he saw on the telly.

His Trafalgar. Nelson's Trafalgar. Nelson, borne up to London by his friend the brown river and now here he was standing on this tall tube of stone. Once again B marvelled at how often things were connected, lines running into other lines, making patterns, making shapes. The Meridian Line connecting countries all over the world. Railway tracks and the river winding their way to London. Lines and connections. They searched the stars at the observatory to save the sea captains and Nelson was a famous sea captain. A hero.

And so, up from the steps from Trafalgar Square, this was how B first entered London's National Gallery. A little boy overflowing with questions about the world.

At such a tender age he had no concept of fate but his young, raw thoughts danced to its exotic tune. On this special day, here with Molly on her special *Funny Girl* day, suddenly it seemed as if he was supposed to be here, meant to be. That "muddy" line running right around the world had led him to this place right now. He was sure of it.

Walking into the huge, imposing grey building with absolutely no understanding of what lay inside, no notion of the wonderful but terrible forces hurtling towards him, no idea of how fundamentally his life was about to change, B's heart and mind were primed like parched grass waiting for a spark to ignite and burn. Instantly, he was sucked into the vortex of an utterly different existence. His real world stopped completely. The river, London, the lions, all questions disappeared.

For a long time afterwards it was impossible for B to express what happened over the next couple of hours. Certainly, when he walked out into the capital's summer sunshine again hand in hand with his friend, he could not have retraced his steps or explained in any coherent way what he had seen and experienced. A blur? Yes, he supposed it was. But a blur full of frozen moments, dazzling scenes, sharp sensations and, in sheer torrents making his entire body shake, oceans of colour.

Walking, stumbling, careering through the rooms, floating in an electric and fantastical dream of his own. Lost to Mr and Mrs Larnder's promptings and interpretations. Not even aware of Molly, whether she held his hand or spoke to him. Bombarded by limitless, new dimensions of vision, inconceivable concepts of sound and staggering experiences of light. No sense of place or time, no idea of others, moving by some unanchored will.

A dream-world of hypersensitive vision. Objects, shapes and movement exploding his mind... castles, clouds, a rearing horse, daggers drawn, blood from severed heads, hands aloft in prayer, boats, dresses, cannons and courtyards. Axe, boat, ring, skull, animal fur, the deep unease of violent seas, the glowing embers of evening skies, the gentle sway of flowers, pearls of raindrops running down petals, dark chasms of mountains, the placid peace of fields, the gun, the spear and the cross.

A dream-world sounding fury and action... baying animals, the clamour of battle, the cries of children, crowds in streets, birdsong in the air and storms at sea. The clash of swords, gasps from a dying bird, singing of choirs, bursts of musket-fire, roars of huge waves, sounds of markets, trains, churches and countryside, screams of death, the cacophonies of killers, the laughter of the happy and the sobs of the sad.

A dream-world of light with ever-changing subtleties, stabbing then bathing, blinding then soothing... the sun's haze on lazy water, buildings sparkling in the morning, streetlamps in a night city, the rose on a lady's cheek, a tear's streak in the eye of a man about to die, the shine of a bowl of fruit. The bayonet strike of sunrays on the faces of men, twinkles in the eyes of young children and pretty women, sparkles of rivers in faraway countries, shores of ancient cities at the dying of the day, glints of metal, morning piercing through doors, windows and ruined buildings, evening sunsets cushioning the day from the night and starlight shimmering over the good and evil of life below.

Walking inside so many dreams, all fashioning together as if part of one huge, unbelievable never-ending story. Yet above all of it, above the harmony and the chaos, above the noise and the silence and the light, were the colours. A vast array of them from across B's known spectrum and many, many more. Colours arriving and colliding from every angle, pushing him deeper into hidden depths inside his head far beyond the reach of Molly, her parents or anyone else in that special place on that special afternoon.

Objects of everyday life – fruit, shoes, the moon, pebbles on the beach, flags, books – revealed in totally different colours than normal. Each one appearing new and fresh as if it was the first time B had ever experienced them. Purple trees, white suns, blue women, orange fields. The red plum, the yellow dress and the gold cup. All only now offering up their eternal secrets.

The House of Colours shouting his name.

Colours, with other colours buried deep within them, flooding out of box-like shapes on walls, mixing and oozing into the worlds inside other boxes.

Colours, pouring from every direction – trickles and torrents, ripples and raging waves – through keyholes, doors, flooding down staircases plunging from ceilings, bursting out of floors.

Colours, gushing and swirling and eddying, massing and crashing together.

Colours, rampaging like rampant rivers, joining others and churning headlong towards giant rainbow waterfalls.

Colours, filling everywhere, welling and swelling up as if they were smashing through the roof like a giant paintbox blowing its lid into the sky.

Colours colouring everything. Colours living, breathing, no ending until… until, amidst the tsunami, B began to feel a far distant sense of something very familiar, something he understood and that was very dear to him, something he knew but couldn't quite name. Then, at last, it came.

Kaleidoscope.

B felt no physical contact with any kaleidoscope itself, not even his own, more a sensation of floating inside one. And with this he felt himself being raised up, higher and higher, out of the House of Colours, up into the sky, up, up, past Nelson on his tall column, higher and higher above the whole city and on through clouds and space towards the stars. All about him he saw whole galaxies of colours interweaving and merging, twisting around again and again creating new and spectacular patterns.

Imperceptibly, B began to perceive a tiny change of air within his kaleidoscope universe. At first it was a mere whisper, gently touching his skin, then a light, fresh wind beginning to swirl, building by slow degrees with more and more force, stronger and stronger until with a gigantic crash he felt himself being blown downwards with enormous force. Down and down, a huge power propelling him back, past the stars and the clouds and Nelson right back into the House of Colours. Crashing back inside, the howling, screaming storm continued to rampage, sweeping the galleries clean – colours, boxes and walls falling away, all the kaleidoscope dreams dissolving before him.

Eventually, as silence reigned, from somewhere far away, he thought he heard a voice and strained his ears to hear. Very faint at first, but after a while he thought he began to recognise it. Not yet, not yet. But he had heard it before, yes, he had. Nearer, nearer, then, of course, he knew.

Molly.

B found himself in a wide lobby with light piercing down on him from above. Like at the base of Nelson's Column, he was looking up, neck back, staring at a circle of bright off-white light coming from the underside of the National Gallery's landmark dome. Molly was holding his hand, swinging it back and forth in her usual way.

'So, what was your favourite then?' Mr Larnder was saying.

'Dunno really...' replied Molly. 'There were too many. But I'm hungry! Can we go and have something to eat now? Are you hungry, B?'

Clicking his head back down, feeling like he had just woken up from the deepest sleep he had ever slept, B tried to take in his surroundings and what Molly was saying.

'Are you? Hungry?'

B searched and only just about found his voice.

'Er, dunno...' he stuttered.

Mr Larnder sighed and capitulated. 'All right, let's go then. We'll walk back round to Leicester Square and find something.' He took his wife's arm and started down the stairs to the gallery's front doors.

'You ready?' Molly asked giving B's hand a hefty swing.

'Yeah, think so...' B answered shakily as they both moved off to follow Molly's parents. Outside in the afternoon sunshine on the high, raised portico forming the National's entrance, ahead of them stood Nelson still on his big tube in his victorious square.

'You were dead quiet in there,' Molly laughed. 'Didn't say a thing and you kept wandering off on your own. Lost you a couple of times. Mum and Dad said you probably didn't like it. But, you did, didn't you?'

B was still feeling light-headed but with a squeeze of Molly's hand he nodded.

'Yes. I did. I liked it. I did like it.'

But truth to tell he didn't know what to think. Standing there with Molly, he could hardly feel his feet. He knew the touch of Molly's hand but at that moment it was his only connection with reality. What had he just gone through?

He felt numb and excited, peaceful and agitated, confused and utterly clear all at the same time.

'We can't get left behind!'

Pulling B away and running down the steps of the gallery to the pavement, Molly spun them left and they saw Mr and Mrs Larnder ahead arm in arm standing at a far corner across from a massive church. Looking back over their shoulders, they beckoned to the pair before turning up Charing Cross Road towards Leicester Square.

Arriving at the corner themselves, the famous tall spire of St Martin in the Fields looming larger and larger, they were about to turn left too when B stopped and twisted his face back to the gallery.

All he could do was whisper.

'Kaleidoscope...'

'Come on!' Molly urged. 'I'm starving. It's getting time for *Funny Girl* and I just can't wait!'

She tugged B's hand and the two started to run.

Molly at the centre of B's world

Molly.

Lying down on a low tree bough in Greenwich Park's manicured flower gardens. Such a hot late spring day and she's sleepy in the lazy afternoon. Closed eyes, dreaming of dressing up as the lady from Hollywood she saw on the telly last night.

'I picked this for you!' B announces, handing Molly a large, bowl-shaped tulip. 'The park-keeper was looking the other way. It's red. Masses of different flowers here. Blue, yellow, white and red ones, all in patterns. Must plant them that way. Never see any black flowers. Not sure why. Flowers move around in the wind like they're waves on the river. My mum doesn't like flowers. Never have any at home. But we don't have much of a garden and it's all boring concrete anyway. Would be nice to have flowers in the garden. Better when things are really coloured...'

'Will you marry me?'

B looks straight up into the blue sky and sees a tiny white, wispy stripe of cloud far up above him. Slowly he turns to hunt for another flower.

'Might...'

* * *

Molly.

Leaning back against the railings at the observatory holding B's hand. Nearly 1 pm, waiting for the fiery red ball to go up and down the pole on top of the old building to show the world Greenwich Mean Time and make sure the ships and sailors on all the oceans across the world right down to where the penguins live are kept safe and sound.

Suddenly the ball moves, like some powerful, invisible thing pulling it up. Then with a rush it drops back as if another gigantic force has blown it down again.

One o'clock.

B imagines captains looking out over vast blue waters and breathing huge sighs of relief. He starts to speak – a confession.

'I never lost that picture I did in school after we came here first. I told Miss I did but I didn't. Ripped it up into bits and chucked it in the river.'

Molly turns her head to meet B's profile.

'Why? Why did you do that? She said it was really good. You had to show your mum and dad.'

'I tried to. I did. They didn't care... no one ever does, except you. I did that picture for you, Molly, but they made me feel bad about it and I got angry. I felt good about doing the picture. It was the day we first spoke but they mucked it up. Sorry. I wanted to tell you but we're here so I am.'

Molly turns back.

'Do another one.'

B looks up to the fiery red ball and wonders.

* * *

Molly.

Jumping up as the deafening rush of Niagara Falls jets out into chaos and smashes down to the steam and spray of oblivion below. Her face caught in the white and the blue and the shimmering shimmer of the massive waterfall. She sees the excitement before her and has to react, has to move. She wants to dance. Dance to the music of the water.

B watches her, backlit by cascades. He captures her delight and wonders if she will start howling. A wolf howling at the country Wolfe conquered.

Miss Andrews, now Mrs Hinkley, lately married, asks Molly to sit down again and clicks the button for another photograph to appear on the school hall wall. Here are the pictures from her honeymoon in Canada just like she promised on that day at the observatory.

Photo after photo, colour after colour. Blue water, white spray, grey rocks, sky-blue sky, green grass and dazzling orange sunlight. All the colours of the rainbow in sunbeams on the waterfall. Miss, in a red top and blue jacket, with a black bag slung over her yellow dress and a close-up of her gold ring. A man with silver glasses in a chequered red and white shirt. The glowing dark red of a sunset above the falls. Lovely flowers, a land of colour and B dreams of going there one day.

Canada.

* * *

Molly.

Sitting on a desk, one arm propping her up and the other fully outstretched pointing to the ceiling. Grey jumper, white socks, black skirt, a classroom of children all looking fixedly at her.

Aprons on, white paper, Miss Andrews says 'Begin!' and everyone dips brushes into water, slips them across dry paint cakes and starts their first ever life-class.

Everyone except B.

He stares at Molly, brush in hand, but his hands, his fingers, his heart and the rest of his body hovers. There is so much he wants to say, to shape, to colour, but he cannot do this.

That day, the day he first went to the observatory, he remembers it so vividly. How easy it was, how the picture flowed from him. Molly standing across the Meridian Line, the fiery red ball on the old building, an outpouring. But then there was a howling and he tossed his vision into the Thames in tatters. Good ending in bad. Molly is too precious to risk that again.

Mrs Hinkley walks around the class to see how

everyone is doing. As she turns down B's row, he loads his brush and dabs something vaguely resembling Molly in her pose but it's his friend as viewed by a stranger. The teacher stops at B's desk and looks down, inwardly shaking her head. She repeats one word in her head.

Red.

16 July 1966

Flashbulbs popping sparking a small round of applause from a gathering crowd. Molly standing on her hands on the pavement outside the Prince of Wales Theatre.

Upside down, putting one hand in front of the other, swaying forwards, Molly's blue and pink striped dress falls down to below her thighs. One or two of the onlookers catching a glimpse of white knickers.

The photographers were delighted with their unexpected discovery – a lucky bonus on a big night. Barbra Streisand's last London appearance in her hit show and here was their very own little Funny Girl, a little English Fanny Brice, playing the part. A natural in front of the camera.

Barbra was the young American, the new star, the new voice, the new sensation (rumour was she was earning more than the Beatles!) and *Funny Girl* had proven to be as successful in the West End as it had been on Broadway. *Funny Girl*, the story of Fanny, the boundless New York ball of energy who found fame as a star of the Ziegfried Follies, and Barbra was starring the show on her sheer personality and talent. Getting tickets was like winning the jackpot and on Miss Streisand's *au revoir* a cheeky kid was giving them some nice pictures and a side news angle.

'What's your name, darlin'?' rapped one of the cockney pack as they backed away trying to give Molly as much space as they could to do her stuff. The girl's shape, the curve of her back, her kicking legs and vivaciousness captured in their eyepieces and lenses.

'Not Fanny, is it?' shouted another.

'... or Barbra?'

A hand out just in case his incredible friend toppled over but just managing to keep out of shot, B watched and marvelled at Molly's performance.

'No, it's not!' he shouted, a protective response amongst all these strangers.

'Pity!' and more flashes peppered the scene prompting a few extra people to join the throng to see what was going on.

'OK, love! Keep coming! That's great! Ever been on the stage?'

The crowd rippled with laughter but suddenly the intimate display was cut short. A man broke in from the ranks pulling Molly's skirt back into decency and yanking her to her feet.

'Enough now!' he shouted. 'That's enough! Stop!', the clicking brought to a halt to some choice photographer words. Corralling his red-faced daughter away down the pavement to the side of the theatre, Mr Larnder held Molly against a wall, his heavy breathing revealing the scale of his displeasure.

'What do you think you are doing?' he snapped, running his hand through his thinning hair. 'We were only gone for a few...' but his rebuke was cut short.

His wife hurried up to them. 'What's happening? Why did you run off like that?'

'Molly posing for the photographers... doing handstands, if you please! Her dress all over the place and everything...'

He turned back to face his daughter. 'What on earth were you doing?'

Before Molly could speak, quite forgotten in all the fuss, B suddenly joined them.

'I told them your proper name, Molly. They said it was Fanny.'

Mr Larnder started. 'You did what?'

'They said Molly's name was Fanny but I put them right. And she's eleven not ten!' he beamed.

'You gave Molly's name? I don't believe...' looking around in exasperation to see if any cameramen were still there. 'That was a very stupid thing to do.'

'Very stupid!' Mrs Larnder butted in, an automatic echo of her husband's critique.

Seeing her friend accused, Molly leapt in.

'Look, B saw the big picture on the front of the theatre, the one with the girl upside down, and I bet him I could stand on my hands. So I did. I didn't know the men with the cameras were there and would start taking pictures of me, did I?'

'What picture on the theatre? What are you talking about?'

With that, her arms interlocking theirs, Molly dragged her parents back to the corner of the street towards Leicester Square. Parading out into the middle of the road, she turned them around and pointed up to reveal a huge billboard on the façade of the theatre. Just as Molly had said, it dominated the Prince of Wales depicting the outline of a girl upside down in a little dress. *Barbra Streisand* blared out in huge lettering from the top.

'See?' laughed Molly, still pointing. 'Must be *Funny Girl*, I suppose.'

Mr Larnder understood now. The upside-down image of Fanny Brice, the show's publicity image on posters and advertisements, was all over town. But he was still too put out over his daughter's impromptu showing off of her knickers to the world's press to laugh it off.

'All right! Yes, I see. Well, let that be an end to it. We did ask you to be good while we went to buy Mum a corsage. Come on, come on, can we go in now, please?' and he gently pushed Molly and her mother out in front towards the theatre foyer doors. B made to step after them but a firm hand on his shoulder held him back. A stern face bent down to his.

'Listen. Don't egg Molly on like that. Understand? I don't expect her to get in trouble because of you. I'm very angry you gave her name out to those men. Very silly. Now come on!'

B was confused. Why was putting the photographers right about Molly's name such a bad thing? And why was he to blame over her handstands? That was just Molly doing what Molly usually did, the unexpected. But experience had inured him against such criticism. He was all too used to being told he was in the wrong, his parents made sure of that every day, so this latest blast was like water off a duck's back. Besides, so much was happening today – the train, the river, the lions, the tall tube, the colours everywhere and, most wonderful and mysterious of all, the gallery.

They had eaten at a little restaurant just off Leicester Square and for an entire hour B hardly said a word, his silence unnoticed while Molly talked about Barbra without drawing breath. Munching through his first ever bowl of spaghetti, Mrs Larnder's choice but he didn't want to say no, B retreated into himself and tried to work out just what he had experienced back in the gallery. Most of it was hazy, a sort of dream. He didn't feel frightened, more excited, elated somehow, though a little overwhelmed. The gallery had been a good place to be, he knew that instinctively, even if he couldn't understand why or how.

Coming through the theatre doors, his first vision was of Molly laughing, beaming back at him, and B suddenly felt an echo of something from the gallery. Was it a reflection or a face in a mirror? But the flicker was broken in an instant by Molly's hand in his.

Excitement and expectation pulsated, the two children could feel it through their interlocking fingers. Men in smart black suits, women with tall hairdos in long, swanky dresses, a babble of voices, high-pitched laughter, glinting jewellery, friends embracing and the sparkle from a massive glass light on the ceiling.

Paving a way through the melee, they began to mount some stairs and at a landing Mr Larnder pulled away to buy a small book from a man at a side table. B caught a glimpse of a lady on the front cover, in profile with her hair tied up on top of her head.

Then through a curtain and like the sun coming out from the clouds the auditorium itself opened up. Such an array of colours. A woman in a yellow dress with a deep green broach. Other ladies in blues, reds and whites. Another selling something from a tray tied up with a strap looped around her neck, wearing a black dress with a white apron reminding B of penguins.

The children crept along a row of seats with Mr and Mrs Larnder behind them saying "excuse me" to some people who had to stand up to let them all go past. So it was only when he sat down in a plush chair that B was able to take in the whole view of the stage. A deep and imposing red stage curtain staring back at him – a giant cascade, a sheer waterfall of vivid red.

'I'd like to be called Fanny,' Molly laughed leaning towards him. 'Funny Fanny! What do you think?'

'Perfect!'

A man sitting next to B coughed gruffly. As each turned to one another, eye to eye, the boy caught the familiar glint he got at home. *What are you doing here?... I don't care what you do but keep quiet ...*

But this time B smiled to himself. Tonight, he was here, his mum and dad weren't. He was just about to see

Barbra Streisand, they weren't. Lucky B, unlucky them. Perfect. Tonight was perfect.

As the man looked away, B noticed a copy of the same book on his lap that Mr Larnder had bought. He could see it clearly now, the lady on the front with her hair tied up onto her head. She was very beautiful but didn't look like the usual women he saw. This one had a powerful expression – peaceful, but she looked strong enough to tear your head off in a fight.

'That lady...' he asked loudly leaning across Molly and pointing to her mum's copy, '... who is it?'

Looking up, Mrs Larnder felt the usual irritation. No "please", no manners. The boy had a lot to learn. But how much was Molly learning from him?

'It's pretty obvious, isn't it?'

Was it? B couldn't guess.

'It's Barbra Streisand. This is the programme for the show. She's the star, so she's on the cover.'

Molly couldn't hold herself in and snatched the programme out of her mother's hands.

'Isn't she lovely? I can't believe we are actually going to see her in a minute.'

'Excuse me...' and Mrs Larnder ticked off another black mark against B. Her daughter wouldn't have done such a thing a little while ago.

Suddenly, the red waterfall rose – voices, music and movement – and soon, like a living vision, Barbra was there in person. B turned to Molly. This was all for her, a Funny Girl for *Funny Girl*, and as she gripped his hand tightly he could see she was already in some form of a trance. When Barbra moved, Molly moved in her seat with her. When Barbra sang, Molly's mouth opened and silently sang too. But his friend had been transported to a place none could follow.

B couldn't understand everything going on in the show but the music was so good. Comforting, loud, slow, soft, fast and furious. When the songs ended applause exploded and he wanted so much to clap too but he couldn't because his hand was still being held like a vice. Molly wasn't clapping, just staring and smiling.

There was a song about people – people who needed people and children needing children. Barbra sang that one on her own and B couldn't work out if the people she needed knew she needed them. Well, B needed Molly sure enough and Molly needed him.

The best song was about a parade – someone doing something on a parade. The power of Barbra's voice rocked him in his seat and she was so loud at the end B thought his head was going to explode.

After a long time the red curtain went down, the theatre lights went up, everyone clapped and B thought the show was all over. Molly's spell had finally been broken and she was bouncing up and down and clapping in her seat too. Freed, he dodged her pumping hands and leant across to her mum.

'Is that it?' he shouted against the din. 'Is that the end?'

Mrs Larnder was so absorbed in the whole spectacle, she smiled before realising and put B right in the tenderest of tones.

'No, dear!' she laughed back. 'Only half over, it's the intermission. They'll be back on in a few minutes.'

B slumped back into his seat relieved. He wanted more. Then it hit him. Half over? Life outside *Funny Girl*, galleries and handstands suddenly came flooding back in.

Mexico. World Cup. Wembley. Half-time.

But Molly gave him no time to dwell on England's fortunes. The next twenty minutes was a non-stop barrage of her exalting how great Barbra was and only mouthfuls of ice cream from the tubs her father had bought interrupted her flow.

Eventually, the red curtain rose again, music struck up, Molly stopped talking and once more eased forward to the edge of her seat. B watched her – Molly the nativity angel, the handstand girl, the friend who had knocked to take him out of his deep blue home, the girl at the window. Fanny watching Fanny. Mesmerised.

Finally, unexpectedly, the start of the parade song rang out again. B jumped forward in his seat to match Molly and sensing now that he was there with her, her trance broke and together the two children delighted in the song's reprise.

Here she was… Molly's parade…

The music punched, speeded up and just when it couldn't get any louder the last piercing note hit and the whole theatre shook. Connections. B saw Barbra standing at the Greenwich Observatory, her voice howling out across London, across the river and on and on down the Meridian Line to the end of the world and the penguins.

People were standing and applauding like mad again and in the pandemonium the children had to jump up to see over the people in front.

The audience clapped even harder as different performers on the stage came forward but the noise went sky-high when Barbra appeared to take her bows. Then, just when B thought his hands might fall off, the red waterfall dropped for the last time, the applause died and Barbra was gone.

Buzzing with excitement, everyone started to move out to leave. Molly was so happy she couldn't stop laughing. Playfully, she pushed B back down into his seat.

'Would you rain on my parade, Mr Wood?' she shouted.

'I would, wouldn't I, Funny Girl...?'

'F-u-n-n-e-e-e-!'

Outside the theatre into the roar of London on a balmy night, they started to walk back to Charing Cross. Traffic-light reds, car-headlight whites, yellow tinted streetlamps and a green spotlight placed high up on a building. Passing Trafalgar Square, hordes of people milling about as blue glows lit the water in the fountains from below, B looked back over his shoulder and just made out a lonely, lofty Nelson on his tall tube.

Ten minutes later they were sitting on a crowded train as it started off back to Maze Hill, Molly at the window, B next to her, his mind still racing. What a day! Then looking to his right, he saw three men wearing England football scarves and rosettes sit down.

England. World Cup. Wembley.

'Hey, mister!' B shouted at one of them. 'Did we win?'

'You betcha, Sonny Jim! 2-0!'

B's response was loud, instant, spontaneous, intensely felt, graphic and one he would regret for the rest of his life.

'Fucking hell!'

Silence.

The entire carriage seemed to stand still. Even the rumbling of the train was suspended by the words. The man with an England scarf looked away in disgust and Mr and Mrs Larnder gasped as if they had been slapped in the face.

B's euphoria was very short-lived. The moment he mouthed the words he realised what he had done. The vacuum of sound hung for a few seconds more before Mr Larnder jumped up, lifted Molly out of her window seat and plonked her between him and his wife who put a protective arm around her daughter as if to ward off the nastiness everyone had just witnessed.

Swearing at home was an everyday occurrence. His mum and dad swore all the time. Life in general prompted B to do it every now and then too – the playground, missing an easy goal, howling at the sky – but B had never, ever, sworn in front of Molly and absolutely would never have contemplated it in front of her parents. Now, there it was, on Molly's special day, after *Funny Girl* and the gallery, on the train, when everyone could hear it.

Fuck.

Conversations slowly started up inside the carriage once again and the external trundle of the tracks seeped back in. B looked to Molly but her mum had buried her head into her side so couldn't see her. No face at the window. Instead, he sat gazing through the glass at the blackness beyond.

Nothing more was said until the train pulled up at

Maze Hill where they all got out along with a couple of other passengers. Mrs Larnder opened the door and bounded off with Molly at a sharp pace ahead of her husband with B two paces further behind him.

Once outside the station, Molly and her mum quickly crossed Maze Hill into the walled street alongside Greenwich Park. No goodbyes, nothing, and Mr Larnder, barking 'I'll take him home!', strode off with his disgraced charge trailing like a naughty puppy. Zigzagging the dark back streets to his house, B became more and more wracked with remorse and embarrassment. It just came out, he didn't mean it. England had won. It was just one of those things.

When they reached the alley from the Alamo side, Mr Larnder and B turned into it at pace but slowed sharply, almost stopping. Through low light they saw two women directly ahead, obviously very drunk, both swaying dangerously with linked arms. Molly's dad gasped, almost rearing back, nauseated by the dim spectacle, and at the sound both women spun round peering back. After a few seconds, one of them slurred out a greeting.

'Jesus Christ! *Ish* that you, B?'

Her friend laughed like a hyena and confirmed it.

'Bloody right! *It'sh* your love… *loverly* son!'

Drunk as she was, B's mum assessed the situation.

'Well! If it isn't the man from *Funny*, bloody, *Girl!*' She stood only a few feet away from Molly's dad now. 'Had a good time, darlin'? Christ, by the look of it you bloody well need one.'

Bursting into fits of laughter their condition couldn't

sustain, B's mum wobbled violently and her friend keeled over and rolled across the alley.

Mr Larnder, who had stoically led the foul-mouthed boy back home to discharge his duty while raging inside at his daughter's exposure to such filth, had had enough. He gritted his teeth.

'Are you B's mother?' he demanded.

'Sure am, funny boy!' came the reply, still in hysterics.

'Well, here he is. You're welcome to him!' and turning on his heels he marched off into the lamplight.

B's mum, shouting venomously after the fading figure, ended the encounter with terrible, gin-soaked words, the last one lingering long in its vitriol.

'Well, fuck you too, funny boy! You stupid cunt!'

The alley reverberated with drunken hatred and Mr Larnder disappeared from the alley as if he had been blown away by it.

B was in total shock. Already mortified by his own swearing on the train, he couldn't take in what had just happened. His mum and this thing rolling in the alley were like evil, phantom figures and at that moment the maelstrom of all the things he had seen and done during the day completely overwhelmed him. Coupled with his extreme fatigue, he slumped forward steadying himself to be sick just as his mum sat down with a loud hiss in front of him on the low wall outside his house.

'So you saw Barbra soddin' Streisand, did you? Well, aren't you the fucking lucky one?'

Sickness in his gullet, gathering what strength he had left, her son stood up straight and screamed at her.

'Yes, I fucking did!' and in three steps he had grabbed the key under the mat, unlocked his front door and slammed it shut.

The darkness in the house told him his dad wasn't home and after standing at the door for a few seconds he plunged through the living room, up the stairs and jumped into bed just as he was. Asleep within seconds, his dream was of colours gushing down a waterfall.

The many colours of B

Angry, always angry.

Head down, holding onto the bridge rail with straight-out arms, B looks at the fast-flowing river a few feet beneath him. The river, his friend – a smaller, cleaner friend than the one he left in London. A distant memory now but every time he comes to the Cocker he pays a silent tribute to the brown Thames he once knew.

He's had enough. School, teachers, stupid kids, everything and everyone. It's all a joke. Told them where they can stick it. Just walked right out of the front gate. Sod it! And like a magnet he's drawn to the river, his friend.

Jerking himself up, B twists around and faces upstream. Miles ahead and out of sight lay the lakes and hills – other friends, good friends – and he wishes he was standing on High Snockrigg right now. Directly ahead of him, rising up solid and solitary as if from the river itself, lies the brewery where his mum works. He wonders what she is doing now. Not giving a toss about him that's for sure.

A single swear word rings out, B punches the air and turns back to face downstream. The anger churning, churning, churning. Peering over the side of the bridge and down onto the ripples in the water, he sees the usual silvers, greys, blues and greens.

After a while there's the presence of someone standing behind him and instantly B knows who it is. The river colours are slowly abating his anger by now and he feels a tiny movement on his mouth.

'Throwing yourself in this time?'

His smile grows a shade wider.

'Would you pull me out if I did?'

'No…' comes a careful reply, 'but you could have a towel.'

B turns around.

'Come on. Beans on toast?'

And B walks off the bridge with Miss Hattiemore and turns into the street to her house with its little garden beside the river.

* * *

Bluebells.

Blue all around. A soft, rich blanket of flowers.

Up from Crummock Water and down across the valley from High Snockrigg, between Rannerdale Knotts and the edge of Whiteside, is the sea of spring that Miss Hattiemore has promised him. A thousand different tones of blue – subtle, pastel, solid, transparent.

B falls to his knees captured by the mass, drowning in blue, holding his fingers out to touch the little silky petals, making a physical connection to colour.

There grow the bluebells, surrounding him in a non-stop peel of noise from their ringing.

* * *

Running.

He remembers yet again, running hard through the chaos. The black smoke and orange fire, the dark metal and debris, ignoring the screams, noises he can't hear anyway having been so close to the explosion. Running to where the boy had been on the corner of the street. Black jacket, no more than eleven, winking then shouting obscenities as B walked past going backwards bringing up the rear of the patrol, rifle in hand. So young and the boy knew about anger too.

B's boots skid to a halt reaching the spot and frantically his eyes start searching. Smoke is still dense and a smell of chemicals lies heady in the air. Panic seconds passing then he sees it, wedged in, jammed by the force of the huge blast into the struts of some metal fencing. A severed hand, inches of black jacket sleeve, the other end coated in red. Fingers that had given B the two-finger barely a minute or so ago.

And there lying in the road about twenty feet away is the boy. One of B's ears pops, the sound of the day rushing in, and he leaps off the curb towards the crumpled heap, one of its legs jabbing out at an unnatural angle. Screams, hysterical women, children crying, military commands.

Going down on both knees, B leans forward and cradles the body, a blasted arm dangling lifeless. He puts his face against the dead child's – blood-red blood oozing from a deep neck wound and drizzling down onto his uniform.

A hard hand grabs B's shoulder and shouts at him to get up and move. Urgent, loud, insistent, dominant orders. Yet there's a trace of understanding too – someone's son, someone's child, just a boy, a human being whatever the politics, whatever the circumstances.

Laying the lad down softly, B allows himself to be dragged to the side of the street and against a wall for cover, an officer barracking him telling him to move his fucking arse. Nervous, watchful, breathing heavy, the patrol regroups, rifles drawn. Sirens beginning to sound in the background.

Spots of blood still lie on his face when he looks in the mirror back at base hours later. The bodies counted, the bereaved inconsolable, TV cameras still rolling, another tragedy in the life of the troubled city and as yet no one claiming responsibility.

The red blood of the life the little boy woke up living that morning, his world and his future in his grasp.

* * *

Late for the film, B pushed through the doors into the black night of the cinema. Someone big appears out of the darkness, collects them up and by a zigzagging torch beam dancing on the floor steers them down the aisle. His mum and dad tut-tutting, forcing their way into the middle of a row.

Flopping back into the soft padding of his seat, B looks up and sees the big screen. His first ever film at the cinema and he simply gapes, gasps and gawps. Incredulous. Gigantic. Leg-kicking, heart-stopping. Unbelievable. He sits bolt upright, his mouth jaw-slack open-wide and gazes between the gap made by two people in the row in front.

The colours. Such crystal clarity and on a scale he has never seen before in his short life. So vivid, so real, as if Father Christmas himself has just walked up and said "Hello". Too much, too fantastic. Out of the blackness that bathes him, B marvels at this Technicolor dream, unconsciously storing every single colour.

A black-haired man in a white jacket, a red and orange explosion, a lady painted all over in gold, a Japanese-looking man in a black suit with a bowler hat that can kill, a sleek grey sports car with machine guns and an exploding front seat that sends a man soaring into the air…

After a very long time, the big screen becomes full of letters, lights go on and everybody starts to stand up and talk. B blinks and feels his mum's rough hand on his arm dragging him along the row trailing after his dad.

Out of the cinema, crowds dispersing, the cold night, walking back home, he hears "*Goldfinger*", "James Bond", "Sean Connery"…

Neon lights gleaming along the road but B is still inside, back with the cinema colours.

* * *

White stone, white man.

A statue looms above him as B stands in the middle of Main Street. He thinks of Wolfe on his high white plinth scanning the vastness of London. Years ago? No, only two months. That was Greenwich, this is Cockermouth. South, north, before and after.

Wolfe, conqueror of Canada, all in black, ominous, his three-cornered hat, great and powerful. B reads the chiselled-out words on this other man's stone as best he can. They say he is "Mayo", or is it "Lord Naas"? And are they the same person?

MP for Cockermouth and *Viceroy of India.*

What's an MP? He knows India is a country but no idea about a viceroy. Wolfe was a general. Is a viceroy better than that? Questions, more questions.

Cars passing on both sides of the road, inching by more sedately, less hurriedly than in London, B looks away from Mayo and takes in all the shops running away right to the top of Main Street – the angled lines of tiled roofs, the browns, greys, blacks and whites of this little town he has come to live in with his mum.

Cockermouth. Home now. Somewhere north, that's all he really knows. B still can't take in the massive changes in his life in so short a time. Stolen from London and all he had come to know – the park, the observatory, the swings, his friend the brown Thames, even his school – all gone.

White man, and B pictures all those men and women in black. The black jacket he had to wear sitting in the long black car as it drove slowly down the road from the bottom of his alley. Standing in the church as a man said prayers and talked about God and told everyone what a good man his dad had been. His dad, dead.

Called into his headmaster's room, B comforted for an hour not knowing why until a man who said he worked with his dad came to collect him and drove him back down to his deep blue home. And there, walking into the living room seeing his mum crying on the settee, having to wait ten long minutes before she spoke to him. First a statement then a formal dismissal.

'Your stupid father decided to die today. Now go away.' His dad's workmate taking him out again for fish and chips to gloss over the embarrassment.

B didn't cry like the other people – people he didn't know. He knew his dad, knew what he was. The religious man didn't. B had seen too much, heard too much, felt too much. No tears from him but there were plenty from his mum. Black coat, scarf, hat, shoes and handbag, her sombre widow's weeds relieved only by the wild lipstick red of her mouth and fingernails.

After the man in the white cloak threw some mud down on the box that contained his dad, everyone walked away from the hole in the ground and got back into the black cars to drive away. B's mum faced the car window and didn't say a single word to him on the journey home, nor at any time for the rest of the day. Tired and sleepy, he hauled himself to his bedroom at ten o'clock as she drank from yet another bottle in the kitchen, her usual retreat.

Then within three days they were in another car, a blue one this time, speeding to another but unknown life. Hours and hours, miles and miles away. B's mum's sister had a house in a place called Cockermouth and that's where they would live now. The husband of the aunt he had never seen, or even heard of, would pick up their stuff in a van at the weekend.

Turning again, B faces the white man and decides he isn't a patch on Wolfe. Not so high or mighty standing up there. Like everything else in Cockermouth, he's smaller, less imposing, different. B looks hard into the man's blank white stone eyes and feels he had been cast adrift in a deep blue sea.

* * *

'Are you going to jump off?'

B keeps staring into the silvers, greys, blues and greens of the river not realising at first that the words are meant for him.

'Yes or no?' a voice says more intently.

Streams of colours continue to run under the narrow bridge over the Cocker, water from the hills that B doesn't know about yet. Turning around to face the voice, he finds a lady, her arm on the opposite metal rail – white coat, black and brown patterned skirt, deep red soft hat, white bag. He looks at her face and sees deep green eyes – piercing, penetrating green – locked onto his.

'Jump?'

'Yes, you!'

The lady moves over closer to B on his side of the bridge.

'You… you're here all the time. I've seen you from over there…' pointing to a small garden terrace down the river a little, its edge looking directly over the water. 'Always talking to yourself, shouting sometimes. What are you going on about?'

The question is asked very kindly and B hasn't heard kindness for a while. Taken off guard, he answers from his heart before he realises.

'The river… I like to talk to the river. I like it. Helps. It's something I did before.'

'Before?'

'Before, when I lived in London. My house was right near the Thames. I used to go down there and I dunno, talk. Was good.'

Edging closer to him. 'So you talk to the Cocker now?'

'Cocker?'

'Yes. That's the name of the river. You don't know? You talk to it all the time and you don't know its name?'

B feels a bit silly and turns his head in the other direction for a second.

'I dunno. Nobody said. I know this place is called Cockermouth. So is that it?'

The lady can see B is embarrassed. 'Yes. This is the River Cocker and this town is at the mouth of it. This is the last little bit as it joins that river over there. That's called the Derwent.' And she points to another hard-flowing river beyond the other end of the bridge.

'Oh …'

A few seconds of silence before another question.

'Helps?'

'What?'

'You said it helps. Talking to the river helps. Helps what?'

B goes red, feeling unsure. But looking more closely at the lady's face and meeting her green eyes, he relaxes and speaks in a free sort of way which until now had only been possible in Molly's company.

'Helps me sort things out, all the things I can't get right. When I was in London it was just nice being down by the Thames. We moved here a little while ago and I found this bridge and I like the water running under it. It's not as big as the Thames but it's good. The Thames was dirty, brown and oily. But this one is cleaner and I can see lots of colours in it. My dad died and my mum moved us here. London's a long way away…'

B stops mid-sentence, broken from the lady's green spell for an instant.

'Sorry, miss, but is something wrong? Am I in trouble?'

The lady smiles and shakes her head. 'No, you're not in trouble. I just see you from my little garden there and wonder. That's all.'

Then Miss Hattiemore tells B her name and over the next half hour talks about the river, explaining where the water comes from and a little about hills and lakes not too far away. B has never visited them but Miss Hattiemore says he should.

Eventually, she says she has to go home now and that B had better do the same. He nods but it's better standing talking to her.

'I haven't even asked. What's your name then?'

'B.'

The green eyes blink. 'B? Is that it?'

'B. My mum says B for bastard.'

Ten seconds of silence except for the gush of the rushing river.

'B for bridge, B for boy, B for bye!' and Miss Hattiemore touches her new friend on the shoulder and walks off. Two minutes later when she emerges out onto her tiny back terrace beside the river, he is still there. She waves to him, B waves back and he starts to run off back into town.

December 2006

Venus.

A sparkling planet on which it would be death to tread, a tennis champion, some plant that eats things...

Why call herself that? Where has it come from? Vanity, a stage name, a *nom d'amour* from an old affair?

Sitting in the rear stalls of the New Theatre in Hull, a three-hour drive across the north of England from the Lakes, B pondered these questions as the Thursday-night audience thickened preparing for the performance. Questions which had taunted him since learning a little more about Molly's life journey from the girl he had waved goodbye to all those years ago.

Nerves and anticipation waved through him, an inner undercurrent matching the growing excitement of the theatregoers. A yellow ticket stub in one hand, the white and black contrasting on the cover of the show programme he held in the other, a large lady in a mustard top sitting next to him, the burgundy of the soft, black-buttoned beret worn by the young woman in front, and somewhere beyond the heavy red curtain shutting off the stage he knew was his childhood friend. A Funny Girl, who, like him, was now a middle-aged stranger. A lifetime lived down other country lanes, in different worlds, on different planets.

Ever since his arrival back in England and those first hours of contemplation on High Snockrigg, B had been visualising this moment. Tonight was a reunification, the chance to catch a trace of his past, to hold it in his hand and raise it to the light. Since Villers-sur-Mer, he had retraced his life back bit by bit like a crime investigation. Evidence had been weighed, arguments considered, courtroom exhibits sifted – A, B and C – and with time and due diligence he had reached a verdict, a final judgement.

He must begin with Molly, the fountainhead.

Located on the square before Notre Dame's famous twin spires in Paris, all distances in France are measured from Point Zero. B had stood on that spot many times enjoying the colours of the capital all around him, the serene Seine flowing nearby, and it was what he had come to believe Molly represented now – his own Point Zero.

The analysis, cut to its basics, was quite simple. Paris and its ultimate nightmare had been the culmination of his professional life. That career had begun in the army, an escape from his crushing teenage anger, and that anger was rooted in him being cast adrift in Cockermouth. And before it all? Molly.

Until he met her, B's younger years had been lonely and unhappy yet as he couldn't remember any details with clarity they didn't really count. After her, his life had been first an angry red mist then from his army days one lived through, and for, other people. Stumbling upon the Meridian Line again at Villers-sur-Mer had convinced him, however fancifully, that such needless death in Paris tracked back in a complex, but direct line to the little girl in Greenwich. And he was equally sure a connection had to be made with her again if he was to start moving forward with his life.

Here tonight, in this theatre in Hull, watching her as the actress she was always born to be, he hoped for some form of reaction, a sign or clue that would help him plot his road ahead. Was it so silly to contemplate this? So ridiculous to think that merely by being in Molly's presence again a thunderbolt could point a way? Stupid it may be but all B knew was he had to be here to find out.

Of course, it was all a one-sided affair. He had vital reasons for wanting to see, hear and experience Molly again but these were selfish imperatives. She had her own life, her own drives and motivations, all stretching back over the many years separating the two former school friends and they didn't remotely involve B. He was a mere fragment of her history, drowned out by decades. There was no intention, nor should there be, of actually meeting her again.

Of today's Molly he still knew little really, just bare facts which couldn't tell the whole story. Divorced, that strange new name, where she lived (although that wasn't a surprise) but apart from these snippets she was a mystery. The Molly of Greenwich, in the 1960s, of the river and the swings, the girl he had met at the observatory, Funny Girl, this was the source he wanted to tap again. Point Zero. Just perhaps, reunited in her presence tonight, albeit as part of a large crowd, that Greenwich spirit might touch him again and centre things.

Reunifications.

B had already made two of them this week. The biological mother who deserted him at birth and the surrogate mother who wanted him to leave her, the hills and all his anger behind and never look back. What altogether contrasting meetings they had been. For her age, the still strikingly beautiful woman greeting him on her doorstep with a silent shrug, turning and leaving the door open for him to follow her inside like some errand boy, her first words asking him for money. Then later, the pitifully infirm old lady, wracked by Alzheimer's, sitting silently in the nursing home, the font of all his old Lakeland knowledge, his revered companion on valley and mountain pathways, now a lost and pale shadow of that strong, resilient force he had loved. B held her frail, crinkled hand, an unknown, unrecognised visitor, with her still vivid spring-green eyes the only overt connection to the past.

Faded yellows, stained reds and dusty blues in the old living room confronted B when he sat down opposite his birth mother. They hadn't seen each other since he was sixteen, although they had spoken at intervals on the phone over the years, usually when she was in some sort of trouble needing cash – her last-chance-saloon son suddenly becoming useful, remembered. And despite everything, he always succumbed to the ridiculous guilt she could conjure in him. The money was nothing he told himself, it kept her quiet and he could forget her until the next time. His Belfast-born need to protect, to save, always awakened by some atom of maternal gravity left inside him.

'Hundred quid would be good...' she proposed after a thirty-second silence, half-smiling and looking into the middle distance. 'Two would be better...'

B continued to look at her, studying the face from all those bad dreams across the decades since leaving the three-storey Cockermouth town house that morning – bags all packed, standing in the musty-brown hallway, hearing the parting shot he took with him on the bus all the way to training camp.

'Kill someone for me, won't you!' and without any form of goodbye or shred of emotion, she had turned on her heels and disappeared like the day she deposited him on Miss Andrews for his first day at school.

'How have you been, Mum?' B enquired, slowly reaching for his inside jacket pocket. 'You look well. How's life been treating you?'

'Do you *really* want to know?' Late-seventies and her acerbic tongue still a weapon.

'What should I say after all this time? Fantastic, sheer bliss, an absolute scream?' Then getting up and walking to the side table, picking out a cigarette and lighting it languidly in her old style, she let him in for the tiniest of instants, the first time she had ever done so.

'Fucking nightmare, actually, fucking nightmare. It's a big, empty old house this. Too many ghosts and too much dust. You made a good move getting out, leaving your dear old mum behind. Fucking good move!' Yet as quickly as she had opened it, she flicked her eyes and closed the door again.

'Turning up here, always were a mystery, you. Bleeding mystery. What did you come back for, huh? Am doing just dandy, don't worry about that,' and sitting down on a side chair, gazing at an imaginary object across the room the way B remembered, she said with cold finality. 'Just leave the money and go. Nothing for you here, boy. Nothing ever was.'

Nothing.

B placed £5,000 in £50 notes on the table (he had been to the bank in Main Street knowing what was coming) and storing the sight of his mother's lipstick-red mouth, her colourful trademark, he left her alone in the house once more.

'Bye, Mum!' before turning in the hallway to give a long-delayed riposte. 'I did kill a few. But have the lives I saved.'

Fresher colours, light pinks, lilacs and creams, welcomed him an hour later as he stepped into the small but newly-refurbished nursing home out of Cockermouth on the road towards Carlisle. He had phoned ahead, explained and they said he could have a little time with her. She would get tired quickly. The nurse was very kind and helpful.

'Hello, Miss Hattiemore…' B said softly with a gentle brush of his lips on her age-spotted forehead, his former mentor and advisor allowing herself to be kissed in her deep confusion. 'It's good to see you... so good.' He took her hand in his and stroked it.

For the next half an hour, B kept up a one-sided conversation, feeling many mixed emotions through her brittle fingers. 'Why did I always call you Miss Hattiemore? It was never Dorothy, was it? Can you remember High Snockrigg? You said it had the best view in the Lakes...'

B apologised for never coming back, for deserting her even though he was only doing what she had told him to do. The army was the right choice. 'Made a man of me!' he chuckled. He talked of the old days caught in mists and rains on mountainsides, of her little house by the River Cocker and the little bridge she had discovered him on. His brief time too soon over, he gave her another peck on the cheek, left his second mother of the day and sitting in silence in the car for a long time afterwards eventually felt tears fall in salty streams down his face. After fifteen minutes, with a head swimming in memories, he drove away down the gravel drive looking ahead to the third reunion he had to make.

By now the auditorium was heaving with noise and colour – children shouting and electronic flashes from their glow toys purchased in the foyer. On-off red, white, blue and green glitter tiaras on little girls' heads and boys wearing fiery red-eyed monster face masks. But when drum rolls and crashing music started to play, the din, glitter and fierce eyes were dimmed, the audience went quiet and the red theatre curtain rose.

A mass of dry ice enveloped the whole stage set and began to cascade forward to the first rows of the stalls. Scanning with trained eyes for movement, B leaned forward in his seat. There, there and there… bodies came out of the artificial mist, a castle scene, and he probed, processed and analysed in search of her.

At last, simply and silently, she appeared, entrancing right and walking up to a group of characters placed centre stage. Long white dress, a royal blue tunic with gold buttons, she was clad in the fashion of times long ago in lands far, far away when the fear of hideous creatures in the night could grip rural townsfolk by the throat.

Molly.

He knew her, knew her movement, knew her shape as if the years counted for nothing. That jump in her stride at the midway point the give-away, like reading a book you could never forget. B studied her. Even at some distance he could see a face with the same impish qualities – fast, cheeky eyes and an eager, smiling mouth. Yet despite all his expectation, there was no shock at the sight of her. The visual connection made, it was her voice he had not been prepared for and when she first spoke her sound made him gasp out loud. A deeper voice than he had known, an adult's voice, the voice of a mature woman with a long history behind her, a failed marriage for a start, but unquestionably the voice he remembered. The voice that had made him laugh, had comforted, praised and made him feel special when he had been a deep blue little boy so much in need of its tender timbre. The voice of the girl at the window.

Rapt in the sound and reality of Molly before him,

B sat back in his seat lost in a separate world, his eyes never leaving her. Laughter, shrieks, clapping and boos reverberated around the auditorium, the pantomime continuing on its own inexorable path – heroine, monster, songs and the promise of love in the end – yet Molly was his only focus. The vivid colours of the production, the silver castle walls, the rich greens of the woods, the multicoloured spotlights picking out details on the stage, were for once only at the edge of his consciousness.

In his reverie, he remembered another time and another theatre, watching Molly in a trance, her vice-like grip on his hand while Barbra Streisand sang and the audience pulsated to her song. The day Funny Girl saw *Funny Girl* and the world was perfect.

In time, B's reminiscing was finally and roughly broken when the lady in mustard next to him started to squeeze by followed by her two large children. The music had stopped and the red curtain was down. It was the interval and ice creams and drinks beckoned.

Gathering himself, B shook his head in amazement at where he was. A provisional English theatre, a damp December day, being transfixed by a phantom of his childhood, another spectre of his past like his mother and Miss Hattiemore earlier. What changes Villers-sur-Mer had wrought. What a far cry from his former life not so long ago, flying in and out of exotic cities and countries around the world, every waking hour fixed on the safety of his Principal and his family.

Feeling a momentary sense of awkwardness sitting alone and surrounded by so many families and friends,

B picked his way to the toilet and on returning to his seat took out his theatre programme to check Molly's description until the show resumed. Looking at the cover, the black and white outlines of the two principal pantomime characters, the beautiful girl and the terrible looking half man-half animal in a tender embrace – love conquering difference – his eyes strayed from the overall design and focussed on just the words. Then suddenly, with incredible force as if poleaxing himself, he slammed the booklet to his chest.

He had seen the name of the pantomime before, lots of times, while booking his ticket from an ad in a newspaper and, of course, since arriving at the theatre with its billboards scattered everywhere. He had seen the old Walt Disney cartoon and knew the David Bowie song. But somehow the title hit him only now and with utterly unexpected and staggering power. With the sight and sounds of Molly heavy in his head, her presence so real, the simple and familiar words took on an utterly different conceptual interpretation.

Beauty and the Beast.

The thunderbolt.

Beauty.

How piercing and with such dagger-like precision the word struck home. Eyes screwed shut, face clenched, hardly breathing, B was pounded by a concussion of images – a kaleidoscope in his mind, colours twisting and darting, displaying at huge speeds. Shapes, patterns, lines and images appearing and vanishing hundreds to the second dredging up pixels of memory.

Only very slowly, after several minutes, could B begin to absorb outside sensations, light and motion. Movement in the theatre, a spotlight's beam, the burgundy beret in front of him twisting to face friends on either side. His mind pounding, in time he started to hear music from the orchestra pit and with his shaking hands still holding the programme, he felt the audience perk up.

With cheers and a few whistles, like a red mist lifting before him, the stage curtain rose. There was laughter, waves of applause, a child screamed, and in the light of a completely new dawn, B watched as Molly as Venus, Venus as Molly, entered again and started to speak – new colours, a change of clothes, orange, gold, a red tunic. He sat up, set his full gaze on her, a fixed point, and saw the naked truth.

Somehow, for incomprehensible, inexplicable reasons, B had expunged from his entire history, his complete memory, any connection to beauty and what it had once meant to him. His mum and dad's excesses, their terrible insults and punishments, their cruel blows and torments, the trauma of losing Molly... "You'll never see her again!" A lonely August spent in agony, shutting it all out – gone, gone, gone, quite forgotten. Beauty had been lost on the waves of his young despair, never to be recaptured.

A mind game, a mental rejection? Beauty, the force that once inspired and consumed him, had torn his young life apart. Beauty, in all its naked glory, had been driven out of him. Beauty, once so real, so certain, the answer to so many questions, had abandoned him on what he believed would be his greatest day and through the long, arid, intervening years had never found him again.

The pantomime worked towards its climax – a terrifying beast with the heart of a prince, a beautiful girl, steadfast and true, loving in the face of ugliness. The orchestra reached its final and deafening crescendo, the audience clapping, stamping its feet and whistling in wild appreciation. The actors appeared one by one to cheers and playful boos with Molly taking the bows she had always craved.

B had returned to what he thought was his Point Zero but now understood it was a stepping stone to the true source. Remaining silent in his seat as everyone started to leave, he knew with utter clarity what he must do.

Return to the House of Colours.

The many colours of B

High on High Snockrigg.

The deep reds of the evening sun burning its last of the day. Some sheep, no wind for a change, deep down below the comfort of Buttermere and the anger still inside him. Churning, churning.

Questions, as always. Why has he done it? What's going to happen now? Who has seen him? What are they doing and saying?

B jumps up from the tight, tufted hillside grass, paces around for a few steps and falls back down again. Angry at the bastards, angry at himself.

The man and his poxy son ribbing him for weeks. He hasn't a clue what it's all about but every time he sees them in the street or outside his house they tear him to pieces – laughing, mocking. It's not as if they have anything to laugh about or mock. The dad's an out-of-work waste of space and his son's useless at everything – school, football, girls, the lot. B could tear the boy apart, the dad too probably, but they are a tight family and they know too many people, a few you wouldn't want to cross. Well, too late now, B is well and truly in it – up to his red neck.

Red.

He doesn't know where Dave got the bottle from but there was a suggestion about an abattoir further up towards Carlisle. B gave him a quid for it. Blood. Redder than the late September dusk gathering down in Buttermere. How he enjoyed emptying the bottle over the bloke's car, that poxy light blue Ford Escort, with its poxy, look-at-me white lines down the side. Red gushing over the roof and down the bonnet – blue to red. Blood dripping off the Ford. A minute of sheer ecstasy. Dancing around it howling his head off like a wolf, something he remembers doing back in Greenwich.

Then a shout from the top of Waterloo Street, a way past Miss Hattiemore's house, and B flying to his bike, pedalling like a bat out of hell out of there, all the way, miles and miles, lanes and villages to his high, safe place where he can look down on the world and nobody can touch him. High Snockrigg and its huge views out to all the fell tops he knows so well – the Gables, the Scafells, High Stile, High Crag and Red Pike.

Red.

B sits and watches in stillness for another hour as the last reds of the sun disappear. A long night awaits but he isn't concerned, he's been here before, he knows his space and what to expect. It isn't that cold. He'll be OK in his padded jacket. No, night will be the enjoyable bit.

Morning will be the killer. There'll be consequences no doubt, sooner or later.

Bloody hell.

* * *

Black guns held aloft by masked men painted green, military-style. Aiming skywards. Aiming to kill or be killed.

B holding his own gun in his hands, a rifle, standing to the back of the patrol while a yellow car is being checked out ahead of him. He stares at the mural. A simple home to someone but its entire flank wall displaying a tribute to a complex cause. A celebration of a fight claiming so many victims – one of them a little boy blown apart on a street corner just seconds after B walked by.

Hardened now to the role he is playing – protector, alert, aware, conscious of risk – for a few, brief moments B is captured by the colours on the wall. Letting his mind wander, he is fascinated by traces of white, flashes of orange and steel greys in the faces of the men and women – heroes to some, monsters to others.

His daydream shattered by the hard crack of a brick thrown at his feet. A group of boys down the street flexing their muscles, reminding the patrol where they are, as if they need that. B walks a few paces towards them and they all run off laughing, the mural at that instant backdropping him. A soldier who can see comfort in colour even on a black day in Belfast.

* * *

Dark-blue door, white wooden surround, gold lock, silver key, hideous pink wallpaper in the hallway.

B slams the door shut, treads over some mail on the brown entrance mat and huffs and puffs into the living room. Stained red carpet, faded cream glass lamp on a side table and heavy brown furniture, the interior is lightened only by some afternoon rays piercing the half-drawn, seaweed-green velvet curtains. A house of gloom.

A packet of crisps on a chair for some reason and B snatches it up, tears open the paper and takes a mouthful of smoky bacon. Sodding school. Sent home, told to cool off. His mother "will be told". Fat lot of good that's going to do.

Then, silently, ghost-like, the mother who will be told walks into the room herself. Breezing past B, she slinks into the dark brown sofa. No hello, no recognition, he looks at her staring into mid-space as usual, her eyes fixed on a distant want or need. Lipstick – red lipstick.

There is no shock as B absorbs her nakedness, full breasts lifting with her breathing, hair disappearing down between her legs and the sofa seat cushion. There is nothing except for a nagging sensation, however sickening, that his mother, despite it all, is beautiful.

'In here!' she calls suddenly and the next moment a tall man with a black beard walks into the room. Slowly, delicately, like a prowling animal. Naked.

'Oh!' he purrs… 'We have company.'

B's mother laughs for a second and holds out her lithe right arm to the man. He responds by walking behind the sofa taking her hand in his and cupping her left breast with the other, squeezing slightly. He bends down, kisses her briefly on the lips, his eyes staring at B, his hands still full of their property.

A distant memory flashes through B's head – a man holding a lady's tit.

B takes another handful of crisps and catches a brief glimpse of the red nail polish on his mother's toes. Toenail red. He looks up.

'Does he know he's the third one this week?'

* * *

Green.

Clean, sharp, hypnotising, a huge carpet crossed with brilliant white lines spreads out from goal to goal. The crowd building, a smell of food in the air, nervously paying his money at the turnstile, hurrying past programme-sellers across the concrete forecourt leading to the Covered End, stepping up the white-walled stairwell and with his view peaking, looking out over the lush, vivid green grass stretching out forever.

The pitch is lit up by four high corner floodlights, like mighty electric suns beating down, and B breathes in savouring the taste of his first real-life football match on a crisp, cold night. The valley of green, Charlton Athletic in their ground called The Valley some three miles east of his alley.

All those lies and deceptions – an imaginary friend's house, fake schoolwork and the non-existent boy's parents who said he should stay and have tea. His own mum and dad just pleased to have him out of their way, out of their hair. He'll be back home late. Yes, after the game and a bus ride home late.

Standing on a low terrace step at the eighteen-yard line, the crowd swelling in expectation minutes before kick-off, a man selling peanuts, chanting and rattle noise, loudspeakers and some old-fashioned band music starts as the two teams come out… *When the Red, Red Robin…*

Charlton's red shirts and white shorts bobbing around on the green.

* * *

Rainbows skimming the water.

Sparkling, glittering, layers of rich arcing, darting colour in the spray.

After lunch, the laughter and chatter gone, a quiet time aboard. His Principal and his wife resting in the master bedroom, their boy playing in his side cabin. B taking half an hour out looking over the bows of the gratefully loaned, year-old luxury yacht as it glides smoothly across the blue Mediterranean.

Bow-spray generating thin rainbow beams – colours emerging from the white. B puts his hand out as if to touch them, fingering the phenomenon. Questions. How do they appear? Where do the rainbows go when they vanish without warning only to reform seconds later? B watching and waiting before finally a hiss in his earpiece calls him back to life.

Going below, he reaches his own cabin. Preparations to be made, more meetings in the stateroom later, his

Principal's tricky encounter at their destination across the waves the next day.

Suddenly, a thought, and opening up a small drawer next to his bed, B retrieves his old gift of colours, the present he has kept all these years. Putting it to his eye, he looks through the glass, twists the body of the object and delights as always in the many worlds held within – shapes, colours, lines, patterns… and rainbows.

23 July 1966

Going to sea as a twelve-year-old boy, just a year older than B now, and a life full of danger, derring-do, glory and duty. Becoming the most famous man in the country, dying a hero, a lord, loved by his men, his "Band of Brothers" and an entire nation. Their saviour from the French and the terrible Bonaparte, Britain ruling the waves, an empire building beyond measure.

Sitting on the head of a lion in Trafalgar Square, just like Molly had done a week ago, B looked up at the tall tube once more. A week ago, he had no idea who Nelson was. Now with his legs propped up on the lion's mane, the heat of the morning beginning to strengthen and all the noise and bustle of the city bursting around him, B felt he knew this man-o'-war better than he knew anyone, except Molly of course.

School had broken up on Wednesday for the long summer holidays and in three stretched-out days B had retreated to the sanctuary of a slim book he found in the classroom bookcase. Monday morning, his teacher finally answered a barrage of insistent questions, revealed where to find a book to help him and urgent fingers picked it out in seconds. Retreating to a window alcove, B started to devour the words and imagined every full-page coloured picture coming to life.

The Ladybird book, *The Story of Nelson*, made everything real – the waves and ships, the pomp and ceremony, the battles, the missing arm, the lost eye – and B was happy to lose himself in his reading, not merely over a growing obsession with this hero but because he was alone, worried and confused.

Deepest blue alone, at home with his parents. Butterflies inside worried, because of his indiscretion on the train and his mum's even greater foul-mouthed onslaught in the alley. Tailspin confused, from the after-effects of visiting that strange and exhilarating world inside the gallery.

Alone.

The day after *Funny Girl*, Sunday, as already planned, Molly had gone on a fortnight's holiday with her parents to Aunt Meg's house by the sea at a place called Hastings so she wouldn't be coming back to school. Walking out of the gates for the last time together on Friday, she and B had felt a little sad but with such an exciting prospect of tomorrow in London, Barbra and *Funny Girl*, they didn't linger over farewells. Lovely Mrs Hinkley had left to teach somewhere in the country three months ago so there were even fewer emotional ties.

There was no talk of September either. After dual exam successes, in recent weeks they had come to terms with the fact that they were going to different secondary schools in the autumn and faced a future education apart. One mixed-sex school had been possible but Molly's parents had been adamant about where she was going. So a particularly sad visit to the observatory had ended with spoken and hand-held promises of unswerving loyalty. B was unaware of Mr and Mrs Larnder's great satisfaction with these arrangements of course. The long-awaited break-up in the relationship was now certain and Molly and B would drift apart sure enough.

For teachers and pupils alike, there was no real work to be done on these end of term days and for B there was little enjoyment either without his friend. And not just at school. No playing together down by the river or in the park, no laughter and nobody to do stupid spur-of-the-moment things. Funny Girl had gone away and in her absence he began to feel his old unease and worry. For the first time he feared how he would cope at his new school without her constant presence.

But the Ladybird book gave some unexpected compensation and he was quickly absorbed in Nelson's life. Hours sped by reading and he surfaced only to play football in the playground after dinner or in special playtimes as end of term treats to both pupils and hard-working teachers. World Cup fever was everywhere too and goal after goal B was Bobby Charlton, Roger Hunt or Jimmy Greaves – heroes all, just like Nelson.

Worried.

What would be the consequences of his swearing on the train and his mother's terrible insults in the alley? B had already known Mr and Mrs Larnder didn't like him but now they had every good reason. There was no doubt when they came back from Hastings Molly's dad would give him a strict telling off just like he did before *Funny Girl*. He certainly didn't think he would be getting any more invitations to days out for a while. He had better keep his head as low down as possible. Doubtless he would have to apologise, for himself and on behalf of his mum too. But how best to do that?

Confused.

What had actually happened in that art gallery? The sheer force of his visit to the National had deeply unearthed him. It was like he had been allowed to glimpse through the peephole of a secret wonderland, a magical place where anything could happen, where colours came alive. But with Molly in Hastings, B couldn't talk it all over or share his thoughts with her. Bereft of help or guidance at home, he had no hope of comfort except from the river.

So first thing on Sunday after *Funny Girl*, he left the house with his mum and dad still sleeping off their respective hangovers and ran to the riverfront. Reaching the spot where he had once howled in rejection, tearing his picture up into tiny bits, he turned to look up at the alley building's riverside wall. Sure enough, there it was in all its historical and nautical glory. Big bold letters. *Trafalgar.*

The word reverberating in his brain, B dashed down the river walk-way gulping in fresh summer morning air until he reached the black gates of the Royal Naval College. Here they had borne him then, down to the Thames for his last voyage up to London. Here where once B had placed a golden crown on top of Molly's head in the twilight. He looked across the river and imagined funereal ships, decked with sailors clad in respectful black, saluting their hero.

And it was on Nelson's steps that by questioning, searching and probing his friend the river, B tried to make some sense of what he had experienced in the gallery. A full tide lapped only feet below him, images and patterns bubbling up on its oily surface, and slowly, gradually, in its own rolling time, in its own brown way, the Thames began to suggest answers, to water a secret seed in the boy's mind. Reluctantly trotting back past the Trafalgar building for lunch, B couldn't put any form or meaning to the seed yet. It would take another English victory over the old enemy across the English Channel to do that.

Tuesday was just like Monday, more of the Ladybird book and football, and, apart from the term ending, Wednesday was the same again except for the heavy anticipation of that night's World Cup tie. England against France at Wembley.

B felt very strange. A potent mixture of missing Molly, growing anxiety over England and his continuing inner turmoil about the mysteries at the National Gallery. All day his mind swam constantly from one to the other so that by the time the big game came around in the evening, he was a jangling bag of nerves in front of the telly.

His mum had already announced she'd had enough of the "bloody ball", so blue dress, white cardigan, light brown shoes and lipstick-red lips, she'd gone out very noisily with her new friend Brenda, the thing in the alley, leaving her husband sitting grumpily in his grey armchair as usual predicting England would lose.

Kick off, some nervous probing from both teams, a Gordon Banks save from a nasty French shot, some mounting English pressure, then suddenly the boys broke through. A wobbly Jack Charlton header hitting the post and as the ball bumped along the goal-line sure enough Roger Hunt pounced to stab in. B's heady mixture of extreme nerves, a mind in disarray and this being the first World Cup England goal he had seen live (news of the two against Mexico, including a wonder strike from Bobby Charlton after a heart pumping thirty-yard dance with the ball, had prompted his abomination on the train), drove him to jump up with both hands in the air. And in that moment two things happened simultaneously.

First, he totally destroyed the glass lampshade hanging from the centre of the living room, and second, he understood completely what the river had been telling him earlier in the day, the seed instantly flowering in his head. He would go back to the National, take the train again, cross the sparkling river once more, return to the tall tube and find out for himself if that kaleidoscope world he had glimpsed in the gallery was real. All on his own, no one else, just him.

By the end of the game, Roger securing the win heading in from close range, and the smashed glass swept up to his father's incandescent rage, B had it all fixed. Go on Saturday, tell his parents he was watching

England's quarter-final against Argentina at another boy's house, they wouldn't care anyway, and be there and back without them ever knowing. As the referee blew time at Wembley and the nation exhaled with relief, B left his dad begrudgingly giving Alf Ramsey, the England manager, some faint praise and skipped off to bed.

Molly, Nelson, England and that magical world in the gallery, the prospective adventurer had a lot to think about between now and the weekend. Even his mum's return and inevitable fury over the lampshade didn't bother him. And now it was Saturday and here he was in Trafalgar Square sitting on a lion's head.

Lying to his parents about today had been easy. His mum was going out to escape yet more football, his dad was going to do whatever his dad was going to do so, as expected, they hadn't given their son a second thought.

B had emptied the extremely meagre contents of his money box, significantly enhancing it when the coast was clear with a raid on the housekeeping tin he knew was kept in the kitchen and, equally successfully, and with no little measure of boldness, had bought a return ticket to Charing Cross at Maze Hill. He remembered how Mr Larnder had done it while simultaneously managing to stare out the man at the ticket counter who eyed a young boy travelling alone very suspiciously.

The same closed compartment, the same magic tunnel, the same bridge over the Thames and the same glistening river in the sunshine. Only Molly was missing. Molly at the window. B wondered again where Hastings was.

London.

Slipping down from the lion with the same Molly-like agility as last week, B didn't jump to the ground like she had then. Instead, he clambered up a couple of very large steps and walked around the base of Nelson's Column itself until he was standing immediately below the large, imposing plate of the hero's death scene that had captivated him before. Up close, Nelson stricken, it was as if B was trying to make physical contact with a story he had come to know so well that week. In an almost religious gesture, he jumped high to touch the bottom edge of the plate to do just that before climbing back down onto the pavement.

After taking a deep breath, B walked to the opposite side of the column to take in the full panoramic view of the National Gallery building, its distinctive black dome and frontage spreading the full width of Trafalgar Square. Under a pure blue sky, red buses and black taxis passing by in summer procession, for the first time since leaving home he felt the magnitude of his adventure. He'd never done anything like this before, never gone so far on his own. Even his clandestine trip to an evening game at Charlton Athletic a few months before was nothing on this. He didn't feel any sense of danger yet he understood he was far beyond his normal boundaries. Even his parents would be very angry at what he was doing, probably, but the demand to discover, to know, was overcoming everything.

'Kaleidoscope…'

B spoke aloud as he started walking towards the gallery but suddenly, out of nowhere, he was felled by an enormous force hitting him sideways on. Crashing to the ground, badly dazed and winded, he lay gasping until a huge maw of a hand hauled him up to his feet with uncanny strength.

'Sorry, son...' came a rich, deep, resonant voice, 'not looking... trying to see where my mate's gone. You hurt?'

Gasping, B couldn't answer. No voice came but his vision returned just enough to see a mountain of a man. A huge, hairy creature carrying a large Union Jack on a pole, wearing a white singlet vest over grubby black trousers and a yellow straw hat bearing the name "England" on it in red letters. Backlit by the glinting sun, the giant seemed almost as big as Nelson's Column itself.

'You all right, son?'

This time B had enough breath to speak.

'Yeah, think so...' he wheezed, rubbing the side of his head. Then in the simplicity only the young can muster added, 'You're big!'

The giant chuckled and a gigantic fist mock-punched B's chin.

'I suppose I am, son, I suppose I am.'

B saw the red, white and blue of the Union Jack flutter in a breeze then noticed a familiar shape drawn on the man's arm – a skull and some bones crossed beneath it. A memory of seeing it once before on the telly.

'You a pirate?' B asked, pointing. 'They have shapes like that.'

The giant made a big belly laugh. 'A pirate? Me? No, son, no pirate.' But crouching down to B's face level, he took in the boy's eyes. 'I was a sailor once though. Got this tattoo years ago on a trip to South Africa.'

B's mind moved into overdrive... sailor, ships, sea,

Nelson, time… he couldn't believe it. Everything connecting up again just like a week ago. Was South Africa one of those countries on the Meridian Line down at the end of the world?

Leaning so far back B thought his hat would fall off, the giant looked up to the top of the column and with a laugh announced, 'I'll tell you what, son. As an old sailor, if England beat Argentina today I'm going to climb right up there and give the old admiral a kiss! How about that?'

The Union Jack swayed just by B's head and in an unconscious movement he took a corner between his fingers and rubbed it together, feeling the colours. England. World Cup. Glory. He grinned at the man's massive bulk, his black belt spun around an overhanging belly and the ends of black, wiry hairs poking out from coalmine armpits.

'You going to Wembley?'

'Sure am, son!'

B laughed. 'Then that'll be great. Yesiree! A big kiss!'

'If we win… all the way to the top!' and with a shrug of his heavy, bare shoulders, the mighty man carrying the red, white and blue rumpled B's hair and stomped off in search of his mate.

Big and small, fat and skinny, dark, blonde, rough and fine – entirely opposites – but B had seen a welcome piece of Molly in the giant, something spontaneous. Molly would climb Nelson's Column too if she could and as B turned again to face the National Gallery, this echo of his absent friend gave him even greater courage, a steely resolve to revisit that new but unreal world he had glimpsed on the day Funny Girl saw *Funny Girl*.

B walked purposefully through the square. The azure of the fountains on each side, the slightly darker blue of the clock on the big church he and Molly had seen last week, its gold numbers shining like the clock on the tower of the Alamo – the old white fort, John Wayne, "buying" time.

Mounting a stone staircase, he crossed the road to the gallery – more red buses, a green single-decker one too, the gold of the letters on the front of the building glinting in the sun. Up more steps and as he walked onto the National's high portico entrance, B's eyes traced its black and white tiled floor, the colour of penguins. For a full minute he stood still taking in the wonder of where he was and what he was about to do and see.

Then he was through the doors.

Inside a dream.

The many colours of B

'What?'

B flicks his eyes up to her face, instantly embarrassed and feeling very unprofessional.

'What? Come on, what?'

She's laughing now, a laugh on a high generated not by drugs or booze but by something the beautiful people receive – an Oscar nomination. In the back seat of a sleek black limo gliding through downtown Los Angeles en route to the red carpet.

Sitting in a jump seat in front of the star, her tuxedoed beau on her left, B has let his eyes roam just a bit too long over her very low-cut and staggeringly expensive Armani dress. It wasn't her ample, bronzed cleavage he'd fixed on, however, but the vivid red of the dress itself. For a few seconds more than any protector should have been gazing at a principal's assets, even those as stunning as hers, B was lost in a sea of red... the observatory's fiery red ball, his Renault back in Paris, his mother's lipstick.

Red.

'I look good, don't I? You were peeking! Yes, you were! Old granite face was peeking! Well, it's OK, man, go ahead and peek. I look great, I feel great and tonight's gonna be...'

'Great?'

'Well, what about you tonight? Leering over a pretty fine set of goods...' curving her hands over her breasts to ram home the point, 'and right on cue with the chat too. What's up? Got a woman in your life?'

She leans up and blows B a kiss. He has protected her on a number of occasions now, once saving her from serious harm when a fan-turned-stalker lunged at her with a knife while exiting a Cannes Film Festival restaurant. So he's part of her life now – a friend, not just a hired gun.

'Save that for when you win. Now, hold on to Robert there and let me do my job.'

In five minutes the limo stops in line at the start of the red carpet approach and B fires off some instructions into his microphone to his team working tonight – the front-seat passenger and two men already beside the carpet. Handing the star out to Robert in a kaleidoscope of paparazzi flashlights, he lets go of her with a wink, and in a flamboyance of red she walks a red walk towards her second Oscar.

* * *

Rolling to B's feet, the ball comes to a halt a pace away. Shouts from the boys playing a little way over in Memorial

Gardens urging him to kick it back. The game awaits and he looks down.

A lost longing pulls on him – football, World Cup, Bobby, Charlton, the red, red robin – but that was another time, another life. It's been a long while since B has kicked a ball in anger – over a year in fact. He had been so good, understood every dynamic, every spin and angle. Knew it and loved it.

Bending down, amidst ever-impatient voices from the suspended match, B picks the ball up and quietly rolls it back to a boy advancing towards him. He rubs off a little brown mud from his hands, puts them into his blue jeans' pockets and walks off towards the bridge over the River Cocker.

* * *

'*Qu'est-ce que c'est?*'

'*Un kaléidoscope.* Put this end to your eye, look through… twist like this and… lots of patterns, shapes and colours… *toutes les couleurs.* I've got one just like it. Had it from when I was a boy too. *C'est bien!* Lots of fun!'

The boy takes the gift of colours and follows B's instructions. Moments later there are hisses of joy and squeals of delight. Patterns and colours, shapes and images all afternoon and into the evening, right up until the birthday boy falls asleep.

'Very kind of you. Really. He is thrilled.' Grateful thanks from B's Principal, the boy's father, as they both look on the small and intimate birthday party. A chic, comfortable Parisian home. A family secured by their shared love and B's professional expertise.

The protector nods accepting the compliment.

'Is it true? Do you have one just like it?'

B is silent for a few moments, remembering.

'Yes…' he replies slowly, looking down at the boy, his co-conspirator of red, 'I got mine at a birthday party once too.'

* * *

Grey, heavy, wet-heavy grey mist.

A silent and ghostly world. Jet black and grey stones underfoot, slippery and shiny with the surface water. Each step leaving tiny rivulets after the crunch, crunch, crunch of four feet pulling up the track. England's highest mountain, mighty Scafell Pike, away over the unseen bulging rock wall of Great End.

Faith. B has faith in his leader. He has followed her across the fells every weekend since they met and every day in his school holidays. So many wonderful things, such secret sights, such gateways to colours, keeping him safe in dangerous situations and hostile weathers. Faith. She will always know how, when, where and if. Few paths unknown to her, no valley a stranger, all tops conquered.

A single track bending upwards and to their left they strike the gentle ripples at the edge of Sprinkling Tarn. In days of sunshine, green grass and blue skies, the water glistens and glitters. But not today. Dank clouds meet the tarn's surface and its beauty is lost under a thick blanket.

'Not the best. Want to go on?'

'I'm all right if you are. How far?'

'Another fifteen minutes or so up here... across the hause then up... an hour or so to the top at least.'

'Like this?'

'Seems so. Pretty grim.'

'Don't want to go back.'

'Let's keep going then.'

Sure as her word. Fifteen-ish to the hause, the usually beautiful view there directly ahead to Esk Pike and Bowfell now cloaked in deep mist. In the silence they bend to the right, first to an easy track then onto boulders, an ocean of them. Up even more, another descent, then up and up again, slowly, grey figures in the gloom, legs pulling harder and harder before, finally, an enclosure of stone peeks out of the murk – the roof of the world, Scafell Pike summit, England's highest point.

Standing with his arms outstretched, B hoots and shouts. Howling. All anger gone, for now.

Tutoress and boy sit down with their backs against large stones and drink Thermos-flask tea with a piece of cake. Mentor and mentee talking about hills, tarns and old Lakeland stories. B's knowledge expanding and deepening, his education continuing.

Suddenly, the mist dissipates just enough to reveal the upper day piercing through, and B sees the blue of the sky and the orange of the sun.

* * *

Red.

A red coat, stand-out red against the black and white.
A black day seen from a white horse on a hill. A rifle blasts
a boy, women argue over sanctuary beneath floorboards
and sporadic gunfire peppers the town amidst a cacophony
of screams and pleading for pity. A day of death and agony
as soldiers come to clear the homes of vermin and shred
the houses of humanity.

A girl in red nobody seems to see. Not a lipstick red
but a sadder tone, merging into the cold, merciless grey
of the chaos. Clothes thrown from balconies, furniture
smashed, memories dashed, lives ending as the little girl
runs to hide under the bed, anything to kill the terror. Red,
the red getting away.

The killing continues, through the streets, in the dark
and dingy corners, right onto the trains and on and on
to the black-smoked terminus where hair is cropped, all
hope and dignity severed, and women are herded like
naked cattle into a long, metallic-sounding chamber.
Arms to arms, legs to legs, thin vulnerable bodies, breasts
and pubic hair. Faces awaiting whatever fate has in store.

But suddenly there's water from jets in the roof
and a tiny, tiny measure of relief. Screams of a hell not
yet reached. Survival weighed on luck, the balance of
Schindler's gift of the gab and his industrious deals with
the monsters.

Black and white, but a red coat. Not like the first film
B ever saw at the cinema in all its brilliant Technicolor.
Goldfinger.

Those who remember Oskar Schindler the hero place

pebbles on his grave and sad violin music ends Steven Spielberg's epic movie of tragedy and hope, of human potential, lost and found. B leaves the cinema, striking out into the cold New York night, his Principal protected tonight by the rest of B's team – a long week of meetings at the UN.

Hailing a cab to his hotel, B sits back in the yellow car and disappears into the coloured lights of the city.

23 July 1966

Standing in the entrance lobby, screwing his face up tight, holding his breath. Motionless, waiting, not knowing what to expect. One minute? Two, three? Endless.

People passing, low murmurings, muffled footsteps and from somewhere far away within the building a screech like a chair being scraped along the floor. Even at the observatory where he always experienced such great excitement standing on the line that circled the Earth, he never felt like this. Every nerve tingling.

Eventually, his eyes opening, his lungs expelling air, B smiled as the first colours hit, pouring in all about him. He was back in the National, once again in an intensely heightened state of awareness, but this time all was calm – no chaos, no gushing torrents.

And encouraged by this unexpected zone of clarity, B ascended the steps into the main part of the gallery to begin a journey over the next few hours which would generate so much energy, joy and opportunity, but within days consign him to years of anger and pain, and decades of denial.

At first, B was attracted by what he saw on the floor at the top of the steps – multicoloured pieces of stone forming intricate pictures of women like they were sunbathing on a beach. He had no vocabulary for many of the things he would see during the day so he didn't know what a mosaic was. Looking down, he simply liked how the picture came together as a whole from all the tiny bits and instantly thought of raindrops, their colours hitting the floor, spilling out making pictures of pretty ladies.

Exploring up more steps on his left to a landing, there were other pictures on the floor with words styled underneath them. A man lying down looking through a telescope. Connections – observatory, time. Then, unbelievably, just above it a round-shaped picture of a woman contorted like an acrobat with the word *Theatre* below. Connections – *Funny Girl*. Lines running into other lines. Perfect.

When he was able to lift his gaze from the floor, B slowly backed away from the mosaics, turned to open some big wooden doors and stepped into a gallery.

Once inside, he stood perfectly still half-expecting the fantastic dreams of before to come rushing back making everything mad and impossible again. But the calm clarity remained, steady and tranquil. Focussing his eyes down through the vast room, slowly, slowly, click-click slowly, he began to recognise fragments of last week's kaleidoscope blur.

The boxes he remembered seeing on the walls were

not now merging together or flooding their colours into waterfalls, and they weren't boxes at all but picture frames – ornate, carved, thick, strong and imposing – each containing a painting. All around him were a myriad of scenes. He walked up to one and studied it. How the colours stood out – fresh, vibrant, deep and penetrating.

Passing carefully from one painting to another, B stood in front of each one for a long time, his eyes dancing over them. A group of people pulling and tugging at each other (what were they running away from?), fruit and vegetables arrayed on a cart (where were they going?), the outline of clouds in the sky, the lines of sheer cliffs. Colours, shapes and patterns...

A group of adults were bunched around one painting, a lady talking to them obviously saying something important. But he was too impatient to linger with them, he had to see more, he had to move. The paintings went on seemingly forever, stretched out before him, waiting.

Some pictures stood out more than others. The look of a face, the way a mother cradled her child, the ruins of an old building by the seashore. Completely unaware of its title or artist and lacking the maturity to interpret any of its symbolic complexities, B was captivated by Holbein's large masterpiece of the British Renaissance, *The Ambassadors*. To him it looked like two mates standing on each side of a cabinet having a chat, dressed in very old-fashioned clothes with one of the men holding what he thought was a telescope. He looked just like a king. Was he one of the kings who wanted the observatory to see what the stars did?

Lots of paintings had men and women in them with no clothes on, or hardly any. Sometimes people had bits of blanket around them but mostly they were completely naked. Questions. Why? How? Nobody walked around like that today.

B had hardly experienced nudity before and never at home so all the flesh on view was a lot to take in. Boys at school often talked about bums and tits, secretly with knowing nods, and it was funny to see them on show for everyone to see. Confusing too. But it must be allowed because this was a grown-up's place.

The painting with the man holding the lady's tit for instance. B stood in front of it for ages trying to understand. First off he thought the man looked like a boy but that couldn't be right because no boy would ever be allowed to do that. B knew nothing about sex, it would have been an alien concept despite the odd loose word or snigger in the playground, so all he saw in the painting were two people showing affection, probably about to kiss. The lady held a golden ball in her hand and perhaps the man had given it to her as a present. A kiss to say thank you?

But why didn't anyone in the picture have any clothes on? The lady, the man, the little boy holding a pink flower in his hands and even the bald man with the white beard holding up the lovely blue curtain in the background, none of them had a stitch on. Nothing.

Standing back from the famous allegoric painting by Bronzino, staring and staring, at length B's curiosity about its nudity gradually diminished. Instead, he began to lock his gaze onto just the boy-man and woman as their faces came together. A look of love, holding the lady so tenderly, one hand on her tit, the other cupping her red hair behind her head. He wondered if his mum and dad ever looked at each other or kissed like this. If they did he had never seen it. He could imagine Molly's parents doing so though. Lucky Molly.

In a little while B came to a painting with a woman sitting on a little stool in front of it. She wore a bright red jumper, the colour of London buses, a large sketchpad was balanced on her knees and she was stroking the white paper with a yellow pencil. Realising B was there, she glanced up.

'Hello!' she breathed, before bending down to her work again.

B raised his eyes to take in the painting the lady was drawing from and his reaction was immediate and profound.

'Molly!'

The artist looked up again. 'Excuse me. What did you say?'

Embarrassed, a blush ran through B's face.

'Sorry, miss…' he mumbled, 'sorry I mucked you up.'

Obviously the boy was shy. She smiled, speaking softly.

'No, you didn't muck me up. It's fine. I just wondered what you said.'

B was reminded instantly of Mrs Hinkley, her gentle way with him. Nice, the same soothing tone. But this lady sounded different, a voice like the people he heard in films. American, John Wayne, Alamo. He pointed to the picture.

'This reminds me of my friend Molly.'

The lady put her pencil to her mouth. Now it was she who felt a bit awkward. This was Velázquez's Venus, *The Toilet of Venus*, the so-called *Rokeby Venus*, one of the most recognisable paintings in the world. Velázquez the master. There was the goddess, naked, reclining on a bed, unadorned, unabashed, displaying her luxurious charms albeit with her back to the viewer. A voluptuous bottom, a sleek, sensuous, seductive back with her delicate arm propping up her head. Staring into a mirror held by a winged Cupid, reflecting a pink-cheeked, alluring face. But Venus didn't look out at the world for its opinion or consent. She watched you while you watched her. She knew it and so did everyone who gazed on her comely body.

The lady in the red jumper cleared her throat.

'Molly? You think this looks like Molly, do you?' Then a pause. 'How old is she?'

B put both his hands on his head to consider this in great depth while still keeping his eyes on the painting. The reds of the curtain hanging in the background, the folds of the sheets the naked lady was lying on.

'She's eleven like me. We go to school together... well, we did, but we're going to different big schools next year. We'll stay friends though. She's gone away on holiday now.'

Still rather uneasy and moving a little on her stool, the lady probed further.

'Why do you think the picture reminds you of Molly then... sorry, what's your name?'

He turned for a moment to look at the lady's face, before spinning back to the Velázquez.

'B.'

'Sorry?'

A repetition.

'B.'

An eye was raised.

'Hello B. I'm Barbara.'

He turned again and stared. 'Barbara? Like Barbra Streisand?'

The Barbara in red grinned in surprise. 'I… I suppose so.'

'She's great!' B continued without pausing, 'We went to see her. Molly, her mum and dad and me, at a big theatre here in London. *Funny Girl*. We went because that's what her parents call Molly, because she does funny things all the time. Barbra Streisand was great.'

B took his hands down from his head. 'And you talk like her!'

This Barbara (with the extra "a") responded, 'I probably do. I come from Canada. It's next to America and we talk in a similar way.'

Canada!

B couldn't believe it. Why did this always happen? This must be some sort of game. Connections – Wolfe, Mrs Hinkley, Niagara Falls, the lady in the red jumper, his favourite colour, Barbra, Barbara…

'General Wolfe won a war in Canada and I saw some pictures of Niagara Falls once. My teacher went there.'

Barbara was laughing now finding it a little difficult to keep up with the boy.

'You know a lot, don't you? General Wolfe, Niagara Falls, *Funny Girl*.'

B looked embarrassed and turned once more to the painting.

Barbara was intrigued. A certain vulnerability, an eager imagination. It was the same unknown something that had once caught the then Miss Andrews's fancy. A light that dimmed when B hadn't recreated his remarkable first drawing although it lingered with her right up until the teacher left the school.

'You saw Barbra Streisand in *Funny Girl*? You're very lucky!'

'I know. We went to see the last show ever last week. Her name was Fanny in it. She's a great singer.'

Red Barbara tried not to get distracted and pushed a little more. 'So, B, why does the painting remind you of Molly?'

She could see him weighing this up. Then the boy spoke, almost whispering.

'It's the way she's looking in the mirror. Looks like a window and I always think of Molly sitting at the window of her house when it was her birthday. She was on the window ledge and waiting for me to come along. She's got a house just by the park and that's where we play a lot.'

Relieved, Barbara sat back on her stool. Some uncomfortable thoughts dissipated and a faint shadow of shame crossed her mind for even thinking such things. Shifting her gaze, she studied the Velázquez herself again. That face in the mirror, those pink cheeks and quizzical look, her hidden left arm she assumed covering her breasts. The wanton sexual connotations of the painting were not lost on her despite B's answer and a stray thought went out to James back in Toronto.

'Why hasn't she got any clothes on?' B asked. 'The boy with the wings hasn't got any either. There's loads of paintings in here with people with nothing on.'

Barbara laughed and her sensual reverie of the man she hadn't seen for months faded. Holding her drawing pad to her chest, she stood up and moved forward to stand next to the boy – her red sweater beside his blue shirt. She thought hard. Where to start? Even in her classes, where most of her young pupils were knowledgeable about the history and concepts of art, such a question could be interpreted in many ways. She opted for simplicity.

'Yes, it is a bit strange. It's difficult to understand but it's all to do with how people thought of gods and important people who lived a long, long time ago. This lady was a goddess and artists believed if they painted them with no clothes on then it would be the best way to show how beautiful they were. They wanted to paint "beauty". Can you follow that?'

B gave a nod of sorts. He thought he got the gist, a bit like when the old man at the observatory talked about time and kings and queens. Complicated, but he grasped the general idea.

'So,' he answered with a question, 'having no clothes on is like telling people they are beautiful?'

Barbara hesitated deciding not to go deeper. 'Almost, B, almost. Something along those lines.'

'But people with clothes on can be beautiful too, can't they? I mean, I think Molly is beautiful and she has clothes on.'

'Yes,' said Barbara grinning again, 'yes, people with

clothes on can be beautiful too. I'm sure Molly is very beautiful indeed.'

'She is,' B declared stepping closer to Venus. 'She is.'

'And do you like paintings generally, B? Is that why you've come to the National Gallery today?' But before she let B answer, she realised something. 'Who's with you, by the way? Are you here with your mum and dad?'

B felt a sudden sick sensation in his throat. He got that sometimes when he became really worried, like the time he had to tell Mrs Hinkley he'd lost his drawing. He thought fast.

'Yes,' he lied, pointing through some big doors at the end of the room, '… er… they're down there somewhere.' How could he explain his adventure today? He changed the subject quickly.

'Your jumper is a lovely red. Red's my favourite colour. I don't know why. I look at colours all the time. So I like it here. There's lots of colours all over the place. They sort of come out of the pictures at you. Don't know what all the pictures mean though. This one with the lady lying down who looks like Molly, not sure what she's doing, but I feel good looking at it. It makes things nice. It's like my kaleidoscope that Molly gave me on her birthday. Every time you turn it there are new patterns and colours. That feels good too. Your jumper, it's the same as the red buses…'

Barbara held her pad tighter taking in what the little boy was saying. His ardent innocence and evident passion for what he saw was palpable. In some ways he was revealing more feeling and deeper, inner appreciation than many of the would-be artists she taught, or some of the professionals she knew across the art world come to that. A boy relishing the simple joy of the art all around him. As simple as a child's kaleidoscope.

'Have you ever tried to draw or paint, B?' she asked.

Draw, paint...

Suddenly, a bright light switched on in B's head. A flash into a completely forgotten chamber, a lightning strike into deserted cells deep within his brain.

Locked away...

Molly at the observatory, fashioned in charcoal, the fiery red ball, Miss Andrews saying how good it was and that light-headed, happy and joyous feeling when he looked at what he had created. Ripped to shreds, he had tossed the pieces into the brown river, the waves sinking those heady sensations.

His picture...

Lying to his teacher the next day and covering up his howls of anguish. Never chancing to rediscover his new-found creative spark for fear of things going wrong and losing his best friend. Too afraid to try again, even after that day at the Meridian Line when Molly said he should draw another picture.

Now, as he faced the Velázquez, the forgotten chamber was revealed at last, opened up by a lady in red from Canada. Suddenly, he felt the first faint welling of tears since that day he sat at the table in his living room, rejected by a mother who never even bothered to see what her son had rushed home to show her.

'I drew a picture once... at school. It was the day I

went to the observatory and talked to Molly for the first time. My teacher said it was great. I remember running all the way home. I just wanted to show my mum. I wanted her to see it and like it. Like it the way I liked it.'

B was crying now, inwardly, to himself. He kept looking at the goddess picture, staring away from Barbara. Taking a deep breath, fists clenched, he continued.

'No one was interested. Mum walked way. So I ran to the river and tore it to bits. Chucked it in the river, got rid of it. I felt bad about telling my teacher I lost it and dunno if she believed me. I told Molly though. She said I could do another one, but I never did...'

Then real tears began to fall, the howling of a need so long neglected, and a little boy in a blue shirt on a big adventure to see if his dream was true just couldn't face turning round and seeing the lady in red. B felt so empty, so sad, trapped inside his eternal maze. Gasping for breath and mumbling something, he started to dash off down the gallery towards the doors his imaginary parents had passed through.

'Hey, hey, hold on! Wait a minute!' but he was away, through the doors and out of sight in a trice.

In a while, sitting back down on her stool, Barbara looked up at Venus and stared at the painting for a very long time deep in thought. She knew the Velázquez like no other, she had copied it many, many times. But what did she see now, what did it really tell her? With all its majesty and power had it made a little boy cry? A quarter of an hour passed before she placed her pad back down on her knees and started to draw again. The familiarity of Velázquez's wonderful hand. Love waiting back in Toronto.

Elsewhere in the gallery, it was only as Barbara resumed her work that B raised his reddened eyes to the paintings once more. His quiet sobs subsiding, he had gradually regained control of himself, glad that nobody had asked him what was the matter as he sat slumped on a bench in one of the rooms.

Stretching as he stood up, B shuffled forward to take a closer look at the picture on the wall right before him. It was a strange painting, one unlike any in the gallery he had seen so far, the scene difficult to make out. Probing very hard, eventually he began to feel as if the dark colour at its centre was coming out of the picture straight at him. Was it a train? Yes, a train, speeding towards him. He thought of the one he caught that morning, chugging through the magic tunnel to London.

Other elements of the painting started to mesh together. Railway tracks running over a bridge, emerging out of what seemed like dense fog – dark, billowing, erupting. B scanned further, an eerie mix of subtle colours – blues, yellows, browns and whites – and out of this deep mist, he felt movement and light bursting forth.

So absorbed was he by J. M. W. Turner's *Rain, Steam and Speed – The Great Western Railway*, that when at last B moved away from it he failed to notice much of what he passed on the walls for a while. Quickly through some more Turners, floating by Constables and Gainsboroughs, a huge Stubbs, he sauntered into another large room – Goya, Ingres and other marvels – then into another, until finally he entered a room where the immediate, staggering impact of its colours ripped him awake.

He was surrounded by many famous impressionist paintings, works by artists the world lauded and revered every day but whose names meant nothing to him. The shock of their rioting colours was intensely physical. Colours screamed at him, they cavorted, they pierced his skin, and for a few seconds the madness of his first visit to the National returned – colours flowing, gushing, cascading. But slowly, slowly, this new wildness subsided, his vision cleared, and he began to smile as he let himself wallow in this new, living kaleidoscope. Enough reds as he could wish for, banks of blues, fields of yellows, gardens of greens, and so many individual specs of colours in one particular painting as the number of stars in the sky he saw at night down by the river.

Inside this rainbow room, B lost all track of time and sense of himself. No food for hours but he didn't feel hungry. A bottle of fizzy orange back on the train but he wasn't thirsty. Any link to the outside world had disappeared altogether and it was only when at long last he walked through some gallery doors and found himself back out in the entrance lobby that he saw daylight once more and realised where he was.

On the floor before him there were more stone raindrop scenes. Peering down, he saw a picture with the one word, *Football,* and his mind raced. Connections – England v Argentina, the giant with the red, white and blue flag, kiss the admiral, Bobby, Roger, World Cup.

Another momentous day and yet again he had forgotten what was at stake at Wembley. What time was it? Sunshine streamed into the entrance hall. He knew it must be the afternoon sometime so were they playing yet?

B ran down the steps and out of the National's entrance doors. Bursting forwards, placing his hands on the high portico balcony, he looked out over the crowds swelling in a hot Trafalgar Square. Beads of sweat began to form on his brow and upper lip. There was the column – Nelson at Trafalgar – and England were at Wembley. Both had beaten the French.

He was just about to ask a man for the time when he noticed in the distance, beyond the tall tube, a tower with a clearly visible clock face. It read three o'clock but he was too far away to hear the chimes of Big Ben ring out as if telling the referee miles away across a hazy London town at Wembley Stadium to blow his whistle for kick-off. And in that moment, gazing over the square with its four lions and azure blue fountains, as the hum and bustle of the capital teemed with life on a brilliantly sunny Saturday afternoon, B came to a profound decision.

That lost, secret chamber had been opened up at long last and he knew beyond a doubt what had been hidden there should now be set free. Molly had wanted him to draw again and now he would – he most certainly would, Mr Wood! In that instant he also knew his theme – beauty, goddess. B didn't know the name of the lady in the painting but he would draw Molly as Venus because Molly was beautiful.

Pushing off the stone balustrade ready to run back to the train station and home, B almost collided headlong with a woman standing behind him. Snatching out an apology, he saw her and recoiled.

'Still running?' the lady in the red jumper laughed.

B didn't know what to do. Barbara smiled back at him but he was cornered. It was now very hot and he could feel his face sweating hard.

'Hello,' he said meekly. 'Er... just going home.'

'Home? With your parents? Where are they?'

B was confused, he didn't sound convincing.

'Er... down there in the square. I dunno... got to catch them up...'

Crouching down, Barbara slowly held out her hands to him. They bore her drawing pad and a large packet of coloured pencils and she was offering them up in the same way B had once presented his school picture to his mum. But this time he heard kind and soft words.

'Listen, B. Listen. Listen to me. Don't worry. I know, I know, really, really I do ... Look, these are for you. For you, understand? From me to you... I want you to have them.'

Then the art teacher from Canada who over the last hour or so had begun to miss her James back home so much, who had finished drawing her Venus and had looked around the galleries in a vain search for the boy, who had hung around the entrance just in case and who finally had seen him tearing out of the building as fast as he had run away from her earlier in the day, said what she had waited to say.

'Draw the beauty you see, B. Never, ever, forget how beautiful everything is. The whole wide world. Can you understand? You can capture it all with these. Beauty is everywhere. Draw your beautiful Molly and don't let anybody ever stop you.'

A few seconds of complete silence between them – red jumper, blue shirt – B swallowed hard and took the gifts, holding them close to his chest. He wanted to draw Molly and now he could.

Connections – Barbara, Barbra, *Funny Girl*, Molly.

The next moment he was running full pelt down the street towards Charing Cross grasping his new treasure tight. Barbara moved to the balustrade herself, looked out across Trafalgar Square and made her own momentous decision – a ticket back to Canada.

Ten minutes later, having negotiated the confusion of the station concourse, B was seated in a small train compartment on his own. The sound of wheels on tracks flooded in through the open carriage window as he opened up the drawing pad.

He stared at the page and gasped. There she was, Venus, and beneath the drawing were written the words.

'*Beautiful Molly. B*'.

Sometime in 2003 – then December 2006

Sunshine glinting off sloping glass. Ominous banks of buildings encircling the pyramid.

A summer city drone, bright T-shirt colours in the afternoon heat, milling crowds, children shouting, city-circling buses.

Paris, August.

Half-standing, half-sitting against a bollard. Behind him the green of the *Jardin des Tuileries* leading up to *Place de la Concorde* and the *Champs Élysées*. Ahead, the wide-open paved space before the *Louvre*.

Hands held high on the back of his head, eyes tracing the lines of the pyramid's many diamond shapes. The glass modernity of the famous public entrance to the city's historic museum surrounded by the classical brick and stone of the rest of its huge bulk. The "new" allowing you to see within. The "old" shutting you out.

What has come over him? Sweeping past lines of tourists queuing to see the treasures, waving to greet a member of the curator's senior staff for this special VIP visit, suddenly something is very wrong. The Principal's lovely wife – tanned, white dress, blue shoes, black headband – and her son with a piece of red amber in his pocket showing concern for their protector in his obvious but mysterious distress.

It is the boy's birthday and his first tour of the galleries – the *Mona Lisa*, objects, art and beauty – but somehow, for some inexplicable reason, B knows he cannot enter the pyramid and explore with him. Glass beckoning them down to vast, ancient stores below but it is impossible. Sincere apologies, a glance of true regret to the boy who is so disappointed, his deputy feeling awkward as he arrives to take his place and B reels away disappearing into the Parisian throng.

Bringing his hands down to hold his shoulders, a girl in an orange dress walking towards him, her ultramarine clutch bag, B has absolutely no idea what has happened. An invisible line he couldn't cross, an internal voice telling him "no", a distant feeling so familiar but one he cannot name. One he is profoundly afraid of.

London... Trafalgar Square... years...

B looked up at the stone pillars and gables of another national treasure house and realised like the lifting of a veil what it was that Parisian day. The sharp return of memory. Such a long time since he had stood where he was standing now.

Nelson... Funny Girl...

In 1966 it was high summer, sunshine and heat. Now it was December, clouds and chill. In the square stood a mighty Christmas tree, tall and cheerless in the morning gloom, Norway's annual gift to Britain as gratitude for World War II help. Behind it, surrounded by his four lions, stood Nelson, still up there on his column. Ahead lay the panoramic sweep of the National Gallery building.

Back then B had discovered beauty only to have it turned to ashes in his mouth by childhood demons – beauty banished, expunged, obliterated – and whether by fortune or unconscious design, he had never been near an art gallery since. Until Paris and the *Louvre* confronted him that day and some deeply repressed phobia must have reared its terrible head and forced him to stay outside.

The little birthday boy's artistic education had continued at the *Metropolitan* in New York, in Amsterdam's *Rijksmuseum*, at the *Prado*, across Venice, and in great establishments across the world, yet, how strange, these itineraries always seemed to clash with B's Principal's more pressing needs.

Now today, with the chimes of Villers-sur-Mer still ringing in his ears, with beauty's mirror cracked at the theatre in Hull, and after an all-night drive to London from the stage door, B stood ready to face his long-hidden nemesis.

Nervously mounting the steps of the National, he strode across those same black and white portico floor tiles and once again stood at the balustrade looking out across Trafalgar Square. Big Ben displayed 10.30 am on this Friday morning – a different epoch – as he remembered the gifts given on this very spot. Paper and pencils from a lady in red. After a few minutes B turned, his phobia so far at bay, and stepping aside to let an elderly couple pass – white raincoats, brown checked hat, navy blue handbag – he opened the doors to the gallery and walked through.

Inside the wide foyer, unshaven, a little dishevelled, B slowly let the breath out of his body. Hungry and tired from his journey south yet too tense to rest, too full of the past to grab breakfast, he closed his eyes taking in this momentous moment. And, in the kaleidoscope twist of these few seconds, he realised he had finally made the journey back. Villers-sur-Mer to Honfleur, his rapid return to Paris, France to England, and although the Lakes had been his immediate target, it was not the place. His mother, Miss Hattiemore, both on the way to Molly, and even she wasn't his real destination. Here, here it was. B sensed it, smelt it, opened his eyes and saw it.

Answers.

B found them in every room, before every painting and every colour. Answers tumbled headlong from the walls and from each imaginary landscape or stern portrait. They shone from the numerous homages to Christ and depictions of the divine. They leapt out from skies and forests, ships and horses, saints and monsters and from the many images of peace and war, life and death.

Reading pictures like simple books, B followed their stories and understood what the scenes and colours were saying to him. He didn't know how he could, he just did – instinctive, automatic, natural. In the shuffling quiet of the

National, answers spilled right out of thick picture frames and fell about him.

Answers he craved.

Why light contrasted with darkness, how good pitched against evil, how day battled with night and most of all how artists used colours to tell a story, to create an atmosphere, to make a statement or a confession, to glorify or to condemn, to make you laugh or cry and, yes, to ask questions.

Colours as tools, colours as conduits.

B saw the nakedness around him and remembered how deeply its beauty had affected him as the little boy on a wild World Cup day adventure to London, and how, with such tragic consequences, it resulted in his childhood friend being driven away. Bodies, torsos, breasts and crucifying Messiahs at every turn, now as a grown man B could see these images in utter clarity. They were indeed truly beautiful – beauty in glorification, reverence, admiration, love and commitment.

In one room, B turned to greet a scene which with such instant recognition forced his hand to his mouth in wonder. So long ago but a sight so familiar. Yesterday into today, the past coming alive, a phrase echoed up from a secret place inside him. A man holding a lady's tit. Exotic colours, nakedness, dominating flesh tones. B inched up to be face to face with the look of love, the golden ball, the luxuriant blue background and the old man with white hair. Swathed in memory, how vivid that Argentina day was now.

In time, B moved his head to one side to read the

painting's grey rectangle description panel but reeled back clenching his eyes in disbelief at the words. The new knowledge simply not computing.

An Allegory with Venus and Cupid

Molly, Venus.

Venus, Molly.

It took twenty minutes for B to be released by the Bronzino, his mind still buzzing from this fresh, inexplicable link to his childhood friend. It was incredible. Then, propelled by an intense, inner imperative, he set out at speed in search of another painting, one he knew was somewhere in the gallery. Driving through the night, floodgates of memory opening wide by the revelation of beauty in the theatre, the image of this other picture had kept coming to him. He saw it in headlight beams, from the twinkle of streetlamps, in the red, amber and green sparkle of traffic lights. Crystal clear, a spectre in sharp focus. A lady lying down, a boy with wings, a mirror, naked. He had arrived at the National wanting to see it again but the Bronzino had multiplied this into an urgent, desperate need.

At length, walking down a long room – deep red walls, wooden floors – B glanced to his left and gradually, slowly, deliberately, his eyes focussing closer and closer, he saw what he was searching for.

A large group of schoolchildren in red sweaters and white shirts with yellow and blue ties were seated in front of the painting. To one side of it a grey-haired lady was talking to them, pointing, seeking to explain and illuminate its glories. A Miss Hattiemore of the arts.

Unable to get close, his eyes helplessly fixed ahead as if in a trance, B hunched up close to a small boy sitting on a viewing bench some way back from the picture. The educator's voice continued but he heard it only as a distant background hum.

Eventually, it was the boy who brought him round. B felt the lad shuffle in his seat as he balanced a small sketchpad on his knees twiddling a yellow pencil in his fingers and tapping the end of it on his lips. No more than ten or eleven, brown eyes and blonde hair, he was a boy in the same place but in another time. B awoke turning to watch him put the pencil to the paper and write down in individual letters a word at the top of the page before leaning back contemplating what to do next. The shock as B read the word was so great he snatched the pad out of the lad's hands.

'Sorry! Sorry!' he exhaled rapidly, handing the pad back. 'I'm sorry. I just wanted…'

The boy looked warily for a second or two before, without any hint of surprise or nervousness, he turned the pad around so B could see it clearly.

'Venus!' he announced. 'Is it spelt right?'

B looked at the boy and back to the word three times before he felt in control of himself enough to answer.

'Er, yes, yes… it is… yes, that's right…' he choked.

Grinning, the boy jabbed his finger up to the painting in front of him and pointed.

'There!'

B's world had been on an emotional switchback for weeks. Death, guilt, escape and denial, rage, red-driven delirium, ghosts reborn and recaptured. Lakeland memories rediscovered, heartless and heart-wrenching reunions, then a long-lost friend seen again and only last night as he read a theatre programme his lost childhood sense of beauty had been reawakened. A cautious man, one who could always see the right move after the next, steady, dependable, no surprises, taciturn, on the level, B had been through such highs and lows since the bullets rang out in Paris, he wondered if he could take any more. But as he tore his head away from the boy and fixed onto the painting before him, he believed he had crossed over to a place way beyond feeling, somewhere not touched by the extreme physical fatigue hitting him at that moment with a vengeance.

Venus? The spectre was Venus?

Beauty defined, goddess soft skin, a hazy reflection in a mirror, it was a red, blue and white madness. All those years ago, two paintings, two Venuses and now Molly was herself Venus. Utter madness. Just how could this be?

The boy spoke again. Red jumper, the lady from Canada was in bus-red too.

'She's beautiful!'

B fought to speak, succeeding at length.

'Do you like to draw?'

Taking his pencil off the paper, the boy tapped his lips once again and grimaced.

'I'd rather sing,' he answered, 'I like singing.'

'Are you any good?'

'Me?'

'You!'

'The best!'

B couldn't stop himself.

'Yesiree!'

The boy's hand covered his face to stop his giggles as B stood up. Her sleek lines, the sumptuous ruffles of the fabric on the bed, deep velvety colours, he started to pick his way through the thick carpet of children on the floor edging up to the painting's description panel. Sure enough, there was the truth. *The Toilet of Venus*, the so-called *Rokeby Venus* because it had been kept at Rokeby Hall in Yorkshire for many years. Velázquez. B had heard of him but wouldn't have been able to recognise any of his work. Paintings weren't a part of his practical life.

Standing in a red, white and yellow sea of boys and girls, suddenly the teacher stopped explaining to her class and barked at the man with arms opened wide seeking an explanation herself. What did he think he was doing? Suddenly made aware of where he was, B turned to see everyone's eyes, including Venus's in her mirror, on him. All he could do was mumble an apology and in red-faced embarrassment tiptoe out of the children before retreating in utter confusion down the long gallery, the boy on the bench throwing him a quick, unseen, wave of goodbye.

Through some heavy wooden doors, down through some more, B stumbled into a small corner gallery, the paintings here more modern, more colourful than those back with the *Rokeby Venus*. A round red leather bench stood in the middle of the room and he plonked down hard on it, his mind spinning. Leaning forward, he put his head in his hands and looked out through the prison bars formed by his fingers straining to make sense of what was happening, fighting to understand the National's tricks and disorientation.

Everything since Villers-sur-Mer, all the twists and turns, had driven him to be here, right now, at this time and place. But what was this enormous game being played on him, what did it all mean?

Throughout his life, B had always had a recurring dream. It took on various forms but in each version, whether as a boy or a man, eventually he would walk round the corner of a street and see a girl sitting at an open window. Whenever he thought about the dream, either on waking or when it just sprang into his head, he understood who the girl was and remembered the scene happening in his life – Molly, on her birthday, the day she gave him his kaleidoscope. Yet despite the dream's regularity over the years, his thoughts never went any deeper than simple recognition that such an event had actually taken place. Each recurrence left him momentarily sad, a dull longing, but his mood recovered and moved on. Yet since rediscovering the line that ran round the world, a line that ran directly back to his childhood, the dream had taken on fresh impetus and meaning. Only three, no, two nights ago, B had woken in the small hours having walked around that corner once again, seen the birthday girl, pictured the whites of her dress and with his sleepy head in sweaty early morning hands, so wished he could go back in time and relive that majestic day.

Now, sitting on the red bench, he opened his eyes, peered forward through his fingers and saw the much-repeated dream actually being played out right before him. His dream had become reality. A small painting on the wall, only a foot or so high, a girl all in white sat at a window looking out onto the world exactly like Molly had done all those years ago. An eyeglass onto the past and a lightning rod onto the future. B pulled his fingers away from his face, hardly able to breathe and knew.

A life spent in colours, conscious of them every second, his kaleidoscope by day and the film projector behind his closed lids at night. Colours living with him and through him. Colours his life. Meeting someone judged by their colours – clothes, hair, make-up, skin. His passing world experienced by colours – cars going by, action on the TV, the magic on the movie screen, rivers flowing, waves crashing, seconds, minutes, hours. Colours dominating when meeting his mother on the doorstep, red lipstick still, and later when remembering with Miss Hattiemore – those spring-green eyes. Colours screaming at the pantomime – Molly's red and gold.

Colours were how he understood the world.

Colours formed the fundamental fabric of his soul.

As B sat up on the red bench laying his hands by his sides to face this extraordinary little painting, incongruously a work in monochrome except for a light grey-blue border, he felt it answer eternal questions at a stroke.

Tools, conduits.

B had never looked at colours in this way. For him colours simply were. They existed, they were witnessed and experienced, he didn't use, direct or exploit them. Except, of course, he had done so once – a long time ago when he took the pencils he had been given and made them work for him. Now he knew with utter certainty this was what the National was telling him today, what this incredible picture was revealing, what the game was all about. The ultimate answer.

Take all the colours and create beauty. Again. Try again.

Draw the beauty you see, B. Never, ever, forget how beautiful everything is. The whole wide world. Can you understand? You can capture it all with these. Beauty is everywhere. Draw your beautiful Molly and don't let anybody ever stop you.

B sat before *A Girl at a Window* for a fathomless time, a girl showing him a light in a darkened place, a sunbeam through a dusty curtain, a candle in his night. Beauty had not been destroyed as he once believed. Crushed and broken sure enough, but beauty had survived, it still lived, it had remained with him as a boy among the hills and lakes and he had witnessed it across the world ever since. He had seen it in people throughout his life – from Miss Hattiemore to the boy with red in his pocket – and proof lay all around him today in the National Gallery, in the Venuses and in all the other paintings on the walls. Beauty continued to talk to him, through colours.

Suddenly, how angry B was that it had taken him so long to appreciate this. A lifetime. Those old, lost teenage feelings of acute anger welled up inside him once more as he clenched his fists at the acute pain they inflicted. How inconceivable to have lived a life in colours but to have lived it staked at bay in a perpetual fog of black and white. Look at him… ex-army, protector, the practical man, his days full of colourless things – plans, details, timings, backups, risks, entrances, exits, a mind alert for mechanical issues, the mundane practicalities of saving other people's lives. Colours in his every movement but colours always denied. Colours defining his principal persona but never his principal driving force.

Standing up at long last from the red bench, B stepped unsteadily towards Louis-Léopold Boilly's mesmerising girl. White dress, white shoes, her head tilted towards him, she was the embodiment of his recurring dream and the spark of a new and wonderful idea.

Like when Molly sat at her window on her birthday, B looked on and simply absorbed this new spectacle. And only when his eyes were finally released did he probe further into the room behind the girl and realise that, inside, in the shadows yet out of the sunlight, was a little boy looking up at the stars through a telescope.

Or, B wondered, was it a gigantic kaleidoscope?

30 July 1966

Sitting on Molly's doorstep, his back against her big black door, all sorts of questions running around B's head.

Where is she right now? How far away is Hastings? What if they don't get here before the kick-off?

After all, this is the day. THE day! England v West Germany. Wembley, Bobby, Roger, Gordon and the rest of the heroes.

Every five minutes or so B got up and walked the twenty yards to the top of Molly's street where it met the narrow road flanking Greenwich Park. Behind the expansive house facing him and to his left the sombre, high brick wall running off towards Maze Hill Station, lay the swings, the gnarled ancient trees, the observatory, the bandstand and all the other special places he and Molly knew so well. Like him, the park was waiting.

Every day since she had gone on holiday, B had missed his friend with an ever-mounting sense of loss. Now today, despite her imminent arrival, the aching was unbearable, the pain on waking hitting him like a physical blow. He'd lain in bed for minutes stricken with the sheer impact. Then, as quick as blinking, another hammer slammed into him. It was Saturday, 30 July, the World Cup Final. Dragging himself up to look at his reflection in the mirror, the double significance of the day was almost too enormous to take in.

It was still only 10 am and already he had been outside Molly's for over an hour. Molly and Wembley, the anticipation and nerves were driving him to distraction. He couldn't think straight, his stomach felt tight and his knees wobbled like jelly. More questions. Was Molly all right? Will we win? How can we stop Franz Beckenbauer, the marauding German? And the deepest one of all. What will she think of it?

Every time he reached the park road he looked in both directions hoping desperately to see Mr and Mrs Larnder's red car come into view. Nothing. Even more disappointed on each occasion, he moped back to Molly's and slid down dejectedly on the doorstep.

Originally, B had decided to walk up to Molly's house at about midday (she would have to be home by then, surely) and they could have a couple of hours together before he went home to watch the final on the telly. His house was off limits to her and Mr and Mrs Larnder were as likely to be watching the match as was Nelson himself to come sailing back down the Thames. But they could meet up again when the game was over and whether in joy or despair they could share the historic moment together.

Gulping down some breakfast cereal, he thought he would head to the river, see what was happening, mess around to while away the time and take his mind off it all. As he ate, he certainly wanted the savage atmosphere in the house to be gone by kick-off at three o'clock.

B was surprised all hell hadn't broken loose already because the morning tension between his parents was at breaking point. A husband, unshaven in his white vest, slumped in the grey armchair, running his hands through his hair and hissing. A wife, blue towel to her head, puffing viciously on her fag, looking like she was ready to kill someone and there was no doubt who that was.

His dad had finally got home in the early hours of the morning, drunk and very noisy from a pre-World Cup Final binge with his mates. B hadn't been able to sleep at all and as he twisted his kaleidoscope in solace he felt the full force of the ensuing row downstairs. Even by his parents' standards the fighting was extreme.

Eventually, somehow, he had drifted off to sleep and didn't know how the battle had ended. Yet clearly it hadn't because the two of them were visibly itching to resume. So with the twin drums of Molly and Wembley pounding his head, B just left them to it and headed for the sanctuary of the river.

The tide was out and at first the therapeutic pleasure of hurling stones into the calm Thames in the morning air was enough, the odd chunk of driftwood and a curiously-shaped red glass bottle washed up on the shore adding interest. But these diversions were short-lived and in fifteen minutes B's mind was firmly back in the Molly v

Wembley firing line. It was impossible to think of anything else.

Vainly, he tried another tack. Leaping up Nelson's funeral steps before the Royal Naval College, B nodded at the memory of crowning his River Queen and sprinted off to his right down the river path towards *Cutty Sark*. Running fast, by the time he reached the ship he was panting hard and had to put his hands on his knees to recover. Yet by the time he had, he knew it wouldn't do. The change of scene wasn't helping, his thoughts were still in chaos. Nothing for it. He knew where he needed to be. Molly was on her way home and how he needed her. There was just too much to say, to explain and to show.

Still ignorant of its revered history, B craned his neck up to look at the front of the famous old ship. Above him the bare-breasted white witch figurehead stared blankly away across the river and his mind went back to the National Gallery. The Bronzino painting, the loving man holding the lady's tit. Connections. The witch decided everything and B sprinted off again for home.

A half mile's dash down the river walkway, up past the Trafalgar building then a quick left into his alley, B held a stitch in his side with one hand as he grasped the house-key under the mat with the other. Heart hammering, he unlocked the door straining his ears for any warlike noises from within. Nothing came. But bursting through, what had been obviously a momentary lapse in hostilities abruptly ended.

'You bastard!'

His mother's scream shot out from behind the half-open kitchen door over the sounds of a physical scuffle and crockery smashing. The vision of both of them in that tiny space, red-faced and hating, flickered across B's mind as he tore up the stairs to his room. Quickly falling to his knees, he reached with both hands under his bed, pulled out what he needed, tucked it under his arm with a little difficulty and sped back to the front door. Opening the latch all he could hear from the kitchen was the sound of sobbing – a deep, guttural heaving giving B no clue if it was male or female. Slamming the door and shoving the key back under the mat, he spun-turned in the alley taking in gulps of air. Here was his deep blue home with its red-hot, real-life conflict raging inside but breathing hard he realised he didn't care. Only two things mattered on this day of days. Molly and Wembley.

Minutes later, B was standing in front of Molly's door. The absence of the red car told him they weren't back yet but he rang the doorbell all the same as, who knows, Mr Larnder could have gone out again.

Silence.

So, every few minutes, B's restlessness got the better of him and he walked to the top of the street hoping a car would hove into view. But with a heavy sigh after his latest return trip, he turned, dropped to the ground, let his head fall back against the door and closed his eyes. The lost hours of sleep, his morning exertions so far and the raw, gnawing tension inside him kicked in all at once and in his darkness he felt exhausted.

After a few unconscious minutes, B roused blinking in

the sunlight and looking down spread his hands out over the large rectangle pad lying across his knees, moving over the surface like a caress. Inside was Molly, his week's work, his first attempts to capture beauty like Barbara at the gallery had said he could.

Delicately, with great care, B opened the pad out making sure he didn't crease anything. There on the first sheet was Barbara's Venus, *Beautiful Molly. B*. A fine-line drawing with the flanks of the goddess's body styled simply and the mirror held by Cupid sketched in hazy strokes. No colouring and no great detail but the essence of Velázquez was reflected cleanly as the Canadian art teacher had wanted.

B ran his fingers over the figure, an almost erotic gesture had it been made by an adult. Pleasing shapes, curves and the warm feeling glowing inside from what this scene now meant – the core of his adventure to London a week ago today and his inspiration to demonstrate his gratitude to Molly for being his friend.

Turning another page, again smoothing the sheet down carefully, B beheld a second Venus but a completely different type of drawing, one with incredible detail and colour. Pinks for cheeks in the mirror, reds for the luxurious curtain, flesh tones for the sensuous body, deep browns for the hair, as sophisticated a palette of strong and subtle colours as could be wrung from the pack of pencils Barbara had given him on the balcony overlooking Trafalgar Square.

B considered his work carefully. A return-gift for his kaleidoscope and he smiled to himself, his first show of ease and happiness so far on this chaotic day. He was very satisfied with what he saw. Molly lying there with no clothes on because she was beautiful. The shape of her body, the turn of her neck, the texture of her hair, her obvious playfulness even with her back to the viewer. Molly's natural elements.

So young, B could not appreciate or interpret his picture in the seasoned, intellectual way of an art lover, critic or experienced artist. He knew what he knew and saw what he saw very simplistically with an intrinsic understanding of what was true to his eye, guided by innocence and a talent he couldn't yet recognise or acclaim in himself. A talent, though green, evoking a maturity far beyond his years. That keen vision and sharp eye Miss Andrews once detected and which had now been unleashed with great virtuosity.

B had started the next morning, Sunday, sitting on Nelson's funeral steps – a low tide, a light breeze and a little traffic out on the river. The growing void caused by Molly's holiday aside, B felt as good as he possibly could. He knew what he needed to do, the National Gallery and Barbara's gifts had shown him his task and the way. But there was more, much more.

England had beaten Argentina at Wembley, a neat, twisting second-half Geoff Hurst header securing the win, and now they were in the semi-finals against Portugal on Tuesday night. A small boat went chugging past on the water trailing a Union Jack at its rear and for the umpteenth time B wondered if the giant in the white vest and yellow hat holding the red, white and blue, had really climbed the tall tube to kiss Nelson. He said he would.

Although the World Cup was a competition, the

possibility of actually winning it hadn't really hit B until the win against Argentina, a victory confirmed when he returned home from London with, as suspected, neither parent paying him the slightest atom of attention as he walked in carrying a large pad and a pack of coloured pencils.

To him the games so far against Uruguay, Mexico, France and Argentina had been exciting, but without specific consequence. Now all of a sudden England were only one match away from the World Cup Final itself. Bobby, Roger and the rest could really do it. Portugal couldn't be that good despite this Eusebio bloke who was scoring all the goals. Every time B thought about Molly coming home, he shook his head at what a great day Saturday could be. His friend back with him and England world champions.

Turning a page in the pad, a blank white sheet glared back in the sharp morning light. He picked up the pack of pencils, flipped the top down and looked at the colours. A vast array to choose from, a rainbow in his hand. Automatically, B pulled out one of the reds and held it loosely in his fingers. Lipstick red.

He put the pack back down on the step and hovering the pencil over the page looked into the distance along the river as it bent eastwards. To his right, beyond the Trafalgar building, was Greenwich Power Station with the unseen white Alamo beside it. Directly ahead lay the vast grey-black gas tanks of Blackwall and somewhere running under the mud and bed of the river itself were the car fumes and noise of the road tunnel connecting life north and south of the Thames. Thus absorbed in his surroundings, feeling an acute sense of where he was as the world turned and the river ran, at that moment a boy who was always asking questions was supremely calm and in control.

Without knowing how he started or any deliberate thought about what he might draw first, B had begun and his lipstick red was already creating shapes, patterns, lines and meaning on the white.

From the beginning he was making essays of the goddess. A folded arm, some fingers stretching out from a hand merely suggested by a few lines. A long, languid leg slightly bent at the knee, a back curving against an imagined bed below. More and more exercises. A girl's rounded bottom which, on its own and with no legs or torso attached, looked like a red apple. Lines of a face inside a box shape, an early trace of a reflection. Areas filled in with varying shades of red constructed by different levels of force on his pencil – the folds of Velázquez's curtain material. Other patches depicting the fall and crumpling of bed linen, red in line but white in substance. A Cupid's wing, splayed as if ready for flight.

In three hours, hardly raising his head or diverting his gaze, B had filled three or four pages of work and when at last he laid his pencils down, pulling his back straight as he looked at what he had drawn, all the little individual sketches appeared like jigsaw pieces – this with that, parts of a whole. An exhilarating feeling of satisfaction ran through his body and he remembered how good it had felt back in the classroom that afternoon before he destroyed his picture in a howling fury. Happy, proud, like he was beyond being told off or what to do.

But he also felt very tired. Yesterday in London had taken a heavy toll and after such a marathon on Nelson's steps B realised how weary he was. Content with his first ventures, he walked home, hid the pad and pencils under his bed, ate a tense Sunday dinner with his parents during a brittle, unexpected truce then spent the rest of the afternoon at the flower gardens in Greenwich Park dozing on the tree bough where Molly had once asked him to marry her.

The real work started in earnest very early the next day, Monday, and continued right through Tuesday. Life poured into the goddess as B sat at the riverside, on a bench before General Wolfe or at several favourite sites around the park including the Meridian Line itself. Special places for a special task. Pencil to pad, blank white space transformed into beauty. Line by line, colour by colour, shape by shape, B's picture grew into a living, breathing thing. Molly was there on the paper in front of him. An invocation.

No prompt or visual reminder was required. When beholding the original Velázquez at the National, B had unconsciously memorised every detail. Working in deep concentration, his tools in his fingers, colours at his disposal, by day he recreated the picture etched deep inside his head and by night the emerging goddess slept under his bed as he dreamt in it. Wonderful, bright, kaleidoscope dreams.

Four o'clock on Tuesday afternoon, B sat on the grass near the green railings of the flower gardens while a few boys played football an avenue of trees away, their sounds and the heat of summer all around him. He put a grey pencil down and straightened, holding his pad up square before him to look upon the finished work. Many sensations came at that moment but apart from relief at having accomplished his task what he felt most was joy. B would have called it happiness perhaps or feeling nice but joy in all its euphoric and fervent senses was what it was. Now he had something precious to give to Molly. His equivalent of the kaleidoscope she had given him on her birthday at the window.

Laying his pad down, he took a deep breath and was quiet for a minute or two before the single word entered his head.

Portugal.

Too busy with colour and beauty, all thoughts of the World Cup semi-final had been successfully banished from his mind until this moment. Yet now he was free to believe.

Tonight. Wembley.

A shout from the game thirty yards away and realising what they wanted B leapt up in a flash, side-stepped a few yards, ran forwards at full pelt and smashed the football back to the boy in the makeshift, jackets-down-on-the-grass goal. Still in his bubble of joy, B grinned to see the ball crash through the goal as if Bobby Charlton himself had scored.

Back for tea with the parental pugilists, eager for renewed fighting, he twisted his kaleidoscope for a while before steadying himself in front of the telly for the game.

Surprisingly, considering the momentous scale of the match, from the moment England went one up thanks to

Bobby Charlton slotting home from the edge of the box, B lost all his nerves. And when Bobby rattled in a second with ten minutes to go, qualifying for the final on Saturday seemed a mere formality. That was until a Portuguese penalty minutes later, brother Jack Charlton's handball, and the world suddenly turned black.

B let his feelings be known as Eusebio slotted home.

'Fuck!'

Unconsciously done, the act of a true supporter, his aberration on the train had been repeated. B shut his eyes in horror. A line had been crossed and he knew it.

The warring factions were exceedingly displeased. Unfortunately, his mum had been passing through the living room at that precise moment and his dad, morose in his grey armchair, was ready to take his disappointment out on someone. Ears ringing with furious chastisement, B sat out the last few minutes of the game in disgrace, yet thankfully his fears of an even bigger Portuguese revival came to nought. Victorious and back in his bedroom, he heard his dad shout to his wife he was going over to the pub to celebrate and jumping up and down on his bed, his mind swam with amazing possibilities.

Saturday, Wembley, England, World Champions, Molly.

But walking along the riverfront next morning, his thoughts bouncing between Molly playing on a beach at Hastings and him scoring the winning goal in the final, B could not escape the nagging guilt of swearing during the game and, worryingly, his failure to learn the lesson coming back from *Funny Girl*. His loose tongue on the train had considerably deepened Molly's mum and dad's icy regard even before his mum's awful drunken barrage. B felt so bad yet what could he do? Then, blue sky, brown Thames, as another white stone skimmed the water, suddenly he had the way to apologise.

Connections.

Mr and Mrs Larnder loved each other, it was obvious, he'd seen demonstrations of it. He remembered them holding hands on the day in London. It was simple. The Bronzino painting, the look of love. Flicking one last stone across the waves, he laughed and started to run home.

The rest of the day and some of the next were spent on Nelson's steps and on a bench near Cutty Sark. B focussed only on the main figures in the Bronzino, the lovers' look, their nakedness, the woman holding the gift of the golden ball, the man holding the lady's tit.

Unlike his goddess for Molly, this picture was not to be overly detailed or coloured. He wanted to draw in simple outlines, similar to Barbara's tribute to Velázquez at the front of his pad. Again, no visual reference was required, the Bronzino was fully captured in his memory. Pencil colour choices sympathetic to the original, flesh tones merely hinted, the slight blush of red on cheeks. How effortless it was, how easily the lines came together, how utterly absorbed he was in his quiet, happy toil. The picture answering what he demanded of it and himself.

His apology finished if not yet offered up to Mr and Mrs Larnder, B whiled away Friday on more drawing, rigorous swings at the swings and a final saunter past Molly's house just in case she had come home early. Tea over, he spent an evening at the river and kaleidoscope-twisting in his room, both to escape some renewed door-to-door fighting by his parents. But all the time the sheer unknown of what tomorrow held mounted and sleep wouldn't come until that massive row in the early hours. Now, sitting on Molly's doorstep still wracked by nerves, he knew there would be no respite until she was home.

Then suddenly the waiting was over. The sound of an engine, a flash of red and a car swerved into the space in front of the house.

The longed-for arrival came so quickly B didn't have a chance to stand up. Sitting low on the doorstep his presence wasn't noticed either by Mr and Mrs Larnder or, indeed, Molly herself even though she was in the nearside back seat. As the car's front doors opened, B started to hoist himself to his feet hampered a little by the pad under his arms and it was only as he was pulling the driver's seat forward to let his daughter out that Mr Larnder checked at last and saw him. And in that instant, catching mean, angry eyes, recognising the same look his own parents gave him every single day, B realised what a terrible mistake he had made by being there.

'What the hell are you doing?' shouted Mr Larnder letting the car seat fall back down trapping Molly inside. But he gave B no chance to respond.

'Well? What? What's going on? Why are you here?'

Stunned by the venom of the questions, so unexpected and sharp, a sickening lump formed in B's throat.

'Look, you, go home! How can you be here? We haven't even got out of the car!'

Mrs Larnder came up fast on her husband's shoulder as he continued to shout. 'Go home! Go! Do you hear me?'

'Yes! Go home!' echoed his wife with equal spite. 'You can't be a nuisance like this. Leave! Molly can't see you. Do you understand?'

B felt a burning sensation in his face. His heartbeat pounded in his ears. Stepping forward a pace, in a silent almost pathetic gesture, he held his pad up high in front of him.

Molly's dad looked down and snapped. 'What's this? What is it?'

Sound came to B's voice.

'Please, sorry... it's for Molly... for you... sorry...'

Mrs Larnder snatched the pad out of B's hands as her husband turned him around and pushed him away harshly.

'All right. Now, off you go. Go home!'

At that moment Molly got out of the car but before she could speak her mother produced the front door key and ushered her daughter inside. Mr Larnder stepped closer towards B barking out one last order.

'Go!'

Then he too about-faced and disappeared into the house.

More deeply blue than he had ever felt in his life, B shook with the finality of the command and started to walk away. Blue sky, red car, green trees, all colours at that moment fell headlong into black and within a few steps his knees physically buckled under him. Traumatised, he had to hold on to a wall in front of a house to steady himself. Palms down on the rendered surface, he looked up through tears to see a sticker in the front window. Across the small concrete front garden space, Willy, the 1966 World Cup lion mascot, a familiar figure now across the nation, smiled back at him.

Willy, World Cup, the world. Uruguay, France, Mexico, Argentina, Portugal, lands B had never seen and somehow he had been transported to a land he couldn't comprehend.

A pebble rested on top of the wall and without realising what he was doing B grabbed it and threw it as hard as he could. A windowpane shattered and at its crash he broke into a sprint.

December 2006

Red. Rothko.

Thick, dark, hypnotic colours.

The nut-brick colours of the Tate Modern, a massive former power station on the south bank of the Thames just across the river from St Paul's Cathedral, giving way inside to the overpowering rich reds of its renowned Rothko room.

Absolutely still in front of the paintings for over two hours, alternating between sharp concentration and helpless hallucination. Nine Rothkos boring into him from plain white walls. Huge, rectangle and square red eyes – insistent, burning, scouring.

At first they are impenetrable. Blank banks of paint crossed with broad markings, giving up nothing, no signs, no secrets. Then, as B continues to stare into their depths, like the sun burning away dense mist, gradually shapes and patterns open up revealing themselves. Wide, uneven, jagged-edged lines on the paintings now appearing like window frames, inviting and taunting. Looking through them, he can see faces and bodies, lands and seas, the clear light of day and the black fear of night.

Mark Rothko's Seagram murals, works originally for the walls of a flash New York restaurant until the artist thought better of it (you can't eat and take in such beauty at the same time). Some of the collection ending up at the Tate instead, arriving with uncanny finality on the day Rothko commits suicide so he can't be questioned any more about his motives or whether the whole thing is nothing more than a big joke on the rest of the fat-cat world. One that builds expensive restaurants for Philistines to munch in while gawping at a person's soul on the wall... "We have the meaning of life on the menu today."

Extraordinary, powerful canvasses with mysterious, enticing reds sucking B into the room and, once inside, holding him there suspended. Deep velvety maroons, sultry crimsons, peppery purples, bottomless burgundies. Not the obvious, fiery lipstick reds B has always liked so much.

The room Rothko wanted as a treasured space for his murals to breathe and take breath away. The room forcing B to dive deeper into colour than he has ever done before. Down, lower-fathom down, into his core. Mines of colour, layers and layers peeling away, searching out what lies beneath. Even the most vibrant colours he has experienced on this unforeseen odyssey into beauty have never taken him so far. Undiscovered territory, Rubicons crossed, a journey confirming how much and how quickly

B has moved on. No longer can he just acknowledge and simply pass by the colours of everyday life – white coffee cups, red cars, blue plates or green fields. Nothing can be the same again.

Rothko.

Yes, B has heard of him, just like some others, the famous ones – Velázquez, Turner, Van Gogh. TV programmes, radio shows, dinner parties, even some of the few books he has read over the years mentioning them. But they were the stuff of superior conversation, of dinner-party noise, fluff for expensive un-opened coffee table volumes. Hardly relevant in B's practical, A-Z world of protection, plans, security and the dirty business of saving lives.

But not now.

In these last few days, B has come to appreciate a very personal tragedy. Once, as a schoolboy, he made a leap from his deep blue world to the lands of Rothko, Rembrandt, Caravaggio or any of the hundreds of artists he has experienced in this crazy, new afterlife. A leap through a window which opened only very briefly, his one long-lost escape to beauty. But through the ignorance, neglect and cruelty of others, through loss, anger, the passing of time and the sheer day-by-day, year-on-year, drip, drip, dripping onslaught of life, a leap he never made again.

Tuesday morning and sitting once more on the round red bench before Louis-Léopold Boilly's painting, B held a large sketchpad by its upright edge upon his knees with some packets of coloured pencils by his side. He had bought the best quality materials he could find, underlining to himself how serious the task before him was. Plain white paper, colours as tools, his mind was all set after walking into the National just as the doors opened for another bright, new day.

Curious, mischievous, beckoning, tempting, *A Girl at a Window* looked at him the same way as when he had found her. She was the final catalyst, the breaking dam, unleashing an incredible flash flood across London's art galleries. B, drinking in all the beauty they could offer, his lifelong thirst beginning to be quenched. Pad after pad filled with drawings, hands and a mind unable to stop, his hotel room floor strewn with work. Riding a ceaseless whirlwind of inward discovery and outward expression ever since Friday evening when the discovery of the Boilly finally released him and he walked out of the National into the evening chill of Trafalgar Square.

By then it had been thirty-six hours since he had woken in apprehension. A day of reunions, a thunderbolt pantomime, a night's drive to London, the game revealed, Venuses, so many answers found, and once again B stood looking out from the gallery's raised portico. Enigmatically spotlit from below, Nelson looked down towards Big Ben and Westminster, and a raw, natural call was answered. B headed for the river.

The lure of the Thames was as insistent as it had been in his old Greenwich days and within minutes B was standing on the cold, lamp-lit Embankment at high tide, a lumbering swell slapping a few feet below him. Black water under a moonless night, there had been many similar nights down at the riverfront looking up at the stars.

Old strangers, old friends, some clichéd introductions, a few haltering words, so began a renewed acquaintance and while London's traffic droned by and Big Ben chimed in the distance, it was soon obvious the river had lost none of its power to listen. Relieved, B opened up his heart about his personal tragedy. How today the National had proved his drawings as a boy were in truth a beginning not an end. How a fire was now beginning to burn inside him. How he knew, knew utterly, he could use colours, lines, patterns and shapes as conduits and, with sadness mixed with anger, how much time he had lost – a lifetime.

Eventually, his tale told, a way ahead decided, the river and the man said their fond goodbyes and parted. The Thames was left to think about the tide turning once more and B jumped into a black cab back to his car. A fast meal, a hotel, any place, any room, no luggage, no thought but for now, a short, restless sleep, and by 3 am B was sitting up in bed with a pencil in his hand staring down at a piece of guest writing paper, both plucked from the bedside cabinet.

First a simple, tentative, deliberate line. A grey lead trace suggesting a path that could go anywhere. Then another, joining it, anything possible. Yet B was apprehensive, self-conscious, constrained. Just two lines on a piece of paper, he couldn't see what they meant. Bare, thin lines looking forlorn on the page. What did he think he was doing? What was he hoping to prove?

Another line, then another and yet another, forcing them out, grinding them down on the lily-white surface. More and more, until a definite shape, the outline of something. A curve, a shade, the hint of a darker space than before. Incredibly, an image forming in spite of himself, his hand working almost independently, the pencil stroking the paper as if driven by an unconscious power from within. Old pipes in the high-ceilinged hotel room bubbling and gurgling when at last with an audible gasp of release B stopped, held the paper high up in front of him and beheld what he had fashioned.

Stunned.

Shock that the face before him was his mother's. Shock at her invasion even here. Shock at the eeriness of her kindly smile, a softening of her eye and a loving look he had never seen – the face on the other side of her moon. Equally, utter amazement at her physical reality. She wasn't simply represented on the page, no mere reflection, semblance or idea. She actually lived on it, she existed from within it and through it, she radiated from it. Not the shallow, selfish, spiteful but beautiful mother he knew and kept in dark places inside his head. Instead, a comforting, understanding, welcoming and beautiful mother he dreamt of occasionally.

At last B broke his astonishment and spoke. Hushed, slowly, a feeling of vindication.

'Mum. Mum? You see. It was me. Those pictures, all the time. It was me. I did it. I did them. Me. I told you, I told you!'

Picking up his pencil he wrote at the bottom of the paper in big letters, *Nothing for me here!*, before he swept the page away from the bed onto the floor replacing it instantly with a brand new sheet.

A second image appeared in seconds. A tall tube with

a man standing on its top. Nelson, his sword at his side, the height of the column hinted, the tops of the four lion heads suggested. A matter of a few stroked outlines but the moment, the place, the experience, captured. A third picture appearing as quick as its predecessor. A girl from Argentina with long black hair. B was laughing aloud now.

By 6 am the floor was scattered with sheets of paper depicting a host of images – details, ideas and scenes. The outline of hills, an old lady sitting in a chair, an ugly monster and a beautiful girl, a ball, a boy lying in the road, a hand, a bridge over a running river and, on one page, a line running across it with two feet planted on either side and looking from below the soles spelling out the different words, *East* and *West*.

Saturday…

A snatched breakfast over a London guidebook. Cold city air, jumping into a taxi and the need, a hunger, a craving to see more. The same clothes for a man wearing an entirely different perspective.

First stop, Tate Britain beside the Thames at Millbank just down from Westminster's Houses of Parliament, the river now brown in the daylight. An old building looking like a church, feet tap-tap-tapping on the hard floor, voices falling away in the distance. Hushed galleries like the National but a distinctly different feel here – more reverential, more delicate and refined. Yet a cathedral of colour just the same. Glorious paintings and B overwhelmed by the dexterity and passion of the Turners. So many paintings on the walls from England's master of light, sunburst skies and furious seas.

One scene instantly capturing B's imagination, pulling at his heart. Connections – a piercing arc of a rainbow over the green wilds of Buttermere and Crummock Water (*Cromackwater* according to the picture panel), Turner's historic view when on a tour of the Lakes in his younger days. And there peeping at the very edge of the painting, High Snockrigg, his high, safe retreat when anger used to strike. Clearly, B wasn't the first to have been beguiled by the beauty of that place.

Day flowing into evening, his mind teaming with gallery colours. Sketchpads and pencils bought, working on street benches, embankment walls, on breezy bridges across the Thames, in steamy cafes, in the back of taxis, anywhere an image, a view, a colour taking him. Then a whole night working in his hotel room – feverish, intense, a bottle of brandy by his side but in truth such stimulus hardly needed. By morning, light pouring in through the window revealing another carpet of paper on the floor.

Sunday...

The Tate Modern, Rothko, drowning in those reds and a full realisation of his tragedy. He always knew, he did, always. B convincing himself of this more at every picture he sees and with every new colour he subjects to memory. So much to discover here. Challenging New Age work. Strange, often childlike, sometimes confrontational, but shapes, lines and patterns telling him stories, opening up his thoughts, explaining and answering questions.

Monday...

Back at the National, back at the centre of it all. Pad and pencils. Copying, studying, watching other artists with their easels, seeing how they do it. Yet seeing too how their attempts are often lost in translation, the target missed, the idea thwarted. Shapes out of line, patterns blunted. B sensing where things go wrong. The hue of failure. Understanding.

Although he has more time to spend absorbing the Venuses of Bronzino and Velázquez, his origins of beauty, there are so many other pictures, other wonders. The rich red at the imminent beheading of England's nine-day queen Lady Jane Grey and Ingres's stout Madam Moitessier in her pretty coloured dress – comfortable, proud and flirting. The sweep of Constable's Salisbury Cathedral, the precision of the Dutch school and Seurat's cool, pin-prick coloured pointillism depicting Gravelines on the northern coast of France. B's been there. He knows where this is.

Fascination revisited in front of Turner's painting from that long ago trip to London. The black train speeding out of the picture towards him. The railway tracks, the same commotion of blues, whites, browns and yellows merging, creating the mist and smoke from which the powerful engine is emerging. And once again, such nakedness all around him. Smiling at Cézanne's nude *Bathers* – humanity at ease in a theatre of blues. Like the beloved kaleidoscope even now in his pocket, each painting showing him new worlds of colour.

Despite all the awe and instruction, however, inexorably B is drawn back to the Boilly. Whether from the red bench from where he first saw the girl at the window, or away from the other side of the room or up close, piercing his eyes deep into the soul of the painting, it is clear what he must do.

Tuesday, ready to begin…

B visualised the entire concept, the complete picture inside his head at once – a bridge across the past and a giant leap into his future. There were demons to slay, apologies to make, tributes to lay. There were statements to state, doors to close and many more to open. There were lines that should have been drawn in the sand and imperatives representing this new, kaleidoscope life.

A girl at a window. The catalyst to spark off a wildfire…

Boilly's monochrome scene transformed into a sea of colour. Pools, mixtures, overlays, layers of it. Molly in red, a flame red, a blaze of red, a fiery red focal point. Molly the window girl now as a grown-up woman. Substantial, richer, even more vibrant and effervescent. The actress still playing her parts.

'Good morning!' she says, her lips parting, her back just beginning to arch up. Movement and energy as he works.

'Good morning!'

'I knew you were coming. All this time, I knew it.'

'Yesiree!'

Molly's hand that used to hold his, now worldly-wise, mature, not the cool white girlish hand which in Boilly's world gently feels for a telescope on the windowsill. Reaching, reaching. No, now it's a gun. A revolver, a hard, metallic, black thing, so sinister against the hot glow of Molly's dress. But she isn't picking up the weapon to murder someone outside her house. No, she's accepting it in a symbolic gesture, an amnesty for the rest of B's life. No more guns, no more looking at his world through risks and threats and colourless things. A *coup de grâce* on all that. Glints of sunlight on the barrel giving it a shiny lustre. The gun is entrusted to her.

Deep inside Boilly's window is the little boy, tousled hair, gazing through a telescope to see the heavens. It is B as he remembers himself – in the background, overshadowed by the brilliance of the girl in white. Molly, the leading light, his funny, shining star. He, the deep blue boy she kept afloat for a while when he lived by the river. The boy who grew into a man spending his life in shadow. Out of sight, denying the light, taking colours for granted.

But, at last, it was time to climb out of the darkness.

Beyond today's Molly, now sitting in red at B's modern window, sits quite another boy, one who shared the gift of colour with his hero and loved red too. A boy who adored his kaleidoscope like the man who had given it to him on his birthday loved his. A boy B held in his arms as he lay dead in the street.

Colours trace, images form, and the boy is alive once more. The chance to be what he could have been. To win or lose, to pick and choose, to fuse and burn. Protector, deliverer, in his time B has saved many lives and in his picture he has given life back to one who had his stolen.

Echoes of a conversation…

'Your father is very angry with you.'

'*Oui…*'

'And your mother.'

'*Pas juste!*'

'Sometimes life isn't fair.'

'I was angry.'

'I know.'

'I get mad.'

'We all do sometimes.'

'You never do.'

'I used to. When I was about your age I did. It passes.'

'*J'ai vu rouge.* I saw red.'

Molly in red at the window, a multitude of colours telling the story. Conduits to colour B's escape. Boilly's thick, blue-grey border replaced by a kaleidoscopic mix of coloured dots made up from every pencil B has in his armoury. Seurat's effect B liked from pictures in another National room.

A full day in the making of it. People coming and going, nosy peeks onto B's pad to see what he has done. Smiles, nods, looks of respect. One woman coming back time and time again eager to know who the woman in red is. One man asking for a business card and B staying quiet, locked in on his world.

Eventually, when his pencils are laid aside, B stretches his arms and shuts the pad, his task done. A very old feeling of joy emanates from within as he holds his eyes with his fingers for a few minutes before he has to leave. The National closing, shutting out the bright, new day that was.

B walks back through the galleries, passing under the lighted dome where he once snapped awake from a colour storm, descends the steps to the landing and walks over the old, familiar mosaics on the wide floor, their thousands of tiny splashing rain-drops of colour depicting the same beautiful ladies. Through the doors and out onto the black and white tiled portico floor. Nelson, Big Ben, the lions, the fountains and the lady from Canada who said he should draw beauty.

As London's busy rush-hour madness bustles and jostles by, B takes in some cold evening air then sets off at a pace to tell his friend the river all about it.

30 July 1966

Running away.

An animal urge to escape, fear of breaking glass, sprinting down Park Row, blindly dodging traffic across the busy Greenwich road.

Running non-stop until physically crashing into the riverfront railings down by the Trafalgar building. The collision hurting, pain hitting hard. Falling back to the cobbled floor with hands high, gripping the black metal. Face jammed up against the figure-work, kneeling as if in prayer to some river god, arms up reaching for heaven. A heaven that had forsaken him.

At some point a man and a woman passing by from the river path stopped and stooped over B asking if he was all right. Clearly, he was in great distress, blood ran from his hand as he knelt crying. But at a touch on his shoulder, the boy jumped up with wild eyes, backed away facing the couple as if they were hunters, guns cocked, closing in for the kill. Circling them with his arched body, wary, catlike, the man put out a hand to pacify the situation but B screamed at the top of his voice before running off wailing down the river walkway towards Nelson's steps. Low tide, sensing a sanctuary, leaping down the stairs three at a time, he ran fifty yards or so along the river wall before collapsing with his back against the hard Thames bank, his entire body shaking, fists pummelling the shore, yelling obscenities.

Long, agonising minutes passed before B's hysteria gradually began to subside, his knuckles punching their last, the sounds of the river starting to tune in and his breathing becoming more regular. A fraction of control was returning but with this faint hint of order came a chaos of inevitable questions.

What happened? Why did Mr and Mrs Larnder treat him like that? Why were they so angry? What did Molly think? Was she mad at him too?

B understood he had done a very bad thing by swearing on the train coming back from *Funny Girl* and he knew too that Mr Larnder must have been furious over the complete disaster with his mum later in the alley. But that was why he had drawn a picture for Molly's parents, to say sorry and show how their love for each other was beautiful, just like Barbara had said he should. Where did such awful bitterness come from? He was just sitting on their doorstep. Molly was his best friend and they had been apart for so long.

The tide was slowly edging in and slumped in utter misery B watched as the wash of water inched closer and closer. Questions rippled across his mind over and over again and even the river, usually so wise and understanding, could not soothe him this time. Brown waves lapped empty and cold.

Suddenly, B was stabbed by another terror. The trauma of Molly's return had driven it from his mind but through the sounding of some subconscious, inner alarm, it returned with huge force.

Wembley.

A wave of World Cup worry had hit him that morning as he laid in bed aching for Molly and the same rush of anxiety multiplied ten-fold now crashed into him, all on top of this new, bitter anguish. B had to hold his head in his hands at the sheer scale of it. Molly v Wembley. Today was meant to have been the best day of his life but everything had gone utterly wrong and now he was gripped with intense fear for England.

B couldn't guess the time. Sitting against the bank for what had seemed hours, the tide was almost upon him. It couldn't be long before kick-off, could it? Somewhere across the river a siren went off, a sound he had never heard before, and it acted like a starter's gun firing him into action. Leaping back up Nelson's steps, B started to sprint home, the deep blue of his life there matched today by the colour of his life outside it.

Speeding into the alley, everything was normal. The walls to his left, the flagstones on the ground and the row of cottages on the right were just the same. The key under the mat was there as usual and he smelt familiar wafts of food from the Trafalgar building and the pub. The key turned as normal, the door slammed as always, but from the moment he heard raised voices from inside, voices very different from the usual bombs and gunfire of the war, he knew instantly that everything was far from as it should be. His terrible day was about to get even worse.

Walking into the living room, the voices stopped abruptly and three adults turned to him as one. His mum – brown cardigan, lipstick-red lips, gold chain around her neck. His dad – white shirt unbuttoned at the top, jet-black hair, a shaving blood cut on his chin. Mr Larnder – check jacket, light blue V-neck jumper, shiny tanned shoes. All staring. B couldn't believe his eyes.

Under his arm Mr Larnder held B's drawing pad, its pages containing his vision of the goddess, his Molly and his apology. Barbara's gift on a sunny day when a giant had promised to climb Nelson's column, when Geoff scored the winner against Argentina and when the dream in the gallery became reality.

It was obvious the three had been talking for some time and with B's entrance Mr Larnder started to move away towards the door. Deeply hurt and dazed by the events outside Molly's house, wracked with fear over the prospect of West Germany and Beckenbauer and here was Molly's dad in his own house, right here in front of him, telling his parents how bad he was.

'So we understand each other, correct?' Mr Larnder checked, reaching the edge of the room. 'I'm expecting you to deal with this.'

'Yeah, you made your point,' B's dad spat back.

'I don't want a big row. But this has got to stop. I might go to the police.'

'Yeah, you would...'

'Don't think I won't...'

'Look, I told you. We'll handle it.'

And with that Mr Larnder turned and disappeared with the pad still under his arm. B heard the door open, close and never saw him again.

The echo of the door shutting rang around the room for a second or two before his dad started. Flashing his hand, he leapt forwards and struck B around the face so hard he flew backwards onto the floor. Stunned, head bursting, instantly he was dragged back up to his feet again by rough and forceful arms. Holding him by his shoulder, his dad smacked him across the cheek with his ringed hand.

'You stupid sod! You stupid, dirty sod! What's up with you? What's going on? Where did you get all this stuff from?'

From some distant star, one the famous men in the observatory could have gazed at to find time, B heard his mum chime in, her voice radiating not anger but a cool, detached condemnation.

'I knew you were an idiot, always known. Knew you were useless. But now you're a dirty little sod too.'

'And what about the window, for fuck's sake?' his dad shouted. 'You broke their fucking window...'

B was thumped down onto the settee, totally disorientated, his whole body heaving, his face burning from the blows. In absolute shock, his throat blocked, he put a finger to his lip feeling some blood but the tears pouring from his eyes prevented seeing it. Throwing himself down, his dad grabbed his son's hair forcing his head back sharply. Eyeball to eyeball, he hissed in rage.

'Don't you ever touch pictures like that again, do you hear me? Do you? Shit like that. Bloody dirty pictures. What's going on with you? What's her name, the girl? Molly? He says she's crying her eyes out because of you and they're so pissed off they might go to the Old Bill. Coming round here having a go at us like we're rubbish or something.'

He pulled B's hair even harder. 'And you smashed their fucking window. Christ Almighty!'

B's dad lowered his voice making him sound even more threatening – venomous, alcohol breath. 'You go anywhere near dirty pictures again and I'll knock you to kingdom come. Got it? Understood?'

B's head was exploding. He couldn't think, couldn't speak. He lived in a house where his parents fought bitterly with each other constantly, had even come to blows, but he couldn't remember being hit by them before. As he so often believed, he didn't mean enough to them for that. The rarity of the attack was as shocking as its savagery.

His mum joined in again. 'Come on, come on, then. What's the story? Where did you get the pictures from? *Funny Girl's* dad there said you nicked them from somewhere. So where?'

Letting his prey's head go with a slap, his dad stood up causing B to slump down into the space just vacated. Burying his face into the seat, B tried to block everything out but he was yanked back onto his feet again.

'Look, I'm telling you!' his dad shouted, a hand cocked to strike again. 'Tell me or you'll get more.' Looking at his watch, he shook with temper. 'Jesus! It's the final in a minute and I've got to deal with this!' before he lashed out again, this time his ring making contact.

At this last blow, the sting of the ring on his cheek, the complete madness of it all, the blockage in B's voice broke and he let out a loud scream – guttural. The room shook, the walls echoed. Even his attacker flinched. Then a slow, staccato, sobbing whisper.

'No, no… not nicked, not nicked… I… drew… me…'

'What? What? Can't hear…'

'I drew, the pictures, me. I did, not nicked… Molly, beautiful Molly, paintings in the gallery… I saw, Barbara said, beauty…'

The room was silent, there was no interruption. B took a deep breath as his whole body trembled.

'I drew it for Molly… she's my friend, the red curtain, the mirror… I just wanted to, felt good… I drew the other one for her mum and dad to say sorry… swore on the train…'

B's mum reacted first.

'You? So you're telling me you drew them? You did the pictures. You, all on your own.' Her son nodded his head.

'Listen, stupid! Don't lie to me.'

His reply came, louder and more animated. 'Yeah, yeah. I did. I can. Me. I used the pencils Barbara gave me. All the colours. On the pad. I drew it and lots of other things…'

This time his mum bent down to be level with B's face. Her look was granite-cold and ruthless, the look of the white witch on *Cutty Sark*. Lipstick-red lips smiling as she stabbed out the words.

'You are a lying... little... sod. You couldn't draw to save your little... stupid... life. Who do you think you are, bloody Picasso? Nicked, and a filthy mind. Dirty pictures from a dirty little boy.'

'And who's this Barbara?' his dad shouted, jabbing a finger in B's face. 'Who's she then?'

Before B could respond his mum jumped back in.

'Bloody Barbara! Must have a thing for them. *Funny Girl* told you to nick them, did she?'

'No!' B screamed again, so loud his dad hit him hard across the top of his head yet again.

'Right! That's it! Enough! Upstairs, now! And you can stay there for the rest of the day. Think about lying and dirty pictures up there. I told you. I told you. I'm going to make you wish you'd never been born.'

As he dragged his son to the stairs, in a passing shot she couldn't resist, B's mum jibed, '*I* wish you'd never been born.'

Unable to see through his tears and panic, B was pushed upstairs, shoved into his bedroom and manhandled onto his bed. His dad, massive in the small room, was breathing hard now.

'Stay... don't move! Not a word. Understand? Not a bleeding pip.' He looked at his watch and swore again. 'Bloody game's on now!' Then to twist the knife he added, 'And don't think for one minute you are going to watch it. Not on your life. You can think about what you nicked.'

B screamed, not just at the accusation but with the sudden, awful realisation he was not going to see the final.

'I didn't nick 'em!'

No Bobby, no Wembley. He couldn't believe there was an even higher level of misery but incredibly he had reached it.

Screaming, 'I drew it, I drew it, I did!', B rolled off the bed, grabbed hold of what was underneath it and spun round on his knees to face his dad. In the position of prayer for the second time that day, B offered up sheets of white paper and the packet of coloured pencils in raised hands. Once, long ago, he had made the same gesture to his mum when he ran home ever hopeful from school with his picture of Molly at the observatory.

B's dad walked two paces forward, snatched up the precious offerings, and a sneer crept across his face. Without looking at the drawings – scenes of Molly and Barbra, England heroes, Nelson's Column and special places in Greenwich Park – he shuffled the paper from one hand to the other in a show of utter indifference, mocking his son's despair.

'What's this then? More smutty pictures? More filth you stole? Well, you can say goodbye to it.'

On his knees, abject before his father, the sheets were ripped into halves, then ripped again and again before they were scattered over B like confetti. Beauty in tatters, beauty broken.

As the paper fell, the destruction took on another form. Pulling the pencils out of their packet, B's dad snapped them all in half, one by one – green, blue, grey, yellow, turquoise, brown, black, all the colours – and they too rained down on top of him. One piece fell into B's upturned palm. Red. Lipstick red.

Backing out of the small bedroom and pulling the door closed, the tormentor fired a *coup de grâce*. A final gunshot on World Cup Final day.

'There's one thing that stupid bugger and I agree on. You and this Molly? Finished! You'll never see her again.' And the door closed with a tap.

B remained kneeling completely still, the torn remains of his imagination and the broken tools of his creativity all around him. Two, maybe three minutes went by in total silence. No sob, no creak, no breath until at last he heard the TV downstairs burst into life and tinny sounds of crowds cheering and chanting rose up to him. England, West Germany. The game he would never see. Faintly, but as real as the jagged piece of red pencil he now cupped in his hand, B heard the shrill of a whistle. Three o'clock. Wembley.

Wembley v Molly… Molly… never.

The words still echoed across the room but they didn't make sense. How could they? Molly, observatory, swings, river, *Funny Girl*. These were real things. Molly was real. How could they never see each other again?

Then out of the mania, B was suddenly struck by a thought and his head twisted to one side at the sheer enormity of it. What had his dad said? He spoke the words aloud.

'*You broke their fucking window… broke their fucking window.*'

The rush of horror at what he must have done now hit B like a train. The pebble on the wall, World Cup Willy, glass shattering. His head and shoulders sank. He felt crushed. He had smashed Molly's window.

Molly at the broken window.

A little pebble to set off an avalanche...

The glass shattering over Mrs Larnder as she stood at the window to see what was happening outside. B's pad tossed onto the dining table, the gall of the boy. Intolerable. Waiting for them like that. What a family!

Molly, seeing the pad, reaching out for it but her hand stopped by the loud crack at the window and her mother shrieking in the explosion. Leaping to assist, thoughts of the pad lost. Her father running in and shouting in the chaos, cradling his wife in his arms, glass all over her pink sweater, shards in her hair.

A trickle of blood from a cut at the top of Mrs Larnder's eye and, in some odd family unison at that moment, all three seeing the same thing on the wooden floor – a single pebble amidst the broken glass, sparkling in the morning light. Rock-hard proof of the vandal's hand.

Mr Larnder running out of the room again, ripping the door open, yelling after the shadow of the boy. Then returning, the shadow gone, shaking, out of breath, incensed, having to sit down at the table in shock. Molly dabbing her mother's cut with a cloth, her dad glancing down at the pad, unconsciously opening it and after a minute's silence telling Molly to go into the kitchen and wait there.

The bare and unsavoury facts of the pad's contents. B revealed as a nasty little boy, a distinctly unpleasant little boy with an exceedingly dubious side to him.

The first page, the first Venus, Barbara's fine-line

drawing sketched before the Velázquez and her fond dedication to the girl she had never met now giving an altogether different meaning to Mr and Mrs Larnder.

Beautiful Molly. B.

A second page, another Venus, but one far, far more lavish, more detailed and intense. Colours, light, innocence and tenderness. An inner eye far beyond tender years. A talent to be tapped. The assuredness, a teller of simple truths. Yet all the young mastery drowned out in a sea of prejudicial nakedness and disgust at the red words underneath the picture.

My Funny Fanny. B.

Revulsion at uncovering the last insult. B's apology, nude figures, the obvious sexuality of the lovers and the tit being held. Final and damning proof of the boy's lurid mind. The inscription underneath condemning him from his own hand.

Mr and Mrs Larnder are beautiful. B.

The pad snapped up in alarm and parental concern. The daughter at risk, the thought of what damage may already have been done by such lengthy exposure to the boy. The whispered discussions, the hushed options, the opening door and Mr Larnder driving off to do what must be done.

Banging on the door at the house in the alley. The boy's father appearing, dishevelled, wild-eyed, saying something about kick-off. Drunk already? Demanding to talk to the boy's parents, entering the deep blue house, the full story being told, the nakedness, the effrontery, the dirty thoughts, the dark threat to Molly, the very idea. The pictures, the beautiful pictures, unveiled but hastily closed, the angry father's sordid case established. The question of where B had got the drawings from, how he must have stolen them and no idea about who this Barbara was. Her Christian name written at the back of the pad in a neat hand.

Then the family homecoming and B on the doorstep. The absolute cheek of it. The scene in the street, the stone through the window, his wife's cut eye and the only one direct lie – Molly's distress, her tears and her vow never to see B again.

The decision made, friends no more. No more days at the park, at the swings, or together at the river or anywhere else the boy's influence could pollute a daughter's mind. The end of the line for a friendship that first bloomed where a line cut the world in two. New schools in September providing the perfect fork in the road. Boys for him, girls for her. A daughter safe and a son to be punished as his parents see fit.

The business as good as concluded with the door slamming and B entering the room.

September 1966

She gazed at him across the busy morning road. He gazed at her across the weeks of pain and injustice.

Green blazers, white shirts, black sturdy shoes, they echoed each other in their new school uniforms but were heading in entirely different directions, geographically and in the next stage of their young lives.

With her mother at her arm, Molly was being accompanied to school on her fresh first day. Chastened, confused, hurt and lost, B was walking alone to his.

Mrs Larnder, protective, hand on her daughter's shoulder protective, taking no chances protective, steered Molly as they talked. Sunk in their military tactics and constant threat of ambush, B's warring factions had hardly registered the significance of the day for their son. No parental reassurance, no words of wisdom, no goodbyes at the door.

Satchel at her back, taller now after the long summer break, Molly and her mother had strolled down Park Row from their blue house heading for the bus stop, her ride to new friends and a new world. Brimming with anticipation for big-school days, skipping the odd step, Molly was on her way – chaperoned, encouraged and loved.

After a few minutes confiding quietly with his friend the Thames, now his only friend, B had walked back up past his alley to the main Greenwich road heading for the day's big boys' challenge ahead. Head bowed, he moved without focus, carrying a tan-coloured school bag containing only a pencil case. No pencils, just a pen. B had dispensed with pencils.

Reaching the pedestrian crossing on the corner of the Royal Naval College, his path lay straight on up Park Row into the park itself by the National Maritime Museum. He was bound for the far gates at the top of Maze Hill towards Blackheath where they opened out a hundred yards or so from his new school.

Lipstick-red buses, dirty laden lorries and noisy vans thundered past starting their chaotic days below a September sky-blue sky. Westwards, the road passed the regal twin domes of the college to its right and the majestic colonnades of the Maritime Museum's white Queen's House on its left. Eastwards, lay the dense urban sprawl of Greenwich then onwards to Charlton with its red and green Valley. All directions crossing an unseen Meridian Line as it cut its way from the observatory en route to all those countries right down to the bottom of the world where black and white penguins lived. East meeting west over the clamour and clash of yet another day in the life of everyone.

And just then, between the roaring vehicles, a pedestrian crossing apart, the boy who once discovered and created beauty in days of hope and confidence, met the eyes of his goddess, his Funny Girl, his girl at the window. It was the first time he had seen her, seen her shape, her familiar outlines, since that terrible day when his world turned black and beauty abandoned him. Since the day England won the world and he lost everything. Since the nation saw Bobby and Nobby, Bobby and Roger, Geoff and Martin, Alan and George, Jack and Gordon, Ray and Sir Alf all victorious on Wembley's greatest day while B twisted his kaleidoscope in agony in his bare bedroom. Since the day pencils were snapped in two and a hundred visions created in B's inner eye were torn to shreds.

If waiting for his friend to come home from Aunt Meg's at the seaside had been hard, then the weeks of pining for her through the barren school summer holidays had been nothing short of torture. Days of drowning for the air she could give. Hours of hoping she would knock on his door like she did once before. Minutes full of madness kicking walls, running full speed into nowhere, smashing stones on the shore, shouting at boats cruising down the river and howling up at the stars at night. Anything to let his fury and helplessness out.

Now here she was, just like that, out of the morning blue dressed in her green matching his green. Here she stood, a few yards away across a black and white crossed line. His girl at the window, the famous fake violin player, the golden angel, his River Queen on Nelson's steps, the motionless goalpost, the Molly who asked him to marry her, the hopper on one leg, the confider of secrets as the swings swung, his comforter in distress, the lovely voice in front of the Alamo, the friend who had given him his kaleidoscope and with it a world of colours. The goddess of his imagination portrayed in the gallery on an adventure to London.

The pounding traffic didn't let up as Molly and B recognised each other across the crossing. Easing her mother's hand away from her shoulder, Molly slowed to a halt as B stayed rooted to the spot. In spite of everything, all their intense intimacy over the past year, all their shared secrets and memories, their faces gave away no emotion. Instead, acknowledgement was played out in their eyes. B's ached. Molly's shone.

Mrs Larnder felt her arm being lifted off and following her daughter's gaze saw B herself just as the tail end of a lorry rolled past. Her immediate reaction was to pull Molly away but something stopped her. In that moment she saw what this was – a risk, perhaps, but a defining moment. A slight smile turned her mouth up at the sides and she waited while the seconds ticked by, confident the ties that once bound were now broken.

Another set of cars went by before one slowed to let B cross and when the other lane stopped too, the vision between him and Molly was clear and unimpaired. Yards apart, eyes fixed on each other.

B flew back...

Back to the scene of the crimes, to his pictures and pencils scattered in pieces all around him. No more Molly, no more Molly at the window. The broken window.

Kneeling in his bedroom, still stinging from his parents' physical and psychological attack, the blows so painful, sudden and shocking, the prospect of never seeing his precious friend again seemed unimaginable. But the realisation that he had shattered her precious window was a crushing strike to his soul. Inside, he reeled from the mania of this terrible thing he had done as the TV sounds of Wembley's greatest ever game rose from deep below in the house, reverberating upstairs, taunting and mocking him kick by kick.

After an indefinable time, the echoes of the crowd turned wilder and B realised a goal must have been scored. He screwed his eyes up in an agony of suspense. England or West Germany? Bobby or Franz? The telly gave nothing away but his dad's loud and abusive response to Helmut Haller's slanting shot across England's penalty area gave him the answer. B's shoulders sank even further. He had lost Molly and now England were going to lose too. His world had ended and England's World Cup dream was disappearing under Beckenbauer's onslaught.

Opening his fist, B looked at the lipstick-red remnant of the pencil still lying in his palm. Red, the colour of buses, of a flower he once gave Molly, of the fiery ball above the observatory and a colour of beauty. But where was beauty now, where was its power? It didn't exist in this awful place called home. It wasn't with him in this prison bedroom. There was nothing beautiful about his parents and what good was all the beauty now scattered around him in tattered pieces of paper and wood?

For the second time in his life drawing had caused

misery. Once again shapes, lines, patterns and colours had amounted to nothing. Consumed by some inner unknown passion that first observatory day, high hopes had been dashed by a mother who didn't even bother to look at his precious picture. Now, with passion rekindled at the National Gallery, fuelled by Barbara's gifts and stoked by her words, the result was the same. No way out, no answers, everything in ruins. All those hours by the river and in the park were worthless. All week he had been driven by certainty but what was his reward? Molly was lost.

B opened his hand and let the broken red pencil slip to the floor. He would not draw again. It was a fact established. A finality on a Final day. That was that. A passion spent, as if it had never existed.

Slowly, B lifted himself off his knees, opened his bedside drawer, took out his beloved kaleidoscope and lying down on his bed turned to the wall to shut everything out. Yet as he twisted from each colourful new world to the next, the sounds of the World Cup Final wouldn't let him be. The crowd's chants, the piercing shrills of the referee's whistle, the low hum of the commentator bounced off the bedroom walls enveloping him.

Suddenly, there was a loud scream. His dad was banging the side of the sofa downstairs, a deep thumping thud, and B jerked the kaleidoscope away from his eye. It could mean only one thing – England had scored. But who? Bobby? Roger? Geoff? B swallowed hard. 1-1. They had equalised. They just might not lose. Maybe they could beat West Germany after all. Maybe they could actually do it.

B leapt off his bed. A goal, and in that instant his

heart rose. Perhaps things could be different. Perhaps the beatings, the tearing of his pictures and the snapping of his pencils had been enough. Perhaps he had been punished enough. Perhaps B could go on seeing Molly and things could be just like they were – the park, the swings, the bandstand. Reaching his door, he grabbed the handle but it was only to hear a taunting shout from the bottom of the stairs.

'Great game! Shame you'll never see it, Picasso!'

B's hand recoiled as if it had been electrified. A few seconds passed. It was true then. No Molly, no more, beauty gone. Returning to his bed, he faced the wall again, took up his kaleidoscope once more and began twisting.

In time the sounds from the telly changed subtly and B heard his dad moving about. There was no indication his mum was in the house, he hadn't heard her voice and assumed she was probably out with the thing in the alley, exiled by the bloody ball. It had to be half-time. One all.

Back...

Standing at the pedestrian crossing, the traffic waiting, purring, anticipating, B continued to stare into Molly's eyes but he could still feel the cruelty of that second half at Wembley.

Twisting...

Twisting his kaleidoscope as Bobby ran and Nobby tackled, as Roger dodged and Gordon saved. Twisting as Martin stabbed home from eight yards and ran wild across the pitch with his arms in the air in his number "16" shirt. 2-1 England. Twisting and twisting as the minutes ticked by and tired legs thought it was nearly over. Twisting at the bitter shock of Weber rescuing West Germany with a goal in the dying seconds and his dad kicking the walls downstairs in disbelief. Twisting as in extra time Alan crossed from the right, Geoff pounced, swivelled, shot, hit the bar and did the ball cross the goal-line? Twisting as the ref put his whistle to his lips allowing the goal and the West Germans complained bitterly to the linesman while England went berserk with relief. Twisting as the shrill of the telly entered every pore in B's body and reached an even greater crescendo when Geoff picked up a long ball from defence and slammed it home in the magical summer sunshine for his hat-trick. The final won, 4-2, England, World Champions, his dad yelling and yelling and B twisting his kaleidoscope as he twisted in knots inside.

Not being part of it, not feeling the joy and euphoria as everyone else had. Not witnessing the crowning glory when England's blonde-haired captain, Bobby Moore, walked up the famous Wembley steps, took the gold cup from the Queen's outstretched white-gloved hands, faced the crowd, the entire nation, and held it high for all to see and wonder at. Everyone except B.

Twisting still...

An August spent alone. No Molly to talk to. No Molly to talk to about anything. The sentence carried out, the threat made real. Friends no more and B never contemplating going near any place where he might meet her. How could he dare? B had made her cry and she never wanted to see him again. Whole days sitting down at the brown river trying to explain, telling his side of the story, asking questions and demanding answers that never came. Never passing an open window without seeing Molly sitting there.

An August leading into a slightly fresher September and a new school with a new green blazer, new school bag without any pencils, new experiences, new people and new times. But B rejected the new, hated everything new. He stood at the black and white crossing as the morning traffic suspended its thunder and he wanted only old things. He craved for what had been, when everything was better, funnier and happier. He wanted to be back in the world when Molly and he had explored and laughed together. A world when beauty hadn't been explained. Before colours gushed.

What B searched for in Molly's eyes across the baying Greenwich road was just one spark, one tiny sign that she too wanted the world to be as it once was. A world where she would be funny again while he watched her from the wings as a shepherd. When she would tell him Mr Wood would walk in the woods if B would. When she would sit on the windowsill looking out knowing he was about to appear around the corner and her birthday party could begin. A simple sign telling him how terribly alone her August had been too. The smallest signal saying she had forgiven him for making her cry with his dirty pictures.

B searched and searched in those seconds while the traffic began to lose patience, horns blared and drivers tut-tutted and swore. The same tense seconds when Mrs Larnder grew more and more convinced her risk had been worth the taking, that her daughter had moved on, had grown up a little through a difficult August when she had been returned to Aunt Meg's for safety. A month when amidst much manipulation, choice words, false accusations and other adult skulduggery, Molly must have indeed put away the childish thing that was B.

Eyes meeting eyes but B found nothing there, no yearning for the past. Molly's twinkled, perhaps with curiosity at seeing him, yet this was not significant. She simply recognised him, that was all. He gazed at her with earnest entreaty, she gazed at him in simple neutrality.

Raising a hand, an unconscious act spurred by his deepest wishes, B waved for Molly to come back and be friends once again. Slowly, matching his green arm aloft, Funny Girl raised hers too, like the day she played kings and queens at the observatory, but he quickly saw the gesture for what it was. One of goodbye, her hand twisting back and forth saying farewell.

I have to go now and catch my bus to see my new friends.
I hope you like your new school.
OK, Mum, let's go.

And sliding her arm back into Mrs Larnder's, mother and daughter moved off along the street to the bus stop without looking back.

B's arm was still raised when the cars, lorries and lipstick-red buses finally lost patience, roared back into life and sped eastwards and westwards from one side of the world into the other. Remaining at the edge of the road still unable to move, he stood alone, an empty vessel.

After several minutes, another set of traffic stopped

and this time B somehow managed to cross. Head down, meandering up Park Row, trudging through the park gates, he wound his way up wide tree-lined vistas eventually reaching the imposing wall bordering the summit of Maze Hill. Through the gates, he turned right to join a steady throng of boys walking to his new school. Some were just like him, new arrivals, with new bags, new blazers and new shoes. But of course they were nothing like him. They were walking into a new dawn. B was walking away from his brightest days.

Arriving at the school with its white and blue bell tower, B entered the busy playground and while other new boys stopped and wondered what to do, where to go, all nervous, expectant and excited, he didn't linger but aimed straight for a wall on the far side. Brown bricks, daubs of yellow painted lines, when he got there he spun around and sat down on the ground with his back to it, closing his eyes shutting the day out. But snapping back to life as if remembering something, he drew out a folded piece of paper from his blazer's inside pocket, a crumpled double-page section torn from a magazine. He opened the pages out and for the thousandth time looked at the picture facing back.

There it was, all gold, cradled by Bobby Moore, glory gained – the World Cup. Seated and standing alongside the gleaming trophy in a victorious team photograph were all the immortals, the Wembley heroes – Bobby, Roger, Nobby, Gordon…

But more than this, more than the proof this picture demonstrated, that England had beaten West Germany on a terrible but momentous day, more than this, there was the sheer wonder of the colour of the shirts England were wearing.

Red.

Not their traditional white, B had never known England could play in red shirts. How stunned he had been when he first saw the picture and ripped the pages out to prove it was real.

Red.

Lipstick red, fiery ball red, his favourite colour red, England red. Like that day he met Molly and ran down the hill like a mad thing never letting go of her hand, he saw red.

B put the picture of England to his lips and gently kissed it.

December 2006

B gazed across the vast mass of London, the capital spread out as far as the eye could see early on a cold, frosty morning. Pewter-tinted clouds lying low like a huge, sombre blanket, the faintest of hums from the traffic passing far below, the park's greens stretching out and the Queen's House at the National Maritime Museum ghostly-white directly ahead.

December, winter, no life in the trees but shape and colour in B's heart.

Behind him at the top of the hill stood the general, constant as ever, erect on his high plinth. He was gazing out too, his mission since stationed there in 1930 as a gift from the Canadian people. London's gatekeeper, watching and waiting. A Wolfe ready to howl a warning at the right time from the home of time.

Black statue, white stone, just the same, but the old hero's view had changed over the years. Beyond the river, over across the Isle of Dogs, now sprouted an emerging new hub within the greater city. Haemorrhaging commercial life in the days when B lived in his alley, London's docklands had been transformed into a towering metropolis. Banks touching the sky, offices in the clouds, underground trains pumping people in and out, glass and steel. A terrestrial sight the famous people studying time at the observatory over the centuries would have gasped and wondered at.

Time.

Here he had first learnt a little about time as an old man waved his arms around like fury speaking of sea captains, telescopes, kings and queens and a muddy line.

Time.

The years B had lost and those he could now win back. Time for new hopes and dreams. A plain white sheet of paper on which to draw his future.

Time.

And today it was time to go.

B couldn't go "home" because he didn't know where that was. Greenwich, Cockermouth, the army, Paris and the ever-moving world of his Principal, these were all "homes" chosen for him – a life lived for others. So where would B want to live now he was free to choose? At present there was no answer to this question but to start with he would return to the Lakes. If beauty was to be a guiding principle for his life ahead then where better to begin than in the most beautiful place he had ever seen. Back to the Lakes then. But not just yet, no, not quite. There was a task to be done on the way first. An important apology to make.

So much had been revealed in the last few days, about himself, his past denials, his future needs, and much had been answered. But like a sunken guilt that wouldn't die, one thing still troubled B deeply. Something that pierced his soul on that far away day in Greenwich when beauty was crushed and he feared he might never recover from the wound.

Hijacked to the north after his dad's death, the pain inflicted continued to gnaw at him all through his Cockermouth years and into the army, relenting only with the ebbing of his anger on the streets of Belfast leaving the occasional stings whenever his recurring dream disturbed his nights. Then, just a few days ago, the world changed irrevocably and coming face to face with the Boilly, his old, sordid insult to Molly surfaced again. Decades on, and with the rest of his life about to start on an entirely fresh path, B so desperately wanted to make amends, to say he was sorry and to wipe the slate clean.

You'll never see her again.

Those old, spiteful words echoed across his past, flying over the unseen Meridian Line as it ran down from where he was standing now to his tiny alley bedroom still there under a mile away towards the river.

With the mature reasoning of an adult, one given absolution by all the beauty he had seen since Friday, B now understood he bore no blame over his boyhood pictures. Innocent in action and thought, he realised that at the time he had been simply overawed by such rich and intoxicating experiences – that glorious *Funny Girl* day, the sheer impact of the National Gallery, the colours, his wild adventure down the railway tracks, the nakedness, his huge regard for his friend, the incredible giddiness of it all. His pictures were but natural expressions of what he was feeling. True to a childlike idyll, they were dynamic responses to a powerful inner imperative to draw and create. That young and urgent need choked out of him so wickedly the day England wore red and won the world at Wembley. The fundamental part of himself he proceeded to starve until revelation at the National Gallery.

Yes, B was blameless, but a basic fact remained. Molly had hated him, his naked crime compounded by the crack of a pebble thrown through glass. She gave him the gift of colours at that window, his beloved kaleidoscope, and all he had done to thank her was to shatter it and their friendship – a suppressed, lifelong bruise.

Yet just like the docks, B had also been reborn. Villers-sur-Mer, the Lakes, the theatre in Hull, seeing Molly again and everything he had experienced in London had led him to a new, all-encompassing purpose. From now on he would live for colour and beauty – food to feed his hunger – and lying in the boot of his car, mounted in a golden frame, was the first completed work from this new life. A long-overdue apology to Molly, created in front of *A Girl at a Window*.

His first picture of his friend, drawn with raw intensity and conjured by the discovery of the muddy line that day, had been torn up by his own hands and tossed to the river. His second, his Venus, had driven her from him. Now his third, *Molly at the Window in a Red Dress*, was the way he would lay a ghost to rest and go forward with a clean conscience.

His task before he could go "home" to the Lakes was to give her the picture. Anonymously – quietly, no show, *Beauty and The Beast* – it was all planned. Leave the picture at the stage door, no fuss, no pack-drill and he would be happy with that. Rothko red, Turner sunset, Constable wheat-field, green-green Monet lily-pond happy.

B was convinced his new life ahead needed the same complete break he made as a teenager, the cutting of all ties, but this time for colour and beauty not the army. He must be rid of all that bound him to his lost and barren years when colour was denied. He had to admit there was still the tantalising enigma of Molly's new name but the National had given him no answer to this, nor had any form of overt or clandestine research, and he had come to accept this as a riddle that might never be answered. Ask Molly herself? At no time did B consider trying to meet her, introduce himself back into her life, either to find out or even give her his picture in person. He felt he had no right. She had never wanted to see him again, and there were just too many years in between. No, it was time to call a halt. He had a bright new future to carve out and he desperately needed to crack on and start. Give the picture, apologise and finally move on. Cut all ties, the past was the past.

Except one thing. There was one part of the past with an ongoing consequence and he would not shrink from the responsibility of it. Whatever life had in store, wherever it took him in the future – who knows, perhaps the Lakes – B would take care of Miss Hattiemore. Although he doubted it would be for long due to her condition, he would make what was left of her life as happy as possible. She was in good hands at the home, he knew that, but he would play the part of a loving and dutiful "son" until the last.

Driving out across London before heading back up north seemed the most appropriate way to start saying goodbye. The observatory was where it all started, crossing a line, and here was where he would draw a line across his Greenwich days. Over the last two hours he had seen all the old haunts – the alley, the Trafalgar inn, the Alamo, his shore, Nelson's steps. He had jumped a swing, made a few passes until a park attendant shouted they were only meant for children, and had stood astride the "muddy" Meridian Line with a foot on each side of the world. But now it was done. B turned away from the general with a smile, walked to his car parked on the reddish-coloured tarmac over near the bandstand and drove off to make the final cut with the past.

A few hours later, miles and miles north...

B stood outside the stage door of the New Theatre in Hull and held his breath taking courage. Under his arm he held his precious picture wrapped in plain brown paper with *To Venus* written on it in neat red ink.

Red stage door, silver handle, a woman wearing a green coat walking in, B realised how perilously close he was at that moment to re-entering Molly's life. Still quite some time to go before the evening's performance, he was glad she probably wouldn't be there yet, but his body trembled at the enormity of what he was doing. For Molly it would be a nice gesture by an admiring fan, something to show the rest of the cast and, who knows, she might even find a place for it somewhere in her home. It would be good to think that. But for B, leaving his gift meant something fundamental and significant. It was the last link between his old and new lives. The stage door symbolising both an exit and an entry.

As he stepped through soon after the lady in green, B was immediately confronted by someone obviously in charge of things. White hair, hideous multicoloured sleeveless sweater and bulging green corduroy trousers, his voice barked out orders to a couple of younger men hauling a bulky white plastic star-shaped stage prop along on wheels.

'Chaps, I don't give a monkey's. Move it! Now!' Then looking over his shoulder at B he rapped, 'Yeah, what's up?'

B jumped and mumbled looking sheepish.

'I wondered… could I leave this… token of my appreciation… er, I came here last week and wanted to say thank you for a great show…'

'Venus?'

'Sorry?'

'This for Venus?'

Exhaling nervously, B was still not used to Molly's adopted name.

'Yes, Venus.'

The white-haired man detected embarrassment so softened his tone.

'Fan?'

'Sorry?'

'You… fan of hers?' he chuckled. 'Ah! Don't worry, man, we get a few in here. Usually flowers or a bottle of something. What you got?'

B was still unsure of himself, his army training deserting him at this very personal moment. 'Well, I'd rather not say exactly.' Then he came clean. 'Well, it's a picture actually. I hope she'll like it.'

The man raised an eyebrow.

'Can't see it being porn, you don't look the type. Mind you, never know. OK, leave it with me. I'll put it in the dressing room she uses. Is that all?' before he started off abruptly after the two men with the star.

B gestured to the multicoloured back as it disappeared down a corridor.

'Yes, sure, er, thanks…'

Suddenly, he was alone and in silence. Hands free without his apology, B pocketed them in his coat and started to take in the dark grey floor and the off-white coloured walls of the backstage surroundings. A bright yellow plastic sun leaning against a chair, a rack of clothes presumably costumes, a stack of catering glasses. So this was Molly's domain, her world, where the player of parts played parts. He smiled as he mused. She certainly hadn't wasted the intervening years like he had. Lucky Molly, always knowing what she must do and fulfilling her childhood promise.

Job done, his apology made, B about-faced and pushed the stage door open to leave. But as he emerged into the cold, coming straight towards him from across the street was Molly herself. Red gloves, white jacket, a dark headband through her blonde hair, that jump in her step, she was unmistakeable. In the instant of her appearance on stage the other night he knew her as if they had always remained friends – the girl as a woman, the transformation smooth and natural – and now she was right in front of him.

With only a moment to choose, his heart pounding, B decided he couldn't turn away and kept looking ahead holding the stage door open for her. Four yards away, Molly fixed her eyes on him and seeing his gentlemanly act started to smile. Three yards, and he saw her face light up in the playful, carefree way he remembered. Two, and she began to hold up her arm with the hand that had held B's tightly in affection or consolation so many times, the same arm that had waved to him across the street in Greenwich saying goodbye. A yard, and she was so close he could see the texture of her skin, the shine of her hair, the white of her teeth in her smile and the ageless glint in her eye.

At the door Molly passed under B's arm, flashed her face up and gently brushed her hand across his in thanks. Hand to hand, that old sensation, the same touch, a fleeting second, in an instant the door closed behind her and B was left paralysed in shock. A moment so fast but so real, so tender. A flash of memory, her hand on his. He was struck dumb by a dazzling mixture of euphoria and fear.

Three people coming out of nowhere to enter the theatre made B pull away across the pavement, his hands holding his face. Half-staggering, he rounded a corner and glimpsing the faint lights of a coffee shop, blundered in. Dark brown Americano, lighter brown wooden stick, deep red cup, white lettering, he sat on a high stool staring out of the window onto the street desperately trying to gather his thoughts.

A passing instant, their lives coming together, she had absolutely no idea who he was. B shook his head wondering how long it would be until she saw his apology in the dressing room. Right now? Was she opening it up right now? Sorry.

All day he had been ready for "home", however temporary a home back in the Lakes might be. Since finishing his picture, he had believed he would simply leave it for her at the theatre then drive away to continue the rest of his new life. But her hand, her smile, her shape... he simply didn't know now. Seeing her, touching her, had somehow changed the plan, tilted a delicate balance. Sipping his coffee, he began to imagine there might be still something else he must do, another twist to the story. And by the time his cup was empty he knew.

This chance meeting with Molly had to mean the National game was still being played. It wasn't over yet. Venus, that enigma. Was the mystery of her name about to be revealed – a name game for a man with no name? Walking out of the coffee shop, B felt compelled to see the performance again tonight and find out. One thunderbolt had struck him when he first saw her on the stage, did another lie in store?

Luckily there were a few seats available at the box office, the girl behind the glass smiling at B's obvious relief. Long black hair, lipstick-red lips, echoes of an old flame from Argentina and his natural mother.

'Looks like you can't wait,' the girl laughed, handing B some change.

B thought of another game, an old one. Would you wait Mr Wood, would you? Yellow ticket, black lettering, he smiled back.

'No. I don't think I can.'

People were already arriving for the show, the panto rush beginning, and B headed for the upstairs bar. Sitting with a beer at a large window-table overlooking the theatre entrance with a little park beyond, he took up what had become normal practice in any odd moment. A little black sketchpad, a pencil, the red one he always kept in his pocket, he started to draw. An outline of Molly walking towards him, a detail of her profile, two men pushing a star along on a trolley, the face of the Beast from a poster on the wall.

The weekday crowd built quickly and the bar was soon a bedlam of chatter, children and clinking glasses. Whatever the circumstances, whenever he was drawing, B always withdrew into himself, his focus fixed firmly on his subject, a fierce concentration from within. This time too he managed successfully to blot out the din and his inner turmoil, but on entering the auditorium he began to feel very nervous and strange. Sitting down in his seat, the dazzle and glare of the LED and glow toys all around him like before, he realised with mounting trepidation how once again he was being sucked into perilous, new territory. His dash to London, like his flight from France to England and all the other twists and turns in his life recently, all because he had felt driven – answers always around another corner. He had thought there were no more twists to come, yet here he was waiting for the red curtain to go up and still anything could happen.

B sat mid-row surrounded by a noisy bunch. Shouts and whistles, sweet wrappers and crisps, a little punching between some boys and girls and various parents trying to keep order. Then music, lights down, hisses, shushes and dry-ice started to cascade onto the first rows in the stalls. B was much nearer the stage this time so wisps of it drifted back to him.

On cue, there she was, walking to mid-stage to join some other players. The story beginning, the castle and the lush green forest. B scanned Molly's face for a sign, a signal, anything to explain, yet all seemed normal. She entered and exited, stage right, stage left, to the usual cheers, laughter and boos. Everything was as it should be. Christmas was coming and Santa was on his way. B was left wondering and perplexed. Had his imagination got the better of him this time? Was a second thunderbolt mere self-delusion?

Suddenly, there was a missed line, a stumble, one of the cast making a quick joke of it to the audience while Molly ad-libbed to get back on track. Then she did it again, and again, this time more obviously causing a faltering ten-second pause. Some sharp thinking from other actors covered for her once more, a series of outlandish gestures generating laughs which conveniently led into a song featuring lots of the cast on stage together. With safety in numbers, Molly sang and danced playing a full part in the choreography.

A rousing crescendo to the song brought the panto's first half to an end and applause filled the auditorium. Molly finished the number to the rear of the cast but just as they began to exit she pulled through the throng towards the front of the stage and, reaching it, she stopped to stand alone as the red theatre curtain came down behind her. The houselights were already up yet the audience thought the show must still be continuing somehow and kept to their seats. A strange silence held, a curious anticipation in the air. Everyone was wondering what was going to happen next. Was she going to sing or tell a few jokes? But Molly did neither, she just stared into the crowd.

At last, slowly, hesitantly, lifting her arm into the air, Molly started to wave it back and forth as if beckoning to someone. Then after a few more seconds she started to speak, a shaking voice, a mix of desperation and hope.

'B?'

The sound of his name echoed around the auditorium. He heard it but couldn't believe it.

'B? B? Are you there? Are you here?'

There was now absolute silence. No child shouted or cried, no parent pestered or chided, no sound came from the orchestra pit. All eyes were concentrated on Molly. Venus in the spotlight, talking in tongues to the audience.

She spoke again.

'B? B! I know you're there.'

Then.

'I have the picture. I know it is you.'

Colours at life's most momentous moments. A piece of black jacket on a child's severed hand rammed into a fence on a Belfast corner, red blood on a pavement in Paris dripping from the body of a little boy who had hero-worshipped him, the green of the hills where he went to lose his anger.

Rising quietly from his seat, standing to face Molly in response to her sign, B absorbed the colours of this inexplicable moment. Her red tunic, its golden buttons, the deep red of the curtain forming a backdrop to her like a waterfall of blood, a blue spotlight on the wall. Colours of the everyday at an extraordinary instant when the past and present came together. Then he too raised an arm, a reciprocal salute, an echo waving back, identifying himself, answering her call. Hundreds of heads, young and old, swung away from Molly to take in the apparent object of her search.

She gazed at him from the red-draped stage, he gazed at her in complete astonishment that she had called his name, that by some giddy mystery she knew he was there. How was this possible, how could she know? What inexplicable magic was this? Even up so close, earlier at the stage door, she had passed under his arm without a hint of recognition. How could it be otherwise? Yet she said she had the picture. His picture. What could have possibly told her that? There was nothing to link him to her anonymous gift. No name, no clue, nothing.

She gazed at him from across the years, he gazed at her in the wonder of discovery and by some simultaneous understanding they both started to move. B past knees and legs to get to the aisle at the end of his row, Molly to the stairs to the theatre floor at the right of the stage. The audience a mute witness to such a curious public meeting.

Molly and B came together and stood a yard apart. Staring at each other like once before when they were children standing at a road crossing, they played out their emotions through their eyes. His were lost in a fog of incredulity, hers were tearful and glistening in memory. Eventually, like crossing a timeline, a line that had divided their worlds for so long, Molly reached out, scooped up B's hand and held it aloft.

B saw the red of her costume, Molly in red, a bright red, a lipstick red, and with his free hand he gently caressed her cheek, leant over and kissed it.

Part Two

The colours of
the world

1970 – Mexico

England red, West Germany white.

Four years on, the World Cup, Mexico, thousands of miles from Wembley and light years from 1966. Fifteen years old, sadder, more wary and angry. Angry most of the time. Four years since England won the world and B lost everything.

Staring at the colour telly in Miss Hattiemore's home by the River Cocker. Reds, whites, greens, yellows and blues playing out on the screen. A container of colours, like the kaleidoscope twisting in his hands.

Staring at the game, not quite believing what he is witnessing. The past coming around again. Despite everything his parents did to him, here he is, surviving.

Four years on and they can't stop him now. His mum? Out somewhere, not caring less where he is. His dad? Long dead, beyond taunting him this time.

England v West Germany. Reds against the whites. Just as it had been at Wembley.

There's Bobby, the same as in 1966. Glorious, bestriding the pitch, in control, beauty in motion. There's Bobby Moore, Alan, Geoff, heroes all. But Gordon is missing. A stomach bug, the TV commentator says, and Peter Bonetti in goal instead.

No matter, 2-0 up, Mullery and Peters the scorers. Winning again, Mexican glory, heading for the semi-finals and a chance to get back at Brazil for beating England just a week ago in Guadalajara. The blue and gold of Pelé and Rivelino against the English white that day.

Just in from shopping in Main Street, Miss Hattiemore plonks a beaker full of orange squash down next to him and in the time it takes to look up to say "thanks" and back to the telly the ominous tide has begun to turn. Beckenbauer, the nemesis, the cool, calculating threat. Marauding forward he shoots wide across Bonetti from the edge of England's penalty area.

2-1.

Then the unthinkable. What's happening? Bobby is trotting off the pitch, his white number nine retreating to the sideline towards Sir Alf, still the England manager. Injured? No, can't be. But it's true, Bobby's being substituted. Colin Bell is coming on. A great player, one of the best, but he's not Bobby. Shock creeping up B's neck.

Wreaking his own personal revenge for 1966, a freak header somehow curling up into the air going in, Owe Seeler, the old man of West Germany, makes it 2-2. It can't happen, can it?

But it can.

Extra time in the heat and shimmer of León, panic in the English defence. The orange squash untouched. B, who has given up playing football because the joy has gone out of it, a victim of his anger, and who is watching the World Cup out of sheer defiance of his parents, sees the Wembley world champions lose their crown to a Gerd Müller high-kicking volley.

England's net bulges. 2-3. Defeat. White conquering red.

Miss Hattiemore watches as B walks out of the front door and looking from her back window sees him appear soon afterwards on the narrow bridge over the Cocker. B stares into the river flowing from the hills, memories dripping into the blues, greens, greys and whites of the water.

1974 – West Germany

Orange pumping out of the TV stuck on top of a shelf. Barrack-room noise filling the air and chants of *'Tay-lor! Tay-lor! Tay-lor!'* bouncing off the dingy walls, tinny tables and reinforced glass windows of the army mess.

Fifteen feet back, squeezed into the middle of a row of squaddies, all anticipation for the kick-off and B can see the irony. Orange shirts and flags of the Dutch everywhere over in the *Olympiastadion*, Munich and outside the base a flash of the colour can get you killed.

'*Tay-lor! Tay-lor! Tay-lor!*', the chanting continues. The World Cup Final, four years on from Mexico, England humbled in the qualifying rounds. Sir Alf and Bobby Moore no more, finally put out to grass for defeat by Poland. But the boys have to have something patriotic to cheer for. Hosts West Germany versus the young guns of Holland and the referee is, well, English of course. Jack Taylor, the nation's finest, the man with the jet-black Elvis hair, the man in charge.

'Playing by bleedin' English rules, mate!' says the face of the tattooed arms next to B.

'Pay the buggers back for Mexico, Jack!' screams another from the back.

Mexico, Bobby, England. B hasn't forgotten anything. He fully appreciates what today represents. The orange of Johan Cruyff or the white of Franz Beckenbauer might win but B is celebrating his own private triumph. Another World Cup Final he can't be denied. Death just around almost any corner out there in the streets of Belfast but B is living to tell the tale unlike dear old dad. His mum? Well, she can go to hell, anyway.

Orange, white, kick-off, white ball, just a minute in and Jack metes out early justice for a nervy West German trip on Johan in the box. Penalty!

'*Tay-lor! Tay-lor, Tay-lor!*' Everyone joins in, officers too. The entire British Army in the dinner-smelling mess with their arms linked around the shoulders of their comrades in arms and Jack is the hero of the hour. Neeskens takes the penalty, the goal assured, just like B used to think when he took them back when he played – the playground, the park, the swings, history.

Goal! 1-0 to the Dutch and orange pumps out of the TV again.

1978 – Argentina

Her body melting into the barstool as she sits down next to him. A sweet smell of something exotic surrounding her and his attention switches from the TV perched high on the bar wall to a vision in blue.

Ice-blue skirt, a soft, slinky, slightly darker blue strapless top, a delicate silver chain below cascading black hair, there's no doubt to B or anyone else she is beautiful. As usual he stares at her and can't quite believe his luck.

Home on leave for a week in January (Home? What a joke!), a mate in the unit's bedroom floor on the outskirts of some town but a pub, a party and there she was. Argentinian, from Buenos Aires, at university, intellectual, rich parents, lovely smile, sensual mouth, an unforgettable shape, her colours and, as B discovered within half an hour, she found him just as attractive.

A protective arm around her waist as they left the party, B's mate's hard floor replaced by a soft hotel bed for the night and for the few nights they have managed since. Until June, Corfu, together on holiday and as much sun, sand and sex as they can cram in. So tonight, a cool beer before him, a tan developing nicely, a few days left in paradise, a girl to die for and the World Cup up above him on the screen.

'Oh, it's started!'

'Fifteen minutes… don't worry.' B kisses her soft, perfumed cheek. So alive, so tender, sparkling, like a blue waterfall.

'I wish I was at home.'

'No you don't! You love being here with me. It's on the telly. What more do you want?'

'But we are going to win the trophy. I just know it. My country will go mad.'

'Doesn't seem very likely at the moment though. You need to beat Peru by loads to qualify. Brazil will go through instead. Can't see it, sorry.'

'Pah!'

'Hah!'

'Easy! Just wait!' and she bends her head to the bar counter as if committing herself to prayer. Well, Argentina will need it tonight.

Her long, shiny hair parts to reveal the nape of her neck and B recalls how he first realised he was in love. Sitting on the end of the bed stretching her arms out above her, supple back muscles twisting just under the surface of her skin as her shoulder blades and spine moved up and down with the motion. Fumbling to put her bra on, her whole back contracting and then relaxing to complete the task. Her slender fingers clipping the little catches into place.

Arms crossed behind his head on the pillow, B watched the sleek flow of her body, her back revealing so much, until he looked up and saw she was watching him, smiling into the bedroom mirror in front of her. B thought he had seen all this before somehow, a fleeting sensation, no placing it, but he couldn't let the moment pass. Sitting up and moving forward, gently unclipping the bra, black with the faintest of white dots on it, he slipped it to one side, snuggled close and kissing her back took both her breasts in his hands. There it was again, the faintest of memories.

Suddenly a goal, the match commentator going berserk on the TV and the locals shouting. She snaps her face up from the bar and arms in the air breaks out into a chant, the sound singing out from her lipstick-red lips.

'Ar-gen-tina! Ar-gen-tina! Ar-gen-tina!'

1-0. The blue and white striped shirts, black shorts and white socks of Kempes, Bertoni and the rest of the Argentine heroes go on to sweep poor Peru away. The dynamic Gauchos scoring six to go through to the Final. Marching forward to their ultimate victory on home soil.

Just like England in 1966.

1982 – Spain

Hot Bilbao, cold, windswept islands a stone's throw on the map to the bloody South Pole. B knows where he'd rather be and today his heart is far north across the equator in Spain's sticky summer. After everything that has happened it seems a million miles away. The costs of war being counted and somewhere, somehow they are playing football?

Crackly static on the radio but the voice of the commentator coming through clear enough. World Cup, Bilbao's *Estadio san Mamés*, England v France. 1966 all over again? No, never. He has survived his most recent battle and with every World Cup he feels a survivor of his past too.

Things are happening so fast. Seems like yesterday the fleet left Britain, sailing all the way down to the South Atlantic. The planning, the fighting, the killing, his role as defender and protector. The man the nation and his own men can always rely on. And here they are, no time at all, liberation, the Argentine surrender only two days ago. A snap of the fingers and it's done. Blink and he's lying on a bunk with the red of England playing the white of France.

So fast...

One minute making love to her, so in love with her, her smile as sweet as ever, black hair, her shape. The next, Argentina breezes into the Falkland Islands, their Malvinas, his mouth wide open as she tells him on a grubby barracks phone she can't ever see him again if he goes to war with her country.

Ar-gen-tina! Ar-gen-tina! Some things love can't bridge.

Too soon...

No time to work it out, talk it through, reach an understanding, find a compromise. He's at sea, all at sea, but with his first boot on the islands and his first round fired in anger, he knows his duty. Battle, and by default death to the love he has treasured and honoured at every touch and caress of her.

Kick-off...

English red attacking down the right. Off for a throw-in. Coppell takes it, Butcher heads on and there in the box is Captain Fantastic Bryan Robson volleying in from just yards out. England one up after twenty-seven seconds.

So fast...

The boys go wild and dance around the radio. Another victory looks on the cards. First the Falklands and now France. B remains motionless on his bunk. Too fast, too many things. The men he has lost, those he has killed, the love he has kissed goodbye.

Picking out an object tucked into his kitbag, slowly putting one end of it to his eye, he twists its body and colours dance to give him some relief.

1986 – Mexico

115,000 in Mexico City's *Estadio Azteca* when a moment becomes a fixed point in time nobody there will ever forget. All eyes on Diego Maradona, pivoting, pulling the ball one way, dragging it another, breaking free and heading for England's goal. A blue dragon of Argentina with 10 on his back attacking the white knights of St George allayed in front of him.

One part of his life over and another just about to begin. The army in the past, Paris lying ahead. Different people to protect – rock stars, politicians, business people, all those that can afford to pay – but first a holiday, he deserves it. So Mexico, the World Cup, deciding it's about time he actually went to one and experienced it in person. Another little victory, one that will always be a fundamental part of his life. Every World Cup, lay a ghost to rest and repay old scores.

Short, strong, swarthy, ballerina-balanced, dancing feet, a blue blur, Diego is in full flight. The white ball spun to his feet by an invisible silken thread. Inside one white shirt, outside another, breathless Englishmen fading in his wake and those precious seconds are frozen in awe.

It's taken time but B is over her now, so he tells himself anyway. Argentina again. How ironic. All that palaver over those tiny, sheep-filled islands, all those lives lost and here are the two old enemies playing a game. No referees back then. Bet she would love it in Paris though. Her shape still coming into his mind's eye whenever he least expects it.

Swinging past the hapless England defenders, the rampaging blue menace is in the penalty area and Peter Shilton, England's vastly experienced goalkeeper, is moving out to meet him. But these moments are pre-ordained, the goal of the century is already written in the history books. Diego feints to the left and before a lunging England leg can stop him he jabs the ball into the net.

Instant pandemonium, a cacophony of elation and hysteria. The blue genius runs off towards the corner flag as the Aztec worshippers look down, go crazy and acclaim a god raised in a shanty town outside Buenos Aires.

1990 – Italy

B in Turin. His current Principal, a businessman with a long arm of influence all over the world, back in Amsterdam.

Next week is massive. Negotiations are finely balanced and tension is rising. Important men in various countries are getting jittery. Whatever the outcome there will be blood in the boardrooms. But huge sums and dirty politics are involved and the businessman wants to make completely sure he doesn't end up shedding any himself. B will be needed more than ever and this little Italian jaunt hasn't gone down very well. OK but be back pronto. Funny, B doesn't seem to take much interest in football.

It's been a long time coming but the survivor is here now. The real thing. Nobody to stop him tonight. England in white, West Germany in green, the World Cup. Franz Beckenbauer now in charge of the national side, still the thorn in the English side, but the important thing is to be here, to witness it.

The semi-final ebbs and flows, tight and tense. A fluke German goal, a snatched England equaliser from Gary Lineker and finally it's down to a penalty shoot-out. Players score and miss, Franz wins yet again, green beats white and Germany get Argentina in the final.

B smiles, a little twinge of regret. What is she doing these days? B looks around the stadium and breathes it all in before he checks his watch, gets out of the ground quicker than he imagined and within an hour is in his black car speeding towards France.

Amsterdam. Deals to be dealt and a life to be protected.

1994 – USA

Yellow...

Like fields of daffodils, fluttering all over the stadium. Blue...

Regal, rich and luxurious like the deep, deep sea. Like the blue of the sky deeper into the day.

Blue mixing with yellow on a hot summer's afternoon. Copacabana meeting the Azzurri on green turf. A repeat of the 1970 final. Brazil v Italy.

But this isn't Mexico City. Over two decades on and that fabulous Brazilian team of Pelé, Jairzinho, Gerson and Carlos Alberto is long gone. This game is closer, duller than the one he remembers watching in Miss Hattiemore's front room. Brazil won't win 4-1 today. 0-0 and penalties looks a safer bet.

Another World Cup Final, another day to celebrate but B doesn't care less who is victorious. Simply by being here he is chalking up another personal victory.

After a while he stops watching the football and his mind slips away to soak up the colours. Brazilian yellow and Italian blue on Californian green, like a flock of kingfishers diving into vivid river water. Italian supporters banked throughout the ground with scores of their red, white and green national flags waving in the afternoon heat. Cascades of Brazilians all around him, as he stands amidst their exotic drumbeats, whistles and chants. Silver rings on the fingers of the woman next to him sparkling in the sun, clapping her hands, gyrating to the rhythm rocking the stadium.

Across the pitch B zeroes onto a pinprick. Someone dressed all in red, a red dot, a spot of blood, a red rose here at the *Rose Bowl* in Pasadena.

1998 – France

His Principal working his charm, shaking hands, talking sweetly. Important men and women, backs to slap, ears for quiet words. Private confidences to exchange and public compliments to voice while the champagne and five-star finger food is circulated. B is acutely aware that real people, real lives and deaths, lie at the end of each and every smile and gesture. His eyes fixed on every move, on the potential threat on this extraordinary day for France.

Out there on the terraces of the *Stade de France* in Paris the dream is taking shape for a nation. The World Cup Final, *Les Blues* beating Brazil 2-0. The master from Marseilles, Zinedine Zidane, with two almost identical headed goals. Now a resident of the capital, B is happy for his current countrymen and content to be working today instead of just another face in the crowd. Either way he's here, isn't he?

Half-time, official receptions in the corporate function rooms, and B's Principal is doing what he does best in a most political gathering. Friends and enemies mixing freely on a day of sporting immortality.

Suddenly, a slight change in the atmosphere. A raising of a voice, a female hand on a man's shoulder seeking calm. A twist of a head, a foul word spoken aloud. But before the man's head twists to confront his Principal, B is there in control of the situation, his powerful arm on the man's wrist. No personal protector for this objector, a man with a long-held grudge he cannot control even for a football match, and B steers him towards the exit. Near the door, a glass of red wine in the man's other hand is thrown in B's face, the red dripping and staining his white shirt. Momentarily distracted, a long-lost memory of pouring a bottle of blood over an enemy's car stabs into B's mind. Red, he sees red, but just as quickly the memory dissolves.

A pinch of his old anger fully under control, B quietly powers the man out of the room and returns a minute later, unruffled, his suit jacket buttoned up to obscure the red. He dips a quick nod to his Principal who is already working the room with a smile and a shrug of the shoulders.

2002 – South Korea/Japan

'Hello'

'B? Is that you, B?'

'Yes... hello... is something wrong?'

'No, no... can you hear me? No, nothing's wrong.'

'What's up? Is the family OK?'

'Yes. Everything is fine. No problems. I just wanted to check how you were. Great result... for you, I mean... England...'

B smiles, a touch of relief.

'Yes. Thank you. Good game. If you ask me a bit lucky to survive but can't complain. Argentina played well.'

'Always so fair! Can't you gloat, be smug for once in your life?'

Another smile and a warm feeling because he has cared to call him at such a time.

'OK, so I do feel good!'

And B does, in a way. England getting one over on the old enemy after all the battles. Tonight Sapporo, a David Beckham penalty on the stroke of half-time and sweet revenge for the England captain being sent off against Argentina on a balmy night in Saint Étienne back in 1998. Before that, Mexico twelve years earlier, then the Falklands, Wembley in 1966. But he has some regrets too. Her long black hair, her sweet, sweet lips, her shape so real sometimes.

'You and the World Cup. All that way to Korea. You don't give a damn about football but you have to see the finals. One of these days you'll tell me about that.'

'Sure, one of these days…' but B doubts if he ever will.

'I just called to say I hope it's going well. I am being looked after so don't worry about me.'

'Thanks, I won't. Anyway, Louis says you're behaving yourself and doing everything he tells you.'

'But of course! Anyway, I have a little man here who wants to say hello. Shall I put him on?'

B smiles again and hears scraping in the phone's earpiece as his driver pulls up at yet another set of traffic lights.

'Hello?'

'Hello! Is that you?'

'*Oui, c'est moi,*' comes the slightly timid reply.

'Are you being a good boy for your father and mother?'

'*Oui.*' Then. '*Es tu?*… coming home?'

'In a little while, not long now. I am watching the World Cup over here and then I'll be coming back. The winners get a big golden cup and are champions of the world.'

A pause. 'Oh… *comme la France*?'

'Yes, just like France.' Just like England once, B thinks, a long time ago.

'*Apporte moi*… a present?'

'*Bien sur*! It's your birthday… *ton anniversaire*… when I get back. I'll buy you something.'

'OK. *Merci. Au revoir*!'

'*Au revoir*!' and suddenly the phone goes dead.

B looks out of the car window into the crowded, multicoloured night. Spots of colours changing before him, patterns reshaping and reforming at every turn and twist of his head.

He smiles again. He knows what he will buy the boy.

2006 – Germany

Red in his pocket, incredulous, up on his feet, hands jabbing the air. The boy is screaming at the top of his voice.

Like everyone else in Berlin's *Olympiastadion,* he is going mad – as mad as the French master Zinedine Zidane, all shining in white who has just head-butted the blue Azzurri Italian defender Matarazzi and been red-carded from the field. A legend is departing his natural stage. Zidane, the wizard from Marseilles, *Zizou,* the two-goal King of Paris in 1998, ending his illustrious international career in ignominy. Well, ignominy for some but the French and most of the footballing world will remember his years of elan and poetry long after this instant of insanity.

All square, 1-1 after ninety minutes, extra time being played. Tense, tight, tantalising and all to play for still – all the world actually. But despite *Les Blues* going down to ten men it looks like penalties will decide the golden trophy.

Sudden illness has kept B's Principal away but a promise to the boy has been kept and his protector is the father figure tonight. High up in their seats, looking down on the shining green of the floodlit pitch, another World Cup Final and yet another promise kept to himself. Another victory against his parents.

Still screaming – at the game, at the referee, at the night sky and the prospect of France not winning – the boy swivels to face his "father".

'*Incroyable!*'

'You can't do something like that, head-butt someone, even if you're Zidane. Come on, sit down!'

But the boy stays on his feet.

'Zidane… *rouge*… he saw red!'

Part Three

Colours.

Coalescing and condensing.

Colours of a new-dawn life as a creator of beauty.

Precious colours standing tall and proud, dancing in the shadows, floating in on the emerging day and slipping away in the creep of night.

Colours of the past and a story yet to be told. Coming together, intermingling, forming lines, shapes and patterns.

1966 – 2006

As Molly sat on the bus that September morning en route to her new school and in eager anticipation of new friends and fresh experiences, she did not realise how much she had changed over the past few weeks. Her outlook on life and what she now believed was important had shifted significantly (she had indeed put away some childish things) but as cars and lorries whizzed past her window she had little idea of the scale of her evolution or why seeing B again at the pedestrian crossing was already forgotten. He was a friend firmly in the past.

What Molly did know was how much *Funny Girl* meant to her and how it had shown what she wanted to be when she grew up. Barbra Streisand, the music, singing and dancing, the clapping and cheering, the sheer excitement. Since that unforgettable night in London, she had played out *Funny Girl* every day either in her head or in actuality wherever she was, first at the lovely cottage down at Aunt Meg's, then back home on the make-believe stage in her room. Even now, on the bus.

Molly as Barbra as Fanny, over and over again.

Molly's parade... here she was... people...

Funny Girl had pushed everything else to one side, so much so her parents' poisoned words against B in Hastings were hardly required. For those two weeks she barely gave him a thought. All day was a non-stop performance to herself or anyone in her presence, every scene recreated time and time again. Molly bowed to ecstatic audiences, flowers were accepted from adoring fans, curtain call after rapturous curtain call was taken and even in the car going home that World Cup Final Saturday every atom in her body pulsated Barbra and Fanny.

Arriving to see B on the doorstep, all that commotion, B looking as if he was upset, Molly felt curiously detached from what was going on. Hustled into the house by her mother, she supposed she would see B at some point, probably, she didn't know. Then a pebble shattered glass, her mother's eye streamed blood and the sketchpad remained unopened on the table. How very bad of B to break the window, how strange to behave like that, swearing on the train too. By the time her father had returned from wherever he had gone in such a hurry, she was upstairs singing in front of her full-length wardrobe mirror... *my parade...* and B was a distant echo.

With her transformation already well advanced, Molly spent August in star-struck fantasy worlds of her own invention oblivious of B's lonely pain. Fanny was always her main character but she played out many other roles too. A princess, a witch, sometimes a lady off the telly or, occasionally, she roamed the African plains with her lioness.

Part by part, scene by scene, her real world took on a new course and the door closed so far on B that when on her first day of school, arm in arm with her mother, carefree and excited, she saw him from across the pedestrian crossing, she had entirely lost the magic their friendship had once spun. Waving to him was just an acknowledgment of times spent together. For so long her main object of concern and who in a month would find himself cast adrift in Cockermouth, B had been entirely replaced by the lure of the stage.

Molly had always acted, sung and played up to any crowd, loved being the centre of attention. She was the golden angel of the nativity, the handstand girl for the world's press, the entertainer on her birthdays. But all just for fun, for the sheer joy of being Molly, nothing more. It was not enough now. That night at the Prince of Wales Theatre, gripping B's hand while Barbra toyed with the audience, had opened a Pandora's box. *Funny Girl* had given her purpose and ambition, a portent of life as an actress laid out before her like a yellow brick road bathed in footlights.

The bus sped Molly away towards a new life of fulfilment and green blazer, white socks, green and black school tie, she grasped it with passion. She blossomed within a heady mix of academic study and the performing arts. Schoolwork proved easy, tests mere play, exams just games. Classes were topped, gold stars were awarded, teachers loved her and Mr and Mrs Larnder lapped up all the plaudits at every parents' evening and annual prize-giving.

Yet even this bookish success paled to shade compared with Molly's talent as a performer. She carried school plays entirely on her own, she dazzled at every concert and radiated at each review. With a simple dramatic gesture or twist in her voice she could drag laughter from the most po-faced, or wring tears from the bitterest of hearts. Molly was an outstanding prodigy and her future stardom seemed never in doubt. At fifteen she was playing leading roles in amateur dramatics and under the wing of a top talent agency. There had been a couple of lucrative television adverts and small parts in films. She was a serious prospect, no doubt about it, and nothing was stopping her. *Funny Girl* had pointed the way to the stars and that same intense focus which unconsciously had driven B from her life never waned. Eventually, it took Molly from school to the embracing arms of RADA, London's Royal Academy of Dramatic Art, despite warm overtures from Oxford and Cambridge.

RADA proved a hugely invigorating environment in shaping and honing her talents, a rite of passage for Molly's all-round devotion to performing. In such a creative crucible, she gained a thorough and long-enduring appreciation of everything to do with drama. Under the instruction and tutelage of the academy and time spent with other students, she came to respect all elements of the performance, not just the players themselves but all those involved in bringing something to the stage or screen be they writers, designers or directors. Before it had all been about her, what she felt and wanted, the applause she had earned personally. RADA gave Molly a deep insight, a rich love of all the aspects of acting, its history and traditions.

And it was this wide perspective that sustained Molly's motivation in her subsequent acting career and the years of relatively sparse success that came her way. Over the next decade there was solid national and regional repertory company work, a stint with the Royal Shakespeare Company, several half-decent minor films and forays into television, radio and advertising. But the long-predicted glittering stardom never materialised. Molly was good, exceedingly good, absolutely, but the real break never came, the right play was never offered, the right producer never called.

Once, some years after leaving RADA and following a particularly well-reviewed Ophelia in a Canadian-backed production of *Hamlet* in Toronto, she was flown to Hollywood for an audition in a big-budget period piece with an established director. A major, mainly English cast, talk was the part was hers for the taking. Molly duly turned up for the screening, they made her feel a million dollars and the limo back to the hotel seemed an overture of greater things to come. But sadly the phone never rang, or, at least, no one with any clout called, and a month later Molly jetted home in economy to her agent's offer of a good but hardly sensational part in a TV drama remembered only because the tanned Lothario in the lead role was subsequently busted for drugs in a raid on a house rumoured to be frequented by Princess Margaret.

Yet through it all, through every disappointment, through all the very-nearlys and the not-quites, Molly never lost her love of acting, her lasting respect for the theatre or ever doubted that she was in the best possible profession. Whatever she was appearing in, whatever role she took, for her there was always the fundamental thrill of the performance, of being in a make-believe world and of playing to an audience. As time went by Molly still dreamed of stardom but she never became a slave to fame, never craved it or felt parched by the thirst for it. Her insatiable, in-the-moment, carefree nature, always extolled as a child, teenager and student, bore her up and despite celebrity status eluding her Molly remained fulfilled and contented.

Even when she took everyone by surprise, including herself, and in her early thirties married a successful businessman she had met by chance at a dinner one night, acting remained her prime source of happiness. Marriage was a leap in the dark, a Molly-like spontaneous act after a wild, six-week romance – she thought she knew her own mind, she wanted to love her new husband, she believed she did – but whether she had done the right thing or not she knew her heart's core belonged to drama.

A few years later, however, things were different. Her husband's suffocating control had so eroded Molly's spontaneity and effervescence she lived like a kicked cur in fear of the next blow. One day a new wife, loved, cherished and wanted, the next, a mere possession, afraid, whipped and unable to protest. Such dominance was total. It was impossible to understand how she had come to allow it.

The acting lark had continued for a while but in the end he said it had to stop and so it did. Molly's life-force, the stage, the thrill of it all, was summarily extinguished and she retreated to being no more than a house-shadow, a mute adornment to an alpha male's life. Instead of applause, her head rang with insults and incessant criticism. Instead of audiences, she spent her days alone, cooped up at home, abject and intimidated. She could not explain. She could not give reason to it.

Cruel years of emptiness and fear dragged by while Molly, the Funny Girl who used to give pleasure to everyone, who delighted audiences wherever she went, that exuberant free spirit, crept through a dark and dingy life in a cage her husband built for her. By forty, Molly was a pale wraith of the human being, let alone the actress, she had once been. A jackboot had stamped out her flame.

How poignant then to have her life, her true self, restored through the deaths of the very people who had continued to love her throughout her long, dark nightmare. The mother and father who had so doted on their Funny Girl through her budding years of childhood, those flowering seasons at RADA and the blooming of her acting career before their precious daughter's piteous decline during the starvation years of her macabre marriage.

Travelling back from a summer holiday in the West Country, an articulated lorry carrying, ironically, a container full of imported car seat belts, blew a tyre, crossed the central reservation and smashed into Mr and Mrs Larnder's silver BMW killing them instantly. There was little left to identify when Molly was taken to the mortuary by the police unaccompanied by her husband who had an important golf match he couldn't miss and who didn't even bother to turn up at the joint funeral two weeks later.

And so it was that dressed all in black, a small wake at a nearby hotel over, everything in her parents' will left to her, Molly sat alone on the windowsill of the blue-painted Greenwich house she now owned and looked out up the street towards the park. She remembered how she used to adore sitting here and tried to recall the last time she had done so. Not for a very long time indeed and never once since she had been married.

The still familiar rooms were all empty and sad-looking now as Molly tiptoed through them half-afraid her husband might walk in at any moment and demand to know what she was doing. Perhaps, almost trying to hide from the threat of him, she closed the doors behind her as she looked for memories of kinder times in cupboards and drawers.

Here ghosts of the past rose up. Photo-albums full of black and white images, old portraits of long-dead relatives and, to her great delight, mementoes of every production a beautiful and talented daughter had ever been in. Whole shelves stacked full of theatre programmes, ticket stubs and other memorabilia. Autographed cast-lists, magazine articles and a lipstick-red kiss impression planted on a publicity shot. Tokens and tributes, parental pride.

When Molly returned to her once favourite seat in the window, she breathed in the late-afternoon summer air and waited for Harry to turn up. Almost eighty now,

Molly hadn't heard from her godfather and provider of those precious Streisand tickets for some years. In the early days of her acting career he had been quite useful to her, the rumours of his theatrical contacts being true to some extent – Harry did know a few influential people in the business, although as it turned out Noel Coward wasn't one of them. A few auditions and, she was sure, one actual part came her way because of him but he had never owned up to helping her and his influence faded in time. Why then at the wake did Harry ask to meet later at the Greenwich house? Molly could only assume it was something to do with her parents but she had no idea what.

Just before 5 pm a red car appeared around the corner and parked by the house. Harry was let out of the back by the driver and stabilising himself with his walking stick, looked up to smile at Molly at the window.

'I've seen you sitting there so many times… takes me back! Let me in. I have something for you.'

Minutes later Molly sat at the table in the front room, her window still open wide, with Harry propped opposite her and two parcels wrapped in plain brown paper lying between them. She had been surprised when he asked if his driver could bring the packages inside and now, face to face in a silence broken only by an old clock ticking on the wall, coffee or tea having been declined, she looked at her visitor with curiosity and eyes probing for an explanation. How could Molly know then how much Harry's strange, slowly-told story would change the entire course of her life?

Did she remember a childhood friend who went with her to see *Funny Girl*?

'You and the boy were very close at the time. B was his name. How curious to be called simply that!'

Molly did remember him, she did, but now she came to think of it only because he happened to have been there on that night. So many years on, he was no more than a hazy memory as a person, let alone a friend. *Funny Girl* the performance was etched on her memory not the bit-parts by minor players. But why? What had Harry got to do with the boy?

The tale continued, gradually, at the old man's speed and in his faultless, clipped diction. Facts, reports and interpretations Molly had never heard before, revelations entirely new, flashbacks of her life seen from different angles, events running parallel to her known past yet which had never been revealed to her. Accusations that were made, opinions that were changed, first impressions which should have remained unvoiced until more sober and understanding judgements had been considered. Disgust and dismissal replaced by appreciation and acceptance. Eyes and a mind opened.

Astounded, Molly listened as events around the most pivotal episode of her young life and the days and weeks after it were given entirely new twists. Astonished, as her late father's secret concerning the packages on the table was revealed – a hidden obsession, known only by Harry.

'I always believed your father should have told you. I always said you had a right to know.'

The reason why B had been on the doorstep that day. Molly's parents still angry with the boy. Swearing on the train and being what he was, somehow not good enough for their daughter. Discovering the pictures, Molly in the nude, themselves portrayed as naked lovers, the tit being held and deep concern for their girl mixing with such filth. The arrangements made with the boy's parents, the friends split up.

Harry held out a finger and brushed the string wrapping the parcels.

'But, you see, the pictures never were destroyed. They were hidden away for a while in case, your father said, they might be needed for a police investigation or some such nonsense. Then a few weeks later he dusted the pad down and opened it.'

Her father's secret...

His anger now subsided, the chaos of that day now replaced by the Sunday morning peace of his bedroom. Taken down from on top of the wardrobe, the pictures holding a magnetic power over him from the instant he beheld them. Not the first one, *Beautiful Molly. B*. That was good, very good, a very skilled hand, but the page was quickly turned.

What his eyes met next simply took his breath away and for several minutes he sat on the bed just staring at the picture. He knew the scene, the *Rokeby*, a favourite, he had stood before it many times, Velázquez. Yet here was a completely different, fresh and invigorating interpretation. Beguiled in a moment, here was his daughter – naked, open to the world, her arms, legs and bare back, her suggestive pose, the look in the mirror. But it was his own child, his own flesh and blood who was being revered and glorified, his own beautiful girl, the very essence of her, everything she meant to him captured in garlands of colour. Even the dedication, *My Funny Fanny*, seemed apt and true. This was indeed his Funny Girl. There in her reflection and perfection.

At length, he turned the page and it was as if a butterfly had broken free from its pupa. The amorous look, the tender caress, the breast cupped by a hand. But no repugnance this time. From the day they met, he had loved his wife dearly – her looks and intelligence – yet here was that love revealed in a way he had never been able to express. This second picture displayed in its simplicity the very marrow of their passion and their peace, their mutual respect and faith in one another. Hearing her now calling up the stairs for their regular Sunday walk through Greenwich Park, her voice mixing with the pulsating range of emotions evoked by the drawings, his mind swayed with acute sensations and delicate sensitivities. It was a task of great effort and will when finally, after more calls from the bottom of the stairs, he replaced the pad and left the room, all thoughts of destroying the art gone.

In due course, fixed to preserve them and framed, the pictures ended up with Harry. After everything that had happened, Mr Larnder found he could not bring himself to tell his wife or Molly how he now felt about them. So one quiet afternoon, he entrusted them into his friend's hands. At Harry's, safe and hidden, he could see them whenever he wanted which turned out to be often and for the rest of his life.

'They are quite remarkable, quite something. They have so much power, even today. After a while Peter came to believe it was indeed the boy who had drawn them. He used to say he never felt as close to you as when he was looking at your Venus.'

Venus.

Molly stood before the Velázquez at the National Gallery trying to get a sense of what had inspired the boy to recreate her as a goddess in such an electrifying way. For surely the boy had done so. Like her father before her, she couldn't know for certain but the very soul of the picture now hanging on the wall in the front room at Greenwich convinced her B had drawn it. Here right before her was the original but a little boy had produced his own masterpiece many years ago. Exhilarating and hypnotic, a child's masterpiece, pencil strokes of genius she now treasured and which supplied the courage to end her nightmare marriage.

Molly hadn't been home for a week and sure enough her jailer husband came calling with threats and harsh words. But the planets had moved, the stars had realigned. Now he faced a goddess, one with the newly-found might to face down a mere mortal at the doorstep, one with the power to slam the door in his face. His dark spell finally broken, she danced and sang *Don't Rain on My Parade* down the hallway.

So she went back to show business.

It wasn't easy, Molly had been away for a very long time, but finally an audition went well, a director saw something, some old techniques came good. A new start, a new name, then it was back into the old routine – plays, pantomime, the odd film, an advert or radio, whatever came up. Molly was back doing what she loved and each year was better than the last.

And when she was "resting" or fortunate enough to be playing in or around London, home was Greenwich where she was often joined by a housemate, always a fellow actor, both for some company and to share the expenses. Other times, for periods of the year wherever the parts took her, she stayed in digs just like the small house in Hull she walked out of one afternoon eager for the performance that evening.

She felt good, the pantomime was doing well, it was a good company, the audiences liked her. Then, how nice of the man at the stage door to hold it open for her, and how touching, a gift from an admirer in the dressing room she shared with some other members of the cast.

A plain brown paper package with a neat *To Venus* in red letters, a golden frame and without warning, out of the blue, there she was, in a red dress, at a window, gazing out to greet herself. Her body and soul captured in a precious moment. Her very self revealed.

Molly was shaking as she walked on for her first entrance, her legs nearly collapsing underneath her as she walked towards the players mid-stage. Her training and years of experience helped her through her first edgy lines, laughter and applause from the house giving her a boost, yet it couldn't last for long. Confusion, disorientation, cues going astray, she tried to concentrate but she couldn't.

Somehow, she knew. Out there in the blackness he was there. The package, at the window, undoubtedly the same creator. It was him, it had to be. The boy who had given her a new future, a new life. The man she didn't know but whose drawings she would have identified anywhere.

'B… I know you're there… I have the picture.'

June 2007

Arrival

A glass room looking ocean-wide out in every direction onto fields and trees and right up into the air to a clear sky-blue sky.

There was the old man, standing in front of a canvas screen measuring about a metre across and two tall. A large paintbrush hovering in mid-air at the end of one outstretched hand and an unzipped banana in the other. Yellow skin peeling down, the uneaten white curve looking like a dagger unsure whether to strike, or a gun thinking twice about firing. On the floor beside the master's light-brown, lived-in-looking boots stood a tin of household paint. Opened but fresh. Yet-to-be-dipped-in.

Ushered upstairs to this 360-degree lookout onto the world by Hudson, an elfin-sized beauty with jet-black hair who had welcomed him at the front door with a steady smile, the new arrival wasn't sure his entrance had been noticed. Clearly, this was someone in the throes of mid-decision, an answer not yet given, a choice not yet made, and he didn't want to disrupt such obvious mental flow.

Except for the two men the lookout panorama room was empty – just them, the screen, the banana and the paint. Neutral colours inside contrasting with the spectacular, verdant Connecticut countryside outside. Eventually, the old boots started to shuffle and scrape in circles around the tin but came to a halt after half a dozen laps as if their wearer had been struck by a conclusion, a course decided, a route chosen.

Suddenly, the enigma plunged his brush violently into the paint, some of it edging over the sides onto the floor, and began to cover the screen. Chump hands and cucumber fingers working quickly, the brush full and glistening. Backwards, forwards, up and down, and the top half was covered before B heard the rich, gravelly voice for the first time.

'Sometimes you wake up and you never know what to feel… it's raining and you think what the hell, stay in bed, let the day take care of itself, this one's not for me. Or it's fall and the trees are clear, vibrant, so real they just shout at you and you know, you just know, it's easy… candy from a baby.'

The brush was loaded again.

'Today was a difficult day… ever since breakfast I've been changing my mind. Yes, no, maybe, maybe not… is it a green, blue, purple or a pink one? Nah, hate pink, can't be that!'

The chat kept up until the screen's whole surface was coated, wet paint glinting in the sunshine piercing the glass. Apparently satisfied, the painter bent down, laid his brush over the top of the tin and walked over to stand before his guest. Taking a big bite of his banana and gesturing his head back to the screen, he took up his monologue again.

'That's what this is... every day something different, every day a different colour, a different look out on the world. Have I got the blues, is there light at the end of the tunnel... is there anything to look forward to?'

The younger man took the maw of the free hand offered to him and shook it. An old man's face lined with a long life.

'My moods, as I live and breathe, as the sun and moon rise... and as you can see I'm in a red mood today.'

Looking down, he read the label off the tin.

'Well, how 'bout that... an "American Red" mood to be exact!'

There was a wink and a snatch of a smile.

'So whaddya think, a red day today? Whaddya say?... Or is that too obvious, too near the mark, too much of a coincidence?'

Chewing, visibly tasting the fruit, the legend didn't wait for an answer.

'Happy, sad, up, down, contented, at odds, positive, negative, perfect day... moods change, don't they? Blue skies, brown earth, black death, white knight, never the same... but it's a fact you know, yesireee, one thing never changes. Everyone has their own special colour, theirs for life... now that never changes, that's forever!'

Yesireee? This was surreal. Touching his nose knowingly with his banana hand, the icon looked the Englishman squarely in the eyes.

'You, you're a red man… red, that's you, no doubt about it. No, man, that picture you drew, no messing, gave the game away… no going back and no place to hide. That's your colour… you, you're a red man!'

And the two of them smiled at one another as they continued to shake their brushing hands a little harder.

'Hey! Do you like fish?'

December 2006

'This is very strange.'

'Just a little…'

'You said to wait.'

'Yes, absolutely, yes…'

A pause, visible breath from their mouths, three of the company coming out of the stage door and waving goodnight. Keeping her eyes on his, Molly snatched out a "Bye" in return as a light from within illuminated her face – lipstick red on her lips.

'I feel… er…'

B stopped. A silence.

'What should we do?'

Standing to attention, gathering herself to keep her nerves at bay, Molly pointed. 'Tell you what. Let's go to the pub just down here. It's where some of our people go but we can talk.'

B looked relieved.

'OK, sounds good.'

And as one old friend led off with a self-conscious smile, the other fell in beside her. The jump in her step. They always used to hold hands.

'Just here…' pointing again, showing the way.

'Sure, don't worry, I'm going with the flow. Can't believe any of this.'

Molly gave a weak laugh and relaxed slightly. Yes, this was incredible, barely possible to imagine. He had kissed her on the cheek in front of everyone in the auditorium (a few people cheered) then they pulled apart not knowing what to say.

'Kiss her again, mate!' said a man seated at the end of the row, green and blue tattoos on his arm, one the skull and crossbones – the giant, Trafalgar Square, Nelson's column. Both broke out in giggles realising they were the centre of attention for everyone in the theatre.

'Stage door!' Molly whispered. 'Stage door, after…' then disappeared behind a side-curtain.

Finally, painfully slowly, the performance ended. Molly changed out of her costume with hands shaking so much she felt they hardly belonged to her. And right on cue beyond the stage door there he was, as large as life.

The *Old English Gentleman* stood on the corner and they were inside the bustling pub with its smattering of panto-punters before speaking again. B ordered while Molly grabbed a table – a short postponement, a little time to think through teeming thoughts and their mutual awkwardness.

A few minutes later B sat down next to her bearing two gin and tonics but suddenly, at that second, he couldn't bring himself to look at the face of his past. Yellow pieces of lemon, cubes of ice, bubbles down the side of tall glasses, he could feel her eyes on him and he froze.

The years separating their worlds had distilled into this very emotional moment. A woman's blue blouse at the table next to him, blues remembered, bluebells, Azzurri blue in Pasadena, she wore ice blue in Corfu, the blue sky above Scafell Pike when the sun crept through the clouds. At length, B felt Molly's hand slip gently into his, such a familiar feeling even now, even under such extraordinary circumstances. An entirely normal gesture, instantly comforting. She had consoled him so many times – the day he lied to Miss Andrews as she was then after he tore his picture to pieces and tossed it to the Thames.

'I'm not sure I know what to say,' he began, stuttering. 'You… this… it's unreal.'

Molly leaned in a touch closer. 'I knew. I did. I knew.'

'But how? I can't imagine.'

'The picture… I told you… your picture. It had to be you.'

Looking up, finally he met her stare. 'I don't understand.' The face of the woman at the window. 'I don't understand.'

'It's a long story.'

He nodded his head. 'Yes, I've got one of those too.'

A hubbub in the bar, muffled fruit-machine sounds in a far corner, glasses clinking and they began to tell their stories. Only outlines at first, their immediate need to explain and desperate curiosities meant colouring in would have to wait.

Molly spoke first and fast, pouring out revelations at a speed and with implications B could scarcely follow or make sense of. Shaking his head occasionally, he listened in silence, watching her lips, feeling her hand tighten when she found words difficult. The green of her sweater, some deeper green glass beading of a design in the weave, a brown wooden bangle, the faint gold of a delicate chain around her neck.

Secrets, wonders, incredible answers, a side of his life hidden under a shroud, lying dormant for so long. Her father's obsession, knocking on Harry's door over the years needing a viewing like a drug addict craving a fix, wondering sometimes if his daughter and wife were more real to him as Venus than they were in actual life. His treasured Molly never more prized than lying there before her Cupid – red curtains and white linen. His beloved wife never more loved than in the Bronzino – the cupped breast. The two most precious females in his life never more intimate or sensual.

Molly told him of her new life as Venus, his Velázquez changing everything. How it had empowered her to bring about the end of her spiritual and marital darkness and usher in a new age of light. How she had rebuilt her life back in Greenwich, a player again, the stage, her lifeblood rediscovered, and all of it, every single day, traceable back to B's childhood vision of his beautiful Funny Fanny. Her naked exposure now hanging on the wall in that front room where she had given him his kaleidoscope. A constant reminder, a confirmation of her true self, her uniqueness long lost under her husband's hammer. A living statement of her spirit and innocence, her exuberance and endearing spontaneity. Everything that had made her what she was and which she knew she was again today.

And upstairs on another wall, the Bronzino. Beauty in the beholding, the sharp eye, her parents in a rapture and its perpetual assurance that she was born out of their deep mutual love. Uncanny power from the boy artist. The ability to reveal high emotion with such tender simplicity, clarity and precision.

Then just tonight, she opened a brown paper parcel in her dressing room and there was a new, modern Molly, captured at the window. A fresh, penetrating examination of herself brought up to date with the same essences B had infused into his child Venus. Sitting in the chair for her make-up, she could see anew how the world saw her today and how she saw herself – Venus through a prism. Molly in a red dress though a looking glass.

'... I was ill once, I don't know, a bad bout of flu I think, in bed and feeling very sorry for myself. I remember getting up in the late afternoon and going downstairs for some water... sore throat... took it into the front room and as it was hot and summer I sat in the open window to drink. Not sure how long I was there but I just kept looking and looking at your picture. An hour went by, probably, can't say, but when I finally stood up, somehow I was fine, no headache or anything. How strange. But there it was. I felt perfectly OK... so good I went out for a walk in the park.

'… what I mean is, something happens inside me, when I look, every time. Both pictures held a sort of spell over my father, Harry was convinced of that, Dad spoke of that many times. It's not like that for me, not a spell, but the pictures have a profound effect, always, since that first day. My Venus, difficult to explain. It's as if it tells me who I really am. I'm looking into the mirror at myself… the naked truth you might say.

'When Harry gave me the pictures after my parents' funeral I went to the National Gallery the very next day and saw the originals… you can imagine, very emotional, very weird. I stared at the Velázquez for ages but within a couple of minutes I had already decided to change my name… well, my stage name anyway. So obvious. Just the right thing to do.'

A heady mixture – the edges of memory, incomprehension at the new and the dawning of undreamt possibilities.

'The pictures have become a basic part of my life now… a sort of well I go to for replenishment, like water. Don't laugh! It's what I feel, honestly.'

B was smiling but stayed silent. He had never made her cry, he had never hurt her. But even though he feared his head might burst at what Molly was telling him, each second like a new kaleidoscope twist, he understood it wasn't his turn to speak yet.

'Everyone who comes to my house says so… all affected by the pictures in some way. A friend even knocked on the door in the middle of the night once to see the one with my parents in it. She stood there and cried. She told me it was the way her boyfriend used to look at her but how he didn't any more…'

At length she did come to an end, a tone in her voice, some inevitable questions.

'So how did you find me? Why now? Have you always known about me? A film or a play? Have you always been an artist?'

Both their drinks were finished but they hadn't noticed. With a smile and a touch on his shoulder, suddenly Molly broke away to the bar before B could start. It was an intermission, the end of Act 1. Molly's handbag lay on the table – deep maroon leather, Rothko maroon, the maroon in Molly's dress in his picture. A gold clasp. World Cup gold, clock-tower gold as she sang to the men at the Alamo.

She was back soon with two more gin and tonics, a firefly returning. Bobbing the slice of lemon with a finger, B's tale was slower, more deliberate and far leaner.

Despite his life's new benchmarks of beauty and colour, he was still a man of reticence and reserve. So there was less meat on the bones of his story but Molly listened with no less astonishment at his revelations as she twisted a ring on her right hand – silver.

Service in the army followed by a career in commercial security work. No names, no hint of its high profile or proximity over a decade to international power. Then one day a little while ago someone very close to him died and he needed to get away to take some time to think. B picked off each consecutive phase in turn – serendipity at Villers-sur-Mer right through to that afternoon's touch of her hand at the stage door.

'... finding the Meridian Line again like that, a complete coincidence, total chance, and I have been following one path after another to get here. Lines joining up with other lines. That used to fascinate me as a boy...'

B felt her hand squeeze.

'Remember that kaleidoscope you gave me, on your birthday, at your party?' She nodded. 'I've still got it, never go anywhere without it... in the car now.' Her hand tightened further. 'All my life... colours, all around me. People, shapes, all the time, and after everything I have seen in London in these last few days I know I cannot ignore them any more. When I started to draw again it was as if, oh I don't know, as if I'd thrown a switch, walked through a keyhole, passed through a door into a hidden garden... like I'd found what it was I was looking for even though I never knew I was searching...'

The two of them sat in their own silences for a full minute, the woman in blue getting up to leave, a shimmer of blouse material as it caught a beam from a wall light.

Molly took up the flow again. 'So, you have never drawn since then? You have never had the need or the urge? Seems incredible... something like that, I mean, how good they are, the power they have. It's too big to have kept in or blocked off, isn't it? Me, I have to act. If I didn't, I think I would go mad. In fact, I know I did when I was married to that bastard. Acting is part of what I am, it sustains me, defines me, it's what I have to do. But you... you have this, what, this skill, talent, ability and you haven't ever wanted to use it?'

'I never knew I had it.'

'Well...' but he cut her off.

'Anyway, what talent? You're the one with the talent. Actress, professional... all those people tonight, loving what you can do. You've proved that over the years, you've worked at it, you know your stuff, you know how. Me? I've only just started. I know nothing. While these last few days have convinced me that I want to draw, to paint, I have no idea I'll be any good...'

'But you are good!'

'How can I be?'

'Look at the impact on my father. Look at what your drawings have meant to me, what they have done for me... I'm telling you, you can't do that... create like that unless you have real ability, something special?'

B let out a laugh and looked around feeling a mixture of embarrassment and timidity. He certainly believed Molly spoke from her heart, how could he think otherwise? She was the central object of his recurring dream, a subconscious constant throughout his life, the little girl he had transformed into a goddess even in his childhood, a Point Zero that had led him towards a new and meaningful existence after his nadir in Paris. He thought her incapable of deception or conceit and took her compliments as polite flattery.

How vividly he remembered that feeling of joy, of elation on completing his drawings as a boy. The colours pouring from his pencils, reds as he wanted them, whites just so, and certainly the reality on the page met the forms in his head. Yet whatever his delight, he had no concept of his work's quality or merit, his mind hadn't bent that way, no comprehension of how good he might have been, or was now.

'And the picture you gave me today... an amazing story, almost too fantastic to take in. The way you remembered, the window, I don't know what to say, except that it is wonderful. I can't describe what I felt inside when I opened it up. I couldn't speak. I cried. The others thought I had received some bad news. I'm not sure how I dragged myself on stage. Well, you saw the results...'

In an instant Molly jumped up, their hands breaking apart, a glass tumbling from the table, and grabbing her things raced towards the pub door. Taken by surprise, B's rapid reactions saving the falling glass, he only caught up with her back out on the street.

'*Emergency Ward 10!*'

'What?'

'Never mind.'

Still unpredictable.

'I'm sorry. I needed air.'

In the cold night, standing with one hand against her hip, the other running through her hair, Molly started to twirl around in a circle.

'Look, ghosts don't appear every day you know, even friendly ones, bearing gifts.'

B watched her. The way she used to spin around. She was almost shouting.

'It's propped up against my dressing-room mirror you know. I couldn't bring it away, could I?'

The spinning stopped and Molly faced him.

'That picture's told me more about me in a few moments than the bloody mirror ever will.' Then, as quick as a flash, she changed tack and tone.

'Funny, we haven't said a word about when we were children. Those times… the bandstand, do you remember… the shore?'

B nodded noticing out of the corner of his eye a fire station backing onto the New Theatre.

'That day. You saw red.'

Red. Fire engines.

'I want to see my picture again. Come with me?'

Joining hands once again, their outlines completed, the shape of their stories in place, scenes 1 and 2 played out, B and Molly walked back into the night to the stage door. He stayed outside while the actress disappeared into her domain but she was out again in a trice, his apology retrieved.

'There's still a lot to say,' Molly declared, her arms enveloping the frame. 'You're not going away, are you?'

'I thought I had a plan, but…'

'Tomorrow?'

He was helpless. 'Tomorrow!'

Some arrangements quickly made, directions written on a piece of the brown picture wrapping paper, and after self-conscious pecks on cheeks, a lift home politely declined without knowing quite why, Molly jumped a passing cab back to her digs simultaneously elated, confused and extremely tired. Equally exhausted, B returned to his car and drove off in search of the hotel Molly had recommended, his continuing odyssey from Villers-sur-Mer seemingly without end.

Unsurprisingly, despite their fatigue, little sleep was to be had for either of them. The real Molly in her pyjamas and her latest incarnation as Boilly's girl in the red dress stared at themselves for most of the night, while B filled half a sketchpad with images of his long and eventful day then twisted his kaleidoscope before finally dropping off as a church bell struck four o'clock.

A mere six hours later, B called the mobile number Molly had scribbled hurriedly on the same piece of brown paper and told her he was parked outside the house. White raincoat, pink scarf, blue jeans, how excited she was, how animated, straining for the day when she got in beside him.

'Your car, my lady!'

'Thank you, driver!'

'Where to?'

'Now that would be telling!'

'It would, would it, Miss Wood?'

'You remember that too?'

'Yesiree...'

Molly announced they were going on a magical mystery tour and gave directions every so often as they headed out of town. The red of the hazard light switch on the dashboard, a yellow van overtaking, a green road sign, some mixed greys and blues in the sombre Turner sky and in due course it was she who picked up the trail from the previous night.

'Curious how so much comes back. You know, back then, us. Over the years with your pictures I have pieced together some sense of you, some of the places we played, some days and that word game of course. But it's patchy. Time, I suppose... the usual.'

Time. Greenwich. They had met and played at the home of time. Red brake lights in front, a slight drizzle and B turned on the windscreen wipers.

'That day when I found the Meridian again in France, it all came flooding back.'

'I kept asking you to marry me as I recall and that horrible house of yours, I could never visit, could I? Your mum and dad...' Deep blue, the paper in tatters, the broken pencils, twisting the kaleidoscope while England conquered Wembley and the world.

'... down by the shore, throwing stones. Next to you the river was my best friend. I really missed it when I left.'

'You left?'

Gripping the wheel tighter, a large lorry in front, a yellow and orange sign on its rear, B began to tell her about his father's death, the speed of his uprooting to Cockermouth and, briefly, the bare facts of his unhappy life there.

'Like a pack of cards really. A special day in London, you went away and then nothing was ever the same again.'

'*Funny Girl* really changed everything, didn't it? Barbra Streisand has a lot to answer for!'

She started to sing... *people*... but didn't get very far. Jumping forward in her seat, she shouted for B to stop and pull over. Out of the door in a flash, she was hailing him at the top of her voice and circling an arm for him to follow.

'Come on! This is it!'

B caught up with her fifty yards back standing by a sign set a few feet into a grass verge. Fields lay all around them, some black rooks flying around Van Gogh-style.

'Now this is just like old times. You tearing off and me trailing along behind.'

'Look!' she demanded with a huge grin on her face pointing to the sign. 'How about that? I had a brainwave! Checked the Net this morning and thought there had to be something like this around here.'

She had been right. Out of Hull on the winding road towards the bleak North Sea, a little way outside the village of Patrington, there it was. East meeting west. The muddy line running down through numerous countries to the bottom of the world where all those penguins lived. B looked up at the Prime Meridian marker. Connections – observatory, fiery red ball, a line dividing the world in two and criss-crossing his life. As at Villers-sur-Mer, markers like these followed the Meridian all through its course, north and south of Greenwich. 0 degrees. Towns, villages, pubs, grand houses and roads all celebrating the line that was at once very real yet both evocative and imaginary.

'Scary, huh?' Molly laughed starting to jump with both feet together across the hemispheres. 'Come on! For old time's sake?'

Unable to stop himself, B joined in – the bandstand, the swings, *Cutty Sark*.

'You're still mad. Mad as a fruitcake!'

After a while, he laughed. 'My Funny Fanny!'

It was the cue Molly had been waiting for. She stopped jumping and breathing hard laid her hand on B's arm bringing him to a halt.

'Last night you said so much... but those pictures, nothing about how or why. Please!'

And at last, at long, long last, so often denied, so many times wished for, B finally unburdened himself. The words his parents had refused to hear, the words his anger had stopped him sharing even with Miss Hattiemore or whispering to any lover, even the girl from Buenos Aires. White lines in the road, gunmetal grey clouds, a red chocolate bar wrapper on the grass, he spoke the unspoken, his whole truth.

Colours, beauty, a London adventure, gifts, the compulsion to draw, his certainty of it. Pining for her return from her seaside aunt, waiting for her that day, shock at her parents' reaction, her father and his mum and dad standing there. Vicious punishment, beauty crushed, England denied him, Wembley and Bobby without him. A window broken and twisting his kaleidoscope to escape the shame and pain. An August full of agony and a final wave of goodbye at the pedestrian crossing in September.

Pink scarf around her neck, the noise of a black car passing them, he spoke of his young trance of creation, of his utter conviction of purpose, seeing her as a goddess and conjuring her spirit. Lines, shapes and colours flowing out of him like a raging river in flood and onto the page – minimum effort, maximum control, total absorption. All beaten out of him, cast adrift and angry. Until the Boilly, until *A Girl at a Window,* his recurring dream coming true and his conviction returning. A new life in light awaiting him.

B put his hand into his coat pocket and brought out his kaleidoscope.

'The gift of colours.'

Molly took her old birthday present from his hands and looked through the eyepiece. As she handed it back she beamed.

'There's someone you have to see.'

June 2007

Dinner

Wonderful smells wafting through the house drawing B downstairs like a magnet. Sitting in respect at the vast oak table, ancient and gnarled like the old man himself, watching the artist as cook going expertly about his business.

Fragrant and sumptuous aromas vied with an array of mouth-watering kitchen colours. A gigantic, vivid red range stretching from wall to wall, shiny copper pans heating on its hotplates and powder-blue bowls lined up on wood-grain worktops. A flash of gaudy orange apron, a white shirt, the same shuffling brown boots and in those huge, old hands, silver sword-fighting implements dancing through the air as they cut, diced and chopped.

Deep yellow walls contrasted with a black slate clock on one of them and a large oil painting hanging on another (B recognised the old man's seventies' style). Age-worn terracotta floor tiles ran across the whole room, a gold wristwatch draped on the chef's wrist and ripples of grey hair massed on his head. B took it all in as he sat listening to the deep, non-stop voice punching out half thoughts and, after a few seconds of deliberation, rolling out the other halves.

'Told ya! Best fish you'll eat this side of wherever, don't mind saying it myself... pretty damn good with a griddle as you'll find out soon enough. Hudson loves my cooking but she won't ever let on, not to me any road... keeps mum does Hudson. Don't pry, don't peep, got some secrets... never too slow when it's on the table though. Knows which side of her bread is buttered, that one... Hudson, Hudson Bay, Hudson River, good ol' Hudson, I say.

'Got some bass today... silver, scales, and a secret little recipe from yours truly. Bit here, a dab there and whaddyaknow, Yesiree, a miracle on a plate... don't let them tell you I don't know a thing or two. When you get your lips round this baby you'll soon realise... yes, you're gonna love this red, man, yes indeed. Should'a gotcha a red mullet maybe, or a piece of red salmon?... Jesus! That don't go in there, not yet anyhow, er, where's the thing, ah, gotcha... take that out of there, put it over here for a couple of minutes, and bingo, back to normal. So where was I?... Red mullet, no, red salmon... yes, you red, man, that's what I should'a done. But this will be good enough and we can have some red wine...'

He turned to jab a finger at B. 'Ha, ha! Red, red, red.'

'Say that's what you can do... see that bottle there? No, not that one, that's crap... might be red but I ain't giving you that sucker. Yep, that's the one... don't mind sayin' but that's the best in the house. Compliment to you, red man, and you're gonna love drinking it... you do drink, dontcha? Used to drink a lot me, I mean a lot, red man, a long time into the night a lot... you get the picture? Best time for me though, saw the real world, the real things, got it all in the eye, laid it all out, kept the faith while I was making it... you like capers? No matter, gonna be gettin' some anyhow... think that's enough in there... out you come, babies... you can stay on there a while. Yesiree, red man, that was it... singin' and dancin', rockin' and rollin', never ran out of road, never stopped to wonder, saw the full measure and paid my own piper.'

The guest stayed silent and let the one-sided verbal dice roll all through the meal. What happened one day when a bird flew into the kitchen, a few flouncy remarks about a painting on the wall, something about a guy he met once called Teddy, how he must clear up some leaves on the porch, the brilliant colours of the autumn trees and New York's skyline in the mornings. Punching, punching, rolling, rolling.

Thousands of miles from Molly, the kitchen colours streaming into his head, a meandering house with a glass, see-the-stars crow's-nest top to it, and B reckoned his grizzled host would get around to telling him why in his own good time, in his own rambling way.

Why B was here. Why the frantic call across the Atlantic to his little bridge over the Cocker. Why such a famous but famously reclusive master wanted such a novice.

1996-2006

Even as the sun with purple-colour'd face
Had ta'en his last leave of the weeping morn...

Purple, a colour of lust. Feel me, touch it, on my body, through me and into me. Hot rays shining, purple heat on my skin. Smooth, luscious, delicious, tips of the fingers, nerve endings and purple...

Rose-cheek'd Adonis hied him to the chase;
Hunting he loved, but love he laugh'd to scorn...

Rose, pinkness in her cheeks. Rose, a loving colour and the flower of love. Two dozen, three dozen. He loves me, he doesn't know but he loves me. The hunter hunted. Hunt him, hunt him down and take him, the purple burning for the rose...

Sick-thoughted Venus makes amain unto him,
And like a bold-faced suitor 'gins to woo him.

Sick with sex, wide-eyed, legs wide, open-mouthed and dripping. Holding onto the bed. Venus, naked, waiting for him, a lascivious smile in the mirror and she wants to taste him…

'Thrice-fairer than myself,' thus she began,
The field's chief flower, sweet above compare,
Stain to all nymphs, more lovely than a man,
More white and red than doves or roses are…'

Lovely, I am lovely, lovelier than you could ever imagine. The sweetest sweet ready for your tongue. The purest white, the folding bedsheets, the harmony of white below the red curtain. Sensuous red like hot blood, swaying above my beauty…

'Nature that made thee, with herself at strife,
Saith that the world hath ending with thy life.'

Nature made me, nature forces me. Lust and power. Too good to stop, too bad to care…

'Vouchsafe, thou wonder, to alight thy steed,
And rein his proud head to the saddle-bow
If thou wilt deign this favour, for thy meed
A thousand honey secrets shalt thou know…'

Your proud and urgent head, your steed to ride, reining you in, taking your fullest favour and secret sensations. Our milks and flowing honey, a thousand times…

'Here come and sit, where never serpent hisses,
And being set, I'll smother thee with kisses…'

Coming together, snakes in the grass, hissing and writhing, wriggling and licking tongues. In me and in you. The purple, the red, the rose, the white, the colours set, settling down and in their easing. I kiss you, you kiss me and we linger in kisses…

Wanton, carnivorous, open for anything, anyone and with this came an inner, long-wished-for freedom to go wherever her whim took her. The very first time she had experienced such control, such dexterity of spirit, such chameleon-like ability to be whoever she wanted to be. Control in abandonment.

Their eyes and libidos followed her every move and word, her every seductive curve teasing their senses. They wanted a temptress, a siren, a Monroe, a porn star, a goddess and she became a voluptuous Venus, giving them what they craved. They saw her, felt her desire on them, felt their heartbeats race and faces flush and knew they had found exactly who they were looking for.

Deep in reverie, Esmé sat on the sumptuous, champagne-coloured leather sofa lightly fingering a bronze figure on the side table beside her – a half-naked woman perched on a rock with her body arched in a moment of ecstasy. The sofa, so chic, its propped array of rich cushions perfectly matching the sophisticated taste and style of the room. Reserved neutral walls exploding with colour from large abstract paintings decorating them. Deep, rich wooden flooring hues complimenting the considered deployment of flowers and, expertly placed around the space, an eclectic mix of personal items. Many expensively framed black and white photographs, a silver laptop computer, elaborate vases, neat packing cases, piles of extremely expensive books, a refurbished jukebox and, on a tripod as a specific feature in one corner, a working cinematic camera as used on a major Oscar-winning motion picture, its lens fixed on a white marble shelf on an opposite wall bearing the figure of a precious golden statuette the lead role in the same film had won her.

A chance meeting in a coffee shop after auditions for them both, different theatres off London's West End but the same outcomes, "Thank you.", and "Thanks for coming.", meaning "No thanks!" and "No way!", Esmé and Molly had struck up a conversation following their simultaneous order for a last piece of cake which, after a chuckle to hide their individual disappointments of the day, they decided to share at a table by a window.

Over the coveted wedge of Victoria sponge, the next hour saw them disclose their equally shared profession and its common frustrations. How Molly, now reinvented as Venus, was battling to get back onto the stage and how Esmé, a small-time bit player for some years, was still itching for her first substantial role. Laughter and smiles, an instant personality fit, thus by the unexpected magic of such things was a special and enduring friendship born.

The next couple of days saw Molly and Esmé's personal histories outlined further in other cafes and their many theatre-land trials and tribulations recounted with laughter and sighs. Molly's younger-day flirtations with stardom were much admired by her new confidante, eight years her junior, and at length Esmé gladly accepted the offer of a room at the blue Greenwich house – her flat in East London, she confessed, being almost uninhabitable.

So began a few weeks of blissful life together – a time of ease, harmony and deep satisfaction, a period of intoxicating intimacy, shared passions, even shared beds and tender kisses too sometimes, though never shared bodies. Their mutual attraction, sudden and strong, never led them in that direction.

When Esmé could get a job she would be Molly's first paying Greenwich drama-guest. In the past months, the now liberated wife had come to enjoy her independence and solitude away from her husband's iron fist, yet from the very moment Esmé walked through the big black front door everything seemed just right. And dumping her bags down, their young but close bond matured to an even greater strength when Esmé eyed the drawing on the wall. Walking up to the frame, studying the picture, she put her fingers up to touch the glass as if caressing Molly's young body.

'This is you!'

A declaration not a question.

'*My Funny Fanny. B.* Such a beautiful thing! I know it's you. So beautiful.'

She turned to face her new friend. 'How extraordinary. Fanny?'

Molly took Esmé's hand in hers.

'Fanny Brice, you know? Barbra Streisand? *Funny Girl*? It makes me very happy you like the picture.' Then touching the glass with her fingers too. 'Come on, I'll show you the other one.'

Upstairs, Molly's bedroom, the quiet intimacy of the deeply personal – underwear on a seat, bedside books, perfume, a hairbrush – Esmé gazed on the far wall and saw the Bronzino. The look of love, faces of passion caught in the moment, and at once she felt incredibly moved. This was how love was supposed to look. How lovers looked.

Esmé heard the tale as far as Molly could take it. A little boy drew them one long ago summer, Molly's school friend called B, a boy who had loved colours. A wonderful day in London, *Funny Girl*, her father saving the pictures and how they had saved Molly so many years later – not so long ago in fact.

Time together passed gently in Molly and Esmé's newly-found world in Greenwich, the home of time – the park, the river, endless days and carefree nights. No work, no success yet but they both lived in hope and expectation of the next audition. And as time drew on, so B's drawings continued to lure Esmé in – teasing and tempting, revealing and veiling. The Velázquez was amazing, uncanny, but the Bronzino was the insistent, burning image in her mind. Often, she would find herself drawn to it like a moth to a flame. Some nights spent with Molly, sharing, caring, she would awake in their bed as if somehow roused by its intensity.

One night, tiptoeing naked from her room, she crept silently into Molly's. She had been dreaming, erotic, turbulent dreams, the tit being held. As Molly slept she gazed upon the drawing caressing her own breasts and within a minute brought herself to a deep and unashamed orgasm, her moans of passion somehow not waking her friend.

Ten hours later, Esmé stood on the stage of a London theatre auditioning for a new production and ignited by the sensuality of the Bronzino and her sexual oblivion in Molly's bedroom, she recited Shakespeare's poem "Venus and Adonis" in a way which transported her to loftier heights of acting than she had ever known. Esmé felt she could do anything, be anyone, reveal any emotion, touch any heart, laugh, cry and love at her own will and timing. From her core she was able to tap into the lust Venus was feeling in the poem having felt the same such passion herself during the night. Facing the director and producer sitting somewhere out there in the dark from the stage, it was as if overnight her theatrical range had been magnified beyond recognition, revealing a truth within her she had never believed possible.

Still probing the erotic girl on her rock, Esmé was roused by doorbell chimes, the sound echoing around the house as memories echoed around her head. That audition, her first major part, the great success and acclaim it had unleashed followed over the next decade by bigger, better, then leading roles – television, films, huge international fame, and, catching its gleam in the corner of her eye, that Oscar.

Now they were at the door. Molly, and as she understood it from the breathless telephone call yesterday, the man who as a little boy had conjured the Bronzino. The person who had lit the fire in her body that night unlocking the vast well of dormant talent lying so far down inside her all the time. Esmé paused with her hand on the door handle nervously waiting for her inner-director's call, then slowly turned it.

Action.

The two actresses embraced each other on sight then peeling away Molly revealed her living phantom. Blue suit, red and white striped shirt, black shoes, Esmé took

B's outstretched hand, touchingly covering her clasp with her other hand. Despite the performer's renowned control and assuredness, she had been all fingers and thumbs since the phone call. Molly had found him (or rather he had found her), it was fantastic, and rather formally and shakily all she could say was, 'It's an enormous pleasure to meet you.'

Molly was fully aware of the effect B's drawing had had on her friend's life. On Esmé's triumphant return to Greenwich from that career-making audition, they had talked long and late into the night about its impact as an erotic catalyst. Over the years, on other telephone calls, on meeting up if Esmé's hectic schedule could manage it, or for one epic week at home together in Greenwich when the famous film star's love life had turned very publicly sour and she needed a safe retreat, the pair had often discussed how much fame had been triggered by the boy's art.

Esmé's work was non-stop – Hollywood, New York, back to Europe, the Far East – so it had been at least two years since she had seen the Bronzino in person. Yet its power seemed always to be with her, in her heart, to be recalled at will. If a part demanded it or her astonishing ability to meet any acting challenge waned a little, she would often summon the picture's spirit from within and her performance would elevate and astound as the world had come to expect.

'Well, here he is, in the flesh!' Molly giggled at her planned reference to those carnal pleasures of the Bronzino. Esmé knew her playful friend and gave her a wince as she continued to grasp B's hand.

Hardly through the door, B was agape. He was used to big stars and important faces, he had seen many up close, often when they were frightened and weak, so fame usually had little effect on him. But the sudden appearance of such a celebrated face, out of the blue, no hint from his mysterious Molly, had quite thrown him.

He stammered for the right thing to say. 'Er, well, this, I don't know, she never said... er... thanks, delighted to meet you too.'

'Mystery woman meet mystery man!' Molly announced. 'Now let's have some fun!'

B feigned exasperation. 'I have simply no idea what she's talking about. She's an idiot. Nothing can be done for her.'

'I know!' agreed Esmé, grinning. 'Totally beyond help... and that's why I love her.'

B grinned back but his curiosity was mounting.

'Look, OK, so I'm impressed. Famous movie star, very nice house and you are pleased to see me, but can someone tell me what I'm doing here?'

Esmé laughed and pulled B into the main room of her London muse home. Colours hit him immediately and he liked what he saw. Balance, wild shapes from the abstracts, the black and chrome of the movie camera. His eyes darted around and locked onto the golden Oscar.

Molly followed his gaze. 'Now that's impressive!' she declared.

Slowly, B pulled at his chin as if mock-contemplating the question. 'Well, maybe, but it's not the first one I've seen.' He play-yawned. 'One of my former employers you know. Actually, she's won two... sorry to disap...'

Now it was Esmé's turn to pretend and she put her hands to her hips in a fake display of displeasure. 'All right, all right! I know I really should do better!'

'Absolutely!' Molly laughed. 'Now pour us a drink! What have you got?'

'Champagne! What else?'

When three crystal glasses were poured, Esmé raised hers towards her two guests and spoke, something she had been rehearsing all day but had not perfected yet. This was an important and deeply personal moment for her so she hoped her experience would shine through.

'A toast. First, to my agent! He's swung a good deal today and I now have to leave for New York tomorrow so I'm glad to have caught you before I go. I wouldn't have missed this for the world but Christmas in Manhattan does sounds good to me. Second, to Molly! To repeat, I do love her and how wonderful it is to see her again. Funny Fanny! She is and always will be my very best friend. How long has it been? Months? Too long! Too, too long...'

Then Esmé's voice deepened. 'But third, and best of all, a toast to someone I have long longed to meet... never thought I would. How could I? And now here you are. Yes, in the flesh...' A pause. 'You have two women here, sir, two thespians no less, who owe you so much. Molly has already told you her story. Well, she's brought you here so I can tell you mine. I hope you will listen. I hope you will like it. All I can say is that without your pictures, those amazing drawings you created when you were a boy, and especially one of them, I wouldn't have found what it was within me. I'm sure of it. I don't think of you as my creator, no, not that. But certainly my key. Yes, the key to my door and one I will always be eternally grateful I opened. So, a toast to your artistry and for finally, finally, coming alive. To all three of us, but especially to you. B!'

Then glasses were clinked and delicious champagne drunk, and amidst more laughter and embarrassed faces more was poured and as they sat together in the room with the golden Oscar, Esmé told her story – Venus, love, desire, metamorphosis.

Again, B wondered if his odyssey of revelation would ever stop. Listening to this modern icon, hitherto a remote yet magnetic figure seen from a cinema seat, he was amazed at his pivotal part in her history – her talent finding its flower from his. What he had drawn, had drawn from her, launched her ascendancy from the ranks of the ordinary to the stars. His Bronzino capturing a sublime moment and in doing so defining something almost indefinable, sparking a fusion in her years later that still burned today.

B sat deep in an armchair while Molly and Esmé held hands on the sofa – bright lime green glowing from the abstract behind them. Cleary these two had a powerful friendship, one wrapped up with his boyhood pictures – two Venuses – but even while he was trying to absorb what Esmé was telling him, there was a piece of his consciousness able to stand apart, calculating what he thought of Molly being so close to someone else.

A few days ago he would have considered having any right to a morsel of Molly's life absurd – a huge, atavistic imposition. He had his life and she had hers. In trying to sort his future out, B's plans had involved the concept of Molly's past and present but it didn't include her in actuality, despite the then unsolved mystery of her new name. He understood this even when leaving his *Molly at the Window in a Red Dress* for her at the theatre. But now everything had changed. Staying over in Hull, just like their childhood season of friendship, this short, new time had been spent almost exclusively together. Yes, Molly had performed on stage to packed audiences, her days still busy with other people, but essentially their focus was only on each other.

Two not three.

Molly had kept Esmé a secret and now he knew why. She was an important chapter in her story and seeing them so intimate, fingers entwined, suddenly he felt a sharp twinge of envy. It pinched hard and painfully. But then Esmé stopped talking, Molly pulled away quietly, rose from the sofa and kneeling before him took his hand in hers – such expressive, cathartic hands – and his stab of jealousy evaporated.

'You see? You see?' she said softly. 'My father, Harry, then me, then Esmé… all of us touched and changed by what you drew. I can't, we can't describe it, we can't give it a name. I don't know the words but it's real enough. It's in you. It was then and I'm certain it is still.'

Molly continued. 'Your new picture of me at the window is, I don't know, proof. I'm sorry but that's the best word I can think of. You must feel this, you must know now, surely? That's why I brought you here.' She had given him the kaleidoscope. 'I think you have something precious. I think you have to take care of it and use it.'

B had always been a level-headed man, calm under pressure, qualities that had earned respect in the army and later enabling him to snuff out danger and threat for his principals. He could speak and act with total clarity – cool, prepared, detached. Yet since the carnage in Paris he had lived on a high wire of emotion and, exposed there, his skills for maintaining an equilibrium had quite deserted him. B found no voice to answer Molly's analysis. All he could do was shake his head, demonstrating he recognised what she was saying but laying bare his fear at the implications of it.

A deep, inner calling he was powerless to deny had claimed his future. Beauty and colour, the two pillars of his life to come. A lifetime in the building, ultimately revealed to him in London. He was joyous about their discovery. He felt challenged, liberated and elated. But the idea that he possessed any particular power over beauty and colour hadn't crossed his mind. Yes, he could create, he wasn't blind, he always felt he captured the essence of his subject – Molly, a landscape, a sky, whatever he pointed his pencil at. And it was easy, the energy, the ideas, simply flowing from his hand. Yet he felt it purely as an inner satisfaction. So far, he thought of himself as a mere beginner. Molly kept telling him he had a power and he had dismissed her claim as mostly sentiment – such a generous nature – but now there was more evidence. "There's someone you have to see…" Esmé, the abstract lime, the golden statuette.

Living his life through others – his men, his principals – B himself had never been the central factor. Now he felt a fear of being his own principal.

'Will you do something for me?' asked Esmé leaning forward in her chair. 'Please...'

She hesitated. 'Would you draw me?'

Juicy cerise, velvet vermillion, tempting colours around the room, there was a momentary silence before B cracked a small grin. So many years sensing the next threat, he knew a set-up when he saw one and he looked squarely at the two conspirators.

'I've walked straight into this, haven't I? Lamb to the slaughter!'

The plotters looked knowingly at each other.

'All mapped out. Actresses? Never trust them!'

'The thing is,' said Molly, 'Esmé is actually a bit of an art buff. That sort of started with your drawings too. She got into it and now, well, let's say she knows people and what she's talking about. And she can afford it. These here on the walls... pretty expensive stuff, even though I think they are bloody awful...'

'Hey!' cried her friend.

'... so, I thought if she told you, Mr Wood, then you would have to believe it, wouldn't you!'

'I would, would I?' B laughed.

But Molly was serious for a change. 'Yes. You would.'

June 2007

Why

Part of it came, finally, on B's third New England day. His second had been spent almost entirely alone either drawing or pottering about the house and grounds.

That first dinner had lived up to all the cook's boasting. Three beautifully cooked courses, all eaten exclusively to the sound of his host's wild and random outpourings. Sketches of his life in dancing, rolling sentences. Sometimes slow waltzes – 1, 2, 3… 1, 2, 3 – other times fast and furious, jives, swinging high and low. B wondered if the loquaciousness was a kind of catharsis after spending so much time alone apparently cooped up in this house. Hudson, it seemed, was a regular figure in his life although even she had not shown up since letting him in with her name on her lips.

Brandies after the feast and suddenly the throaty voice

stopped mid-sentence and just took off with its owner somewhere deep into the house leaving silence in an instant. Molly should be here, not me, B thought. How they would have made out. The old artist and the actress, both garrulous and unpredictable.

Alone and abandoned, eventually B mooched back to his room leaving the dishes to Hudson or whoever did the housework and absolutely none the wiser as to why he was here. He had hoped rather than expected the morning to give him answers but he was to be disappointed. No old man at breakfast, the kitchen all miraculously spick and span again, and no sign of him during the day either except for the tell-tale sign of a newly painted egg-shell blue coloured screen and a wet brush in the glass panorama room when B popped up to sneak a peek.

Around five in the afternoon, while sketching in one of the sitting rooms downstairs, B caught a quick 'Hi!' from the voice as it passed the doorway but before he could fully react the phantom was gone. At eight he got his own dinner, a far less culinary affair than the previous night, and at ten shuffled off to bed frustrated and confused for another two hours of drawing before falling asleep with a red pencil in his hand.

But waking with a start at six the next morning, there was the old man fixing him from a black wicker chair at the end of his bed. Faded green rain jacket, light and dark blue check shirt below an off-white sweater, a look of deep earnestness stretched across the grizzled face. At first B didn't know where he was. Back with his Principal, nobody would have got within shooting distance of him sleeping.

Always alert, his thoughts only for others, sharp and fast, the protector never really switched off. Now, jolted from sleep by some still lingering sixth sense, he bolted upright but was quelled instantly by a raised arm.

'OK, red man... OK, OK, don't fret yourself now... still, be still, all's quiet in the house.'

There was a very long pause before the voice took up again, deeper than normal but still punching and rolling.

'What you did for Esmé, the look you gave her... everything she is, her pretty mouth, all that glitters, more, much more, and then some. You can do that for me? See me, that way? Catch a fallen star... put it in your pocket. Can you do that? Can you do that... for me?'

21 May 2007 and the day after

The phone, the phone ringing…

Ringing, ringing…

Loud, insistent, taunting, echoing within the house and out through its black front door.

Key in the lock, breathless, fire in his eye, reds, oranges and yellows in the huge billowing flames. Engulfing, overwhelming, a kaleidoscope of destructive colour. Beauty even in calamity. Twisting, twisting, desperate, violently twisting his wrist back and forth to get inside.

The phone. Who? Molly? He has to speak to her, she must be told. How he would like to be holding her hand right now. Knowing and receptive, anticipating his words and thoughts.

Out of the blue house early in the Monday morning, a throwback to his boyhood and a calling still strong.

A waking urgency to say hello to the river. His Thames, Nelson's Thames. Still listening. Molly away filming for a TV ad, some supermarket chain, so he's on his own until she comes back at the weekend. But his weeks are getting busier and busier.

Experimenting, so many colours, such a wide variety of materials. New and exciting media – chalk, pastels, crayons, watercolours, acrylics and recently oils. So much to learn, unlock and express. The deep well inside him and he's only dipping his toe, his imagination, into the gleaming surface. Day by day, week by week, how in control he feels with every line and colour.

Another night half-awake, ideas and possibilities jabbing the patina of sleep. Yet not one scintilla of fatigue. A dynamo on a constant loop, constantly refreshing and recharging himself, running on the perpetual motion of colour and beauty.

Early in the May morning light, down Park Row and across the pedestrian crossing where he once said goodbye to Molly, further down, past the entrance to his old alley, past the Trafalgar building and onto the river walkway. Down the steps there and onto his old shoreline – pebbles, driftwood and even some sand. The brown water just below him – ripples. Then on up Nelson's funeral steps, Molly the River Queen's steps, continuing along the walkway bound for *Cutty Sark*. A fresh new day, familiar noises from the river.

Cutty Sark, the witch, the masthead and the bare white breast. The tit being held. Bronzino. Although life is moving on. Still those tantalising few yards away from the open water she must crave, the old tea clipper is being completely renovated – a huge project making the vessel shipshape for the digital age. New funds for a new life to satisfy all those tourists on the riverbank. A blue wooden fence encircling the maritime icon marking out the restoration site.

But suddenly the air is different.

Emerging from the river walkway as it opens out onto the wide, sprawling pedestrian piazza containing the ship, the scene is almost too bizarre for B to take in. He has seen fires before – bombed houses ablaze in Belfast, a little boy with the severed hand, burning death on the Falklands, a firebomb thrown at a principal in Rome and on 9/11, in New York with his Principal for meetings at the United Nations, standing in sickening awe watching the twin towers burn and fall – so many fires. Yet nothing to match the visceral, physical immediacy and raw, deafening whip-cracking enormity of the inferno ripping through *Cutty Sark*'s wood and metal in front of him now. Searing, burning colours, massive red, orange, yellow and black flames erupting into the sky.

Panic, confusion, rage, incredulity, helplessness all coursing through his brain at the mad spectacle. Holding his head, running around shouting like a real-life Munch scream, long-gone the cool protector and measured saviour. A fiery red fire engine arriving and men jumping out of it, yellow hard hats, black uniforms, leaping into action. Minutes passing and as the inferno leaps higher and higher a rough hand grabs B's shoulder and a gruff voice shouts at him to calm down. Spinning around to be confronted by the stern, ruddy face of a policeman, strong and masterful, the control B used to have. The piazza has to be cleared, he has to come away, unsafe, black fire debris raining down. Quick, quick, and he follows the officer like a dutiful dog down past the pub on the corner into a back street where some police vans are parked. Another fire engine arrives, more red, lipstick red moving towards the chaos.

Gradually, the fire is brought under control and B is interrogated by various officers. Why was he there? What, who did he see? Name, address, occupation (he says "artist" without even realising it). He was, he is, a local, living just up the road. The police will need to speak to him again. He is a witness yet again. The boy and his mother dead.

By late morning *Cutty Sark* is a smouldering, smoking wreck. B wonders how she can survive but the initial word is it may not be the total disaster it looks. The ship's masts and most of its bulk were removed earlier in the restoration so escaping the fire. The bare breast is safe. Why didn't B realise this before? He has seen the renovation going on a number of times over the past months while living at Molly's. Amazing what shock can do. A piece of B's boyhood, his happiest time as a child, going up in flames and his nerves falling to pieces.

Later, walking back to Molly's blue house, this time down the main Greenwich road with its thundering traffic crossing the unseen Meridian Line, his thoughts becoming clearer, colours kicking in. No more panic and his inner dynamo sparking into life again. All the spectacular tones of the fire captured in his head, already wanting to express them on paper through pencils and brushes. Excitement mounting, he has to get back, get back and start. The well erupting. Running up Park Row towards home. The pictures forming. The hot kaleidoscope of colours and he's at the black door, desperately fumbling for the key.

Then he hears it... the phone, the phone ringing.

Eventually, the latch turns, the door springs open and bursting down the hallway, B reaches his mobile left on a side table. Molly will be as shocked as he is but she has to know. He should be the one to tell her before she hears it on the news. Breathless.

'Molly! Molly! Listen, you'll never...'

But it isn't her.

Instead, he hears a deep, sedate, neutral voice at the end of the line and after ten seconds or so working things out B answers that yes it is he. The voice, clear and controlled, tells him it's a sergeant from Cumbria Constabulary at Cockermouth Police Station, the old brownish-black building back up Main Street from the white stone Mayo. He is sorry to call, very sorry indeed, but they have been trying to trace him and he was given this number to try.

'I'm saddened to have to inform you that your mother died in a house-fire in the early hours of this morning...'

A sympathetic yet professional tone, tender but raw. B hears soft words of condolence – heartfelt, loss, understand, at this time – but the sounds hardly penetrate his disbelief.

Red lipstick and nail varnish, the colour of her toes when B last saw her. *Nothing for you here boy...* black dress in the black car, her naked outline on the chair, the white towel around her head. Beautiful, she was beautiful.

Passing into the front room, B's *Rokeby Venus* staring out in front of him, hearing the old words, *Who do you think you are, bloody Picasso?* His fingers touching Molly's body just like Esmé had done the first time she saw it, touching the past where his mother will live from now on, always there in the back recesses of his mind. Nothing for him now but the colours, shapes, patterns and lines of her.

The phone again… the phone ringing, still holding it in his hands, the loud shock making him start in the afternoon stillness of the house.

'Hello. It's me!' greets Molly's cheerful, cheeky voice, happy and carefree in her day without the choking smoke of fire or the bitter-sweet sadness, or release, of death.

Telling her about the two blazes. One consuming their childhood maritime friend, the other snuffing out his mother's bitter indifference and cold rejection. Grey-black Cockermouth plumes of smoke visible a few miles away from the beautiful hills he roamed with a surrogate who loved him as his own flesh and blood never could.

'I'm so sorry, B. All your life…'

Alone in the room where she gave him his kaleidoscope. His eyes meeting another picture on the wall – a new one, Molly in red.

'I'm standing at your window. The sun's shining in and I'm looking out towards the park. This is your special place. Funny without you here, Funny Fanny.'

'Do you want me to come back? Feel awful you being there on your own.'

'No, it's OK. Really. I've told the police I'll go straight up to Cockermouth early in the morning anyway. I'll call you.'

The sergeant had given it to him straight. The body, arrangements to be made and the need to take some decisions about the state of the building. It may have to be demolished. All in all it would be helpful being on the spot.

B sat on the windowsill, Boilly's background boy taking centre stage in the scene, usurping Molly's favourite place. The man stepping into the light.

'I need to capture this, today, what's happened. It's all going around my head... the fires. If I don't put it down on paper I think I'll explode.'

'I know.'

'It's ridiculous, isn't it? *Cutty Sark*'s in ruins, my mum's dead and all I can see are the colours.' Crying silently now, salty tears teasing his lips. 'Is this how you're supposed to feel?'

Molly, switching her mobile phone to her other ear, gesturing to a man wanting to talk, telling him to wait. 'I think it's exactly how you are meant to feel. That's how you see everything now. Nothing is more normal than to want to paint it or draw it.'

A day of crazy abnormality until the paper is before him and his post-Paris, post-Villers-sur-Mer new-world normality can make sense of it all. Finding answers, meaning and, especially today, solace, in the colours and shapes he produces.

Out of a chaotic, watery, Turneresque abyss rises a colossus of flame. Huge orange tentacles, licking red fingers, snapping jaws of fire. And there, emerging high, high above, out of the whole of it, coagulating and massing up into the dark sky, is the beautiful face of his mother. Hot and lovely, fierce and fiery, cold and cruel.

Next day, miles and miles, hours and hours north...

'Excuse me!' said a woman tapping B on the arm. 'Are you the son?'

Two officers had walked B round to his old house from the police station – figures in deep blue contrasting with his white raincoat. Whatever he felt about his mother, whatever form of shock had driven him to create such a penetrating picture of her, he could not wear a mark of mourning.

For some fifteen minutes, B had been standing the short distance he was allowed from the taped-off house. He couldn't go inside for safety reasons and various men were working on the structure at the front. But he didn't want to enter anyway. As the damp, clogging smell of the place hung in the air, B had come only to seek a final resting place for his anger.

He turned taking in the woman's shape. 'Er, yes, I suppose I am.' Then realised what he had said. 'Sorry, yes, I am.'

The woman shifted her handbag to her other hand, B judging it a sort of misty rose and her coat a dull magenta, and resumed tapping on his white arm.

'Your mother was a saint, a real saint. Do anything for anyone. Ask anyone round here. We are going to miss her so much, you know. Only saw her for a chat the day before. Terrible, terrible thing.'

B felt the hand grip his sleeve. There was a shake in the hold, so unlike Molly's certainty.

'She thought the world of you, you know. Talked about you all the time. Couldn't have a better son, she said. She loved getting your letters and cards and was always telling us what you were getting up to.'

The woman must be mad. Letters? Cards?

'Pity you could never visit her...' , a rebuke, a definite rebuke in her voice, 'but she understood, she did, really she did. No need to blame yourself. Artists! Well, you must be busy. Mind you, she kept that quiet for a long time. Still, you're here now, I suppose.'

Crazy, crazy. All at once the sight of the woman was sickening, her hold on him nauseating – a Hogarth hag, a fat Rubens lady, something ugly deep down deep in a Rothko – and suddenly he wanted the river.

B snapped his arm away and without speaking walked off, ignoring the police officers calling out if he was OK. No doubt he had been overcome by grief.

At the top by Main Street, B turned left passing a bunch of fell-walkers with their backpacks and high spirits. Up ahead of him stood the white stone Mayo, but paying the old viceroy no heed, he crossed the road navigating as if by remote control. Instinctively, he took a right into a narrow side street (a familiar scene, the bottle of blood all over the poxy blue car with the poxy white stripes) and continued along past some little houses, then a new development on his right until he walked onto the bridge. The old handrails, the brewery, the rushing of the water, the colours flowing and disappearing under his feet. The Cocker.

B put his hands on the rail and peered over into the river to see them again – the blues, greens, whites and silvers – and gradually, in this well-remembered place, Miss Hattiemore's little old haven just ahead of him, he became calmer seeking to understand what the woman had said.

Lies, crap, it had to be. He knew his mother. Yes, he knew her right enough. If she was a saint then the bastards who shot his Principal's little boy were heroes. Yet even as he batted this back to himself, the thought struck him. As he knew all too well from long experience, for some those killers in Paris were indeed heroes – martyrs, proud warriors for their cause. Over the years he had met many intelligent, rational-thinking people, important people with real power and sway, who could defend even the bloodiest of acts as part of a peace process. However perverse it seemed, B wondered if, in a similar way, this woman could have a completely different perspective. Perhaps she knew a side of his mum he had never seen or contemplated. The light side of her moon.

Pondering the Cocker's colours more closely, the evocative sounds of the running water – cold, fresh from the hills – minute by minute, slowly, B began to entertain a possibility. Had his mum been able to feel something for someone after all? Was it conceivable? Could he even contemplate the word "care" or, for heaven's sake, "love"? If such a remote concept was indeed possible then no doubt it would have been her kind of care, her kind of love, played out on her terms. Giving little and taking everything.

Had she always had the capacity to care or love? The question had simply never crossed his mind before. Her empty, spiteful heart was always such a fixed star in his life.

Certainly, there had never been anything for him. No memory of a single act of maternal tenderness. For his dad? All he remembered were the wars and rows in the night, the blows and sobs in the kitchen. Deep blue on the dark side of her moon. Later there had been the sex, yes, lots of it. An endless trail of men through that dusty house but none of them staying for more than a couple of days. Their bodies, their money and interest soon used up. Love in transit.

She thought the world of you...

This he dismissed totally, just the sort of ruse to get some sympathy, winkle her way in somewhere and find an angle.

A saint, a real saint!

A mother. He would have liked a real mother.

Yet there had been enough miracles over the last few months, so why not another one. Perhaps, just perhaps, a callous heart had at last found the will to shower a little affection, a tiny scrap of humanity on the fat lady and her little Cockermouth circle of friends.

But an artist? How would his mum have known anything about that? For a moment it was a mystery, the Cocker's colours running below his feet without illumination. Then, of course, it was simple. B realised just how quickly things had happened. Even she must have read the papers. His little story wasn't just his any more.

The phone… the phone ringing… ringing, against the rush of the water.

'Hello?'

'Hi, B! Sorry to disturb. Where are you?'

Esmé.

'Er, hi!'

B walked back to the edge of the bridge trying to cancel out the river's background noise.

'Hi, Lake District. You?'

Her sensuous voice, her imposing presence and he visualised the red room at the top of her house deep in the countryside. A cavalcade of reds. Walls, carpets, chairs, and the picture, his picture, now hanging there.

'Switzerland… filming. Not going very well I'm afraid.' Hollywood in the white Alps.

'Listen, B. I've spoken to Molly. She called me last night. I'm so sorry about your mum.' A few seconds of running water down the phone line. 'You never told me everything, not all of it, but I know how difficult this must be for you. Not just the fire but, well, you know…'

B felt her fumbling, hunting for words. Up in the red roof-room at her lovely house in Kent, he had told her some of it all while she sat for him in her low-slung, revealing red dress. He sought to put her at ease.

'It's OK. Esmé, it's OK. A few skeletons in my cupboard but I can deal with them.' Perhaps it was because she was so close to Molly that he felt so comfortable with her. He began to retrace his steps.

'Where I'm standing now, over the river, the Cocker, on a bridge, is where I used to come when I felt mad at things as a boy. Mad as hell. You know, I told you a bit about that. Living here, mad at her most of the time. My mum. And starting to draw again after what happened back then, yes, I have felt angry... angry like that all over again. They... she... all messed up and I lost so much time, so much time. That's been the hardest thing, the wasted years. Things could have been so much different. I could have been so different.'

Back in the middle of the bridge, B now faced upstream. Ahead lay the brewery buildings where his mum worked until she got bored one day and just walked out. He wondered how long his £5,000 had lasted.

'But somehow, I don't know, with her gone now, the fire, this new anger has sort of left me. All burnt away, gone with her. What's done is done and I'm not going to let her mess up the future too. There are too many things to do now, too many pictures.'

'That's good, B, that's good.'

B turned and saw a woman with a boy appear on the river garden of Miss Hattiemore's old house – new residents in his former haven. They were pointing over where the Cocker joined the Derwent. Smiles and happiness, light blue and vivid pink sweaters, the boy no more than eleven or twelve, the woman a reminder of his other mother still clinging on to life.

'Listen, B...' Esmé continued, 'there's another reason I'm calling. Listen now, it's important.' He regained his concentration on her.

'I can't explain too much but you are going to get a phone call in a while. Not sure when. It might be a bit strange, a little far-fetched, but it'll be genuine. Truthfully. I was amazed too. Thought it might be a joke. But it's not.'

Esmé could only give the briefest of outlines, just a snatched call from America and difficult to take in. She apologised for giving his mobile number out but the circumstances were strange.

'This is a very big deal, B, an incredible honour really. You've got to let me know when you get the call. Fascinating!'

After a while they said goodbye and B pocketed his phone. He had no idea what to think but obviously his story had reached a world way beyond his mum.

His story...

Esmé jetting off to Manhattan, B and Molly deciding to spend a short, quiet Christmas together in Greenwich. Their old haunts shared, orphans of their pasts, on common ground, both standing on the Meridian Line looking out on a grey but festive London. Christmas right down to the end of the Earth where the penguins live.

That first week in January, nervous and a little intimidated, B fulfilling his promise. Esmé sitting for him, a week's worth of intensive work in the Kent countryside and one special portrait of her drawn in the top-floor room decorated in red, her special colour too. Tears when the picture is revealed. So many roles, so many characters, but B capturing her simple essence, a quantum particle within her, indivisible, whole, which no one had ever seen before. Not Molly, not her finest director, nor the luckiest of chance paparazzi.

B and Molly beginning a new life in her blue house by the park. Together but not together, mutually respected and revered but never recognising the growing truth between them. Colours, paper, pencils and paints dominating his days and weeks. Molly, his frequent muse. Experimenting, discovering, pushing yesterday's boundaries.

February. Esmé up for a BAFTA, a British Oscar, for her latest film and sailing down the red carpet in that revealing red dress, a tribute to B's special portrait of her. Winning, of course, and in front of a TV audience of millions dedicating the award to a man who gave her the key. An achingly personal acceptance speech choking back high emotion.

'... as artists we all strive to achieve perfection. Inevitably we fail. We are impostors, never attaining the precious thing we seek...'

But B had. Bronzino. And he still was. Red room.

An inevitable media mystery ensuing. The hunt becoming a worldwide chase with Esmé picking up an Oscar later the same month and dedicating that to the boy-man artist too. Finally, reluctantly, B allowing one journalist to tell a little of his story, a Sunday newspaper profile, his mum cracking a sneer as she read the words over breakfast. And a few days later, 3,000 miles away in a house in New England, an old American man of colours looking fathomlessly deep into the photograph of Esmé's portrait in a magazine realising what he must do.

The phone... the phone ringing, ringing over the flowing blues, greens, whites and silvers of the River Cocker.

June 2007

Rothko

'I knew him, at a distance… the same bars, places, the same faces. He was different, to me anyhow… gifted, no doubt at all. Saw things, talent, saw his work whenever I could… he went deep, sometimes as deep as you can go, though reckon I went there too.'

They were talking Rothko and his New York. The old man was younger but their styles not too dissimilar in the early days. Connections, New York, and B remembered coming out of the Schindler movie downtown. The little girl in red fleeing the Nazis, the yellow taxi, lines meeting other lines. Esmé in red, the red man, the why he was here.

'I saw the Seagram murals at the Tate in London a while ago. Difficult to explain, they sort of sucked me in somehow and took me anywhere I wanted to go. How do you know when you have the power to do that?'

But B was pressing too hard, too fast. The old man was still in his slow lane, only ready to go at his own pace.

'Cruising down the same roads, those lil' ol' ways... took a piece of this and little bit of that, built my own heavens, formed my own stars.'

Stars, observatory. Boilly, Molly in red. B, the red man.

'Used to feel in my gut what was right, didn't think twice it was all right... saw something, remembered something, perceived something and I'd do it. Could'a been a girl's face, or the traffic in the street, or Eskimos... had patience when I needed it, could take it easy, nothin' rushin'. Other times the thing would burn red-hot inside and I had to run fast, do it fast, get it done, no tomorrow... you know that feelin', doncha, red man, you know that, doncha, speakin' as a red man?'

Lazing together in the summer sun, sitting in old easy chairs on the wooden terrace overlooking the fields (Hudson had given them both a drink an hour ago), and B thought he was making a glimmer of progress. A tiny foothold on the old man's craggy rock face.

July 2008

The track from Haystacks gently winding down through Warnscale, its beck gushing in the gulley, the sister-waters Buttermere and Crummock clear and in total view. The pathway spinning a turn to the left then veering right and within the zigzag thus created lies a grassy hump, a green oasis of calm for B in his younger Lakeland days. Miss Hattiemore so often with him in this lonely, echoing geological bowl beneath familiar, craggy hills, both contemplating the world.

Today the view was the same as ever. Buttermere, green and luxuriant, then twelve o'clock high at its furthest tip, Turner's "Cromackwater" before it meandered out northwards towards Lorton Vale. But Miss Hattiemore, his faithful walking companion and de facto mother, was not with him on this warm July Thursday. Alas, those beautiful green eyes would never gaze upon this wonderful view again.

Fire hadn't brought B back to the Lakes this time but a sad and respectful telephone call from the home near Carlisle. A hot pain of shock scorched inside him after he answered his mobile at breakfast on the veranda of an elegant waterside house beside Italy's Lake Garda.

Malcesine. The little town's intoxicating colours. Red sail-borders already out on the morning waves, prism sprinkles of sunlight on the early water, grassy shades of Dolomite hills all around, and B was having a few days of ease after a week with a friend of Esmé's in not far away Venice.

She wasn't his artistic pimp, never that, but the friend was close, a serious member of Europe's art establishment, and she persuaded B it would be a good idea to show off his talents. So he had discussed, dissected, debated and drawn with the illustrious friend, a doyen of the City of Water's world renowned *Biennale* art exhibition, and he and his colleagues had been highly impressed. B should come to Venice again. Doors were certainly being opened now, as indeed they had been to the Garda-side beauty-spot house gladly loaned out by another friend of Esmé's eager to do a famous film star a special favour.

Garda's glory froze as B heard the news. The bright crimson of a mountain paraglider sweeping down from his high eyrie on Monte Baldo overlooking Malcesine's picturesque castle faded to black as the sun disappeared behind some clouds at that instant – a sudden sympathetic eclipse. She wasn't very good when he saw her just before leaving for Italy, far more chesty than usual, but things had turned worse very suddenly and the frail, sunken and confused body couldn't fight it this last time. No adieu in a cacophony of flame for her, more a quick and quiet passing into one of the many peaceful valleys she had revealed to him. Now Miss Hattiemore was on a never-ending footpath, one he couldn't follow her on, not yet. How ironic to be told the news on another lake a thousand miles away.

B spent the whole day on the veranda – memories, her colours, her little garden beside the Cocker, the hilltops and lakes they had shared. A son's bitter grief and by nightfall a large collection of sketches seeking to come to terms with all she had meant to him. As stars twinkled on Garda's surface, a firework display boom-booming on the far side before the holiday port of Limone, white car lights peeping on the lakeside edges before disappearing into rock road tunnels, B's table was strewn with drawings of her. Vaulting a stile, walking with her favourite stick, jumping a brook, beside a mountaintop cairn, striking a pose on the Cocker bridge. Her face, the very traces of her, and naturally those penetrating green eyes. Eventually, with a heavy heart, he packed up his memories and images, went inside, toasted Miss Hattiemore with a large brandy and called Molly.

'I feel terrible... never there when these bad things happen.' Outer London playhouse, she was at a little party after the performance.

'Never mind, you don't do it on purpose.'

'How are you?'

'I loved her.'

'I know.'

'But, I'm not sure I realised just how much until today.'

'I understand.'

'My mum, my real mum.'

'Don't tell me, there's a pile of drawings, right?'

B smiled, his first shaft of cheer that day. 'Yes, a pile. Think I caught her in a few too. As she was.'

'Coming home?'

'Tomorrow, booked a flight.'

Then the artist and the actress made their arrangements. B would fly back to London, stay the night at Greenwich and go to the Lakes the following day to oversee the funeral. After another two days of a short run, Molly would join him at the hotel they used a few miles from Buttermere. And there, once more together, they pulled out a box of personal possessions Miss Hattiemore had left at the home. Tender and revealing, its contents proving a spyglass into her past and a surprise reunion with B's youth.

Inside lay a pack of photographs sealed with a gold ribbon and the prints were spread out on the wooden hotel floor like a storyboard. There was B on the hills, standing on High Snockrigg, posing atop Scafell Pike and smiling with his bike in Waterloo Street. There was one of them together on a summit somewhere (Great Gable, B thought) and B standing in the middle of his bridge, his arms holding the rails at the very spot where she had first spoken to him. Snapshots in time, moments from B's angry time, but as he could see now he wasn't always at odds with the world back then. Despite his belief that beauty had been destroyed, there was some light in his young darkness. She had showed him so many beautiful things.

He pulled out a "thank you" note from him to his mentor, a little piece of blue paper still folded crisp and tight. *To Miss Hattiemore, Thank you for the money you gave me at the weekend. You are very kind. B*, and he remembered with a smile the bottle of blood he spent part of that money on. There was a birthday card from her (fifteen, and the same number of "x" kisses, a rare sentimental lapse) and, to B's great surprise, a copy of his birth certificate. There it read in all its brief significance. His Christian name, proof of his mum and dad's eternal joke on him. "B" for bastard. Finally, at the bottom of the box, a brochure on how to join the Forces.

His Lakeland guide had told him to go away to the army and forget her, but as B could now see she had never forgotten him. Cut adrift in her Altzheimer's otherworld, she had never been in control of her mind enough to tell him this, but the tender trappings of her life in the box told him it was so.

The funeral was a very simple affair, just a few acquaintances from the home and a couple of very old friends from Cockermouth who remembered B. Some flowers, some loving words spoken, a few tiny grains of earth brought back from High Snockrigg placed on the coffin and Miss Hattiemore was physically gone forever. But her spirit was alive and well enough the next day as B sat on his little artist's chair placed within the green zigzag of the path down from Haystacks. He could feel her with him as he took in the view, the freshness of the summer's day and the panorama of Lakeland colours.

'Would you like a cup of coffee, Mr Wood, would you?'

B turned and laughed. 'Yes, indeed I would, Miss Wood. And would you be kind enough to pour me one if you would!'

Molly laughed too and knelt down on the grass opening the Thermos flask to sustain the artist's creative juices. When the brew was poured, she walked over and gave B the drink putting a hand on his shoulder.

'Any good? How's it going?'

B put a watercolour paintbrush aside, enveloped both his hands round the hot cup and leaned back into the chair to the feel of her.

'OK, I suppose. Getting there and I want to put a rainbow in if it works. Just like Mr T.'

'Turner?'

'J. M. W.!'

'He who must be obeyed.'

'Well, he was about the best you can get, in my humble opinion. You remember, the rainbow one at the Tate in London?'

Molly moved away and sat down on the grass sipping her own coffee. She had been building up to what she wanted to say and thought now was as good a time as any. The sadness of the last few days had stopped her but the serenity of the view, the sunshine and the twinkling lakes gave her the confidence she needed.

'What's wrong, B?'

B turned and looked at her. He shrugged.

'Well, it's a shock she's gone…'

'No, not that,' she interrupted, 'something else.'

A pause.

'What's wrong? What is it?'

B didn't move for a few seconds then dropped his eyes to the last mouthful of coffee. Taking a gulp, he swallowed and sought to answer as if he had been half-expecting the question. The two of them attuned to each other's ebbs and flows.

'I don't know, I don't, but you're right... something, something. A few things happened in Venice but it's been around for a while. Difficult to explain.'

'Try.'

B said nothing for a full minute, then, 'Not like the old man. I haven't stopped, haven't shut down. Quite the reverse. I still feel full up, raring to go. I just want more, to do more.'

'But?'

'But...' B stood up this time and walked a few paces towards the lakes, keeping his back to Molly. Another long minute passed.

'But I haven't done it yet, haven't got it, not there yet. Hard to say, to put into words.' He spread his arms as if to seek inspiration from somewhere. 'All I have done, all I have produced so far. I am proud, I recognise it, it's what all this has been about since I started. But something's missing and I'm trying to find it.'

Molly felt for him.

'I'm lucky, I think. It's not like that for me. I feel it, whatever it is, every time I go on. I'm there in the moment, the audience, the words, the atmosphere, every minute. I come off, feel happy, I am what I am and I'm thankful for it.'

B kept staring at the lakes. 'Yes, you are lucky and I know what you mean. I see it when I see you. I saw it the very first time in Hull. Born to be what you are. That's what makes you so, I don't know, "cherished" I suppose is one word for it.'

He turned and came back to kneel facing her.

'Esmé is the same but she's writ large. That's what makes her so great.'

Molly responded by leaning forward onto his knees. 'And you are the one who gave that to her!'

B smiled. 'Yes, there is that. Yes, I did.'

Their eyes met. 'So? So! As I keep saying. Whatever you think of yourself, you have this power and everything you do exudes it. That's what everyone says the moment they look. The reaction you've already got is fantastic. People tell me all the time. Nothing you do is ordinary. How can you believe otherwise?'

'I don't. That's not what I'm saying. I'm glad people think what I do is good...'

'Good? Christ, B, you know it's more than that.'

'OK. OK. I know what they mean. I get it. All that for the old man? An incredible reaction really. I couldn't take it all in. Yes, I do know. But for me, it isn't enough.'

'Enough?'

'Yes. Look, you go on stage and it's enough. Your performance is complete for you and it's enough. It sustains you, you express yourself and tell your story. How I envy you that. I know all considered it's not been a long time, despite everything I've only just started really, but for me, it's not enough, not yet.'

Molly took up B's hand the way she always did and together they fell silent. A few birds singing, the rush of the water in the beck and the unique noises of the hills. B was right, it hadn't been a long time and together they sat and contemplated how much had happened...

Esmé's BAFTA and Oscar successes, dedicating both awards to her "key", worldwide public praise for the man who had ignited her talent. His story being told and from the ashes of fires, the famous old man asking to be found again. New England, a month with the master, both teaching the other. Techniques and wisdom from the older red man, stunning natural ability from the younger one from old England.

A set of wondrous drawings, a media frenzy when displayed at a rapidly put together show in New York. The world agog. The famous former master, the celebrity recluse surfacing again after so many years, the Esmé man bringing him back to life. Astonishing, as were the reviews for the drawings. A major new talent had arrived through the resurrection of an old one.

Another show in Chicago a few months later, a selection of pieces including Molly at the window, Esmé, also in red in her white house, and some other famous faces B had captured when they had asked and he agreed. Several movie stars, one a double Oscar-winner who had once worn red on a red carpet, some sports heroes, a prestigious British man of letters and a hot-tip to be the future President of the United States. A portrait too of his old Principal, a widower and a still-mourning father now out of the international fast lane who contacted B one day to say how happy he was for his former protector. Two days in Paris to draw, talk about what happened and remember a loving wife and a sweet little boy.

Not all portraits though. Scenes of the Lakes, the Thames, Niagara Falls and other treasured places. An esoteric amalgam of a show but totally unforgettable for those who saw it. Each drawing or painting telling the viewer something of themselves. Each speaking to them all and each making all of them think more deeply about their lives, the world they lived in and what the future could hold. Different languages and nationalities, different religions and beliefs making little difference. Each viewer served from their own private well and the deep water that washed them flowed with colour and was beautiful to them. Old and young, happy and sad, all came and left changed and different in so many different ways.

Days and days, weeks and months passing and B's creative whirlwind blew with such force until Venice, Malcesine, Lake Garda, the call on the veranda, the death of his true mother and his return to the Lakes.

And what lay in store now? The pace was relentless. A day in the hills, then back to London to plan a repeat of the Chicago show with new additions at a highly influential gallery.

'Come on, enough! J. M. W. can wait. The day's too good. Let's eat in Buttermere, down at the Fish. Would you like that?'

'Yes, Miss Wood, I would!' and they both laughed, pulling each other up from the grass.

Familiar fells looked down as they ate at a wooden table outside Buttermere's white-walled Fish Inn. Robinson, Hindscarth, Dale Head, Fleetwith, Haystacks, High Crag, High Stile and towering immediately to the west, Red Pike, a red vein of syenite running through the ground and surfacing in a sunken bowl beneath the summit giving the mountain its colourful name. Dark bear-brown beer, golden brown chips, lipstick-red tomatoes, deep red wine, their table was laden when, unexpectedly, B took up the subject once again.

'When I played football, it felt right. The ball, always in control, as though nothing could touch me. Didn't have to think about it, everything at my feet. My heroes were so important... Bobby Charlton, Bobby Moore, Roger Hunt, all those 1966 greats. Then one day you were gone and I stopped. By the time I landed up in Cockermouth I didn't want to play ever again. Yes, I know I go to the World Cup but you know why that is. That's a promise to myself. Go, be there, witness it all and win a little victory. But that's not the same as not playing any more. Playing died in me that summer.'

B took a swig of beer and slopped a chip through a small pot of creamy mayonnaise. 'The thing is, I reckon if I hadn't stopped I could have been really good. Who knows, professional perhaps?'

He laughed. 'Imagine! Me at Wembley! How about that?'

Green cucumber, white bread, lemon-yellow cheese, the colours of every day. B continued.

'So that's the point, isn't it? We all have this, what, something inside us and if we never take it where it leads then we will never know, will we? I drew those pictures all those years ago, they were good and I should have kept going. It wasn't right and I know now it wasn't my fault but I never saw it through. And now, here I am, a lifetime away and I'm so lucky I've found the little door into that precious world again. Where I belong.'

He twisted a red pencil in his coat pocket.

'That's what I really mean. That's the missing part. What I haven't found yet. What I haven't been able to capture yet in any picture. Produce something that makes people realise what they can be, even if that's what they are already.'

Molly had let him continue explaining but now she challenged him.

'Believe me, so many who see your work are already realising those things, already asking those questions.'

'Perhaps...' he answered flatly. 'Perhaps. But I can't see it yet. The old man says he saw it and I know he did. But I didn't. And until I can see it, see it for myself, then it won't be enough, not for me.'

Molly's words were slow and cool with reality.

'You know you might never find what you seek, don't you? Gold may never be found at the end of your rainbow.'

Rainbow – connections. J. M. W., a man who had painted beauty in the Lakes. His Tate "Cromackwater" rainbow bending from the heavens right above where he and Molly were sitting now. All its colours lying ready to explode in the kaleidoscope nestling in B's other jacket pocket. And with such words hanging in the air between them, they left the Fish swimming in the verdant pastures between the sister lakes, returned to the hotel and drove the six-hour journey back to the blue Greenwich house. Yet once there, the uneasy tension still troubled them and it was no surprise they made their way to the observatory at the first opportunity, their time-honoured, mutual sanctuary of time.

The courtyard was noisy, full of tourists from all over the world. On the Meridian itself flocks of people were examining some updated, added extras adorning the simple metal line, including international place names marking out their positions on the globe. B stood apart, away at the railings where once he talked of colours with Miss Andrews, his hands like they were then, resting on the metal struts. The observatory's fiery red ball looked down on him and he gazed out across London while Molly was in the toilet across the way.

Two Americans with matching black and white check jumpers, blue denim jeans and sporting green Green Bay Packers NFL American Football caps, were standing next to him talking loudly in hyperbole about the "olde-worldeness" of it all. Did Henry VIII and Anne Boleyn really live here? Or was that Stratford-upon-Avon? And wasn't everything just so darned ancient? B smiled to himself.

'Is that right, the Olympics might be here in this park?'

'That's what the bus driver said on the way over. The equestrian events for London 2012.'

'Yeah, that's it.'

'Well, they got a lot of land here and great views. Sure will be a sight to see!'

But B didn't hear any more. Suddenly the world went crazy. Colours all around him were tumbling like rapid-fire turns of his kaleidoscope. Lines joining other lines, missing pieces fitting together, questions being answered, incredible leaps of imagination at fantastic speeds inside his head.

Molly appeared from across the courtyard waving like that day she played kings and queens, approaching from the same direction. She gazed at him in the simple joy of seeing him again, he gazed at her in a totally new sense of possibility and meeting her halfway across the cobblestones, the one o'clock ball hovering above them like a red sun, B took her in his arms and kissed her as if it would be the last time he would ever do so.

June 2007

Lost

One of his long monologues pouring out. Trickling at first and then rising with a surge, flooding across the wide plains between them. Reasons, heartache, aftermaths and realities hitting home.

In the glass-walled panorama room, just the two of them and the screen newly painted orange. The old man had been looking at the sun for a couple of hours and it matched his mood perfectly – ready to blaze. He put his brush down on top of the tin and facing one another the two sparring partners seemed to sense a moment of truth had arrived.

'An orange day... felt it when I woke up this morning, a tang of orange, a peal of orange bells chiming in the daybreak. Squeezing out the juice... "Oranges and Lemons", ain't that how it goes? Citrus colours, the colours of fruit and zest.'

The old artist walked to the edge of the room and stared out through the glass across the multitude greens of the fields and trees below.

'One day I had it, the next I didn't… had it from when I was a kid, ever since I can remember… here in my head, easy, smooth and natural. At high school, my friends knew, my parents saw it and they let me have my head… so I did what I wanted, day and night, anytime at all. Jesus, what they never knew. But they fell behind pretty quickly… couldn't keep up.'

He shifted an old brown boot and picked at a mark on the glass. 'Always had something in my hands… crayon, pen, paper, a brush, anything I could get. Then art school, you know, early days, New York, never stopped chasin' or runnin', … well, everythin''s history and it's all there in the newspapers and magazines and the galleries and books and collections. People who think they know me, or thought they knew me. Saw what I did… big time, big shot, big cheese.'

B's only words. 'You were.'

'Yeah, well…' and he placed both hands on the glass.

'But that's the point, that's the big, big point, the big zinger. I "was"… whaddya say, past tense, the past reflective. Ain't there a Latin name for it? Yesiree, a Latin word, probably something ending in an "o", more like future imperfect… and what I've got left, it's looking like ending in a big zero… now that ends in an "o", don't it?'

The sun shone in from outside, its rays hitting the orange screen sun he had painted inside, and the rock-edge voice dropped even deeper.

'Everything just sort of went, sort of left me, left me on my ownsome... I was tired, I'd worked my way through and it was all there, all of it, all over the world. Then I went to sleep, woke up one day and nothin'... zero, no sight or sound. Thought it was just a block at first. Happened a couple of times before but only for a day or so. But this was deeper, denser, freefall... my sort of blue period, or my blues period, nothin' there and no sign.

'I did stuff, I worked on this and that and people said it was OK, but it wasn't, not to me... scrambling around in the dark, like a child screaming. You know I have a colour, I do, just like you, red man, just like you, you'll never guess, oh no, never in a million years... yeah, you got it, red, a red man too. Take a look back at it all, you'll see, it's all there... but fact is I woke up and I didn't have the power any more. Upped and left me spittin' and grovelling on the ground. Squalor... red just said that's about enough, man, put your life away now cos it's all gone.'

Tree-trunk hands pushed away from the glass and spun the old man around. His back was now turned against the external sun as he looked over to the internal one from the screen.

'Orange day today... orange, fresh, open, dramatic orange,' and shifting his face towards B there was an earnest entreaty in his weary, frustrated eyes.

'I think you can give it back to me, red man... yes, I think you just might be able to do that, you just damn well might, yesiree. I saw it there on the page and that's why I called you... Esmé... make me see myself like that and I think you can give it me back, give me my promise again. Show me, tell me… I'll know it when you're done, I'll know then, whether it's worked or not. A gamble… a gambit. I've seen you, I've watched you, what you said back on the porch, getting your future back, beauty, colour an' all that… that's what I want too. I want it back… desperate, desperate man, so fuckin' long. I don't care about all those out there. Oh no, not a pigstickin' thing… they have always wanted just one more piece of me, one more masterpiece out of me. Just one flicker that the old man is back in the game… what a story, the hermit who came back, headlines. But I don't care about all that. Nosireebob, it ain't that… I need this for me, just for me.'

Walking up to B he took his hand in his, Molly-style.

'I wanna see a new sun.'

Times in 2007
and 2008

Swarming yellow Fifth Avenue cabs, Central Park greens, the cool white interiors at MoMA, the Museum of Modern Art. The blue-copper patina of the Statue of Liberty B saw on the telly once and Molly resembled as she scavenged for driftwood before Nelson's steps. Multicoloured neon lights in the city's famous Times Square.

Connections, time.

Kaleidoscope New York arrayed all about them as artist and actress go tourist in the Big Apple. Together again after a month's sojourn in the New England countryside with an old man who has been reawakened by the abracadabra of a red man. Flying separately into JFK, embraces at the airport, hands interlocking in the taxi into Manhattan – the same, unique Molly way but there's the tiniest of difference now, a finger probing a palm with subtle variations.

Entering the hotel just off Broadway, laughter and hands on arms, a whisper or two and a head-down, eyes-up look into each other's eyes while signing in. No words from either of them in the lift to the eighth-floor room. Anticipation, tasting the moment. Card entry at the walnut brown door with its brass handle. A huge bouquet of deep red Rothko-red roses and a bottle of Veuve Clicquot on the table – a gift from their Oscar-winning friend fresh from her latest film in the white snows of Switzerland.

Then a flowing out of clothes and a sliding into cool sheets, a wrapping of a leg around another and a twisting of bodies like the twisting of a kaleidoscope as it makes patterns and shapes – the colours of this next special moment. Colours spinning and dancing in his mind, a kiss with slightly parted lips, a hand on a breast with more tenderness than even Bronzino had conceived, her fingers delicately steering him inside her, his inconceivable desire come true, her completeness made real and she has indeed become the living embodiment of the goddess he once created her as.

Many times, night-times, daytimes, so many dreams of that time, in that Greenwich time when a little boy turned a corner and a vision in white at a window made his whole life whole. The time of his life that day, that kaleidoscope day.

Now it was another time, another day, the day of B's return from the Lakes. His lipstick-red mother cremated and, mid-afternoon, a red car turned the corner into the street where the blue house with the black door stood.

Once a different red car had come around that same corner – another time, another life – and B's world was turned upside down. Pain, disbelief, World Cup Willy on a window sticker, a pebble shattering glass and a terrible chain of events leading inexorably to bloody red death in Paris.

But today was a different day. The past in the past and a future to relish. B got out and leaned back on the driver's door absorbing this latest vision – Molly at the window. The claret, burgundy and maroon of her dress in folds about her. Reds howling out of one of Rothko's windows. Venus as Venus.

Molly laughed, nodding her head back to the corner.

'I knew you were coming... I was waiting for you.'

'You said that once before!'

'Yes, I know, F-u-n-n-e-e!'

They gazed at each other. She from the window, he from the pavement, and as those protracted, stretched-out seconds ticked by, bolts slid open, keys turned in secret locks and long-withheld passwords were whispered at the gate. Tick tock, tick tock, and in those precious moments down from the observatory which once mapped and measured time, the last pieces of a jigsaw were finally snapped into place.

Molly stood to greet him as he entered the kaleidoscope room, the voluptuous Venus of Velázquez facing full frontal to the viewer, open and exposed. So impossible for every passing voyeur in the National Gallery, now she was accessible, obtainable, ready. So far out of reach for so long, standing before him. Meeting B halfway across the room, their hands grasping and clasping for the first time in such a knowing fashion, her warm, natural red lips met his.

Colours, always colours at incredible moments, and B's mind teemed with the blues of her eyes...

Blue

Backlit by the thundering cascade, Molly standing arms-in-the-air shouting for pure pleasure. White spray all about her, glistening in the sun, and B trying to take a photograph. Molly bouncing in the bedlam as the foaming, boiling falls threaten to drown the famous little "Maid of the Mist" tourist boat venturing out once more into the frothing jaws of Niagara.

Molly decked out in her thin blue plastic shower cape, like all the other passengers. Most of her body keeping dry but not the rest of her. Hair dripping, lips tasting the raging river as it foams en route to Lake Ontario. Silver droplets covering her bare arms as she keeps them aloft, spinning on her heels and singing.

Click! His snapshot taken. B remembering Mrs Hinkley's slideshow in the classroom, her honeymoon pictures from Canada. The country Wolfe conquered and where the lady in red at the National Gallery came from. After a perfect week in New York, their bodies never apart, either taking in the colours of the city or in their eager nakedness, so next it had to be Niagara. A carefree drive across the state and here is Molly bringing the past to life, the funny maid of the mist letting her arms down at last to take in her lover, also cloaked in blue, now walking up to hold her.

Their first kiss as lovers and beloved. Not the friendship pecks of childhood or the restrained brushes on cheeks as platonic housemates. The kiss of new-found feelings and desires.

Until a few days ago, possibly even yesterday, the idea of kissing her in this way, of needing the want of her, would have been madness. Molly was for revering, for keeping perfect, the beautiful goddess on a pedestal or a pillar of stone like Wolfe or Mayo, not the clinging hands of a mortal. B the saviour, the guardian, would protect her from that. These days he was his own principal but his professional instincts would never be lost as far as she was concerned.

And yet here he was, his clinging hands clinging to her, his mouth hot on hers and feeling for the flesh of her neck, instantly aroused and pushing himself onto her. And here she was, her hands which had so often held his in friendship and concern now feeling for him in a totally different way – frantic and demanding, her lips tight on his, then flashing to his eyes and hair when released. Her body tingling under a red dress, that same abandon Esmé had found for her life-changing audition fresh from an orgasm fingered before the Bronzino.

Suddenly, they broke away gulping down air, sparking apart as if from some bolt of electricity. Silent but for their noisy breathing, speaking from their eyes once more. All they had meant to one another, all their history and shared memories. All their mutual respect and gratitude for what they had done for each other's lives. His pictures dragging her out of a nightmare marriage and putting her back on the stage. Her life force returned to her out of his green genius. Her friendship saving him as a little boy, her spectre at Villers-sur-Mer bringing him home. She, a Point Zero who had pointed him to the lost planet of celestial colour and beauty. The world he now luxuriated in.

All this history, their joint investment in each other, was still as solid as gold. It lay in their personal vaults, weighed and banked. But now there were other feelings too – intense, must have, must do, can't wait, can't deny feelings – and the imperative of these new mutual emotions were being fully recognised and accepted. No awkwardness, no strangeness, no faltering, no misgivings, a codicil to the unique contract between them. The woman in red and the red man acknowledging their love for one another as man and woman, and, having come to such an obvious conclusion, the urgency of the new blotted out the cautious respectfulness of the past, and Molly and B fell upon each other once more with hunger and greed.

Kisses flowing into movement towards the door. Hands held on the stairs to the bedroom and light from a window reflecting off a cut-glass vase.

Colours of reflection

Colours radiating through the stained-glass window in the chapel. Patches of red, blue, green and yellow depicting some ancient scene allowing sunlight to pierce into the modern, sombre setting on a day to say goodbye.

"Nothing for you here, boy..."

But today there is someone to say farewell to – forgiveness in death. The artist son facing the fact that, despite everything, he had loved her all his life. Inexplicable, unrequited love for a parent. Love in the face of constant rejection and neglect but there all the same. His tears before her coffin the salty proof of it all.

The odd bunch of women she had, miraculously, showered some affection on all there in the rows, singing their hymns and dabbing their eyes. The lady with the coat and the bag amongst them, mourning in the morning just like him.

Kind words spoken by the minister and B remembering that first picture in the hotel room in London. Alive on the page not dead in a box, his mother's kindly face smiling out of the paper, the first image he created when he fought to join lines with lines. Of all the subjects to choose, from everything in all those countries right down the muddy line to the bottom of the whole wide world where the penguins live, his subconscious mind had chosen her.

Molly not there but back in Greenwich, waiting around the corner for him. She was his future B had said, his mum his past. Let him draw a line across it alone and he would drive his red car back to her the very next day.

Colours at life's searching moments and B chokes back more tears as he lifts his head to the sunlit stained glass.

Hands together on the stairs, floating on steps, stepping on air and into the bedroom. Bronzino framed on the wall looking down on the lovers as they kiss again, hands straining for straps and buttons. A smile between them, nerves gone, butterflies flown away. Turning away from him, he gently unties the remaining clips, pulls a waist strap off, a red tongue, and slides the dress off her shoulders and down her body. She is wearing nothing below. She had known then. Known while he came around the corner for her. Known while she waited for him.

Hands caressing her skin, a hand delicately on each breast. Arching her neck upwards and feeling herself stroked. Kissing the top of her back, he catches her shape in the full-length mirror. Beauty, she is beautiful. Beauty in a reflecting window. Turning again, she undoes the remaining buttons of his shirt and sweeps it away – blue and red together on the floor. Naked. A confirmation if any were needed that a new level has been reached.

The bed is soft, her skin is softer. The look between their wide-open eyes is hard, he is harder. She sighs beneath him, he moves above her. She twists above him, he lies beneath her. The whites and pinks of her body, some parts of her neck blooming red as in time she shakes on top of him, and after a few minutes coaxing and smiling together, in the sweet blackness of oblivion with its kaleidoscope blots and patches of colours beyond his clenched eyes, he buries his face into her flesh and gasps on the release of his lifetime's love for her.

Black

The men in black. The women, such beautiful women, in so many rich and expensive gowns. A rainbow night at the Oscars. Esmé a dead-cert win and B knows she will tell the world about him again as she did at the BAFTAs. Nervous as some British journalists already want a piece of him and now the rest of the media world will want him too. Twisting his head to seek the comfort of his friend looking back at him, knowing what he is feeling, her dancing eyes already soothing.

She gazes at him, he gazes at her, an ultramarine dress for this red-carpet evening. Bending slightly to kiss her on the cheek, he feels a microsecond want of something more.

White

Her simple white dress on a New York night. His pictures of a long-lost red man who once lit up the skies with colours, shapes and patterns. A chic Lower Westside gallery, the focus of intense worldwide scrutiny. An art world stunned by a sign from an old master beyond his New England grave. A wider world just loving a celebrity resurrection.

Portraits on the walls, the core a group of nine at different turns of the head. Red pencils, pastels and paint, echoing the nine red Rothkos. Living proof that life has been breathed into a dead man.

Deep in discussion with a lady from the Musée d'Orsay in Paris, B suddenly looks up to see Molly at the gallery edge taking a glass of champagne from a waiter.

Sitting by a window.

Connections – Boilly.

Chocolate

Dark hot chocolate in three white china cups on the table. Three voices unable to speak, six eyes looking anywhere but at one another. The still raw tragedy lying between them. Guns in the street, cars screaming across town, the possibilities of life snuffed out in an instant. Dark, dark chocolate and darker memories.

Then a little red stone is placed on the white tablecloth, a piece of red amber like a splash of blood. Slowly, the father who lost his son, the Principal B once followed across the world, picks up the familiar possession and puts it to his lips, the way his little boy had done on the day B had given it to him. Molly reaches over, puts her hand on the father's arm and instantly her magic passes through his body. Easing, he smiles and hands the precious object back to his former protector.

'I know!' she says impishly, 'why don't you let B draw you?'

Perfect! Deep ivory dress, black shoes, dark red band in her blonde hair, perfect. B thinks, where would I be without you?

Silver

A silver pendant hanging from her neck as she leans forward striking a pose for him, a trace of her face reflected. Cold January in Esmé's groomed Kent garden. The film star upstairs in the red room on the phone for her next big thing, leaving her friends alone together for a while amongst the shrubbery.

Red pencil in his hand, lines on the page capturing the Molly moment. Winter beauty all around and B fights another green shoot of jealousy erupting somewhere in his mind. Esmé and Molly, all those years together, their intimacy in the Greenwich house, their hands held across the Meridian Line up at the observatory, their shared past with his pictures. Here, now, at her lovely white house, is Esmé the principal friend, the principal consideration?

Arching towards him, silver shining in the winter morning, Molly reaches out and puts both her hands on his wrists. A long look, understanding, a gradual smile, the red pencil still and waiting.

'I love her. She is so dear to me. We are special she and I. We speak the same language of the performance. She is more fluent than me, I envy her that, yet I rejoice in it for her.'

A pause, then a squeeze from her hands.

'This is a new, unsought-for reality, our coming together again. I am still coming to terms. But I know you are paramount.'

And then she starts to sing softly to him.

'People...'

Funny Girl, silver singing.

Gold

A Cleopatra-gold necklace, the expensive curl of its ornate links as the chain loops down on his chest as she moves above him. Making love in the hotel room, just four hours to go to his Chicago show opening, but they only have time for themselves. Urgent phone calls to their room going begging. Spring in Illinois, springtime as lovers.

She cries out, he cries out, passion for her, cramp in his leg for him and there are no words, just laughter. Molly peels off him catching the bedside light sparkle and B remembers watching her as Archangel Gabriel in the nativity play. Rich gold, like the marmalade he used to love in his deep blue home.

Red

> *The fiery red ball*
> *'Here again, where it all started!'*

B steps over the Meridian Line, east into west, and walks after Molly towards the courtyard fencing where it looks down onto the plain of Greenwich Park. The red sun high above the observatory building a few minutes off its one o'clock journey up and down to save those captains on the high seas.

> *'Where "it" started? Do you mean "it" or "us"?'*

Molly turns to him, walking backwards, the jump in her step still jumping.

> *'OK, "us" then.'*
> *'And the line that brought me back to you.'*
> *'The world's most enigmatic bodyguard!'*
> *'Not any more.'*
> *'But still enigmatic?'*
> *'If you say so.'*
> *'I do, Mr Wood, I do.'*

They both reach the railings. All of London before them, millions of people, thundering traffic, a winding river, a city teeming in motion looking still and placid under Wolfe's eye. Waiting for the red ball to dance up and down to the music of time.

He watches Molly as she looks up to the top of the observatory, the shape of the face he has captured in so many pictures since their very public meeting at the theatre in Hull. Reaching out without thinking, he tries to touch her hair but stops as she turns to face him again, smiling.

Arms and legs entwined, the deed done, their contract updated, fingers holding fingers, realisation sinking in while their bodies recharge. A faint whisper of the outside world fluttering into the room. The call of an old man across the blue Atlantic.

'I said I would be there by the weekend. I promised. He seemed to want a reassurance but I have no idea what to expect or what he wants with me.'

'Esmé really knows him?'

'Sort of. He wrote to her once, after he saw one of her films. He knows she is interested in art. A few letters, I think, but they have never met of course.'

'Bloody hell!'

'Quite!'

Molly gently detached herself, slid out of bed and moved to the window as if she wanted to check she wasn't missing something outside. For an instant she was framed against the glass – the naked Boilly girl, the shape of her outlined. What new window had been opened up for them now? But it was only to draw the curtains and she was quickly back under his arm. Her soft warmth against his skin and her hand already reaching down for him under the duvet.

B flinched a little, the very notion of her doing what she was doing was an unbelievable thing. The Bronzino on the wall, the colours of the room – turquoise picture frame, yellow make-up tube, lemon lampshade, shades of his happiness.

'I'll miss you.'

'I know.'

'New York? When I am done?'

'I love you…'

And he felt himself slip deep into the kaleidoscope she was now conjuring with her touch on him.

June 2007

Another day

Eyes meeting, red men looking hard at one another. One searching for a way out, a solution, a sort of redemption. The other feeling a sense of enormous responsibility. B not at all confident he can do what is being demanded of him but glowing with a rare sensation and amazement that he has been asked.

Grey hair, white teeth inside purpling lips, tiny brown age blotches on his forehead and hands, an azure blue shirt buttoned to the neck, buttons of a deeper deep blue, all B needs to focus on. A portrait from the chest up. He understands the landscape, knows the colours.

All that life lived, all that passion and inner drive. Those carefree days, the driven years, the endless bombardment of ideas and the latter decades of complete emptiness. The loves and lovers loved, the losses lost. The fulfilment and descent. The total control and then the utter helplessness. B sees it all, feels it, all the undercurrents, eddies and vortexes, layer after layer, and in doing so catches glimpses of his own story too.

Slowly, deliberately, more cautiously than he has ever approached a subject before, even with Esmé in her red room, B begins the task. Pencils at hand, pencils the best way to start, coloured pencils holding the old man's future in their hands. Working slowly, carefully, the first sketch an outline. B wanting to speculate and experiment in the beginning and then piece by piece bring the old man down to a human level, put some flesh on his bones and reveal what there is to reveal.

Edges and swirls, dark and light, the hint of the chin, the mark of the eye, a flurry at the neck, the shape of the top oval-shaped shirt button. Shading, and with it a breath of the old painter's cares, a pinched brow of vulnerability, a tear's droplet of regret and the deep longing for change. Pencils probing for renewal. To rekindle an old flame.

Another day, another gourmet meal, a magician...

The familiar colours of the kitchen and the rich, succulent hues of the dishes. The now comforting liquid lyrics of the old man's voice – warbling, trilling, singing like a bird. One still chained to his cage but yearning to be free.

Another day, another colour painted on the screen in the panorama room...

But a subtle change today. Black and white horizontal stripes, a vertical zebra crossing.

'Hope and fear, day and night, maybe, maybe not...
are you a goodie or a baddie, a jailor or liberator? Just what
are you, red man?'

Another day, another lesson...

Water. How to "do" water. Both of them expert in the
field. B with his lifelong fascination of rivers (the colourful
Cocker, the old brown Thames), and the old man who had
caught the Staten Island Ferry and crossed the Brooklyn
Bridge over the East River a million times.

'That guy, Canaletto, the Venice guy, can't do water
for shit... little curls supposed to be waves, load of crap.
Buildings? Yeah, could do buildings, fantastic... but
drowns when he gets to water.'

Sitting in a little boat, down at the dinghy on the lake
at the far edge of the property. Red men.

Another day, another debate about colours...

How he once used them as a man of action. Master
and pupil, walking out in the fields away from the house,
a New England new blue sky in the morning. But each
taking different roles at different times. Both leading and
following at each twist of the kaleidoscope.

Another day, another analysis of an artist's work...

B starting to pin up copies of paintings or drawings
on the kitchen pinboard and force the old man to talk
about them. Once, the picture of the day had turned
into an all-night discussion. Daybreak dawning with
empty bottles on the coffee table and the pair of them

flowing into yellow and white eggs at breakfast still going strong.

Today it was the Boilly, *A Girl at a Window*, but B was doing all the talking.

Another day, another image on the paper...

Red pencil, a smile on his lips, a glint in his eye. Walking over to have a look, the senior red man taking the junior red man's face in his huge hands and kissing him on the top of his head.

'Yesireee! I'm laughin', man.'

The many colours
of summer 2009

Multicoloured poisons, pills of every hue, tint, tone and shade dredged from every bottle and sachet she can find. A rainbow of death lying before her on the coffee table.

Sobs in the lounge on a Friday afternoon. Nothing to make it better, no words of calm to soothe the searing pain and no reason left to live. Tablets and capsules in cascading piles, like children's sweeties, like Christmas treats or Easter egg hunts and those once-upon-a-time happy moments so far removed from the grim reality of life without him.

It is true, no looking-back true, ashes in her mouth, no sleep for days, no answer at the door, no way out true.

From the very moment he died, in her hysteria at that awful second, overcome by incandescent, raging delirium, she understood what she would do, what this would mean. They were one, they lived as one, and it would be wrong to continue alone. Their being was a joint entity. No future apart.

Her life had been spent bringing pleasure to people, her talent a driving force, a natural outflow of what it was that made her. Everyone who saw her work witnessed this, witnessed the passion of it. An artist expressing her soul, baring her all, no matter what the task in hand, be it quick and commercial, studied and deep, on the edge, quirky or just for fun. That long, last breath from the man she loved as he slid from her hands so suddenly and there was the sharp rap of realisation that he was utterly central to it all. No "her" without "him". Her fuel and her reason.

And likewise, in his world of lines and shapes, he had been the consummate virtuoso, able to express his innermost dreams and aspirations creating the worlds he wanted to see, the beauty he wanted to capture. But now he was gone, their sublime partnership torn asunder, their tenderness of togetherness stopped in its tracks. The font frozen.

A handful of colourful oblivion, holding the heap of toxic candy to her lips, opening wide, throwing back her head and taking in a mouthful of chemicals. Running tears flowing in, adding their salt to the glass of gin to wash it down.

But just at that instant… What? Some sixth, seventh, or eighth sense? Some deep-down deep automatic reflux, a microsecond of regret, an imperceptible shiver in her memory? Something. An inconceivable diversion sweeping her consciousness from incoherent misery to the burbling television screen.

A name spoken, a spasm of normality inside her brain. In the throes of her swallow, she spat the alcoholic crunchy mix back out onto the tabletop, saliva spilling from her teeth, tablets still sticking to her tongue until another hawk disgorged them.

... a name.

* * *

Drops of sweat from his chin spotting the pillow around her face. Gun in his hot, wet, shaking hands.

His passion in the night, her peace in sweet slumber. The soft lips he had kissed so many times. Those intoxicating blue eyes now hidden under delicate lids. The blonde hair lying in tresses about her bare shoulders. The sleeping beauty and the incandescent beast.

His Browning Hi-Power pistol, the weapon he had kept hidden since those army days. He has used it before, men lying dead on the battlefield. Now, could he use it again?

Never betrayed by his men, how he feels the acute stab of her treachery. Right now, even in the bed they share, what other body is she reaching and scheming for in her dreams?

Whore.

Cold gun metal, fighting to keep his grip steady. Screwing his face up in his extremis, gritting his teeth. How she has lied, how she has cheated. He has seen the men, those vile men looking at her, has watched her look back at them, wanting them, needing their hands on her.

He feels sick, wanting to pay her back for the way she makes him feel.

But as he closes his finger on the trigger, a whimper in the silent night. Some tiny sound stirring her, a quiet moan, and his wet face turns away. Licking lips, a pout in her rousing, opening her eyes and in a flash the gun is behind his back, his other hand softly caressing the side of her face, a piece of her lovely hair caught between his fingers.

'Sshhh…' he whispers.

'I love you. Go back to sleep.'

* * *

Massive, menacing and mean, towering over the cowering boy, laughing at his misery. Mocking, sneering, hissing, without pity.

Powerful, specks of brown nicotine on his fingers, the tormentor dominating the defenceless lad with his heavy tears streaming down. Beauty broken by the fiend's hands, the pieces tossed to the air around him. Snapping and tearing, little scraps of wood, splinters and shards.

Immune to the boy's magical touch, no ear for the sounds of the truth. Where, where was the boy's mother? A mother would stop this cruelty in its tracks. That smiling, gentle, caring mother he loved so much.

His teacher non-plussed, something quite extraordinary, a remarkable exhibition, a wonderful display on a drab school afternoon in the classroom. Such beauty, on a plane far above this devil's head with his spitting mouth and snarling eyes.

You'll wish you'd never been born...

That was yesterday but the pain still smarted, the reality still hit home. Standing now beside the river looking deep down into its murky colours, desperately seeking solace. Alone, so incredibly alone, and scared. Nobody understood but then nor did he. Just what had been that impromptu spark from within, that mystery power? And why had it brought him terror, a bloodied mouth and the loss of something precious?

In his sadness, beginning to speak to the water running a few feet below him. Little swirls of browns and blacks circling at the muddy bank. And exhausting everything he could say about how he felt, how impossible the days and weeks ahead would be, silently turning away, he followed the river pathway into a wild blue yonder to face the inevitable music.

* * *

Green boy, she is remembering. A shining star on the wing.

Lost shadows, the forever child who will never grow up, who ran away to Kensington Gardens to live a long, long time among the fairies. Flying high above the clouds and the sights and sounds of London, on and on to Neverland. Up, up and away, the tingling sensation of flight, free as a bird, nothing holding her down, tipping her face to the sun, the moon and all the stars in the starry, starry night.

Airborne.

There, way down below, back on terra firma, her parents, looking to the heavens and applauding their daughter as she dazzles the crowded auditorium. Leading part, leading little lady, yet another in a long list of triumphs. On the verge of greatness, a career taking off, feet not touching the ground.

So how can she tell them? What can she say to stop their dreams from crashing? How can she let them down? How can she make them understand?

They have sacrificed so much, taken her everywhere, foregone everything to help her climb the glittering ladder. They expected, they wore their pride on their sleeves, their daughter's flight plan through life was fixed. But it is no use. It cannot do. She wants to reach for a different sky, one far beyond the bounds of the high wire of expectation she has somehow become bound to.

She is no everlasting child, no Pan. She knows what she wants in her future. She felt it in her bones, in the smell of the wind, in the instant of that first escape into the wild. Tinkerbell and all the other characters in all the plays she has ever played in are wonderful, she loves it all, and she knows she is good, exceptional. Yet she yearns for a new part, a new persona, a new course to pilot.

Landing now, dropping back softly to earth, applause ringing out. The Lost Boys, those pirates, Captain Hook and that terrifying, clock-ticking crocodile all to come in the next acts. Touching down on the boards, Wendy and the other darling children gathering around. The natural actress in her striking the famous Peter Pan pose. Hands on hips, chin slanting upwards, the green pointy hat, the green tights and short tunic.

Centre stage and in control, but her heart is back in the air, back up there in the clouds.

* * *

Red, blue, yellow, green and black – symbiosis of potential.

Circles of eternal hope and desire known and understood the world over, right down to the end of the globe and the penguins. The Olympic dream, the torch of achievement, the ultimate goal for so many on each continent, denoted by the five rings of its iconic symbol.

A die-hard romantic since his personal enlightenment, B was a man of grey no more. Gone the mere judger of risks, the calculator of moves and counter-moves like a chess grandmaster on a life-sized board – the Bobby Fischer to the rich and famous, the Tal to the high and mighty, the Alekhine to his Principal. Now he was reborn to a fresh, unexpected life of colour and beauty. Each day living and working to reach even higher aesthetic planes than the last. Ever seeking to express the inexhaustible flood of lines, shapes and patterns continually running through his veins.

Unashamedly a romantic, to the end of his days. Yet one not so blind to ignore the modern-day professionalism and cut-throat realism of the Olympics in the twenty-first century. Stunned in sudden epiphany at the observatory railings that day, finally realising how he could unlock the hidden potential in others, even then the image of the modern Olympic corporate monolith didn't escape him. International big business and politics, hard rules, harsh contracts and bitter legalities ran the games these days, he knew that well enough. At his Principal's side, he had been a first-hand witness to the chameleon connotations and *real politic* behind staging them – dealings with ruthless people and organisations. But at that moment, looking out along the Meridian Line as it ran out across the park down to his old alley then over the river and into the depths of East London, B's head spun with connections that drove through scepticism, cynicism and suspicion.

There, right out there, so close he felt he could almost touch it, just a few miles out along the muddy line, was the site for the 2012 London Olympics. A newspaper article had described it only the other day – stadium, epicentre, velodrome, aquatics, glory, winners, medals, fulfilment. It was so near, and in those moments crystallised by the Green Bay Packers Americans, as he visualised gold, silver and bronze horses galloping through his historic park, the entire concept came to him. The simple beauty of it.

Five circles, kaleidoscopes of colours – keys that would unlock the possibilities in others he so wanted to set free.

Molly was walking over the courtyard beneath the fiery red ball and kissing her was, in that instant, the only way he could stop himself bursting with his certainty.

* * *

Barbara knelt before the TV set brushing her hand over the screen. An interview, a man talking about pictures and paintings on show right now. A man who had been a boy on the day she told him about beauty and gave him the colourful tools to draw it.

Her reed-like fingers probing the lines and curves of the face staring back over the years, her eyes bulging with tears, she held her breath in wonder. Her mouth still tasting the deadly drugs spat out on the coffee table top.

Cameras were rolling about a hot new exhibition in New York. Fame and critical acclaim for a new phenomenon. Revelations of an old man waking from the dead and proof of an emerging talent's touch. She had spent so many hours in galleries in front of the old master's works but one day he was gone, years of silence. Now, incredibly, he was back in the world again.

And this new talent was *him*. *That* Saturday morning boy who loved red, who heard Barbra Streisand sing and knew about Wolfe and Canada? *That* same tearful boy who lit the spark in her that day to fly home to a new life? Her wonderful life that hit a brick wall the day dear James died in her arms. A life which had withered and wasted away ever since. Until today, when she had decided to do what she must. A rainbow cocktail of chemicals. No life without him, no future apart.

Barbara fingered B's TV face, stroking back the decades, his image blurring so close to the screen. The boy as the man today – grown, assured, talking about colours and beauty as she dreamed he might learn to do one day back in 1966 when they stood together on the portico of London's National Gallery.

Somehow, a numberless extra sense had stopped her

taking her own life. Deep within her determined despair, she had caught the sound of his name echoing to her over the airwaves. A tiny name snapping her back to some level of consciousness. The saving grace of a letter.

How many times had she thought of him over the years? Lost in some reverie or catching the eye of a child, she would always wonder what had become of the boy. What had he done with her pencils and pad? Had he really drawn his lovely Molly?

Now here he was, jumping out of the past and talking high art. Her pencils and pad must have paved the way, they must have. This was no coincidence surely. This must be the boy. And convinced that it was so, she found herself actually smiling, her first smile in so long. The smile of the chance speculator eventually proved right, the gambler finally winning through, the laugher of the last laugh.

Touched to her heart that day, that sunny Argentina and Wembley day, she felt sudden empathy with the boy's pain and had innocently invested some capital in his future. Take these gifts and create beauty she told him and now, decades later, here he was coming out of the TV ether to present her with a long-hoped-for but completely unexpected dividend.

It was well over a year later when Barbara took in the lines and angles of the former Palladian mansion that housed the RA, London's Royal Academy of Arts. How James would have loved this grand, imposing building on Piccadilly and how desperately she would have loved him at her side. Her architect husband, a virtuoso, a stylist, a connoisseur of light and space, at once flamboyant yet human with award-winning projects all over Canada, the USA and even some in Europe, all bearing his particular hallmark. A London showcase for art since Victorian times, Burlington House was perhaps a shade gloomy for his iconoclastic taste but it was full of intrigue. Those "nooks and crannies" that would have made him laugh.

The RA was not new to her of course. Back in her England days, an art tutor to the young and hopeful, she was a frequent visitor. Indeed, along with the National Gallery, the Tate and the city's other great collections, this famous institution was a favourite hunting ground in her search for beauty and inspiration.

Although still sad in her widowed loneliness, her daily reality of missing James, today she was energised beyond anything she could have imagined. She felt so alive and her high expectations were incredibly tantalising. She was back in the UK, in her seventies, in very good health, and back because of B. She doubted if he would remember her but she was certain it was those gifts that had put him on the road to his current high status. Her heart beat with the same contented pride as on that near-suicide day when she first saw and heard him again. Many times she had wondered about making contact to remind him, jog his memory and perhaps talk about beauty, but she always talked herself out of it. She hated hangers-on.

B's story was well known now and she was still amazed she had never seen or heard of Esmé's first high praise of him at the awards ceremonies. Those childhood pictures, his years of creativity lost, the career in the army, that sexy life close to fame, fortune and international diplomacy spawning some intriguing media profiles. Parisian tragedy leading to enlightenment and the lighting of an eternal flame now burning inside him. A furnace burning hotter and hotter.

And just through the old doors of Burlington House, in a place of honour under a domed ceiling as part of an exhibition, was what everyone was calling B's masterpiece. Across the world the consensus had already decreed his works so far to be masterful, inspirational. But this new work, this *tour de force*, well, the only way to really understand it, to recognise its fundamental power and comprehend its full measure, was to go and experience it for yourself.

Barbara had packed a bag, ridden a taxi to Toronto Airport, flown first class across the Atlantic, checked into a top London hotel and next morning had caught a big red, bus-red, double-decker red bus to the RA to do just that.

* * *

Sun shining, glare off the traffic running down towards Hyde Park Corner, the green of royal trees just across Park Lane, a day-night job done. Hands sunk in his trouser pockets and a mind swirling with such a heavy burden, Billy ambled out of one of London's finest and most elegant hotels and decided just to walk. Anywhere, anything instead of catching the Tube home.

For the last few hours he had tried to concentrate on his work. Whatever he was doing – wrenching a pick-pocket's arm behind her back and bringing the diminutive Australian girl's rather lucrative day to an abrupt halt, doing the checking rounds on each of the floors, catching up with Scotland Yard detectives in their search for a couple of suspected terrorists who could be a lot more dangerous to the life and people of London than the poor pick-pocket – whatever his task, at least he had been occupied. But the demons had never left his head.

The shock of what, apparently, he had been prepared to do to Alexandria, or himself, last night was numbingly profound. In the cold light of a hot day, he was incredulous at his actions in their bedroom. What utter madness to have been driven to such a brink.

Yes, he could definitely use a walk in the sultry sunshine to try and sort his tangled brain. His hotel security job was an important role, one demanding complete integrity, dependability, calm, balance and a cool head. Falling into a steady pavement pace, Billy wondered what his to-date trusting employers would have made of him last night with his gun poised to blow his wife, or himself, or both to hell.

Each step towards Hyde Park Corner then those turning left into Piccadilly piled on even greater horror at his state of mind as he loomed over her. Such high-minded jealousy. How had he come to be so eaten up with such terrible thoughts of her betrayal so soon, so rapidly? Billy violently yanked his hands out of his pockets and stabbed them into the air at his helplessness.

Married only months ago, their vows were hardly spoken before he began to suspect her. A smile too easily given, a hand held too long against a friend's chest over a joke, the highly suspicious three nights out in a row "with the girls", an unnecessarily nice dress worn to work, the odd no-one-there phone call, his mates' jibes at the gym over her lovely figure, her complimented breasts. He felt the stifling fear of it all, convincing himself of treachery at every twist and turn.

Then the straw breaking his camel's back. A telephone number written down on the back of a bank receipt, the man's voice at the end of the line – a deep, carnal, lustful voice insisting he didn't know her but of course he did, knew her in the biblical sense, the bastard. All the circumstantial evidence piling up and finally cracking the dam of his defences. Falling head-first into the pit, unable to stop or cling on to any handhold.

A bottle of wine while she was "out" again with the girls, a few beers, a brandy, then another one, and another one and yet another, and when she slipped naked into bed beside him just after 2 am thinking he was asleep (but he certainly wasn't, oh no!), he shed silent tears at her soft purr of slumber and suddenly couldn't stand it any longer. Rising silently, swaying because of the booze, he tottered towards a drawer in the wardrobe and took out the Browning.

Walking past Green Park then the Ritz Hotel across the road to his right, Billy's inner struggle continued to rage. He wanted her to be truly true but he kept picturing those sticky-fingered men and her hand on a hairy chest. Never any cause to doubt her in their three years together but who was that son of a bitch on the phone? They made love almost every night but was she just going through the dutiful, wifely motions? She said she loved him but how could he believe her?

With the Royal Academy coming up ahead, he yearned yet again for the life of trust and security he had dreamed of – united, together, children, an unbreakable, timeless, mutual bond, happiness.

Not realising what he was doing, Billy dived left into the Burlington House courtyard and began walking towards the main doors of the RA.

* * *

Najib stared out of the top, red double-decker bus window and looked out on the people walking by in the street.

He was doing all he could to block out the mimicry and jeers coming from the back seats. A boy sat beside him, not a friend, not an enemy, just a boy caught in the crossfire feeling distinctly uncomfortable. He had no place in this dangerous situation. These were bigger boys with bigger mouths, boys you wanted to avoid if you knew what's good for you. Boys that would make your life hell if you became a target and Najib, poor Najib, who had dared to be different, was the latest classroom bullseye. An empty can of Coca-Cola struck the back of his head accompanied by a beefy gaggle of laughter and the boy decided to heed the obvious runes, got up and went downstairs to look for another seat. Better anywhere than here.

Najib continued to cower and cringe. How quickly fate strikes, how suddenly your world can turn upside down, how rapidly life has the capacity to suck. Just a few minutes of weightless ecstasy when he picked the thing up and now a never-ending nightmare at the hands of Jobson and his cronies. You get on the wrong side of Jobson and you can kiss goodbye to life. And Najib had done just that the moment he put the instrument down to a stunned Mr Glue, the music teacher, and looked up to see the gleam of envy and hate from the school's tough guys.

The distant echo of a precocious Mozart, a faint strain of Bruch, a whisper of Stéphane Grappelli were all lost on the boys from the hard stuff. He might be sitting on a bus plying its way around Hyde Park Corner's manic roundabout and then into Piccadilly but Najib was still a dead man walking.

Not a musical family, no piano or stuff like that in the house, even the radio was always on the talk channels, Najib had never tried to play anything before, never given it a moment's thought. Then Mr Glue had this violin in the class along with some other instruments, all shining wood and tan coloured, and it just invited him to pick it up and put it to his chin. Taking up the bow stick thing, he sort of ran it across the strings to see what sound it would make.

Alone in the corner of the classroom while the other boys goaded the teacher at his desk, *"... do you have a big horn, sir...?"*, the beautiful music just flowed out. Fingers natural to the fingerboard – lovely, lilting, lyrical, intense and apparently impossible.

The class crowded around slowly as the music filled the scruffy room, the boy and the violin fusing as one. Then silence, it was over. Najib snapped to reality wondering where he was and laid the violin and bow down nervously as if he should never have touched them in the first place.

Mr Glue simply couldn't speak. His mouth popped

and puffed without voice. Najib? Najib! What? How?

But Jobson and his mates knew a prey when they spied one. Najib the show-off, Najib the swot (classical music, you sure?), Najib the flash wanker and his fate was sealed instantly. An after-school victim just waiting to be crushed.

Mr Glue finally gathered himself and took his new star pupil aside. Najib couldn't help much, he hadn't a clue what had happened, but accepted the teacher's fulsome offer of taking the violin home now it was the end of the day to see how he got on with it. They could talk again first thing tomorrow and try to understand.

But tomorrow, Najib's yesterday as he sat on the bus while being told emphatically from the backseat boys he was a "total moron" and a "waste of space", didn't turn out the way Mr Glue had gone to bed fanaticising about.

Ambushed in the park by the river on his usual way home, Jobson took his disapproval out on his prey with a vengeance. Cutting Najib's lip open with a hard fist, he dashed the delicate instrument into a thousand splinters on the concrete path and tossed the case into the water. Wooden shards all over the ground, pieces in Najib's hair, the brute that was Jobson stood over him, towering, vicious, nicotine hands, red-eyed, seeing red, grinding the wreckage of the instrument under his heels, snapping the bow in two. Walking miserably back to his house, Najib wanted to tell his dear mum but that wasn't right. She was very ill and he couldn't burden her with his troubles. Ten years dead, his dad was of no use.

So in the morning there was no violin to return to the eagerly anticipating Mr Glue. Najib stopped off at the river to rehearse his excuses but the pools of murky, muddy water offered no solace or prospect of a way out and eventually the about-to-be former star pupil made his sad and lonely way back to school to face the music from the music teacher.

In the end, Sir didn't know quite what to think. Falling asleep the previous night after a Scotch or two, he was convinced an almighty practical joke had been played on him, and with Najib's downcast admission of the expensive loss (a loss that would in no uncertain terms have to be repaid), a saddened and still slightly alcohol-induced Mr Glue accepted he had indeed been the victim of a prank. With Najib in detention and duly admonished, he simply went back to the mundane business of enthusing some energy into the third-year class he was taking for the first lesson of the day.

Hurting inside and out, Najib was both confused and in fear. What exactly had happened with the violin? He had a vague idea of playing it but to be honest he had been in a world of his own, though a part of him still sensed how good the music had felt. But the danger he now faced from the terrible Jobson was real enough. Time to keep very low indeed, he thought, just play along and hope he tired of him pretty quickly. Tell Mr Glue or the other teachers? Yeah, sure, like signing your own death warrant.

Najib was a sitting target all day yesterday. Choice name-calling on arrival at school and again at break-time, then beatings at lunch. Going home was almost clear but Jobson appeared out of the blue again and Najib endured another round of being told he was a "complete arsehole" and going to "wish you'd never been born, you prick" before he was repeatedly punched in the back of the head and kicked in the shins.

And what would today have in store? The prospect of a school trip to the Royal Academy in London raised the possibility of escaping Jobson's clutches but he doubted it. Stuck in the close confines of the bus, another Coke can just shaving his ear, he was convinced everything was going to be very bad indeed.

Suddenly, the teacher downstairs shouted they were "Here!" and the bus pulled up at a stop just by the gallery. Jobson and clan forced Najib down the stairs, ruffling his hair and yanking his school tie, and fifteen boys emerged onto the pavement noisy, stroppy and wondering what all this crappy art-world stuff was going to be about.

* * *

Elizabeth popped up from the bowels of Piccadilly tube station and started to jog west along to the coffee shop. She hated being late, a slur on her high standards, and of all people she didn't want to keep Uncle John waiting. Confidant, teacher, her gateway to heaven, dear Uncle John.

Barging in through the door, forcing a man with his hot take-away latte to back-step smartish, she saw him sitting in a corner – her rock, her counsellor, her oracle. Elizabeth kissed a "hello" on his cheek and he stood holding her before him in his straight arms, the bond between them strong, born of a shared love.

'Coffee?'

'Please, just a white Americano... you know!'

John knew. They had shared coffee many times before, the last one on a quick trip to Le Havre. But there had been many other excursions over the last secret year – all over the UK in fact. Abroad a few times too but only to places for the day. And he also knew, within a second of holding her, seeing the welling in her eyes, what she had come to say.

Elizabeth sat down, peeled off her thin jacket and John was back with her drink in no time sitting down on the comfy sofa next to her. The two looked at each other for a long time before Elizabeth eventually broke the silence.

'I have decided to tell them.'

'You are sure?'

'Yes. I decided last night. I just knew. I got home from rehearsals, looked at Mum and Dad and I just knew.' She placed a hand on John's knee, a point of emphasis, a profound moment.

'I so want to do this. I knew it the day you first took me. I feel different now. I don't feel like it anywhere else. I used to, I did. But this is inside me and I need to tell them. Tell them now. You understand, don't you?'

John leant forward slightly and placed his hand on hers. What an extraordinary young woman she had become. The little tomboy who grew into their parents' little princess, the precocious talent who had danced, sung and acted her way into the limelight – school plays, amateur dramatics and now a fledgling star in the making.

'Of course. It's what we have talked about. But I wanted to let you make the decision in your own time. It will hit them, you know that, don't you? Hit them hard. They have no idea.'

Elizabeth took a sip of coffee and nodded. Yes, they had no idea.

A year ago, her favourite uncle had offered to take Elizabeth for a flying trip. He owned a relatively new private four-seater plane out of a local airstrip and the whole family made a day of it. Mum, Dad, Elizabeth and pilot John the family hero – jets, big stuff.

From the moment she climbed into the cockpit Elizabeth was completely enchanted. The sleek shape of the plane, the crisp blue sky waiting above her, the cornucopia of dials and switches, the padded comfort of the seat, the anticipation of intrepid flight, the sexy control of Uncle John's deep voice to the tower as he taxied, the speed on the runway (much, much closer to the ground than on the holiday schedules she was used to). Then the total exhilaration of take-off, bursting into the air, leaping into the sky, the incredible speed of lift and, once she had let out her exhilarated breath, the vast green, brown, blue, white eternity before and beneath her. Nothing, nothing, she had ever done or she felt she would ever do again could compare to it.

Flying.

Elizabeth was back in the cockpit the very next weekend, then the next and the weekend after that. She was hooked. All her thoughts were in the air. It was intoxicating. More intense than any fix in front of an audience, more dramatic than any play, more fulfilling than any applause. Her first impulsive love, of acting – the stage, the wonder – had been replaced by the thrill of it all, on the wing.

John was happy to entertain her ever-deepening enthusiasm. He had a very soft spot for Elizabeth, her strength of character and her talent. Flying with her beside him was fun and she was full of questions and the talk he loved. No wife to keep him tied to the ground, he lived for his plane and here was a young seventeen-year-old prodigy, who like him loved the freedom only flight could give. Gradually, somehow, the trips turned clandestine. Nothing was said, it wasn't done on purpose, but flight days became a silent pact between them. Elizabeth didn't always lie to her parents, sometimes she said she was going "up with John", but the intensity of it all was never shared with them.

Then that night playing Peter Pan, a good break for her in a big production, important people there ready to talk business, Elizabeth looked down on her parents and knew where her heart lay. Not on the stage but in the sky. She knew she wanted to be a flier, it was her destiny, and nothing would stop her. But how to tell them far below? Her decision would shatter their hopes and long-held dreams for their talented daughter, their little baby named after Hollywood's famous child star Elizabeth Taylor. Both Elizabeths even had the same beautiful violet coloured eyes.

Now it was summer, a few months of waiting for the right time to say something, an emerging pilot with many more flights under her belt. But last night, at last unable to fight it any longer, she called John to meet. She needed advice, direction and courage and John could give it all. So wise, so assured, the unflappable ace, her mentor.

'Come on. I saw something yesterday that I simply cannot explain.'

Climbing out of the sofa they left the coffee shop and headed further back up Piccadilly.

* * *

Decades in the making, months in the distilling, weeks in the dreaming and in heady days hard at work, layering, ordering, revealing, coaxing, enticing and persuading colours to come to his aid, come to his party and to his senses.

The endless characters and characteristics of colours. Their inexhaustible subtlety, richness and depth, their ability to tell stories, take you inside, swallow you up and give you answers.

Colours and circles.

Circles of reds, blues, yellows and greens, followed by the infinity of the blacks.

Circles revealing what each viewer must see and witness. Their very selves, their hopes and dreams, their fears and deadliest worries, their false promises and true colours. Secret chances half-imagined and, in the end, the ringing bell of certainty.

Love, loss, hate and heartache
Youth, age, sorrow and sadness
Light, life, laughter and loveliness
Danger, doubt, darkness and death.

Four circles standing head-high, arms stretched-out

wide in a staggered row across the gallery floor. One after the other, pointing the way ahead.

First, naturally for a red man, the reds. So many sucking you in, like a round, red Rothko room. An eternity of reds before, finally, a release into the bottomless ocean bottoms of the many blues.

The second circle dragging you deeper into beautiful depths, letting you drown in wild blue yonders and sky-blue horizons.

The third, the many yellows. Paving paths with gold, lands burning with suns and sunlight, basking summer cornfields, desert sands roasting and the glint of the outlandish and risqué.

The fourth, the infinite varieties of greens. Tree canopies and jungles, grasslands and gardens mixing with human hues of envy and the spring green penetration of Miss Hattiemore's eyes.

Four round galaxies. Celestial reds, blues, yellows and greens, orbiting like sister satellites before a fifth. A black star on the edge of time. Deep into outer space, a chasm of distance separating it, a black all-seeing eye. A black circle of finality.

Black, the fifth circle, and as B first imagined it at the top of the world on the Meridian Line, the circle of revelation.

The thick outer ring mixing the many blacks, but within the interior of the circle itself a chaos of colours like a magical paintbox volcano blowing its lid.

The first four circles – assessing, reviewing, sounding out, tempting, cleaning and preparing you. Then black, telling it to you straight, giving you every answer, showing you what you can be and convincing you it can be so. The fifth circle pouring you forth into the time that's left to you in this world and equipping you with the certainty of what you are.

I am a murderer, I will murder. I am a lover, I will love. I am a runner, I will run. I am a leader, I will lead. I am a teacher, I will teach.

I am a man, I am a woman. I am an unbeliever, I truly believe. I do evil things, I am naturally good. I hate my sister, I still love her. I am a free-thinker, I am a racist. I am a prude, I wish to be ravished.

I will be the best at what I do. I will be the friend I know I can be. I will win the race. I will rob my partner. I will dominate people. I will make my pile. I will destroy. I will cheat. I will give. I will preserve. I will give life.

Four lives.
I will go on creating beauty, despite my loss.
I will trust her and live the happy life I dream of.
I will play such wonderful music.
I will be Icarus.

The final circle, the black ring of truth. Portraits and landscapes, realism, abstracts, and impressions, a teeming collection of scenes yet generating one unified picture.

Rothko like? Yes, but a circle of so many techniques and styles B has blended together.

The precision of a Velázquez or a Dali, the eroticism of a Picasso. The romanticism of a Caspar David Friedrich and the god Turner. The micro-dot intensity and endurance of a Seurat. The starkness of a Hopper, the millisecond detail of a Viola, the colours of a Kahlo and the madness of a Chagall. The spotlight light of a Caravaggio, the spontaneity of a Van Gogh, the *joie de vivre* of a Delacroix, the spirituality of an El Greco, the smoothness of a van Eyck, the extraordinariness of a Durer, the serenity of a Constable, the classical form of a Titian, the stillness of a Sisley, the look of love from a Bronzino and, of course, the truth of the Boilly.

* * *

Barbara entered the room as if it was a place of worship. She had flown halfway across the world to be here but now in the presence of this unknown yet urgently-sought precious thing, she was nervous, apprehensive and respectful.

There were many people in front of, inside, around and in almost physical contact with the work yet at the same time there was a great sense of tranquillity. Just feet-taps on the floor and the rustle of exhibition programmes. Barbara took in the faces, so many demeanours. Happiness, shock, euphoria, acceptance, tears. No individual unaffected. An eclectic mix from many countries, like the elderly Japanese tourists standing in front of her. A congregation constantly being enlightened then replenished by new viewers such as herself.

A few minutes' wait and it was Barbara's turn. She had heard the work was marvellous but had purposefully not read or heard any reviews. Newspapers, magazines, TV, radio and online trumpeting "uncanny", "godlike", but she had shunned all accounts knowing it was waiting for her. She would go to it whatever it was and judge for herself. She had such incredibly high hopes of course, he was her pupil after all whether he knew it or not, but she had no idea what to expect. Now, standing on the brink of discovery and opening her eyes, her heart began to see what B had to show her.

Reds – for the blood-energy pulsating inside her all her artistic life and for every day with her beloved James. Blues – for the colours of her best work (yes, the old man would have known she was a blue woman). Yellows – for the sandy beach they had shared every summer on Cape Cod, and, with a hard swallow, for the cowardice she had shown by thrusting those pills down her throat to take an easy way out. Greens – for her little garden she tended back home and the emerald she wore around her neck, her husband's gift to celebrate his first project of substance which still turned heads in a Boston street.

Swaying from each coloured universe in turn, each telling her story in the tongue of her own personal language, oblivious to anyone else in the room, Barbara climbed the red, blue, yellow and green foothills to her summit of judgement at the black circle.

Instructed by the blacks of the outer ring, she gazed into the interior, into an extraordinary multitude of dazzling colours, and squinting with the brilliance, within seconds she understood the answer. Looking harder, she had known it from the moment of B's face at the TV, known from when she left the house and climbed into the cab to the airport and known as she boarded the plane, sipped the red wine in her first-class seat, arrived at her hotel and entered the hallowed halls of the Royal Academy. In some ways it wasn't a revelation at all, more a confirmation, a lifting of a long-closed lid on the long known. Probing even deeper into the final circle, a trace of green amidst the enormous array of colours sealed her decision in a blinking eye of certainty.

She was an artist, had always been one. She lived for what she created and had always looked forward in life. An eternal optimist, she had always said tomorrow was the "beautiful future", another road, another possibility. That brief narcotic capitulation to grief had been a bogus submission to emptiness at her life's lowest point, and with her mind in chaos, the despair had so, so nearly derailed her. Now the route back to the surface was obvious and the fresh taste of air so sweet. A decision, long put off, long declared as impractical, long ago lost as a pipedream was easily made. Paint her way up the Amazon, an epic South American journey of discovery, an exploration of her soul's constant tenet.

Beauty.

Barbara moved away from the work to leave the hallowed space as more hushed newcomers replenished it, like the man rushing into the room as if he was frantically looking for someone. She smiled and recalled how on that high summer day when she met B, she had left the National Gallery and within a week was sitting on a plane bound for home and her future. Out into another sunny London summer afternoon, tomorrow Barbara would be on another flight, this time to face her ultimate destiny.

* * *

Billy was so blinded by his raging inner struggle, he had no idea where he was until he stood inside the foyer. Never an art gallery man, suddenly he computed it was the Royal Academy from the wall posters and spun around to leave, shaking his head in confusion. But somehow, something stopped him. A peripheral vision? A trick of the sunlight? He recoiled from the door, his outstretched arm frozen.

To his left in some wall racks, he saw the cover of a leaflet and automatically picked out a copy. Gazing at it open-mouthed, everything went silent, the day stopped and the people around him evaporated. He turned, bought a ticket, took a deep breath and flew up the steps to the exhibition carried along by the madness of a moment.

The picture of a woman so like his Alexandria looked out at him from the paper in his hands. Her eyes, her hair, her shape, her mouth, it was uncanny. She must be here, somewhere in the gallery, she must be. Billy's mind reeled, he had no self-control, feeling compelled to chase down this incredible moonbeam.

Starting to hunt through the people-packed rooms, Billy's eyes darted everywhere. No thought for anything on the walls, fathoms deep out of his depth in this art world, suddenly there was a flash, a glimpse of hair disappearing into another room. He followed quickly but the figure was already half-passing into the next. Billy wanted to run but a group of aged Japanese tourists blocked his way, cameras necked. Bolting into a room full of architectural models and on past some objects made of stuff like papier-mâché, the elusive woman never seemed any nearer. Taunting, tantalising, she looked like her, moved like her, swung her hair like her. It *was* Alexandria.

Dodging more crowds, Billy rushed into another room frantically looking from side to side. Then suddenly there she was – sleek, slim and beautiful – standing in front of a tall circle of different coloured reds, so near her nose was almost touching it. Breathing hard, his heart pumping in his ears, Billy came up to stand behind her and just at the very point of touching her shoulder, whispering her name, the figure dissolved...

Sunburst, sunset. The dazzle of a fireball, hot embers. The first circle. Confronted with such force, like a physical blow, Billy lost all thought of the blonde and stood motionless before the reds for a full twenty minutes. All was stripped bare – the terror of his struggle over her, his pain and frustration, the utter helplessness of last night and the blood he had nearly shed.

At long last came the blue circle. Relief, the peace of the way things had been before, the colour of the dress she had worn on their first date, the sense of her touch, the flick of her lips on his. Next, the yellows. Relief becoming illumination. The stupidity of his recent fears, the innocence behind her hand on his friend's chest, the telephone numbers of women he had by everyday chance in his own wallet and who Alexandria could have called at any time. Then the greens, illumination merging into understanding. Those evil eyes of envy he had succumbed to. Now he could see them for what they really were – harbingers of needless self-induced pain.

Finally, the black circle and through its colours he saw the future. His whole life running ahead, years of happiness and security. Together, true to each other, bonded, locked and loving.

Moving away from the work after an unknown time, walking to the gallery exit, Billy looked down at the leaflet he still gripped in his hand. There was no blonde lady on the front but instead a jumble of red, blue, green, yellow and other coloured lines. A map of the London Underground train network. Lines connecting other lines.

Out of the RA and into Piccadilly, Billy turned left and hurried for the Tube station and home.

* * *

Najib broke away from the class as soon as he could. An hour or so of torture in this art gallery was too much. So what if he bunked off early, went home and got into trouble, he didn't care. He was in deep do-do with Jobson anyway.

As the rest of the class grouped together at the end of the first main room, Najib slipped off unnoticed in the opposite direction using a group of old Japanese tourists as a diversion. At that moment the bullyboys were too interested in taking the piss out of the stupid pictures on the walls than to pay him any mind. They would soon enough though and turn to him in their boredom, rabid for sport.

Working his way through the galleries, Najib didn't stop to look at the exhibits but, head down, he soon became disorientated. Panicking he might run into the school mob again, he dived into the next room to think. There were lots of people inside but in spite of his anxiety there was an immediate sense of reverence here like he'd walked into a church. Standing with his back to the side wall, he slowed his breathing and basked in a few moments of ease for the first time that day. Nobody to fear just yet, no one throwing cans at his head or calling him names. He closed his eyes in luxurious respite.

When he opened them again, he was looking straight at a man standing before a painted circle of reds. In fact, Najib could see from his angle at the wall that the room had five similar-sized, free-standing round structures. Many people were walking in and around them but for some reason Najib zeroed onto this one man who stood for ages just staring as if in a trance before suddenly he seemed to wake up and move on. Despite his quest for anonymity, Najib was intrigued and after a while broke cover, pulling away from the wall to stand and look at the circle himself. Then he thought he felt a touch on his hand…

A high-pitched and constant note piercing out of the reds, enveloping everything. A beautiful, delicate, yet immensely powerful sound from which there is no escape, ever, but one so essential you could never contemplate flight. The note developing into many, all offshoots of the main. Liquid. Then each taking their own paths and creating new tones. Building, flying and falling inside the many reds.

Blues. Walking down the river path with Jobson, the tide of power having turned. Najib the master, Jobson the supplicant. Najib the power, Jobson the fearful. The gravitational balance between them fixed by a new sense of awe and respect. One has the magic, the other doesn't. One has the stars, the other hasn't. A Pied Piper with the monster in his tow. One on his way to wherever he wants to go, the other going nowhere.

Yellows. The feel of the instrument in his hand, the texture of the wood, the dexterity of his fingers, pulling and pushing the bow at his will. His eyes shut, his whole mind and body living the union of sound and spirit.

The many greens. The infinite possibilities and opportunities of music.

Najib looked upon the black circle and within the innermost depths of its many colours he saw a portrait of himself. Musician, player, master, a reflection of what he was and what he would become. He saw, understood, felt his heavy chains loosen and walked out of the room and out of the gallery in total control and at peace.

The next day, when eventually Mr Glue gave in and allowed Najib to take up another violin, his reward was extraordinarily sweet and proof he hadn't been fooled.

The room swam with exquisite sound. It was transported. And, utterly helpless, all Jobson and his cronies could do was stand, stare and listen.

* * *

Elizabeth lost in the blues. That same sheer exhilaration she always felt in the air – speed, motion, freedom. The hues of the sky and the hopes held within her.

Blues confirming her course was right and her flight from acting correct. Blues of a cool conviction that her parents would understand and accept her choice. That they would see in their daughter's determined face the faith she held in her own destiny. One laying with aircraft and clouds, not greasepaint and applause.

Blues of the wide oceans she would cross, the seas she would see and the heavens she would live in. Blue horizons stretching out before her. Horizons to be touched and explored.

Down Piccadilly and into the RA, weaving through crowds, John had led Elizabeth to the circles. He had warned her this was something miraculous, told her to be prepared, but they took her breath away all the same. Standing at the first circle, unconsciously taking a schoolboy's hand in hers, they leapt into the unknown together although they had no physical sense of each other.

Reds. Preparing the way, giving hot courage and strength, before belief in blues.

Yellows. The deserts she would fly over, the suns that would rise and set as she circled the globe chasing and escaping time zones. A captain offering her thanks to the famous people who found out about time at the home of time.

Greens. The forests she would look down on at mighty heights, the fields she would watch vanishing far below as she travelled at tremendous speeds.

Deep in the black circle, deep down in its many tones, down to the lights they shone and the shadows they threw, Elizabeth found the words to say to her parents and the ways to soothe. And when at the end she was ready to join him, John was waiting for her at the entrance surrounded by a posse of elderly Japanese tourists.

'Thank you,' she said simply and took his hand.

There was no other way to mark the moment. A Tube, a train, John's car and they were at the airfield in no time. Elizabeth sat at the controls and knew her place in the world just as she knew her future above it.

Speed, thrust, noise and lift, she flew into the blues she had touched in the gallery. A nose towards the horizon, her life's audition over, she had landed the part in which she never wanted to land.

* * *

The millionaire banker seeing circles, knowing he can sing like Sinatra.

The nurse watching a favourite patient die, still certain she has chosen the right path.

The con man seeing even more tricks, leaving the colours with a wider grin.

The politician, discovering she is flying the wrong

colour, knowing she must leave the party.

The royal looking into the deepest blues, realising his blood runs red and recognising the possibility of change.

The redundant man seeing a business opportunity in the sands of yellow.

The vain, selfish girl not seeing beyond her own sickly surfaces and becoming only more selfish.

The builder wanting to build and finding the plot.

The boy B met on another trip to an art gallery who loved to sing joining a choir that very day.

The thief, realising she will always be one, enjoying the fact, lifting a purse from a bag before she has left the building.

The runner seeking glory and knowing she can live with the best in London 2012.

The young scientist mixing colours and chemicals together fusing ideas.

The elderly man weeping for his youth in a pool of greens. There with his daughter and sitting at a piano later that day for the first time since he was sixteen playing as if he had never left the keyboard.

The mother-to-be holding her tummy, knowing.

The blind boy being told about the beautiful colours by his mum, creating poetic words to make the world cry.

The young woman's invention coming to life within the black circle.

The student fearing for her country and through a kaleidoscope of colours seeing how she can lead it to change.

The tech man seeing beyond the possible, walking back into Piccadilly full to bursting.

The brother swallowed by blues now understanding

what his sister is seeking and that afternoon doing the one thing to make all the difference.

The man preying on children and faced with his grim truth walking out of the gallery, riding a red bus home to his little flat and hanging himself.

The wife with no future then realising one in her next-door neighbour.

The famous artist not believing what he is seeing, deciding a new path.

The man deep within the red labyrinth finding the courage to act.

The woman falling in love before the blues.

The boy seeing how he will score the winner on the green, green grass of Wembley.

The girl at the yellows seeing her way past her nihilistic, abusive home.

The man who shot B's little boy with red in his pocket coming to London for curiosity sake having learnt of the artist's story and walking from the Royal Academy with a compassion he had never felt before.

The Principal free to marry again.

Mrs Hinkley, who saw something, looking into the reds and feeling vindicated.

An old red man who crossed the Atlantic incognito with good ol' Hudson, yesireee, and in tears witnessing the full deliverance of promise.

A famous movie star who can touch the hearts of any audience, giving thanks again for how her power was ignited.

Molly visiting the RA on her own and smiling.

Men... seeing the big thing whatever their age, taking a gap in the road, making their jobs work, leaving dead-end or great jobs to do the thing they had always dreamed about, going home and beginning to encourage their children, plucking up the courage to ask women and men on the bus or the train or the shopping queue for a date, vowing never to take another drink, forgiving the wrongs of the past and moving on, saying sorry to their wives, leaving their wives, facing the truth, starting anew, returning and seeing a shambles for the chance of what can be...

Women... deciding not to take it any more, mending fences, or breaking them, suddenly able to acknowledge their talent, telling the guys and women at work, or on the train, or at the gym they like them because nothing will ever happen if they don't, leaving barren homes, making new ones, realising the power they have and seeing their boundaries for the bogus prison bars they always were...

> Ambition, hope, talent and risk
> Life, death, endurance and task
> Potential.

The Line to the End of the World

Summer 2010

She gazed at him. He gazed at her.

Across the Meridian Line at *Place Greenwich,* holding hands, jumping from hemisphere to hemisphere, east to west, west to east. Childhood friends, once adult strangers, then lovers and very recently man and wife, together on the line that ran through their lives. The line forming the shapes and patterns of their union.

A group of small children looked at them in astonishment. Music and dance were in the very fabric of their country but these two foreigners were dancing to a very strange tune indeed. Only one little boy was laughing and joining in, working his way into Molly and B's closed hands, the black and white trio dancing from one half of the world to the other in joy and abandon.

Venus and the man without a name had married in the Queen's House at the National Maritime Museum looking out up to their treasured observatory on the hill.

Esmé, Harry and a few friends there, no fuss, just a lovely, colourful day with the black circle of revelation acting as a wedding altar. And fresh from reception, the newlyweds set out on their honeymoon of discovery. The journey they had talked about for so long even back in the days of the swings, the bandstand and *Cutty Sark*.

Follow the line down through all those countries right down to the end of the whole wide world where the penguins live. Follow it down and see all those herds of wild animals and rushing rivers. Follow the long-held and long-interrupted dream. Down along the imaginary line that splits the globe in two.

Of course, the Meridian Line really starts, or ends, at the poles, not in Greenwich. Descending from the North Pole, it cuts through the Arctic and then launches over the Greenland, Norwegian and North seas before first finding land in England. Thus to start their journey properly, the wedding couple travelled north to the eroding coast near Tunstall in the East Riding of Yorkshire, the line's first touch on English soil, and only then did they begin their long trek south.

Within a few short miles they reached Patrington just outside Hull where the recently re-introduced friends had danced their hemisphere dance once before. Down through many more Meridian landmarks – Louth, Tetford, the village of Somersham, onto Swavesey, Royston, on and on through Greenwich itself and finally to Peacehaven in East Sussex where the line left England's shores as did they themselves at the ferry port of Dover a little further along the coast.

Villers-sur-Mer once again, the line's first point of contact in France, but no red to flee this time. Every colour was now accepted, welcomed, encouraged – an essential part of B's new life just like his unpredictable wife. There was the blue line still running down the low, curved wall and the pay-to-view telescope still looking out to sea. The storm that night a distant memory – a metaphor for the personal storms he had weathered to stand there now.

Working their way through France, more markers, *Méridien de Greenwich*, on through Gavarnie in the Hautes-Pyrénées, into Spain then down to the line's most southern European mark at Pueblo Mascarat. Sailing across the Mediterranean, at length striking Africa, continuing through parts of Algeria before entering the huge expanse of Mali.

And here they were now, to the north of the sprawling town of Gao near the flowing brown River Niger, dancing at the upright obelisk Meridian marker at *Place Greenwich*.

Next on the journey lay Burkina Faso, then by the eccentricities of national borders they would follow the line as it dipped in and out of Togo and Ghana, until they reached the Meridian's last land point in Africa on the coast at Tema.

From there, once more spanning out over vast tracts of water across the Atlantic and Southern oceans, the line keeps going until its final arrival in Antarctica and all those penguins.

So where next for the travellers after Tema? They hadn't ruled out Antarctica in due course, but it was 2010, another four years on, and first there was another chance for B to lay a ghost to rest, this time with Molly by his side. They had decided to kill two birds with one honeymooning stone. Two personal pilgrimages – the Greenwich Meridian and the World Cup. Lines meeting other lines. In July they would fly down to the World Cup Final in Cape Town.

After a while the hemisphere dance came to a halt and Molly took up a cheery conversation with the little boy and his group of friends – her easy, magic touch, language barriers of no consequence, the children knowing Molly as she knew them. And with such happy voices in his ears, the children's laughter reminding him of that first day at the observatory in 1965, B turned to face the tall Prime Meridian marker basking in the glory being spun by his new wife.

Hooking off his backpack, B opened it up with a smile and pulled out the envelope for the umpteenth time since his wedding day. Scrawny handwriting on the cover, there was the wonderful treasure inside and carefully, inch-by-inch carefully, he eased it out needing to look once again. With the same sense of awe he felt every time, he read another line of scrawny words on a piece of card – a blessing and a plea.

Congratulations, Red Man! Now get yourself a name!

Flipping the card over, B's eyes fell upon the old man's gift to him on his marriage. A piece of the master's new life – a portrait of B drawn in red, a response to the younger artist's now famous pictures which had received so much worldwide acclaim since their unveiling in New York. Red lines depicting red men, their true shared colour and innate feature of their souls. Everyone has their own special colour.

B had spoken to him some weeks ago and knew he was working hard in his glass panorama room studio, taking inspiration from the trees, the fields and the Connecticut sky. B's red, full-sized portrait of him was still propped up against the huge windows, the picture the old man said had defined the barren years behind him and staked out the unknown days, months, perhaps even years of creation now lying ahead. A picture representing a new, golden time B had forged for him. One the reborn legend vowed over another culinary *tour de force* he would not waste.

B had read the message many times along the Meridian Line, under hot midday suns and in dark nights whenever he couldn't sleep – felicitations from a famous friend. But standing at that moment in Gao, somehow the implication of the words seemed to hit home for the very first time. The plain reasoning. The utter logic.

Under a towering sun, stowing the postcard away, B came to a sudden and epic decision, one he realised with complete simplicity he could now allow himself to take. Walking forward to where Molly was still playing with the children, he called out to the boy.

'Hey! You! Yes, you! Listen… do you speak English?'

The boy continued to laugh. It was very clear he did not and Molly looked at her husband as if to say he must be crazy to ask. But B was too full of his new determination. Pulling away, he stopped a string of adults passing by until he found one who did speak English, a middle-aged woman, and he as much as dragged her over to the lad.

'Can you ask him, please… what's his favourite colour?

Do you understand? Did you get that? What his favourite colour is.'

The woman was taken aback to be so promptly hijacked but she sensed it was all in fun and was laughing herself. She nodded, understanding the request, and in the rapid fire of her mother tongue gunned off the question.

The woman turned to B still laughing.

'*Bilenman*! He says *bilenman*. Red!'

Red man, old. Red man, young. Red boy, even younger.

B swallowed hard and felt into his pocket to bring out a piece of red amber, a gift he once gave to another little boy. The red man held it in his hands for a few last seconds, brought it to his lips, kissed it as his former Principal's precious son had once done, and holding the red jewel out he whispered softly to the woman.

'Tell him, this is a present from me. My favourite colour is red too. Tell him to take great care of it. It is a very, very special thing.'

The hushed message passed on, the little boy continued to smile as he took the proffered piece of amber graciously in his fingertips, put it to his lips and kissed it too. Then, as if the day now had far too many adults in it, he shouted something and fled away at top speed followed by his shrieking friends, just like Molly had done that day she called to see B in his deep blue home. *"Emergency Ward 10"*, sprinting down the alley wailing like a banshee. B saw them all fly away before turning to speak to the woman again.

'What did you say it was? Red?'

She laughed again. '*Bilenman*!'

'*B-i-l-e-n-m-a-n*?' he repeated.

'Yes. *Bilenman*. Red!'

A childhood in rejection, a brief summer of happiness with a young Funny Girl, a few angry years, a life spent protecting people, a devastating death in Paris before attaining much-belated enlightenment through colour and beauty. A journey of discovery from the Meridian Line at Villers-sur-Mer, then to Paris, the Lakes, Hull, London and Connecticut before embarking on an amazing adventure which had stretched all over the world to today's dust in Gao. All of it without a name. His life as an initial letter. That birth certificate copy in Miss Hattiemore's box detailing the impersonal proof.

But now he had it. Now he knew it.

Colour at life's most defining moments and B saw the colours of beauty all around him. Molly's simple white dress, the woman's gold chain around her neck, the cinder brown dirt of the street and the T-shirt by sheer happenstance he was wearing – red.

Red man.

Bilenman.

Molly gazed at him, he gazed at her and she knew what had happened. Softly, she took his hand in affirmation of her husband's decision and kissed him lightly on his cheek.

And suddenly Bilenman wanted the river.

Like that first day when Molly had dragged him away to tear down the green, grassy green observatory hill, although this time their roles were reversed, the red man with a new name pulled his wife into a steady run towards the Niger. Hand in hand, fingers interlocked.

'Would you run all the way, Mr Wood?'

'I would if you would, Mrs Wood!'

But the heat of the day was too fierce and they fell into a giggling walk after a mere hundred yards. Continuing on amongst the beautiful colours of the day, they passed laughing faces and noisy disputes, sellers on every corner and carts carrying everything from fruit and vegetables to livestock, before eventually, rearing up ahead of them, they caught the sway and shimmer of the Niger. Boats out on the flow, people in the water.

Soon they came to its bank, yet another river, a new friend, and Bilenman and Molly turned to each other still holding hands. Playing out their wish in their eyes, they took off their shoes and walked forward together, the browns and greens of the land far over on the opposite shores heading off towards the Meridian Line's African finale.

They looked down and saw their feet. And yes, they were indeed muddy.

Acknowledgements

With grateful thanks to the National Gallery, London; the Royal Observatory, Greenwich; Prince Of Wales Theatre, London; the Barbra Streisand Archives; Douglas Cornelissen, Funny Girl stage production, London 1966; the Mander & Mitchenson theatre collection.

Also to my family and friends for their input and encouragement and not forgetting the countless coffee bars, hotels, trains, boats and planes for being there to write in.